Sensation Stories

Wilkie Collins
Sensation Stories
Tales of Mystery and Suspense

Edited and with an introduction by
Peter Haining

Peter Owen
London and Chester Springs

PETER OWEN PUBLISHERS
73 Kenway Road, London SW5 0RE

Peter Owen books are distributed in the USA by
Dufour Editions Inc., Chester Springs, PA 19425-0007

This collection first published in Great Britain 2004 by
Peter Owen Publishers

Text illustrations by A.H. Dalziel, S.L. Fildes, G. Hine, Anne Scott,
Ernest Wallcousins and Frederick Walker

Photograph on page 18 courtesy of the National Film Archive, London
Photograph on page 19 courtesy of *The Times*

ISBN 0 7206 1220 9

A catalogue record for this book is available from the British Library.

Printed and bound by Bookmarque Ltd, Croydon, Surrey

Contents

'The Master of Sensation', a sketch of Wilkie Collins by Adriano Cecioni for *Vanity Fair* (February 1872)

Introduction

Wilkie Collins is regarded as the founding father of the "Sensation Novel", a literary phenomenon generally agreed to have been inaugurated in 1860 by his best-seller *The Woman in White*, although he had already been writing realistic stories of suspense laced with mystery and thrills for at least a decade previously. In dramatic plots that revolved around hidden secrets, bloody crimes, villainous schemes and clever detective work, all occurring in everyday settings, he helped to shape a new genre that was different from anything being written by his contemporaries – and one that was to have a far-reaching influence.

If this literary development can be said to have a birthplace, then the honour belongs to the isolated hamlet of Winterton on the windswept coast of East Anglia. Wilkie Collins had first been taken there as a child by his artist father, and the bleak landscape and grim legends of the desolate Norfolk community at once filled his imagination with thoughts of mystery and suspense that would later inspire his fiction. It was at Winterton, too, that he met a young woman who would become his mistress and an important part of his life and work.

Situated in a bay just north of Yarmouth, Winterton is an ancient fishing village with a wide sweep of beach and sand dunes that David Yaxley in his *Portrait of Norfolk* (1977) describes as having in winter "all the odd attractiveness of a deserted site like a ghost town of the Gold Rush". It is sheltered on the north-east by a promontory, Winterton Ness, the most easterly spot on the coast of Britain and was, according to William White in his *Gazetteer of Norfolk* (1845), "famous to mariners as the most fatal headland between Scotland and London". Daniel Defoe, who passed through in 1724, was just one of many visitors who have testified to the dangers of sailing along this coast:

> The farmers and country people had scarce a barn or a shed or a stable, nay not the pales of their yards and gardens, not a hogstye, not a necessary-house, but what was built of old planks, beams and timbers,

etc., the wrecks of ships and ruins of mariners' and merchants' fortunes, and in some places were whole yards filled and piled up very high with the same stuff.

Defoe also mentioned that over two hundred colliers and corn ships had been lost at sea during a storm in a single night in 1692 and described how the huge waves that crashed on the sands were regularly throwing up mysterious fragments of wood and bone that bore witness to drama and death at sea. Not surprisingly, the area around Winterton has for centuries suffered from erosion by the sea, and in December 1791, for example, what William White described as a "monstrous" high tide actually breached the sandhills and flooded land all the way to Yarmouth and Beccles.

The buttressed stone tower of Winterton's Holy Trinity Church stands nearly 130 feet high and can be seen for miles around on land and at sea. Wilkie Collins may well have climbed to the top during one of his visits – many tourists do – although whether he experienced the strange sensation described by W.G. Clarke in *Norfolk & Suffolk* (1921) is not recorded: "This prominent landmark is said to sway backwards and forwards in a gale to such an extent that a tombstone at the base is alternately visible and obscured to an observer on the summit."

Collins's interest in the locality had been made all the greater because of his love of the works of Defoe, in particular *Robinson Crusoe*. Ever since he had read the classic, the fact that Crusoe's first voyage had ended in disaster at Winterton Ness was for ever etched in his memory. On several occasions during his life Collins sailed in the same waters as his literary hero – although always when the sea was calm.

In all probability he heard about other sea tragedies from some of the 150 fishermen who lived among Winterton's population of eight hundred souls in the middle of the nineteenth century. Probably, too, he would have heard about a number of huge bones found near the ness. The largest of these, weighing fifty-seven pounds and measuring three feet by two inches, "was pronounced by the faculty to be the leg-bone of a man", according to a contemporary report. What *kind* of man, no one could be sure.

Small wonder, then, that such a unique spot should have proved irresistible to someone with Collins's imagination, and specific references to the area can be found in his novels *Armadale* (1866), a mystery drama set on the Norfolk Broads, *The Moonstone* (1868), in which Gabriel Betteridge shares his author's passion for *Robinson Crusoe*, as well as several of his essays and short stories. Collins's sexual emotions were equally aroused when he first saw the attractive and independently minded local girl Martha Rudd, probably in 1860. Indeed, there are those in Winterton who have suggested that their first encounter – and its implications – might just have inspired some episodes in *The Woman in White*.

Martha was one of eight children of a shepherd, James Rudd, and his wife, Mary, who lived in a tiny, squalid cottage in Black Street. Although it is probable that she received a basic education at the National School, by the age of sixteen she was working as a barmaid in a local inn, the Fisherman's Return. With her dark, smouldering eyes, high cheek-bones and full red mouth, she caught the eye of many a customer – not the least of them, it seems, the successful author up from London on holiday. She was then nineteen years old. Catherine Peters in her biography of Collins, *The King of Inventors* (1991), says that Martha appears to have drifted into Collins's life "as casually as a stray kitten" but that her determination and strong character and his idiosyncratic if caring sense of responsibility propelled them into a relationship that would last throughout the author's life. Peters adds:

> If Wilkie had been writing his life, instead of living it, he would have married Martha Rudd. Her archetype was, after all, the Wronged Maid rather than the Dream Woman. But the King of Inventors who did not hesitate in the didactic fiction of his later years to arrange marriage for prostitutes (one of them to a clergyman), or to match an elderly aristocrat with the mother of a (stillborn) illegitimate baby and a well-born young man with a lively country girl much like Martha, was himself content with a "morganatic family". It was his own phrase for Martha and the three children [two daughters and a son] she bore him.

9

Theirs was a partnership guaranteed to shock in prudish Victorian times. Yet this combination of a single-minded young girl from a poor backwoods family and a writer from a prosperous city background driven by a curiosity about the strange and the mysterious was to form a unique element in the creation of the Sensation Novel – a genre short-lived in itself but ultimately the inspiration of the modern story of mystery, detection and suspense.

William Wilkie Collins was born in 1824 in London, the son of William Collins, a noted landscape painter and member of the Royal Academy. It is evident that Collins senior had an abiding love for East Anglia, and, indeed, his artistic fame dated from 1818 when his main exhibit at the academy's annual show, *Scene on the Coast of Norfolk*, was bought by the Prince Regent and became part of the Royal Collection at Windsor.

Collins began his education at the Maida Hill Academy, but when his father was urged to visit Europe to broaden his knowledge of art for his work the youngster spent two years with his parents in France and Italy. In Rome Collins never forgot his father employing several models for his paintings, including a beautiful young man who posed as either a cupid or an angel and yet – in Collins's own words – "was in private life one of the most consummate rascals: a gambler, thief and a stiletto-wearer, at twelve years of age!"

From childhood, Collins was an avid reader – and soon proved to be a born storyteller, too. After his Grand Tour of Europe he was sent to a private boarding-school in Highbury and there often entertained the other boys with stories based on his travels or drawn from his imagination. This budding talent enabled him to save himself from beatings by the school bully, whom he amused each night with a story. One of the most popular of these tales apparently concerned a boy "who made a business out of swallowing spiders". Collins's ability to come up with entertaining stories at short notice would later stand him in good stead.

Collins left school in 1840, just before his seventeenth birthday. Not interested in going to university or entering the Church – his father's preferred options – he settled instead for an apprenticeship with a London firm of tea importers. The job was undemanding and scarcely fulfilling, and Wilkie admitted that instead of concentrating on bills of lading and invoices he wrote a string of "tragedies, comedies, epic poems and the usual literary rubbish accumulated about themselves by young beginners".

Collins's long-suffering father tried instead to encourage him to enter the legal profession. Wilkie sat the customary examinations and was called to the Bar at Lincoln's Inn but never practised. The ambition to be a writer was already burning in him too strongly to be ignored.

In fact, not all of the compositions he had written during these years were "rubbish". In 1843, when he was just nineteen, one of his stories, "The Last Stage Coachman", was accepted by *The Illuminated Magazine* and published in the August issue. The magazine was edited by Douglas Jerrold, author of the great theatrical success *Black-Eyed Susan* and a prolific contributor to *Punch*. He was evidently impressed by the story of a phantom stagecoach with its hapless passengers and, in particular, its author's ability to conjure up an engrossing macabre situation.

There are certainly several influences at work in this story, which has never been reprinted. Collins had ridden on the Winterton stagecoach to Yarmouth several times and regretted the demise of this form of transport in the face of the ever-growing competition from the railways. He had also endured a terrifying trip with a surly conductor on a diligence between Paris and Chalon-sur-Saône during his travels in Europe with his father. "The Last Stage Coachman" bears traces, too, of "The Story of the Bagman's Uncle" from *Pickwick Papers* by Charles Dickens, another of Collins's literary idols and soon to become one of his closest friends.

Exactly a year after the publication of this story Collins went on holiday to Paris and there gathered the details for what would become one of his most famous short stories, "A Terribly Strange Bed". An artist he knew named William Herrick told him about a den in Paris where the proprietor kept a mechanized bed that smothered anyone who slept in it. The account had the feel of an urban myth about it, but Wilkie busied himself around the back streets of the city looking for authentic

A poster for two plays (above) in which Wilkie Collins appeared with
his close friend, Charles Dickens (facing page)

detail to use in the story, which would again display his reading of other
writers, namely the French author Erkmann-Chatrian and Sir Walter
Scott.

In the story Collins mingles the fantastic and the realistic in a manner that lays the foundations for the Sensation Novel, as N.P. Davis has
written in *The Life of Wilkie Collins* (1956):

> His purpose was to impart a new sensation to his readers by a combi-
> nation of the startling and the familiar, to lay before them a situation as
> weird as anything that might have occurred "in the lonely inns of the
> Hartz Mountains" but to build it up out of absolutely commonplace and
> convincing properties that any one could actually see for himself "in the
> nineteenth century, in the civilised capital of France".

"A Terribly Strange Bed" was not only a ground-breaking story, it was
also the first of Collins's tales to be published by Charles Dickens in his

magazine *Household Words*, in the issue of 24 April 1852. Subsequently, critics have described it as "almost a throwback to the Gothic story of terrors with its machine of torture" or, alternately, a pioneer of the "locked room mystery".

Collins had met Dickens in 1851 through their shared love of amateur dramatics. Wilkie joined the circle of admirers surrounding Dickens – then enjoying the acclaim for *David Copperfield* – to appear in the satire *Not So Bad As We Seem* to raise money for the Guild of Literature and Art. The two men appeared in several more productions – notably the "petite comedy" *Used Up* (1852) – became firm friends and began a literary association writing stories and essays for Dickens's magazines that would last until the great man's death in 1870.

With the publication of "A Terribly Strange Bed" Collins at last began to feel confident that he could be a successful writer. In the interim his pen had been busy with other contributions, notably with a trio of stories for the popular magazine *Bentley's Miscellany*. These were a romance, "The Twin Sisters" (March 1851), a Dickens-inspired comic saga, "A Passage in the Life of Perugino Potts" (February 1852), and a gruesome mystery, "Nine O'Clock" (July 1852), that was another significant step for Collins, although, surprisingly, it, too, has never been reprinted.

"Nine O'Clock" is essentially a story of precognition and out-of-body experience set during the French Revolution. It had been inspired partly by Collins's visits to Paris and more especially by his interest in the new craze for hypnotism and clairvoyance. The previous winter he had attended a number of gatherings in London and contributed a series of articles, "Magnetic Evenings at Home", to *The Leader* newspaper. From these interests he wove the story of a curse that condemns the members of a family to certain death at the fateful hour.

Despite Dickens's enthusiasm for "A Terribly Strange Bed", he was not an editor easily satisfied. When, the following spring of 1853, Collins's offered him a second story, "Mad Monkton", it was rejected. Dickens explained that he could not publish the tale of hereditary madness as it might cause distress to those of his readers "in the numerous families in which there is such a taint". (As a result of this rejection, Collins put the story to one side, and it was not printed until 1855 in *Fraser's Magazine*, since when it has been endlessly anthologized.)

Dickens was, though, at pains to encourage his new friend and invited him to submit a story to the interlinked series of tales he was preparing for the special Christmas 1854 issue of *Household Words*. The series was called *The Seven Poor Travellers*, and Collins broke new ground again with "The Fourth Poor Traveller" in which a clever lawyer-detective recounts to an artist who is painting his portrait how he went about recovering a stolen letter from a man intent on blackmailing one of his clients. Robert Ashley, author of *Wilkie Collins* (1955), claims the tale is the first *British* detective story and has commented: "It utilises more successfully than any other Collins's narrative of the fifties his favourite theme of hide and seek and employs many of the devices of the modern detective story."

Collins followed this success with "The Dream Woman" for the next Christmas number of *Household Words* in 1855. It was the first time he used a technique of foreshadowing events and creating an atmosphere of suspense through expectation that would become such a feature of his later major novels. The story is also a daring departure with its description of a middle-aged man who has a nightmare about a murderous female and then becomes infatuated with and marries the ladylike Rebecca Murdoch, while remaining completely unaware of her real intent. It proved uncomfortable fireside reading and was later described by a critic of the *New York Herald* as "a mixture of voluptuousness, cruelty and horror". In 1874 Wilkie expanded the original version to three times its length as "A Mystery in Four Narratives" and changed the thought-provoking ending for a finale of mayhem and murder which is far less satisfying.

On 19 July 1856 Wilkie added another first to his literary achievements with "The Diary of Anne Rodway" for *Household Words*. A remarkable first-person tale, it relates in diary form a young working-class girl's attempt to hunt down the killer of her friend, making her *the* pioneer female detective. The narrative had an extraordinary effect on Dickens, and as soon as he had finished the manuscript he scribbled a hasty note to his friend:

I cannot tell you what a high opinion I have of "Anne Rodway". I read the first part at the office with strong admiration and read the second part on the railway. My behaviour before my fellow passengers was weak in the extreme, for I cried as much as you could possibly desire. I think it is excellent, feel a personal pride in it which is a delightful sensation, and know no one else who could have done it.

Curiously, the significance of the story as both a new step in detective fiction and for accurately describing the emotions of a simple but whole-hearted young working-class girl – perhaps subconsciously revealing Collins's own feelings towards females such as Martha Rudd who he would soon meet in Winterton – had to wait years to be recognized. For the author's part, he had latched on to an idea that he would soon develop further.

If there is ever a short story in a writer's life that can later be seen to presage one of his great works, then Collins's "A Marriage Tragedy" – which was first published in the USA in *Harper's Monthly Magazine* in

Title page of the first edition of *The Woman in White* (1860)

February 1858 – fits the description perfectly. Apart from being one of his best mystery stories, it is written in a similar style and with similar revelations about the characters as his novel *The Woman in White*, which would appear two years later.

There have been many suggestions about the inspiration for *The Woman in White*, a book acknowledged as a classic and one that has never been out of print and which has been translated into every major language. One source is said to have been his meeting with Martha Rudd; another a chance purchase of some old books in France, about which he wrote to a friend many years later:

> I was in Paris wandering about the streets with Charles Dickens amusing ourselves by looking into the shops. We came to an old book-stall – half shop and half store – and I found some dilapidated volumes with records of French crime – a sort of French Newgate Calendar. I said to Dickens, "Here is a prize!" So it turned out to be. In them I found some of my best plots.

The dramatic poster for the first stage production of
The Woman in White in London in 1871

The books were entitled *Recueil des Causes Célèbres* by Maurice
Méjan and, according to Collins's definitive biographer, Kenneth
Robinson, in *Wilkie Collins* (1951), the tattered old volumes remained
on his library shelves until his death. "But for them," says Robinson,
"*The Woman in White* would probably never have been written."

A still more dramatic source was said to be the events when Collins
was walking down a darkened lane in north London one night and he
saw a beautiful, terrified young woman dressed all in white running for
her life. When he stopped the girl and calmed her she revealed a terrible
story of having been imprisoned by a man against her will for months on
end. Wilkie combined this dramatic encounter with one of the cases
from Méjan's book to create the novel of an heiress, Laura Fairlie, who
becomes the victim of a plot to declare her mad by her debt-ridden
husband and the villainous Count Fosco in order to seize her property
rights.

The Woman in White was first serialized by Dickens in his new

The classic movie version of *The Woman in White*, made in 1948
with Eleanor Parker and with Sidney Greenstreet as Count Fosco

magazine *All The Year Round* and in the USA by *Harper's Weekly*. Such
was its immediate popularity that on the day of publication of each new
weekly episode huge crowds thronged outside the publisher's offices in
London. A cult quickly grew up around the story, as the social historian
S.M. Ellis has written in *Wilkie Collins, Le Fanu and Others* (1931):

> All through 1860 every possible commodity was labelled "Woman in
> White". There were "Woman in White" cloaks and bonnets, "Woman
> in White" perfumes and all manner of toilet requisites, "Woman in
> White" waltzes and quadrilles. There were also a host of imitators with
> stories of women in black, grey, green, yellow, blue and everything else,
> and so the "Sensation Novel" was born.

The circulation figures of *All The Year Round* exceeded even those
for the serialization of Dickens's *A Tale of Two Cities* which had preceded it, and Wilkie Collins found himself being praised by leading

Helena Bonham Carter in the 1988 London stage production of
The Woman in White

writers – including William Thackeray and Edward Fitzgerald, who
reread it four times – while the story was known to be a favourite of
both Prince Albert and Prime Minister William Gladstone. With *The
Woman in White* Collins found himself on a par with his mentor.

It was only a matter of time before the novel was being adapted for
the other forms of entertainment. Collins himself was commissioned to
write the theatrical version that was first staged at the Olympic Theatre,
London, in October 1871, opening a year later on Broadway. This
adaptation has been produced on numerous occasions, most recently
in December 1988 when Helena Bonham Carter took the title role in
the Greenwich Theatre production in London.

The story was first filmed as a silent movie by Pathe in 1917, and in
1929 Herbert Wilcox directed Blanche Sweet, Cecil Humphreys and
Frank Perfitt as the three main protagonists in the British and Dominions
Film Corporation version. The British master of melodrama, Tod
Slaughter, starred in a 1940 adaptation for Ambassador Films retitled

Crimes at the Dark House, and this was followed by the lavish 1948 Warner Brothers version with Eleanor Parker, John Emery and Sidney Greenstreet playing the oily and loathsome Count Fosco.

The Woman in White has also been adapted for television in both Britain and the USA, notably in April 1982 when Ray Jenkins scripted a five-episode series for the BBC starring Diana Quick, John Shrapnel and Alan Badel. It was again serialized by the BBC in November 1997 with Susan Vidler, Ian Richardson and Simon Callow. Now Collins's masterwork is to be adapted as a musical by Andrew Lloyd Webber who believes the plot has all the originality and theatricality of his greatest triumph *The Phantom of the Opera,* which was also based on a nineteenth-century classic novel, *Le Fantôme de l'Opéra* by Gaston Leroux.

Several authorities on Wilkie Collins have drawn parallels between the short story "A Marriage Tragedy" and *The Woman in White.* In both, the plot is activated by a complicated family conspiracy, and the villain in the short story, James Smith, bears a striking resemblance to the evil-hearted husband, Percival Glyde, of the novel. "A Marriage Tragedy" also has its private investigator, the sharp-witted, tireless Mr. Dark, who foreshadows the hawk-like Sergeant Cuff, and whose battle of wits with the sinister Josephine resembles that between the heroine of *The Woman in White* and her scheming husband and Count Fosco.

Collins also adapted the incident of the bloodstained nightgown in "A Marriage Tragedy" to a paint-stained gown in his second great Sensation Novel *The Moonstone,* published in 1868. This, according to T.S. Eliot, is "the first, the longest and the best of modern English detective novels", and, while this claim is open to dispute, the Sergeant is unquestionably the first and most significant detective in English literature. Few who have read the book would argue with Dorothy L. Sayers's verdict that it is "probably the very finest detective story ever written".

Again *The Moonstone* had a basis in fact – the case of 21-year-old Constance Kent acquitted of murdering her half-brother in Wiltshire in 1860 and which she later confessed to having committed – plus a complex plot featuring a priceless Indian diamond stolen from a religious idol and now the object of a relentless search by a trio of fanatical worshippers determined to retrieve it from the young woman to whom it has been given. Anxious to see justice done is, once again, the intrepid Sergeant Cuff whom Collins based on Jonathan Whicher, the Scotland Yard inspector who investigated the Constance Kent case and whose reputation was ruined by the not-guilty verdict.

Like *The Woman in White*, the story was hailed by the reading public and critics alike, an anonymous reviewer in *The Times* declaring that "*The Moonstone* will remain, as long as sensation novels are read, as a model of all that is most sensational, most thrilling, and most ingeniously probable in the midst of improbability." The novel also introduced a number of classic features to the novel of detection: a country-house robbery, false suspects, a final twist in the plot and an eccentric, celebrated detective to solve the mystery.

This novel, too, has been filmed several times. First in 1915 as a silent movie by Pathe, then in Monogram's 1934 version starring Charles Irwin as a very correct Cuff and again in 1972 by Columbia Pictures, with Maurice Denham interpreting the Sergeant as a fidgety and rather garrulous officer of the law.

Some ten years before writing *The Moonstone* Collins had demonstrated that crime could be amusing as well as deadly serious in a little tale entitled "Who Is the Thief?" published in April 1858 in a newly launched US magazine, *The Atlantic Monthly*. The story recounts the mishaps of a bungling new detective tracking some suspects through London and is noteworthy on two counts: as the first humorous or satirical detective story and the first detective story to be written in the form of letters exchanged by the policemen involved in the case. "Who Is the Thief" again contains a number of the elements found in the Sensation Novel before it was established as such.

Although Wilkie Collins wrote several ghost stories as well his tales of sensation, they are not among the best of his work. The supernatural is to be found in "Mad Monkton" (1855), "John Jago's Ghost" (1873) and "Mrs. Zant and the Ghost" (1887), but probably the most accomplished is "The Clergyman's Confession", written in 1875 and originally published in *Canadian Monthly*, which had been reprinting the author's earlier work. The story of a ghost who helps to solve a murder, it stirred up controversy because of the sensual elements in the plot. Indeed, the theme may well have made Collins's usual British publishers nervous about publishing it.

The clergyman of the title is tormented by an affair he had as a young man with a petite Frenchwoman, Miss Jéromette, despite the fact she admitted to him she was the "love slave" of another man who deserted her. Some years later her ghost appears to the man of the cloth revealing that her other lover has murdered her, leaving him with a dilemma to resolve. What makes the story unique among supernatural stories of the time is that Collins describes a seamy, physical side to erotic relationships, all the more powerful in the character of a student of divinity.

Three years after the publication of this story Collins returned to the supernatural again, albeit rationalized, in *The Haunted Hotel* (1878), which most critics agree was probably his last good novel. His health had been poor for years and by this stage of his life he was heavily dependent on opium: "Laudanum – divine laudanum – was my only friend", he was to confess in his diary. Later still, in a "note made on a spring morning" in 1883, he professed his addiction ever more forcefully:

> Who was the man who invented opium? I thank him from the bottom of my heart. I have had six delicious hours of oblivion. I have woken up with my mind composed and dawdled over my morning toilet with an exquisite sense of relief – and all through the modest little bottle of drops which I see on my bedroom chimney-piece at the moment. Drops, you are a darling! If I love nothing else, I love you!

There was a price to pay for his addiction, however. As the doses grew larger so did Collins's grip on reality diminish. He claimed to see a green woman with tusks waiting to bite a piece out of his shoulder, and one visitor to his home in 1885 – four years before his death – said that his eyes had become "enormous bags of blood".

Collins's last years were, indeed, a sad climax after the ground-breaking achievements of his early stories and the success of his two great novels. Indeed, as the Sensation Novel gave way to the story of mystery and suspense, so his own reputation declined. Where once he had been compared with his friend Charles Dickens, Collins would now have to wait for years to be recognized as a great writer. It was as late as 1976 that his qualities began to be reappraised, when Chris Steinbrunner and Otto Penzler in their *Encyclopedia of Mystery and Detection* awarded Collins the following accolade:

> He ranks with Dickens as the best popular novelist of his time, and, although his characterisations do not approach those of his friend, his carefully worked-out plots, complete with red herrings, cliff-hanging miniclimaxes, multitudinous suspicions and evasive alibis, are superior to those of any novelist of the nineteenth century.

Collins continued writing to the bitter end, however, and found his most ready sales to American magazines with stories such as "The Magic Spectacles" (*The Seaside Library*, June 1880), concerning the mysterious powers of a pair of glasses, a romance, "The Fair Physician" (*Pictorial World*, 23 December 1882), and one final mystery story, "Love's Random Shot" (*The Seaside Library*, August 1884). This is a rather melancholy account of a Scottish police officer's last case, and it reads as if both the detective and his creator are aware that their best days are behind them. None the less, it provided the title story for the last collection of Wilkie Collins's work, *Love's Random Shot & Other Stories*, issued posthumously in New York in 1894 by George Munro's Sons and reprinted here for the first time since.

Wilkie Collins once asked that his epitaph should read "Author of *The Woman in White* and other works of fiction". Such a statement, though, ignores his major contribution to the Sensation Novel as well as the pioneering nature of the best of his short fiction. Without either, the modern mystery story might have been years – even decades – later in its development.

THE LAST STAGE COACHMAN

The Last Stage Coachman

I walked forth one autumn evening to observe the arrival of a stage coach. I wandered on, yet nothing of the kind met my eye. I tried many an old public road – they were now grass-grown and miry, or desecrated by the abominable presence of a "station". I wended my way towards a famous roadside inn: it was desolate and silent, or in other words, "To Let". I looked for "the commercial room": not a pot of beer adorned the mouldering tables, and not a pipe lay scattered over the wild and beautiful seclusions of its once numerous "boxes". It was deserted and useless; the voice of the traveller rung no longer round its walls, and the merry horn of the guard startled no more the sleepy few, who once congregated round its hospitable door. The chill fire-place and broad, antiquated mantel-piece presented but one bill: the starting time of an adjacent railroad, surmounted by a representation of those engines of destruction, in dull, frowsy lithograph.

I turned to the yard. Where was the ostler with his unbraced breeches and his upturned shirt sleeves? Where was the stable boy with his wisp of straw and his sieve of oats? Where were the coquettish mares and the tall blood horses? Where was the manger and the stable door? – All gone – all disappeared: the buildings dilapidated and tottering – of what use is a stable to a stoker? The ostler and stable boy had passed away – what fellowship have either with a boiler? *The inn yard was no more.* The very dunghill in its farthest corner was choked by dust and old bricks, and the cock, the pride of the country round, clamoured no longer on the ruined and unsightly wall. I thought it was possible that he had satisfied long since the cravings of a railway committee; and I sat down on a ruined water-tub to give way to the melancholy reflections called up by the sight before me.

I know not how long I meditated. There was no officious waiter to ask me "What I would please to order?" No chambermaid to simper out "This way, Sir," – not even a stray cat to claim acquaintance with the calves of my legs, or a horse's hoof to tread upon my toe. There was nothing to disturb my miserable reverie, and I anathematized railways without distinction or exception.

The distant sound of slow and stealthy footsteps at last attracted my attention. I looked to the far end of the yard. Heavens above! a stage coachman was pacing its worn and weedy pavement.

There was no mistaking him – he wore the low-crowned, broad-brimmed, whitey-brown, well-brushed hat; the voluminous checked neckcloth; the ample-skirted coat; the striped waistcoat; the white cords; and last, not least, the immortal boots. But alas! the calf that had once filled them out, had disappeared; they clanked heavily on the pavement, instead of creaking tightly and noisily wherever he went. His waistcoat, evidently once filled almost to bursting, hung in loose, uncomfortable folds about his emaciated waist: large wrinkles marred the former beauty of the fit of his coat: and his face was all lines and fur-rows instead of smiles and jollity. The spirit of the fraternity had passed away from him – he was the stage coachman only in dress.

He walked backwards and forwards for some time without turning his head one way or the other, except now and then to peer into the deserted stable, or to glance mournfully at the whip he held in his hand: at last the sound of the arrival of a train struck upon his ear!

He drew himself up to his full height, slowly and solemnly shook his clenched fist in the direction of the sound, and looked – Oh that look! it spoke annihilation to the mightiest engine upon the rail, it scoffed at steam, and flashed furious derision at the largest terminus that ever was erected; it was an awfully comprehensive look – the concentrated essence of the fierce and deadly enmity of all the stage coachmen in England to steam conveyance.

To my utter astonishment, not, it must be owned, unmixed with fear, he suddenly turned his eyes towards my place of shelter, and walked up to me.

"That's the rail," said he, between his set teeth.

"It is," said I, considerably embarrassed.

"Damn it!" returned the excited Stage Coachman.

There was something inexpressibly awful about this execration; and I confess I felt a strong internal conviction that the next day's paper would teem with horrible railway accidents in every column.

"I did my utmost to hoppose 'em," said the Stage Coachman, in softened accents. "I wos the *last* that guv' in, I kep' a losing day after day, and yet I worked on; I wos determined to do my dooty, and I drove a coach the last day with an old hooman and a carpet bag inside, and three little boys and seven whopping empty portmanteaus outside. I wos determined my last kick to have *some* passengers to show to the rail, so I took my wife and children 'cos nobody else wouldn't go, and then we guv' in. Hows'ever, the last time as I wos on the road I didn't go and show 'em an empty coach – we wasn't full, but we wasn't empty; we wos game to the last!"

A grim smile of triumph lit up the features of the deposed Coachman as he gave vent to this assertion. He took hold of me by the button-hole, and led the way into the house.

"This landlord wos an austerious sort of a man," said he. "He used to hobserve, that he only wished a Railway Committee would dine at his house, he'd pison 'em all and emigrate; and he'd ha' done it, too!"

I did not venture to doubt this, so the Stage Coachman continued.

"I've smoked my pipe by the hour together in that fire-place; I've read *The Times* advertisements and Perlice Reports in that box till I fell asleep; I've walked up and down this here room a saying all sorts of things about the rail, and a busting for happiness. Outside this wery door I've bin a drownded in thankys from ladies for never lettin' nobody step through their band-boxes. The chambermaids used to smile, and the dogs used to bark, wherever I came. But it's all hover now – the poor feller as kep' this place takes tickets at a Station, and the chambermaids makes scalding hot tea behind a mahuggany counter for people as has no time to drink it in!"

As the Stage Coachman uttered these words, a contemptuous sneer puckered his sallow cheek. He led me back into the yard; the ruined appearance of which, looked doubly mournful, under the faint rays of moonlight that every here and there stole through the dilapidated walls of the stable. An owl had taken up his abode, where the chief ostler's bedroom had once rejoiced in the grotesque majesty of huge portraits of every winner of every "Derby", since the first days of Epsom. The bird of night flew heavily off at our approach, and my companion pointed gloomily up to the fragments of mouldy, worm-eaten wood, the last relics of the stable loft.

"He wos a great friend of mine, was that h'ostler," said the Coachman, "but he's left this railway-bothered world – he was finished by the train."

At my earnest entreaty to hear further, he continued:

"When this h'old place, wos guv'up and ruinated; the h'ostler as 'ud never look at the rail before, went down to have a sight of it, and as he wos a leaning his elbows on the wall, and a wishing as how he had the stabling of all the steam h'ingines (he'd ha' done 'em justice!) wot should he see, but one of his 'osses as wos thrown out of employ by the rail, a walking along jist where the train was coming. Bill jumped down, and as he wos a leading of him h'off, up comes the train, and went over his leg and cut the 'os in two – 'Tom,' says he to me when we picked him up, 'I'm a going eleven mile an hour, to the last stage as is left for me to do. I've always done my dooty with the 'osses; I've bin and done it now – bury that 'ere poor 'os and me out of the noise of the rail.' We got the surgeons to him, but he never spoke no more, Poor Bill! Poor Bill!"

This last recollection seemed too much for the Stage Coachman, he wrung my hand, and walked abruptly to the furthest corner of the yard.

I took care not to interrupt him, and watched him carefully from a distance.

At first, the one expression of his countenance was melancholy; but by degrees, other thoughts came crowding from his mind, and mantled on his woe-be-gone visage. Poor fellow, I could see that he was again in imagination the beloved of the ladies and the adored of the chambermaids: a faint reflection of the affable yet majestic demeanour, required by his calling, flitted occasionally over his pinched, attenuated features and brightened the cold, melancholy expression of his countenance.

As I still looked, it grew darker and darker, yet the face of the Stage Coachman was never for an instant hidden from me. The same artificial expression of pleasure characterized its lineaments as before. Suddenly I heard a strange, unnatural noise in the air – now it seemed like the distant trampling of horses; and now again, like the rumbling of a heavily laden coach along a public road. A faint, sickly light spread itself over that part of the Heavens whence the sounds proceeded; and after an interval, a fully equipped Stage Coach appeared in the clouds, with a railway director strapped fast to each wheel and a stoker between the teeth of each of the four horses.

In place of luggage, fragments of broken steam carriages and red carpet bags filled with other mementos of railway accidents occupied the roof. Chance passengers appeared to be the only tenants of the outside places. In front sat Julius Caesar and Mrs. Hannah Moore; and behind, Sir Joseph Banks and Mrs. Brownrigge. Of all the "insides", I could, I grieve to say, see nothing.

On the box was a little man with fuzzy hair and large iron grey whiskers, clothed in a coat of engineers' skin, with gloves of the hide of railway police. He pulled up opposite my friend, and bowing profoundly motioned him to the box seat.

A gleam of unutterable joy irradiated the Stage Coachman's countenance as he stepped lightly into his place, seized the reins and, with one hearty "good-night", addressed to an imaginary inn-full of people, started the horses.

Off they drove! my friend in the plenitude of his satisfaction cracking the whip every instant as he drove the phantom coach into the air. And amidst the shrieks of the railway directors at the wheel, the groans of *James Watt*, the bugle of the guard and the tremendous cursing of the invisible "insides", fast and furiously disappeared from my eyes.

A Terribly Strange Bed

Shortly after my education at college was finished, I happened to be staying at Paris with an English friend. We were both young men then, and lived, I am afraid, rather a wild life, in the delightful city of our sojourn. One night we were idling about the neighbourhood of the Palais Royal, doubtful to what amusement we should next betake ourselves. My friend proposed a visit to Frascati's, but his suggestion was not to my taste. I knew Frascati's, as the French saying is, by heart; had lost and won plenty of five-franc pieces there, merely for amusement's sake, until it was amusement no longer, and was thoroughly tired, in fact, of all the ghastly respectabilities of such a social anomaly as a respectable gambling-house.

"For heaven's sake," said I to my friend, "let us go somewhere where we can see a little genuine, blackguard, poverty-stricken gaming, with no false gingerbread glitter thrown over it at all. Let us get away from fashionable Frascati's to a house where they don't mind letting in a man with a ragged coat, or a man with no coat, ragged or otherwise."

"Very well," said my friend, "we needn't go out of the Palais Royal to find the sort of company you want. Here's the place just before us; as blackguard a place, by all report, as you could possibly wish to see." In another minute we arrived at the door, and entered the house, the back of which you have drawn in your sketch.

When we got upstairs, and left our hats and sticks with the door-keeper, we were admitted into the chief gambling-room. We did not find many people assembled there. But, few as the men were who looked up at us on our entrance, they were all types – lamentably true types – of their respective classes.

We had come to see blackguards, but these men were something worse. There is a comic side, more or less appreciable, in all black-guardism – here there was nothing but tragedy – mute, weird tragedy. The quiet in the room was horrible. The thin, haggard, long-haired young man, whose sunken eyes fiercely watched the turning up of the cards, never spoke; the flabby, fat-faced, pimply player – who pricked his piece of pasteboard perseveringly, to register how often black won and how often red – never spoke; the dirty, wrinkled old man with the vulture eyes and the darned greatcoat, who had lost his last *sou* and still looked on desperately after he could play no longer, never spoke. Even the voice of the croupier sounded as if it were strangely dulled and thickened in the atmosphere of the room. I had entered the place to laugh, but the spectacle before me was something to weep over. I soon found it necessary to take refuge in excitement from the depression of spirits which was fast stealing on me. Unfortunately I sought the nearest excitement, by going to the table and beginning to play. Still more unfortunately, as the event will show, I won – won prodigiously; won incredibly; won at such a rate that the regular players at the table crowded round me and, staring at my stakes with hungry, superstitious eyes, whispered to one another that the English stranger was going to break the bank.

The game was *Rouge et Noir*. I had played at it in every city in Europe, without, however, the care or the wish to study the Theory of Chances – that philosopher's stone of all gamblers! And a gambler, in the strict sense of the word, I had never been. I was heart-whole from the corroding passion for play. My gaming was a mere idle amusement. I never resorted to it by necessity, because I never knew what it was to want money. I never practised it so incessantly as to lose more than I could afford or to gain more than I could coolly pocket without being thrown off my balance by my good luck. In short, I had hitherto frequented gambling-tables – just as I frequented ball-rooms and opera-houses – because they amused me, and because I had nothing better to do with my leisure hours.

But on this occasion it was very different – now, for the first time in my life, I felt what the passion for play really was. My success first bewildered, and then, in the most literal meaning of the word, intoxicated me. Incredible as it may appear, it is nevertheless true, that I only lost when I attempted to estimate chances and played according to previous calculation. If I left everything to luck, and staked without any care or consideration, I was sure to win – to win in the face of every recognized probability in favour of the bank. At first, some of the men present ventured their money safely enough on my colour; but I speedily increased my stakes to sums which they dared not risk. One after another they left off playing and breathlessly looked on at my game.

Still, time after time, I staked higher and higher, and still won. The excitement in the room rose to fever pitch. The silence was interrupted by a deep-muttered chorus of oaths and exclamations in different languages every time the gold was shovelled across to my side of the table – even the imperturbable croupier dashed his rake to the floor in a (French) fury of astonishment at my success. But one man present preserved his self-possession; and that man was my friend. He came to my side and, whispering in English, begged me to leave the place, satisfied with what I had already gained. I must do him the justice to say that he repeated his warnings and entreaties several times, and only left me and went away after I had rejected his advice (I was to all intents and purposes gambling-drunk) in terms which rendered it impossible for him to address me again that night.

Shortly after he had gone, a hoarse voice behind me cried: "Permit me, my dear sir! – permit me to restore to their proper place two Napoleons which you have dropped. Wonderful luck, sir! I pledge you my word of honour, as an old soldier, in the course of my long experience in this sort of thing, I never saw such luck as yours! – never! Go on, sir – *sacré mille bombes!* Go on boldly and break the bank!"

I turned round and saw, nodding and smiling at me with inveterate civility, a tall man, dressed in a frogged and braided surtout.

If I had been in my senses, I should have considered him, personally, as being rather a suspicious specimen of an old soldier. He had goggling blood-shot eyes, mangy mustachios, and a broken nose. His voice betrayed a barrack-room intonation of the worst order, and he had the dirtiest pair of hands I ever saw – even in France. These little personal peculiarities exercised, however, no repelling influence on me. In the mad excitement, the reckless, triumph of that moment, I was ready to "fraternize" with anybody who encouraged me in my game: I accepted the old soldier's offered pinch of snuff, clapped him on the back and swore he was the honestest fellow in the world – the most glorious relic of the Grand Army that I had ever met with.

"Go on!" cried my military friend, snapping his fingers in ecstasy – "Go on, and win! Break the bank – *mille tonnerres!* my gallant English comrade, break the bank!"

And I *did* go on – went on at such a rate that in another quarter of an hour the croupier called out: "Gentlemen! the bank has discontinued for to-night." All the notes, and all the gold in that "bank" now lay in a heap under my hands; the whole floating capital of the gambling-house was waiting to pour into my pockets!

"Tie up the money in your pocket-handkerchief, my worthy sir," said the old soldier, as I wildly plunged my hands into my heap of gold. "Tie it up, as we used to tie up a bit of dinner in the Grand Army; your winnings are too heavy for any breeches pockets that ever were sewed. There! that's it! – shovel them in, notes and all! *Credié!* what luck! – Stop! another Napoleon on the floor! *Ah! sacré petit polisson de Napoléon!* have I found thee at last? Now then, sir – two tight double knots each way, with your honourable permission, and the money's safe. Feel it! I feel it, fortunate sir! hard and round as a cannon ball – *ah, bah!* if they had only fired such cannon balls at us at Austerlitz – *nom d'une pipe!* if they only had! And now, as an ancient grenadier, as an ex-brave of the French Army, what remains for me to do? I ask what? Simply this: to entreat my valued English friend to drink a bottle of champagne with me and toast the goddess Fortune in foaming goblets before we part!"

"Excellent ex-brave! Convivial ancient grenadier! Champagne by all means! An English cheer for an old soldier! Hurrah! hurrah! Another English cheer for the goddess Fortune! Hurrah! hurrah! hurrah!"

"Bravo! the Englishman; the amiable, gracious Englishman, in whose veins circulates the vivacious blood of France! Another glass? *Ah, bah!* – the bottle is empty! Never mind! *Vive le vin!* I, the old soldier, order another bottle, and half a pound of *bonbons* with it!"

"No, no, ex-brave; never – ancient grenadier! *Your* bottle last time; *my* bottle this. Behold it! Toast away! The French Army! – the great Napoleon! – the present company! the croupier! the honest croupier's wife and daughters – if he has any! The ladies generally! Everybody in the world!"

By the time the second bottle of champagne was emptied, I felt as if I had been drinking liquid fire – my brain seemed all a-flame. No excess in wine ever had this effect on me before in my life. Was it the result of a stimulant acting upon my system when I was in a highly excited state? Was my stomach in a particularly disordered condition? Or was the champagne amazingly strong?

"Ex-brave of the French Army!" cried I, in a mad state of exhilaration, "I am on fire! How are *you*? You have set me on fire! Do you hear, my hero of Austerlitz? Let us have a third bottle of champagne to put the flame out!"

The old soldier wagged his head, rolled his goggle eyes, until I expected to see them slip out of their sockets; placed his dirty forefinger by the side of his broken nose; solemnly ejaculated "Coffee!" and immediately ran off into an inner room.

The word pronounced by the eccentric veteran seemed to have a magical effect on the rest of the company present. With one accord they all rose to depart. Probably they had expected to profit by my intoxication; but finding that my new friend was benevolently bent on preventing me from getting dead drunk, had now abandoned all hope of thriving pleasantly on my winnings. Whatever their motive might be, at any rate they went away in a body. When the old soldier returned, and sat down again opposite to me at the table, we had the room to ourselves. I could see the croupier, in a sort of vestibule which opened out of it, eating his supper in solitude. The silence was now deeper than ever.

A sudden change, too, had come over the "ex-brave". He assumed a portentously solemn look! And, when he spoke to me again, his speech was ornamented by no oaths, enforced by no finger-snapping, enlivened by no apostrophes or exclamations.

"Listen, my dear sir," said he, in mysteriously confidential tones. "Listen to an old soldier's advice. I have been to the mistress of the house (a very charming woman, with a genius for cookery!) to impress on her the necessity of making us some particularly strong and good coffee. You must drain this coffee in order to get rid of your little amiable exaltation of spirits before you think of going home – you *must*, my good and gracious friend! With all that money to take home to-night, it is a sacred duty to yourself to have your wits about you. You are known to be a winner to an enormous extent by several gentlemen present to-night, who, in a certain point of view, are very worthy and excellent fellows, but they are mortal men, my dear sir, and they have their amiable weaknesses! Need I say more? Ah, no, no! you understand me! Now, this is what you must do – send for a cabriolet when you feel quite well again – draw up all the windows when you get into it – and tell the driver to take you home only through the large and well-lighted thoroughfares. Do this, and you and your money will be safe. Do this, and to-morrow you will thank an old soldier for giving you a word of honest advice."

Just as the ex-brave ended his oration in very lachrymose tones, the coffee came in, ready poured out in two cups. My attentive friend handed me one of the cups with a bow. I was parched with thirst, and drank it off at a draught. Almost instantly afterwards, I was seized with a fit of giddiness and felt more completely intoxicated than ever. The room whirled round and round furiously; the old soldier seemed to be regularly bobbing up and down before me like the piston of a steam-engine. I was half deafened by a violent singing in my ears; a feeling of utter bewilderment, helplessness, idiocy, overcame me. I rose from my chair, holding on by the table to keep my balance, and stammered out that I felt dreadfully unwell – so unwell that I did not know how I was to get home.

"My dear friend," answered the old soldier – and even his voice seemed to be bobbing up and down as he spoke – "my dear friend, it would be madness to go home in *your* state; you would be sure to lose your money; you might be robbed and murdered with the greatest ease. I am going to sleep here: do *you* sleep here, too – they make up capital beds in this house – take one; sleep off the effects of the wine, and go home safely with your winnings to-morrow – to-morrow, in broad daylight."

I had but two ideas left: one, that I must never let go hold of my handkerchief full of money; the other, that I must lie down somewhere immediately and fall off into a comfortable sleep. So I agreed to the proposal about the bed, and took the offered arm of the old soldier, carrying my money with my disengaged hand. Preceded by the croupier, we passed along some passages and up a flight of stairs into the bedroom which I was to occupy. The ex-brave shook me warmly by the hand, proposed that we should breakfast together and then, followed by the croupier, left me for the night.

I ran to the wash-hand stand; drank some of the water in my jug; poured the rest out, and plunged my face into it; then sat down in a chair and tried to compose myself. I soon felt better. The change for my lungs, from the foetid atmosphere of the gambling-room to the cool air of the apartment I now occupied; the almost equally refreshing change for my eyes, from the glaring gas-lights of the "salon" to the dim, quiet flicker of one bedroom candle, aided wonderfully the restorative effects of cold water. The giddiness left me, and I began to feel a little like a reasonable being again. My first thought was of the risk of sleeping all night in a gambling-house; my second, of the still greater risk of trying to get out after the house was closed and of going home alone at night, through the streets of Paris, with a large sum of money about me. I had slept in worse places than this on my travels; so I determined to lock, bolt, and barricade my door and take my chance till the next morning.

Accordingly, I secured myself against all intrusion; looked under the bed, and into the cupboard; tried the fastening of the window; and then, satisfied that I had taken every proper precaution, pulled off my upper clothing, put my light, which was a dim one, on the hearth among a feathery litter of wood ashes and got into bed, with the hand-kerchief full of money under my pillow.

I soon felt not only that I could not go to sleep, but that I could not even close my eyes. I was wide awake and in a high fever. Every nerve in my body trembled – every one of my senses seemed to be preternatu-rally sharpened. I tossed and rolled and tried every kind of position, and perseveringly sought out the cold corners of the bed, and all to no pur-pose. Now, I thrust my arms over the clothes; now, I poked them under the clothes; now, I violently shot my legs straight out down to the bot-tom of the bed; now, I convulsively coiled them up as near my chin as they would go; now, I shook out my crumpled pillow, changed it to the cool side, patted it flat, and lay down quietly on my back; now, I fiercely doubled it in two, set it up on end, thrust it against the board of the bed, and tried a sitting posture. Every effort was vain; I groaned with vexation, as I felt that I was in for a sleepless night.

What could I do? I had no book to read. And yet, unless I found out some method of diverting my mind, I felt certain that I was in the condition to imagine all sorts of horrors; to rack my brain with forebodings of every possible and impossible danger; in short, to pass the night in suffering all conceivable varieties of nervous terror.

I raised myself on my elbow, and looked about the room – which was brightened by a lovely moonlight pouring straight through the window – to see if it contained any pictures or ornaments that I could at all clearly distinguish. While my eyes wandered from wall to wall, a remembrance of Le Maistre's delightful little book, *Voyage autour de ma Chambre*, occurred to me. I resolved to imitate the French author, and find occupation and amusement enough to relieve the tedium of my wakefulness by making a mental inventory of every article of furniture I could see and by following up to their sources the multitude of associations which even a chair, a table or a wash-hand stand may be made to call forth.

In the nervous unsettled state of my mind at that moment, I found it much easier to make my inventory than to make my reflections, and thereupon soon gave up all hope of thinking in Le Maistre's fanciful track – or, indeed, of thinking at all. I looked about the room at the different articles of furniture, and did nothing more.

There was, first, the bed I was lying in: a four-post bed, of all things in the world to meet with in Paris! – yes, a thoroughly clumsy British four-poster, with the regular top lined with chintz – the regular fringed valance all around – the regular stifling unwholesome curtains, which I remembered having mechanically drawn back against the posts without particularly noticing the bed when I first got into the room. Then there was the marble-topped wash-hand stand, from which the water I had spilt, in my hurry to pour it out, was still dripping, slowly and more slowly, on to the brick floor. Then two small chairs, with my coat, waistcoat and trousers flung on them. Then a large elbow-chair, covered with dirty-white dimity, with my cravat and shirt-collar thrown over the back. Then a chest of drawers, with two of the brass handles off, and a tawdry, broken china inkstand placed on it by way of ornament for the top. Then the dressing-table, adorned by a very small looking-glass, and a very large pincushion. Then the window – an unusually large window. Then a dark old picture, which the feeble candle dimly showed me. It was the picture of a fellow in a high Spanish hat, crowned with a plume of towering feathers. A swarthy sinister ruffian, looking upward, shading his eyes with his hand, and looking intently upward – it might be at some tall gallows at which he was going to be hanged. At any rate, he had the appearance of thoroughly deserving it.

This picture put a kind of constraint upon me to look upward, too – at the top of the bed. It was a gloomy and not an interesting object, and I looked back at the picture. I counted the feathers in the man's hat – they stood out in relief – three white, two green. I observed the crown of his hat, which was of a conical shape, according to the fashion supposed to have been favoured by Guido Fawkes. I wondered what he was looking up at. It couldn't be at the stars – such a desperado was neither astrologer nor astronomer. It must be at the high gallows, and he was going to be hanged presently. Would the executioner come into possession of his conical-crowned hat and plume of feathers? I counted the feathers again – three white, two green.

While I still lingered over this very improving intellectual employment, my thoughts insensibly began to wander. The moonlight shining into the room reminded me of a certain moonlight night in England – the night after a picnic party in a Welsh valley. Every incident of the drive homeward, through lovely scenery, which the moonlight made lovelier than ever, came back to my remembrance, although I had never given the picnic a thought for years – although, if I had *tried* to recollect it, I could certainly have recalled little or nothing of that scene long past. Of all the wonderful faculties that help to tell us we are immortal, which speaks the sublime truth more eloquently than memory? Here was I, in a strange house of the most suspicious character, in a situation of uncertainty, and even of peril, which might seem to make the cool exercise of my recollection almost out of the question; nevertheless, remembering, quite involuntarily, places, people, conversations, minute circumstances of every kind, which I had thought forgotten for ever, which I could not possibly have recalled at will, even under the most favourable auspices. And what cause had produced in a moment the whole of this strange, complicated, mysterious effect? Nothing but some rays of moonlight shining in at my bedroom window.

I was still thinking of the picnic – of our merriment on the drive home – of the sentimental young lady who *would* quote *Childe Harold* because it was moonlight. I was absorbed by these past scenes and past amusements, when, in an instant, the thread on which my memories hung snapped asunder; my attention immediately came back to present things more vividly than ever, and I found myself, I neither knew why nor wherefore, looking hard at the picture again.

Looking for what?

Good God! the man had pulled his hat down on his brows! – No! the hat itself was gone! Where was the conical crown? Where the feathers – three white, two green? Not there! In place of the hat and feathers, what dusky object was it that now hid his forehead, his eyes, his shading hand?

Was the bed moving?

I turned on my back and looked up. Was I mad? drunk? dreaming? giddy again? or was the top of the bed really moving down – sinking slowly, regularly, silently, horribly, right down throughout the whole of its length and breadth – right down upon me, as I lay underneath?

My blood seemed to stand still. A deadly paralysing coldness stole all over me, as I turned my head round on the pillow, and determined to test whether the bed-top was really moving or not by keeping my eye on the man in the picture.

The next look in that direction was enough. The dull, black, frowsy outline of the valance above me was within an inch of being parallel with his waist. I still looked breathlessly. And steadily, and slowly – very slowly – I saw the figure, and the line of frame below the figure, vanish, as the valance moved down before it.

I am, constitutionally, anything but timid. I have been on more than one occasion in peril of my life, and have not lost my self-possession for an instant; but when the conviction first settled on my mind that the bed-top was really moving, was steadily and continuously sinking down upon me, I looked up shuddering, helpless, panic-stricken, beneath the hideous machinery for murder, which was advancing closer and closer to suffocate me where I lay.

I looked up, motionless, speechless, breathless. The candle, fully spent, went out; but the moonlight still brightened the room. Down and down, without pausing and without sounding, came the bed-top, and still my panic-terror seemed to bind me faster and faster to the mattress on which I lay – down and down it sank, till the dusty odour from the lining of the canopy came stealing into my nostrils.

At that final moment the instinct of self-preservation startled me out of my trance, and I moved at last. There was just room for me to roll myself sideways off the bed. As I dropped noiselessly to the floor, the edge of the murderous canopy touched me on the shoulder.

Without stopping to draw my breath, without wiping the cold sweat from my face, I rose instantly on my knees to watch the bed-top. I was literally spellbound by it. If I had heard footsteps behind me, I could not have turned round; if a means of escape had been miraculously provided for me, I could not have moved to take advantage of it. The whole life in me was, at that moment, concentrated in my eyes.

It descended – the whole canopy, with the fringe round it, came down – down – close down; so close that there was not room now to squeeze my finger between the bed-top and the bed. I felt at the sides, and discovered that what had appeared to me from beneath to be the ordinary light canopy of a four-post bed, was in reality a thick, broad mattress, the substance of which was concealed by the valance and its fringe. I looked up and saw the four posts rising, hideously bare. In the middle of the bed-top was a huge wooden screw that had evidently worked it down through a hole in the ceiling, just as ordinary presses are worked down on the substance selected for compression. The frightful apparatus moved without making the faintest noise. There had been no creaking as it came down; there was now not the faintest sound from the room above. Amid a dead and awful silence I beheld before me – in the nineteenth century, and in the civilized capital of France – such a machine for secret murder by suffocation as might have existed in the worst days of the Inquisition, in the lonely inns among the Hartz Mountains, in the mysterious tribunals of Westphalia! Still, as I looked on it, I could not move, I could hardly breathe, but I began to recover the power of thinking, and in a moment I discovered the murderous conspiracy framed against me in all its horror.

My cup of coffee had been drugged, and drugged too strongly. I had been saved from being smothered by having taken an overdose of some narcotic. How I had chafed and fretted at the fever-fit which had preserved my life by keeping me awake! How recklessly I had confided myself to the two wretches who had led me into this room, determined, for the sake of my winnings, to kill me in my sleep by the surest and most horrible contrivance for secretly accomplishing my destruction! How many men, winners like me, had slept, as I had proposed to sleep, in that bed, and had never been seen or heard of more! I shuddered at the bare idea of it.

But, ere long, all thought was again suspended by the sight of the murderous canopy moving once more. After it had remained on the bed – as nearly as I could guess – about ten minutes, it began to move up again. The villains who worked it from above evidently believed that their purpose was now accomplished. Slowly and silently, as it had descended, that horrible bed-top rose towards its former place. When it reached the upper extremities of the four posts, it reached the ceiling, too. Neither hole nor screw could be seen; the bed became in appearance an ordinary bed again – the canopy an ordinary canopy – even to the most suspicious eyes.

Now, for the first time, I was able to move – to rise from my knees, to dress myself in my upper clothing – and to consider of how I should escape. If I betrayed, by the smallest noise, that the attempt to suffocate me had failed, I was certain to be murdered. Had I made any noise already? I listened intently, looking towards the door.

No! no footsteps in the passage outside – no sound of a tread, light or heavy, in the room above – absolute silence everywhere. Besides locking and bolting my door, I had moved an old wooden chest against it, which I had found under the bed. To remove this chest (my blood ran cold as I thought of what its contents *might* be!) without making some disturbance was impossible; and, moreover, to think of escaping through the house, now barred up for the night, was sheer insanity. Only one chance was left me – the window. I stole to it on tiptoe.

My bedroom was on the first floor, above an *entresol*, and looked into the back street, which you have sketched in your view. I raised my hand to open the window, knowing that on that action hung, by the merest hair's-breadth, my chance of safety. They keep vigilant watch in a House of Murder. If any part of the frame cracked, if the hinge creaked, I was a lost man! It must have occupied me at least five minutes, reckoning by time – five *hours*, reckoning by suspense – to open that window. I succeeded in doing it silently – in doing it with all the dexterity of a housebreaker – and then looked down into the street. To leap the distance beneath me would be almost certain destruction! Next, I looked round at the sides of the house. Down the left side ran the thick water-pipe which you have drawn – it passed close by the outer edge of the window. The moment I saw the pipe, I knew I was saved. My breath came and went freely for the first time since I had seen the canopy of the bed moving down upon me!

To some men the means of escape which I had discovered might have seemed difficult and dangerous enough – to *me* the prospect of slipping down the pipe into the street did not suggest even a thought of peril. I had always been accustomed, by the practice of gymnastics, to keep up my schoolboy powers as a daring and expert climber; and knew that my head, hands, and feet would serve me faithfully in any hazards of ascent or descent. I had already got one leg over the window-sill, when I remembered the handkerchief filled with money under my pillow. I could well have afforded to leave it behind me, but I was revengefully determined that the miscreants of the gambling-house should miss their plunder as well as their victim. So I went back to the bed and tied the heavy handkerchief at my back by my cravat.

Just as I had made it tight and fixed it in a comfortable place, I thought I heard a sound of breathing outside the door. The chill feeling of horror ran through me again as I listened. No! dead silence still in the passage – I had only heard the night air blowing softly into the room. The next moment I was on the window-sill – and the next I had a firm grip on the water-pipe with my hands and knees.

I slid down into the street easily and quietly, as I thought I should, and immediately set off at the top of my speed to a branch "Prefecture" of Police, which I knew was situated in the immediate neighbourhood. A "sub-prefect," and several picked men among his subordinates, happened to be up, maturing, I believe, some scheme for discovering the perpetrator of a mysterious murder which all Paris was talking of just then. When I began my story, in a breathless hurry and in very bad French, I could see that the sub-prefect suspected me of being a drunken Englishman who had robbed somebody; but he soon altered his opinion as I went on, and, before I had anything like concluded, he shoved all the papers before him into a drawer, put on his hat, supplied me with another (for I was bare-headed), ordered a file of soldiers, desired his expert followers to get ready all sorts of tools for breaking open doors and ripping up brick-flooring, and took my arm, in the most friendly and familiar manner possible, to lead me with him out of the house. I will venture to say, that when the sub-prefect was a little boy, and was taken for the first time to the play, he was not half as much pleased as he was now at the job in prospect for him at the gambling-house!

Away we went through the streets, the sub-prefect cross-examining and congratulating me in the same breath as we marched at the head of our formidable *posse comitatus*. Sentinels were placed at the back and front of the house the moment we got to it; a tremendous battery of knocks was directed against the door; a light appeared at a window; I was told to conceal myself behind the police – then came more knocks and a cry of "Open in the name of the Law!" At that terrible summons bolts and locks gave way before an invisible hand, and the moment after the sub-prefect was in the passage, confronting a waiter half dressed and ghastly pale. This was the short dialogue which immediately took place:

"We want to see the Englishman who is sleeping in this house."

"He went away hours ago."

"He did no such thing. His friend went away; *he* remained. Show us to his bedroom!"

"I swear to you, Monsieur le Sous-prefect, he is not here!

"I swear to you, Monsieur le Garçon, he is. He slept here – he didn't find your bed comfortable – he came to us to complain of it – here he is among my men – and here am I ready to look for a flea or two in his bed-stead. Renaudin," (calling to one of the subordinates, and pointing to the waiter) "collar that man, and tie his hands behind him. Now, then, gentlemen, let us walk upstairs!"

Every man and woman in the house was secured – the "Old Soldier" the first. Then I identified the bed in which I had slept, and then we went into the room above.

No object that was at all extraordinary appeared in any part of it. The sub-prefect looked round the place, commanded everybody to be silent, stamped twice on the floor, called for a candle, looked attentively at the spot he had stamped on, and ordered the flooring there to be carefully taken up. This was done in no time. Lights were produced, and we saw a deep-raftered cavity between the floor of this room and the ceiling of the room beneath. Through this cavity there ran perpendicularly a sort of case of iron thickly greased; and inside the case appeared the screw, which communicated with the bed-top below. Extra lengths of screw, freshly oiled; levers covered with felt; all the complete upper works of a heavy press – constructed with infernal ingenuity so as to join the fixtures below, and when taken to pieces again to go into the smallest possible compass – were next discovered and pulled out on the floor. After some little difficulty, the sub-prefect succeeded in putting the machinery together, and, leaving his men to work it, descended with me to the bedroom. The smothering canopy was then lowered, but not so noiselessly as I had seen it lowered. When I mentioned this to the sub-prefect, his answer, simple as it was, had a terrible significance. "My men", said he, "are working down the bed-top for the first time – the men whose money you won were in better practice."

We left the house in the sole possession of two police agents – every one of the inmates being removed to prison on the spot. The sub-prefect, after taking down my *procès-verbal* in his office, returned with me to my hotel to get my passport. "Do you think," I asked, as I gave it to him, "that any men have really been smothered in that bed, as they tried to smother *me?*"

"I have seen dozens of drowned men laid out at the Morgue," answered the sub-prefect, "in whose pocketbooks were found letters, stating that they had committed suicide in the Seine because they had lost everything at the gaming-table. Do I know how many of those men entered the same gambling-house that *you* entered, won as *you* won, took that bed as *you* took it, slept in it, were smothered in it and were privately thrown into the river with a letter of explanation written by the murderers and placed in their pocket-books? No man can say how many or how few have suffered the fate from which you have escaped. The people of the gambling-house kept their bedstead machinery a secret from *us* – even from the police! The dead kept the rest of the secret for them. Good-night, or rather good morning, Monsieur Faulkner! Be at my office again at nine o'clock – in the meantime, *au revoir!*"

The rest of my story is soon told. I was examined and re-examined; the gambling-house was strictly searched all through from top to bottom; the prisoners were separately interrogated; and two of the less guilty among them made a confession. I discovered that the old soldier was the master of the gambling-house – *justice* discovered that he had been drummed out of the army as a vagabond years ago; that he had been guilty of all sorts of villainies since; that he was in possession of stolen property, which the owners identified; and that he, the croupier, another accomplice, and the woman who had made my cup of coffee, were all in the secret of the bedstead. There appeared some reason to doubt whether the inferior persons attached to the house knew anything of the suffocating machinery – and they received the benefit of that doubt, by being treated simply as thieves and vagabonds. As for the old soldier and his two head-myrmidons, they went to the galleys; the woman who had drugged my coffee was imprisoned for I forget how many years; the regular attendants at the gambling-house were considered "suspicious", and placed under "surveillance"; and I became, for one whole week (which is a long time), the head "lion" in Parisian society. My adventure was dramatized by three illustrious playmakers

but never saw theatrical daylight, for the censorship forbade the introduction on the stage of a correct copy of the gambling-house bedstead.

One good result was produced by my adventure, which any censorship must have approved: it cured me of ever again trying *Rouge et Noir*
as an amusement. The sight of a green cloth, with packs of cards and
heaps of money on it, will henceforth be for ever associated in my mind
with the sight of a bed-canopy descending to suffocate me in the
silence and darkness of the night.

Nine O'Clock!

The night of June 30th, 1793, is memorable in the prison annals of Paris, as the last night in confinement of the leaders of the famous Girondin Party in the first French Revolution. On the morning of the 31st, the twenty-one deputies who represented the department of the Girdone were guillotined to make way for Robespierre and the Reign of Terror.

With these men fell the last revolutionists of that period who shrank from founding a republic on massacre; who recoiled from substituting for a monarchy of corruption a monarchy of bloodshed. The elements of their defeat lay as much in themselves as in the events of their time. They were not, as a party, true to their own convictions: they temporized, they fatally attempted to take a middle course amid the terrible emergencies of a terrible epoch and they fell – fell before worse men, because those men were in earnest.

Condemned to die, the Girondins submitted nobly to their fate; their great glory was the glory of their deaths. The speech of one of them, on hearing his sentence pronounced, was a prophecy of the future, fulfilled to the letter.

"I die," he said to the Jacobin judges, the creatures of Robespierre, who tried him. "I die at a time when the people have lost their reason; *you* will die on the day when they recover it." Valazé was the only member of the condemned party who displayed a momentary weakness: he stabbed himself on hearing his sentence pronounced. But the blow was not mortal. He died on the scaffold, and died bravely with the rest.

On the night of the 30th the Girondins held their famous banquet in the prison; celebrated, with the ferocious stoicism of the time, their last social meeting before the morning on which they were to die. Other men, besides the twenty-one, were present at this supper of the condemned. They were prisoners who held Girondin opinions but whose names were not illustrious enough for history to preserve. Although sentenced to confinement they were not sentenced to death.

Some of their number, who had protested most boldly against the con-
demnation of the deputies, were ordered to witness the execution on
the morrow, as a timely example to terrify them into submission. More
than this, Robespierre and his colleagues did not, as yet, venture to
attempt: the Reign of Terror was a cautious reign at starting.

The supper-table of the prison was spread; the guests, twenty-one of
their number stamped already with the seal of death, were congregated
at the last Girondin banquet: toast followed toast; the *Marseillaise* was
sung; the desperate triumph of the feast was rising fast to its climax,
when a new and ominous subject of conversation was started at the
lower end of the table, and spread electrically, almost in a moment, to
the top.

This subject (by whom originated no one knew) was simply a question as to the hour in the morning at which the execution was to take
place. Every one of the prisoners appeared to be in ignorance on this
point, and the gaolers either could not, or would not, enlighten them.
Until the cart for the condemned rolled into the prison-yard, not one of
the Girondins could tell whether he was to be called out to the guillotine soon after sunrise or not till near noon.

This uncertainty was made a topic for discussion, or for jesting on
all sides. It was eagerly seized on as a pretext for raising to the highest
pitch the ghastly animation and hilarity of the evening. In some quarters, the recognized hour of former executions was quoted as precedent
sure to be followed by the executioners of the morrow; in others, it was
asserted that Robespierre and his party would purposely depart from
established customs in this, as in previous instances. Dozens of wild
schemes were suggested for guessing the hour by fortune-telling rules
on the cards; bets were offered and accepted among the prisoners who
were not condemned to death, and witnessed in stoical mockery by the
prisoners who were. Jests were exchanged about early rising and hurried
toilets; in short, every man contributed an assertion, with one solitary
exception. That exception was the Girondin, Duprat, one of the
deputies who was sentenced to die by the guillotine.

He was a younger man than the majority of his brethren, and was
personally remarkable by his pale, handsome, melancholy face and his

reserved yet gentle manners. Throughout the evening, he had spoken but rarely; there was something of the silence and serenity of a martyr in his demeanour. That he feared death as little as any of his companions was plainly visible in his bright, steady eye; in his unchanging complexion; in his firm, calm voice, when he occasionally addressed those who happened to be near him. But he was evidently out of place at the banquet. His temperament was reflective, his disposition serious; feasts were at no time a sphere in which he was calculated to shine.

His taciturnity, while the hour of the execution was under discussion, had separated him from most of those with whom he sat at the lower end of the table. They edged up towards the top, where the conversation was most general and most animated. One of his friends, however, still kept his place by Duprat's side, and thus questioned him anxiously, but in low tones, on the cause of his immovable silence:

"Are you the only man of the company, Duprat, who has neither a guess nor a joke to make about the time of the execution?"

"I never joke, Marginy," was the answer, given with a slight smile which had something of the sarcastic in it. "And as for guessing at the time of the execution, I never guess at things which I *know*."

"Know! You know the hour of the execution? Then why not communicate your knowledge to your friends around you?"

"Because not one of them would believe what I said."

"But, surely, you could prove it. Somebody must have told you."

"Nobody has told me."

"You have seen some private letter, then, or you have managed to get sight of the execution-order, or –"

"Spare your conjectures, Marginy. I have not read, as I have not been told, what is the hour at which we are to die to-morrow."

"Then how on earth can you possibly know it?"

"I do *not* know when the execution will begin or when it will end. I only know that it will be *going on* at nine o'clock to-morrow morning. Out of the twenty-one who are to suffer death, one will be guillotined exactly at that hour. Whether he will be the first whose head falls, or the last, I cannot tell."

"And pray who may this man be, who is going to die exactly at nine o'clock? Of course, prophetically knowing so much, you know that!"

"I *do* know it. I am the man whose death by the guillotine will take place exactly at the hour I have mentioned."

"You said just now, Duprat, that you never joked. Do you expect me to believe that what you have just spoken is spoken in earnest?"

"I repeat that I never joke; and I answer that I expect you to believe me. I know the hour at which my death will take place to-morrow, just as certainly as I know the fact of my own existence to-night."

"But how? My dear friend, can you really lay claim to supernatural intuition, in this eighteenth century of the world, in this renowned Age of Reason?"

"No two men, Marginy, understand that word, supernatural, exactly in the same sense; you and I differ about its meaning, or, in other words, differ about the real distinction between the doubtful and the true. We will not discuss the subject: I wish to be understood, at the outset, as laying claim to no superior intuitions whatever; but I tell you, at the same time, that even in this Age of Reason, I have reason for what I have said. My father and my brother both died at nine o'clock in the morning, and were both warned very strangely of their deaths. I am the last of my family; I was warned last night, as they were warned, and I shall die by the guillotine, as they died in their beds, at the fatal hour of nine."

"But, Duprat, why have I never heard of this before? As your oldest and, I am sure, your dearest friend, I thought you had long since trusted me with all your secrets."

"And you shall know this secret; I only kept it from you till the time when I would be certain that my death would substantiate my words, to the very letter. Come! you are as bad supper company as I am; let us slip away from the table unperceived, while our friends are all engaged in conversation. Yonder end of the hall is dark and quiet We can speak there uninterruptedly, for some hours to come."

He led the way from the supper-table, followed by Marginy. Arrived at one of the darkest and most retired corners of the great hall of the prison, Duprat spoke again:

"I believe, Marginy," he said, "that you are one of those who have been ordered by our tyrants to witness my execution, and the execution of my brethren, as a warning spectacle for an enemy to the Jacobin cause?"

"My dear, dear friend! it is too true; I am ordered to witness the butchery which I cannot prevent – our last awful parting will be at the foot of the scaffold. I am among the victims who are spared – mercilessly spared – for a little while yet."

"Say the martyrs! We die as martyrs, calmly, hopefully, innocently. When I am placed under the guillotine to-morrow morning, listen, my friend, for the striking of the church clocks; listen for the hour while you look your last on me. Until that time, suspend your judgement on the strange chapter of family history which I am now about to relate."

Marginy took his friend's hand, and promised compliance with the request. Duprat then began as follows:

"You knew my brother Alfred when he was quite a youth, and you knew something of what people flippantly termed the eccentricities of his character. He was three years my junior, but from childhood he showed far less of a child's innate levity and happiness than his elder brother. He was noted for his seriousness and thoughtfulness as a boy, showed little inclination for a boy's usual lessons and less still for a boy's usual recreations. In short, he was considered by everybody (my father included) as deficient in intellect, as a vacant dreamer and an inveterate idler, whom it was hopeless to improve. Our tutor tried to lead him to various studies, and tried in vain. It was the same when the cultivation of his mind was given up and the cultivation of his body was next attempted. The fencing-master could make nothing of him; and the dancing-master, after the first three lessons, resigned in despair. Seeing that it was useless to set others to teach him, my father made a virtue of necessity and left him, if he chose, to teach himself.

"To the astonishment of every one, he had not been long consigned to his own guidance, when he was discovered in the library, reading every old treatise on astrology which he could lay his hands on. He had rejected all useful knowledge for the most obsolete of obsolete sciences – the old, abandoned delusion of divination by stars! My father laughed heartily over the strange study to which his idle son had at last applied himself, but made no attempt to oppose his new caprice and sarcastically presented him with a telescope on his next birthday. I should remind you here of what you may perhaps have forgotten, that my father was a philosopher of the Voltaire school, who believed that the summit of human wisdom was to arrive at the power of sneering at all enthusiasms and doubting of all truths. Apart from his philosophy, he was a kind-hearted, easy man, of quick rather than profound intelligence. He could see nothing in my brother's new occupation but the evidence of a new idleness, a fresh caprice which would be abandoned in a few months. My father was not the man to appreciate those yearnings towards the poetical and the spiritual, which were part of Alfred's temperament, and which gave to his peculiar studies of the stars and their influences, a certain charm altogether unconnected with the more practical attractions of scientific investigation.

"This idle caprice of my brother's, as my father insisted on terming it, had lasted more than a twelvemonth, when there occurred the first of a series of mysterious and – as I consider them – supernatural events, with all of which Alfred was very remarkably connected. I was myself a witness of the strange circumstance, which I am now about to relate to you.

"One day – my brother being then sixteen years of age – I happened to go into my father's study during his absence, and found Alfred there, standing close to a window which looked into the garden. I walked up to him, and observed a curious expression of vacancy and rigidity in his face, especially in his eyes. Although I knew him to be subject to what are called fits of absence, I still thought it rather extraordinary that he never moved and never noticed me when I was close to him. I took his hand and asked if he was unwell. His flesh felt quite cold; neither my touch nor my voice produced the smallest sensation in him. Almost at the same moment when I noticed this, I happened to be looking accidentally towards the garden. There was my father walking along one of the paths, and there, by his side, walking with him, was *another Alfred!* – Another, yet exactly the same as the Alfred by whose side I was standing, whose hand I still held in mine!

"Thoroughly panic-stricken, I dropped his hand and uttered a cry of terror. At the loud sound of my voice, the statue-like presence before me immediately began to show signs of animation. I looked round again at the garden. The figure of my brother, which I had beheld there, was gone, and I saw to my horror that my father was looking for it – looking in all directions for the companion (spectre, or human being?) of his walk!

"When I turned towards Alfred once more, he had (if I may so express it) come to life again, and was asking, with his usual gentleness of manner and kindness of voice, why I was looking so pale. I evaded the question by making some excuse, and in my turn inquired of him, how long he had been in my father's study.

" 'Surely you ought to know best,' he answered with a laugh, 'for you must have been here before me. It is not many minutes ago since I was walking in the garden with –'

"Before he could complete the sentence my father entered the room.

" 'Oh! here you are, Master Alfred,' said he. 'May I ask for what purpose you took it into your wise head to vanish in that extraordinary manner? Why you slipped away from me in an instant, while I was picking a flower! On my word, sir, you're a better player at hide-and-seek than your brother; *he* would only have run into the shrubbery, *you* have managed to run in here, although how you did it in the time passes my poor comprehension. I was not a moment picking the flower, yet in that moment you were gone!'

"Alfred glanced suddenly and searchingly at me; his face became deadly pale, and, without speaking a word, he hurried from the room.

" 'Can *you* explain this?' said my father, looking very much astonished.

"I hesitated a moment, and then told him what I had seen. He took a pinch of snuff – a favourite habit with him when he was going to be sarcastic, in imitation of Voltaire.

" 'One visionary in a family is enough,' said he. 'I recommend you not to turn yourself into a bad imitation of your brother Alfred! Send your ghost after me, my good boy! I am going back into the garden, and should like to see him again!'

"Ridicule, even much sharper than this, would have had little effect on me. If I was certain of anything in the world, I was certain that I had seen my brother in the study – nay, more, had touched him – and equally certain that I had seen his double, his exact similitude, in the garden. As far as any man could know that he was in possession of his own senses, I knew myself to be in possession of mine. Left alone to think over what I had beheld, I felt a supernatural terror creeping through me – a terror which increased when I recollected that, on one or two occasions, friends had said they had seen Alfred out of doors when we all knew him to be at home. These statements, which my father had laughed at, and had taught me to laugh at, either as a trick or a delusion on the part of others, now recurred to my memory as startling corroborations of what I had just seen myself. The solitude of the study oppressed me in a manner which I cannot describe. I left the apartment to seek Alfred, determined to question him, with all possible caution, on the subject of his strange trance and his sensations at the moment when I had awakened him from it.

"I found him in his bedroom, still pale, and now very thoughtful. As the first words in reference to the scene in the study passed my lips, he started violently and entreated me, with very unusual warmth of speech and manner, never to speak to him on that subject again – never, if I had any love or regard for him! Of course, I complied with his request. The mystery, however, was not destined to end here.

"About two months after the event which I have just related, we had arranged, one evening, to go to the theatre. My father had insisted that Alfred should be of the party, otherwise he would certainly have declined accompanying us, for he had no inclination whatever for public amusements of any kind. However, with his usual docility, he prepared to obey my father's desire, by going upstairs to put on his evening dress. It was winter-time, so he was obliged to take a candle with him.

"We waited in the drawing-room for his return a very long time, so long, that my father was on the point of sending upstairs to remind him of the lateness of the hour, when Alfred reappeared without the candle which he had taken with him from the room. The ghostly alteration over his face – the hideous, death-look that distorted his features I shall never forget – I shall see it to-morrow on the scaffold!

"Before either my father or I could utter a word, my brother said:

" 'I have been taken suddenly ill; but I am better now. Do you still wish me to go to the theatre?'

" 'Certainly not, my dear Alfred,' answered my father; 'we must send for the doctor immediately.'

" 'Pray do not call in the doctor, sir; he would be of no use. I will tell you why, if you will let me speak to you alone.'

"My father, looking seriously alarmed, signed to me to leave the room. For more than half an hour I remained absent, suffering almost unendurable suspense and anxiety on my brother's account. When I was recalled, I observed that Alfred was quite calm, though still deadly pale. My father's manner displayed an agitation which I had never observed in it before. He rose from his chair when I re-entered the room, and left me alone with my brother.

" 'Promise me,' said Alfred, in answer to my entreaties to know what had happened, 'promise that you will not ask me to tell you more than my father has permitted me to tell. It is his desire that I should keep certain things a secret from you.'

"I gave the required promise, but gave it most unwillingly. Alfred then proceeded.

" 'When I left you to go and dress for the theatre, I felt a sense of oppression all over me, which I cannot describe. As soon as I was alone, it seemed as if some part of the life within me was slowly wasting away. I could hardly breathe the air around me, big drops of perspiration burst out on my forehead, and then a feeling of terror seized me, which I was utterly unable to control. Some of those strange fancies of seeing my mother's spirit, which used to influence me at the time of her death, came back again to my mind. I ascended the stairs slowly and painfully, not daring to look behind me, for I heard – yes, heard! – something following me. When I got into my room and had shut the door, I began to recover my self-possession a little. But the sense of oppression was still as heavy on me as ever, when I approached the wardrobe to get out my clothes. Just as I stretched forth my hand to turn the key, I saw, to my horror, the two doors of the wardrobe opening of themselves, opening slowly and silently. The candle went out at the same moment, and the whole inside of the wardrobe became to me like a great mirror, with a bright light shining in the middle of it. Out of that light there came a figure, the exact counterpart of myself. Over its breast hung an open scroll, and on that I read the warning of my own death and a revelation of the destinies of my father and his race. Do not ask me what were the words on the scroll, I have given my promise not to tell you. I may only say that, as soon as I had read all, the room grew dark and the vision disappeared.'

"Forgetful of my promise, I entreated Alfred to repeat to me the words on the scroll. He smiled sadly, and refused to speak on the subject any more. I next sought out my father, and begged him to divulge the secret. Still sceptical to the last, he answered that one diseased imagination in the family was enough, and that he would not permit me to run the risk of being infected by Alfred's mental malady. I passed the whole of that day and the next in a state of agitation and alarm which nothing could tranquillize. The sight I had seen in the study gave a terrible significance to the little that my brother had told me. I was uneasy if he was a moment out of my sight. There was something in his expression – calm and even cheerful as it was – which made me dread the worst.

"On the morning of the third day after the occurrence I have just related, I rose very early after a sleepless night and went into Alfred's bedroom. He was awake, and welcomed me with more than usual affection and kindness. As I drew a chair to his bedside, he asked me to get pen, ink and paper, and write down something from his dictation. I obeyed, and found to my terror and distress, that the idea of death was more present to his imagination than ever. He employed me in writing a statement of his wishes in regard to the disposal of all his own little possessions, as keepsakes to be given, after he was no more, to my father, myself, the house-servants and one or two of his own most intimate friends. Over and over again I entreated him to tell me whether he really believed that his death was near. He invariably replied that I should soon know, and then led the conversation to indifferent topics. As the morning advanced, he asked to see my father, who came, accompanied by the doctor, the latter having been in attendance for the last two days.

"Alfred took my father's hand, and begged his forgiveness of any offence, any disobedience of which he had ever been guilty. Then, reaching out his other hand and taking mine, as I stood on the opposite side of the bed, he asked what the time was. A clock was placed on the mantel-piece of the room, but not in a position in which he could see it, as he now lay. I turned round to look at the dial, and answered that, it was just on the stroke of nine.

" 'Farewell!' said Alfred, calmly; 'in this world, farewell for ever!'

"The next instant the clock struck. I felt his fingers tremble in mine then grow quite still. The doctor seized a hand-mirror that lay on the table, and held it over his lips. He was dead – dead, as the last chime of the hour echoed through the awful silence of the room!

"I pass over the first days of our affliction. You, who have suffered the loss of a beloved sister, can well imagine their misery. I pass over these days and pause for a moment at the time when we could speak with some calmness and resignation on the subject of our bereavement. On the arrival of that period, I ventured, in conversation with my father, to refer to the vision which had been seen by our dear Alfred in his bedroom, and to the prophecy which he described himself as having read upon the supernatural scroll.

"Even yet my father persisted in his scepticism; but now, as it seemed to me, more because he was afraid, than because he was unwilling, to believe. I again recalled to his memory what I myself had seen in the study. I asked him to recollect how certain Alfred had been beforehand, and how fatally right, about the day and hour of his death. Still I could get but one answer; my brother had died of a nervous disorder (the doctor said so): his imagination had been diseased from his childhood; there was only one way of treating the vision which he described himself as having seen, and that was not to speak of it again between ourselves, never to speak of it at all to our friends.

"We were sitting in the study during this conversation. It was evening. As my father uttered the last words of his reply to me, I saw his eye turn suddenly and uneasily towards the further end of the room. In dead silence, I looked in the same direction and saw the door opening of itself, the vacant space beyond was filled with a bright, steady glow, which hid all outer objects in the hall, and which I cannot describe to you by likening it to any light that we are accustomed to behold either by day or night. In my terror, I caught my father by the arm and asked him, in a whisper, whether he did not see something extraordinary in the direction of the doorway?

" 'Yes,' he answered, in tones as low as mine, 'I see, or fancy I see, a strange light, the subject on which we have been speaking has impressed our feelings as it should not. Our nerves are still unstrung by the shock of the bereavement we have suffered: our senses are deluding us. Let us look away towards the garden.'

" 'But the opening of the door, Father. Remember the opening of the door!'

" 'Ours is not the first door which has accidentally flown open of itself.'

" 'Then why not shut it again?'

" 'Why not, indeed. I will close it at once.' He rose, advanced a few paces, then stopped, and came back to his place. 'It is a warm evening,' he said, avoiding my eyes, which were eagerly fixed on him. 'The room will be all the cooler if the door is suffered to remain open.'

"His face grew quite pale as he spoke. The light lasted for a few minutes longer, then suddenly disappeared. For the rest of the evening my father's manner was very much altered. He was silent and thoughtful, and complained of a feeling of oppression and languor, which he tried to persuade himself was produced by the heat of the weather. At an unusually hour he retired to his room.

The next morning, when I got downstairs, I found, to my astonishment, that the servants were engaged in preparations for the departure of somebody from the house. I made inquiries of one of them who was hurriedly packing a trunk. 'My master, sir, starts for Lyons the first thing this morning,' was the reply. I immediately repaired to my father's room, and found him there with an open letter in his hand, which he was reading. His face, as he looked up at me on my entrance, expressed the most violent emotions of apprehension and despair.

" 'I hardly know whether I am awake or dreaming; whether I am the dupe of a terrible delusion or the victim of a supernatural reality more terrible still,' he said in low awe-struck tones as I approached him. 'One of the prophecies which Alfred told me in private that he had read upon the scroll, has come true! He predicted the loss of the bulk of my fortune – here is the letter, which informs me that the merchant at Lyons in whose hands my money was placed, has become bankrupt. Can the occurrence of this ruinous calamity be the chance fulfilment of a mere guess? Or was the doom of my family really revealed to my dead son? I go to Lyons immediately to know the truth: this letter may have been written under false information; it may be the work of an impostor. And yet, Alfred's prediction – I shudder to think of it!'

" 'The light, Father!' I exclaimed, 'the light we saw last night in the study!'

" 'Hush! don't speak of it! Alfred said that I should be warned of the truth of the prophecy, and of its immediate fulfilment, by the shining of the same supernatural light that he had seen – I tried to disbelieve what I beheld last night – I hardly know whether I dare believe it even now! This prophecy is not the last; there are others yet to be fulfilled – but let us not speak, let us not think of them! I must start at once for Lyons; I must be on the spot, if this horrible news is true, to save what I can from the wreck. The letter – give me back the letter! – I must go directly!'

"He hurried back from the room. I followed him, and, with some difficulty, obtained permission to be the companion of his momentous journey. When we arrived at Lyons, we found that the statement in the letter was true. My father's fortune was gone: a mere pittance, derived from a small estate that had belonged to my mother, was all that was left to us.

"My father's health gave way under this misfortune. He never referred again to Alfred's prediction – and I was afraid to mention the subject – but I saw that it was affecting his mind quite as painfully as the loss of his property. Over and over again, he checked himself very strangely when he was on the point of speaking to me about my brother. I saw that there was some secret pressing heavily on his mind, which he was afraid to disclose to me. It was useless to ask for his confidence. His temper had become irritable under disaster; perhaps, also, under the dread uncertainties which were now evidently tormenting him in secret. My situation was a very sad and a very dreary one at that time: I had no remembrances of the past that were not mournful and affrighting remembrances; I had no hopes for the future that were not darkened by a vague presentiment of troubles and perils to come; and I was expressly forbidden by my father to say a word about the terrible events which had cast an unnatural gloom over my youthful career, to any of the friends (yourself included) whose counsel and whose sympathy might have guided and sustained me in the day of trial.

"We returned to Paris, sold our house there and retired to live on the small estate, to which I have referred, as the last possession left us. We had not been many days in our new abode, when my father imprudently exposed himself to a heavy shower of rain and suffered in consequence from a violent attack of cold. This temporary malady was not dreaded by the medical attendant, but it was soon aggravated by a fever, produced as much by the anxiety and distress of mind from which he continued to suffer as by any other cause. Still the doctor gave hope; but still he grew daily worse – so much worse, that I removed my bed into his room and never quitted him night or day.

"One night I had fallen asleep, overpowered by fatigue and anxiety, when I was awakened by a cry from my father. I instantly trimmed the light, and ran to his side. He was sitting up in bed, with his eyes fixed on the door, which had been left ajar to ventilate the room. I saw nothing in that direction and asked what was the matter. He murmured some expressions of affection towards me and begged me to sit by his bedside till the morning, but gave no definite answer to my question. Once or twice I thought he wandered a little, and I observed that he occasionally moved his hand under the pillow, as if searching for something there. However, when the morning came, he appeared to be calm and self-possessed. The doctor arrived and, pronouncing him to be better, retired to the dressing-room to write a prescription. The moment his back was turned, my father laid his weak hand on my arm, and whispered faintly:

" 'Last night I saw the supernatural light again – the second prediction – true, true – my death this time – the same hour as Alfred's – nine – nine o'clock, this morning.' He paused a moment through weakness; then added: 'Take that sealed paper – under the pillow – when I am dead, read it – now go into the dressing-room – my watch is there – I have heard the church clock strike eight; let me see how long it is now till nine – go – go quickly!'

"Horror-stricken, moving and acting like a man in a trance, I silently obeyed him. The doctor was still in the dressing-room. Despair made me catch eagerly at any chance of saving my father; I told his medical attendant what I had just heard, and entreated advice and assistance without delay.

" 'He is a little delirious,' said the doctor, 'don't be alarmed: we can cheat him out of his dangerous idea and so perhaps save his life. Where is the watch?' (I produced it.) 'See: it is ten minutes to nine. I will put back the hands one hour; that will give good time for a composing draught to operate. There! take him the watch, and let him see the false time with his own eyes. He will be comfortably asleep before the hour hand gets round again to nine.'

"I went back with the watch to my father's bed-side. 'Too slow,' he murmured, as he looked at the dial, 'too slow by an hour – the church clock – I counted eight.'

" 'Father! dear Father! you are mistaken,' I cried. 'I counted also: it was only seven.'

" 'Only seven!' he echoed faintly, 'another hour then – another hour to live!' He evidently believed what I had said to him. In spite of the fatal experiences of the past, I now ventured to hope the best for our stratagem as I resumed my place by his side.

"The doctor came in; but my father never noticed him. He kept his eyes fixed on the watch, which lay between us, on the coverlid. When the minute hand was within a few seconds of indicating the false hour of eight, he looked round at me, murmured very feebly and doubtingly: 'Another hour to live!' and then gently closed his eyes. I looked at the watch, and saw that it was just eight o'clock, according to our alteration of the right time. At the same moment, I heard the doctor, whose hand had been on my father's pulse, exclaim:

" 'My God! it's stopped! He *has* died at nine o'clock!'

"The fatality, which no human stratagem or human science could turn aside, was accomplished! I was alone in the world!

"In the solitude of our little cottage, on the day of my father's burial, I opened the sealed letter, which he had told me to take from the pillow of his death-bed. In preparing to read it, I knew that I was preparing for the knowledge of my own doom; but I neither trembled nor wept. I was beyond grief: despair such as mine was then is calm and self-possessed to the last.

"The letter ran thus: 'After your father and brother have fallen under the fatality that pursues our house, it is right, my dear son, that you should be warned how *you* are included in the last of the predictions which still remains unaccomplished. Know then, that the final lines read by our dear Alfred on the scroll, prophesied that *you* should die, as *we* have died, at the fatal hour of nine; but by a bloody and violent death, the day of which was not foretold. My beloved boy! you know not, you never will know, what I suffered in the possession of this terrible secret, as the truth of the former prophecies forced itself more and more plainly on my mind! Even now, as I write, I hope against all hope, believe vainly and desperately against all experience, that this last, worst doom may be avoided. Be cautious; be patient; look well before you at each step of your career. The fatality by which you are threatened is terrible; but there is a Power above fatality; and before that Power my spirit and my child's spirit now pray for you. Remember this when your heart is heavy, your path through life grows dark. Remember that the better world is still before you, the world where we shall all meet! Farewell!'

"When I first read those lines, I read them with the gloomy, immovable resignation of the Eastern fatalists; and that resignation never left me afterwards. Here, in this prison, I feel it, calm as ever. I bowed patiently to my doom when it was only predicted: I bow to it as patiently now when it is on the eve of accomplishment. You have often wondered, my friend, at the tranquil, equable sadness of my manner: after what I have just told you, can you wonder any longer?

"But let me return for a moment to the past. Although I had no hope of escaping the fatality which had overtaken my father and my brother, my life, after my double bereavement, was the existence of all others which might seem most likely to evade the accomplishment of my predicted doom. Yourself and one other friend excepted, I saw no society, my walks were limited to the cottage garden and the neighbouring fields and my everyday, unvarying occupation was confined to that hard and resolute course of study, by which alone I could hope to prevent my mind from dwelling on what I had suffered in the past or on what I might still be condemned to suffer in the future. Never was there a life more quiet and more uneventful than mine!

"You know how I awoke to an ambition, which irresistibly impelled me to change this mode of existence. News from Paris penetrated even to my obscure retreat and disturbed my self-imposed tranquillity. I heard of the last errors and weaknesses of Louis the Sixteenth; I heard of the assembling of the States-General; and I knew that the French Revolution had begun. The tremendous emergencies of that epoch drew men of all characters from private to public pursuits, and made politics the necessity rather than the choice of every Frenchman's life. The great change preparing for the country acted universally on individuals, even to the humblest, and it acted on *me*.

"I was elected a deputy, more for the sake of the name I bore, than on account of any little influence which my acquirements and my character might have exercised in the neighbourhood of my country abode. I removed to Paris and took my seat in the Chamber, little thinking at that time of the crime and the bloodshed to which our revolution, so moderate in its beginning, would lead; little thinking that I had taken the first, irretrievable steps towards the bloody and violent death which was lying in store for me.

"Need I go on? You know how warmly I joined the Girondin party; you know how we have been sacrificed; you know what the death is which I and my brethren are to suffer to-morrow. On now ending, I repeat what I said at the beginning: Judge not of my narrative till you have seen with your own eyes what really takes place in the morning. I have carefully abstained from all comment, I have simply related events as they happened, forbearing to add my own views of their significance, my own ideas on the explanation of which they admit. You may believe us to have been a family of nervous visionaries, witnesses of certain remarkable contingencies; victims of curious, but not impossible chances, which we have fancifully and falsely interpreted into supernatural events. I leave you undisturbed in this conviction (if you really feel it); to-morrow you will think differently; to-morrow you will be an altered man. In the mean time, remember what I now say, as you would remember my dying words: last night I saw the supernatural radiance which warned my father and my brother, and which warns *me*, that, whatever the time when the execution begins, whatever the order in which the twenty-one Girondins are chosen for death, I shall be the man who kneels under the guillotine, as the clock strikes nine!"

It was morning. Of the ghastly festivities of the night no sign remained. The prison-hall wore an altered look as the twenty-one condemned men (followed by those who were ordered to witness their execution) were marched out to the carts appointed to take them from the dungeon to the scaffold.

The sky was cloudless, the sun warm and brilliant, as the Girondin leaders and their companions were drawn slowly through the streets to the place of execution. Duprat and Marginy were placed in separate vehicles: the contrast in their demeanour at that awful moment was strongly marked. The features of the doomed man still preserved their noble and melancholy repose; his glance was steady; his colour never changed. The face of Marginy, on the contrary, displayed the strongest agitation; he was pale even to his lips. The terrible narrative he had heard, the anticipation of the final and appalling proof by which its truth was now to be tested, had robbed him, for the first time in his life, of all his self-possession. Duprat had predicted truly. The morrow had come, and he was an altered man already.

The carts drew up at the foot of the scaffold which was soon to be stained with the blood of twenty-one human beings. The condemned deputies mounted it and ranged themselves at the end opposite the guillotine. The prisoners who were to behold the execution remained in their cart. Before Duprat ascended the steps, he took his friend's hand for the last time.

"Farewell!" he said calmly. "Farewell! I go to my father and my brother! Remember my words of last night."

With straining eyes and bloodless cheeks, Marginy saw Duprat take his position in the middle row of his companions, who stood in three ranks of seven each. Then the awful spectacle of the execution began. After the first seven deputies had suffered there was a pause; the horrible traces of the judicial massacre were being removed. When the execution proceeded, Duprat was the third taken from the middle rank of the condemned. As he came forward, he stood for an instant erect under the guillotine, he looked with a smile on his friend and repeated in a clear voice the word "*Remember!*", then bowed himself on the block. The blood stood still at Marginy's heart, as he looked and listened during the moment of silence that followed. That moment past, the church clocks of Paris struck. He dropped down in the cart and covered his face with his hands; for through the heavy beat of the hour he heard the fall of the fatal steel.

"Pray, sir, was it nine or ten that struck just now?" said one of Marginy's fellow-prisoners to an officer of the guard who stood near the cart.

The person addressed referred to his watch, and answered: "NINE O'CLOCK!"

The Fourth Poor Traveller

I served my time – never mind in whose office – and I started in business for myself in one of our English country towns – I decline stating which. I hadn't a farthing of capital, and my friends in the neighbourhood were poor and useless enough, with one exception. That exception was Mr. Frank Gatliffe, son of Mr. Gatliffe, member for the county, the richest man and the proudest for many a mile round about our parts.

Stop a bit, Mr. Artist! you needn't perk up and look knowing. You won't trace any particulars by the name of Gatliffe. I'm not bound to commit myself or anybody else by mentioning names. I have given you the first that came into my head.

Well, Mr. Frank was a staunch friend of mine, and ready to recommend me whenever he got the chance. I had contrived to let him a little timely help – for a consideration, of course – in borrowing money at a fair rate of interest; in fact, I had saved him from the Jews. The money was borrowed while Mr. Frank was at college. He came back from college and stopped at home a little while, and then there got spread about all our neighbourhood a report that he had fallen in love, as the saying is, with his young sister's governess, and that his mind was made up to marry her.

What! you're at it again, Mr. Artist! You want to know her name, don't you? What do you think of Smith?

Speaking as a lawyer, I consider report, in a general way, to be a fool and a liar. But in this case report turned out to be something very different. Mr. Frank told me he was really in love, and said upon his honour (an absurd expression which young chaps of his age are always using) he was determined to marry Smith the governess – the sweet darling girl, as *he* called her; but I'm not sentimental, and *I* call her Smith the governess. Well, Mr. Frank's father, being as proud as Lucifer, said No as to marrying the governess, when Mr. Frank wanted him to say Yes. He was a man of business was old Gatliffe, and he took the proper business course. He sent the governess away with a first-rate character and a spanking present, and then he looked about him to get something for Mr. Frank to do. While he was looking about, Mr. Frank bolted to London after the governess, who had nobody alive belonging to her to go to but an aunt – her father's sister. The aunt refuses to let Mr. Frank in without the squire's permission. Mr. Frank writes to his father, and says he will marry the girl as soon as he is of age or shoot himself. Up to town comes the squire and his wife and his daughter, and a lot of sentimentality, not in the slightest degree material to the present statement, takes place among them; and the upshot of it is that old Gatliffe is forced into withdrawing the word No, and substituting the word Yes.

I don't believe he would ever have done it, though, but for one lucky peculiarity in the case. The governess' father was a man of good family – pretty nigh as good as Gatliffe's own. He had been in the army; had sold out, set up as a wine-merchant, failed – died. Ditto his wife, as to the dying part of it. No relation, in fact, left for the squire to make inquiries about but the father's sister – who had behaved, as old Gatliffe said, like a thorough-bred gentlewoman in shutting the door against Mr. Frank in the first instance. So, to cut the matter short, things were at last made up pleasant enough. The time was fixed for the wedding, and an announcement about it – Marriage in High Life and all that – put into the county paper. There was a regular biography, besides, of the governess' father, so as to stop people from talking – a great flourish about his pedigree and a long account of his services in the army; but not a word, mind ye, of his having turned wine-merchant afterwards. Oh, no – not a word about that!

I knew it, though, for Mr. Frank told me. He hadn't a bit of pride about him. He introduced me to his future wife one day when I met them out walking, and asked me if I did not think he was a lucky fellow. I don't mind admitting that I did, and that I told him so. Ah! but she was one of my sort, was that governess. Stood, to the best of my recollection, five foot four. Good lissome figure, that looked as if it had never been boxed up in a pair of stays. Eyes that made me feel as if I was under a pretty stiff cross-examination the moment she looked at me! Fine red, fresh, kiss-and-come-again sort of lips. Cheeks and complexion –. No, Mr. Artist, you wouldn't identify her by her cheeks and complexion, if I drew you a picture of them this very moment. She has had a family of children since the time I'm talking of; and her cheeks are a trifle fatter, and her complexion is a shade or two redder now, than when I first met her out walking with Mr. Frank.

The marriage was to take place on a Wednesday. I decline mentioning the year or the month. I had started as an attorney on my own account – say, six weeks, more or less – and was sitting alone in my office on the Monday morning before the wedding-day, trying to see my way clear before me and not succeeding particularly well, when Mr. Frank suddenly bursts in, as white as any ghost that ever was painted, and says he's got the most dreadful case for me to advise on, and not an hour to lose in acting on my advice.

"Is this in the way of business, Mr. Frank?" says I, stopping him just as he was beginning to get sentimental. "Yes or no, Mr. Frank?" rapping my new office paper-knife on the table to pull him up short all the sooner.

"My dear fellow" – he was always familiar with me – "it's in the way of business, certainly; but friendship –"

I was obliged to pull him up short again, and regularly examine him as if he had been in the witness-box, or he would have kept me talking to no purpose half the day.

"Now, Mr. Frank," says I, "I can't have any sentimentality mixed up with business matters. You please to stop talking, and let me ask questions. Answer in the fewest words you can use. Nod when nodding will do instead of words."

I fixed him with my eye for about three seconds, as he sat groaning and wriggling in his chair. When I'd done fixing him, I gave another rap with my paper-knife on the table to startle him up a bit. Then I went on.

"From what you have been stating up to the present time," says I, "I gather that you are in a scrape which is likely to interfere seriously with your marriage on Wednesday?"

He nodded, and I cut in again before he could say a word:

"The scrape affects your young lady, and goes back to the period of a transaction in which her late father was engaged, don't it?"

He nods, and I cut in once more:

"There is a party, who turned up after seeing the announcement of your marriage in the paper, who is cognizant of what he oughtn't to know and who is prepared to use his knowledge of the same to the prejudice of the young lady and of your marriage, unless he receives a sum of money to quiet him? Very well. Now, first of all, Mr. Frank, state what you have been told by the young lady herself about the transaction of her late father. How did you first come to have any knowledge of it?"

"She was talking to me about her father one day so tenderly and prettily that she quite excited my interest about him," begins Mr. Frank, "and I asked her, among other things, what had occasioned his death. She said she believed it was distress of mind in the first instance – and added that this distress was connected with a shocking secret, which she and her mother had kept from everybody, but which she could not keep from me, because she was determined to begin her married life by having no secrets from her husband." Here Mr. Frank began to get sentimental again, and I pulled him up short once more with the paper-knife.

"She told me", Mr. Frank went on, "that the great mistake of her father's life was his selling out of the army and taking to the wine trade. He had no talent for business; things went wrong with him from the first. His clerk, it was strongly suspected, cheated him –"

"Stop a bit," says I. "What was that suspected clerk's name?"

"Davager," says he.

"Davager," says I, making a note of it. "Go on, Mr. Frank."

"His affairs got more and more entangled," says Mr. Frank. "He was pressed for money in all directions; bankruptcy, and consequent dishonour (as he considered it), stared him in the face. His mind was so affected by his troubles that both his wife and daughter, towards the last, considered him to be hardly responsible for his own acts. In this state of desperation and misery, he –" Here Mr. Frank began to hesitate.

We have two ways in the Law of drawing evidence off nice and clear from an unwilling client or witness. We give him a fright or we treat him to a joke. I treated Mr. Frank to a joke.

"Ah!" says I. "I know what he did. He had a signature to write; and, by the most natural mistake in the world, he wrote another gentleman's name instead of his own – eh?"

"It was to a bill," says Mr. Frank, looking very crestfallen, instead of taking the joke. "His principal creditor wouldn't wait till he could raise the money, or the greater part of it. But he was resolved, if he sold off everything, to get the amount and repay –"

"Of course!" says I, "drop that. The forgery was discovered. When?"

"Before even the first attempt was made to negotiate the bill. He had done the whole thing in the most absurdly and innocently wrong way. The person whose name he had used was a staunch friend of his, and a relation of his wife's – a good man as well as a rich one. He had influence with the chief creditor, and he used it nobly. He had a real affection for the unfortunate man's wife, and he proved it generously."

"Come to the point," says I. "What did he do? In a business way, what did he do?"

"He put the false bill into the fire, drew a bill of his own to replace it, and then – only then – told my dear girl and her mother all that had happened. Can you imagine anything nobler?" asks Mr. Frank.

"Speaking in my professional capacity, I can't imagine anything greener?" says I. "Where was the father? Off, I suppose?"

"Ill in bed," says Mr. Frank, colouring. "But he mustered strength enough to write a contrite and grateful letter the same day, promising to prove himself worthy of the noble moderation and forgiveness extended to him by selling off everything he possessed to repay his money-debt. He did sell off everything – down to some old family pictures that were heirlooms, down to the little plate he had, down to the very tables and chairs that furnished his drawing-room. Every farthing of the debt was paid, and he was left to begin the world again, with the kindest promises of help from the generous man who had forgiven him. It was too late. His crime of one rash moment – atoned for though it had been – preyed upon his mind. He became possessed with the idea that he had lowered himself for ever in the estimation of his wife and daughter, and –"

"He died," I cut in. "Yes, yes, we know that. Let's go back for a minute to the contrite and grateful letter that he wrote. My experience in the Law, Mr. Frank, has convinced me that if everybody burnt everybody else's letters, half the courts of justice in this country might shut up shop. Do you happen to know whether the letter we are now speaking of contained anything like an avowal or confession of the forgery?"

"Of course it did," says he. "Could the writer express his contrition properly without making some such confession?"

"Quite easy, if he had been a lawyer," says I. "But never mind that; I'm going to make a guess – a desperate guess, mind. Should I be altogether in error if I thought that this letter had been stolen, and that the fingers of Mr. Davager, of suspicious commercial celebrity, might possibly be the fingers which took it?"

"That is exactly what I wanted to make you understand," cried Mr. Frank.

"How did he communicate the interesting fact of the theft to you?"

"He has not ventured into my presence. The scoundrel actually had the audacity –"

"Aha!" says I. "The young lady herself! Sharp practitioner, Mr. Davager."

"Early this morning, when she was walking alone in the shrubbery," Mr. Frank goes on, "he had the assurance to approach her and to say that he had been watching his opportunity of getting a private interview for days past. He then showed her – actually showed her – her unfortunate father's letter, put into her hands another letter directed to me, bowed and walked off, leaving her half dead with astonishment and terror. If I had only happened to be there at the time . . . !" says Mr. Frank, shaking his fist murderously in the air, by way of a finish.

"It's the greatest luck in the world that you were not," says I. "Have you got that other letter?"

He handed it to me. It was so remarkably humorous and short, that I remember every word of it at this distance of time. It began in this way:

To Francis Gatliffe, Esq., jun. – Sir – I have an extremely curious autograph letter to sell. The price is a five hundred pound note. The young lady to whom you are to be married on Wednesday will inform you of the nature of the letter, and the genuineness of the autograph. If you refuse to deal, I shall send a copy to the local paper, and shall wait on your highly respected father with the original curiosity, on the afternoon of Tuesday next. Having come down here on family business, I have put up at the family hotel – being to be heard of at the Gatliffe Arms.

Your very obedient servant,

ALFRED DAVAGER

"A clever fellow that," says I, putting the letter into my private drawer.

"Clever!" cries Mr. Frank, "he ought to be horsewhipped within an inch of his life. I would have done it myself, but she made me promise, before she told me a word of the matter, to come straight to you."

"That was one of the wisest promises you ever made," says I. "We can't afford to bully this fellow, whatever else we may do with him. Do you think I am saying anything libellous against your excellent father's character when I assert that if he saw the letter he would certainly insist on your marriage being put off, at the very least?"

"Feeling as my father does about my marriage, he would insist on its being dropped altogether if he saw this letter," says Mr. Frank with a groan. "But even that is not the worst of it. The generous, noble girl herself says that if the letter appears in the paper with all the unanswerable comments this scoundrel would be sure to add to it, she would rather die than hold me to my engagement – even if my father would let me keep it."

As he said this his eyes began to water. He was a weak young fellow and ridiculously fond of her. I brought him back to business with another rap of the paper-knife.

"Hold up, Mr. Frank," says I. "I have a question or two more. Did you think of asking the young lady, whether, to the best of her knowledge, this infernal letter was the only written evidence of the forgery now in existence?"

"Yes, I did think directly of asking her that," says he, "and she told me she was quite certain that there was no written evidence of the forgery except that one letter."

"Will you give Mr. Davager his price for it?" says I.

"Yes," says Mr. Frank, quite peevish with me for asking him such a question. He was an easy young chap in money matters, and talked of hundreds as most men talk of sixpences.

"Mr. Frank," says I, "you came here to get my help and advice in this extremely ticklish business, and you are ready, as I know without asking, to remunerate me for all and any of my services at the usual professional rate. Now, I've made up my mind to act boldly – desperately, if you like – on the hit or miss, win-all-or-lose-all principle – in dealing with this matter. Here is my proposal. I'm going to try if I can't do Mr. Davager out of his letter. If I don't succeed before to-morrow afternoon, you hand him the money, and I charge you nothing for professional services. If I do succeed, I hand you the letter instead of Mr. Davager, and you give me the money instead of giving it to him. It's a precious risk for me, but I'm ready to run it. You must pay your five hundred any way. What do you say to my plan? Is it Yes, Mr. Frank, or No?"

"Hang your questions!" cries Mr. Frank, jumping up. "You know it's Yes, ten thousand times over. Only you earn the money and –"

"And you will be too glad to give it to me. Very good. Now go home. Comfort the young lady – don't let Mr. Davager so much as set eyes on you – keep quiet – leave everything to me – and feel as certain as you please that all the letters in the world can't stop your being married on Wednesday." With these words I hustled him off out of the office, for I wanted to be left alone to make my mind up about what I should do.

The first thing, of course, was to have a look at the enemy. I wrote to Mr. Davager, telling him that I was privately appointed to arrange the little business-matter between himself and "another party" (no names!) on friendly terms, and begging him to call on me at his earliest convenience. At the very beginning of the case, Mr. Davager bothered me. His answer was that it would not be convenient to him to call till between six and seven in the evening. In this way, you see, he contrived to make me lose several precious hours, at a time when minutes almost were of importance. I had nothing for it but to be patient and to give certain instructions, before Mr. Davager came, to my boy Tom.

There never was such a sharp boy of fourteen before – and there never will be again – as my boy Tom. A spy to look after Mr. Davager was, of course, the first requisite in a case of this kind; and Tom was the smallest, quickest, quietest, sharpest, stealthiest little snake of a chap that ever dogged a gentleman's steps and kept cleverly out of range of a gentleman's eyes. I settled it with the boy that he was not to show at all when Mr. Davager came, and that he was to wait to hear me ring the bell when Mr. Davager left. If I rang twice, he was to show the gentleman out. If I rang once, he was to keep out of the way and follow the gentleman wherever he went till he got back to the inn. Those were the only preparations I could make to begin with, being obliged to wait, and let myself be guided by what turned up.

About a quarter to seven my gentleman came.

In the profession of the Law we get somehow quite remarkably mixed up with ugly people, blackguard people and dirty people. But far away the ugliest and dirtiest blackguard I ever saw in my life was Mr. Alfred Davager. He had greasy white hair and a mottled face. He was low in the forehead, fat in the stomach, hoarse in the voice and weak in the legs. Both his eyes were bloodshot, and one was fixed in his head. He smelt of spirits, and carried a toothpick in his mouth.

"How are you? I've just done dinner," says he – and he lights a cigar, sits down with his legs crossed and winks at me.

I tried at first to take the measure of him in a wheedling, confidential way, but it was no good. I asked him, in a facetious, smiling manner, how he had got hold of the letter. He only told me in answer that he had been in the confidential employment of the writer of it, and that he had always been famous since infancy for a sharp eye to his own interests. I paid him some compliments, but he was not to be flattered. I tried to make him lose his temper; but he kept it in spite of me. It ended in his driving me to my last resource – I made an attempt to frighten him.

"Before we say a word about the money," I began, "let me put a case, Mr. Davager. The pull you have on Mr. Francis Gatliffe is that you can hinder his marriage on Wednesday. Now, suppose I have got a magistrate's warrant to apprehend you in my pocket? Suppose I have a constable to execute it in the next room? Suppose I bring you up to-morrow – the day before the marriage – charge you only generally with an attempt to extort money and apply for a day's remand to complete the case? Suppose, as a suspicious stranger, you can't get bail in this town? Suppose –"

"Stop a bit," says Mr. Davager. "Suppose I should not be the greenest fool that ever stood in shoes? Suppose I should not carry the letter about me? Suppose I should have given a certain envelope to a certain friend of mine in a certain place in this town? Suppose the letter should be inside that envelope, directed to old Gatliffe, side by side with a copy of the letter directed to the editor of the local paper? Suppose my friend should be instructed to open the envelope and take the letters to their right address, if I don't appear to claim them from him this evening? In short, my dear sir, suppose you were born yesterday, and suppose I wasn't?" says Mr. Davager, and winks at me again.

He didn't take me by surprise, for I never expected that he had the letter about him. I made a pretence of being very much taken aback and of being quite ready to give in. We settled our business about delivering the letter and handing over the money in no time. I was to draw out a document, which he was to sign. He knew the document was stuff and nonsense just as well as I did, and told me I was only proposing it to swell my client's bill. Sharp as he was, he was wrong there. The document was not to be drawn out to gain money from Mr. Frank, but to gain time from Mr. Davager. It served me as an excuse to put off the payment of the five hundred pounds till three o'clock on the Tuesday afternoon. The Tuesday morning Mr. Davager said he should devote to his amusement, and asked me what sights were to be seen in the neighbourhood of the town. When I had told him, he pitched his toothpick into my grate, yawned and went out.

I rang the bell once – waited till he had passed the window – and then looked after Tom. There was my jewel of a boy on the opposite side of the street, just setting his top going in the most playful manner possible! Mr. Davager walked away up the street, towards the market-place. Tom whipped his top up the street towards the market-place, too.

In a quarter of an hour he came back, with all his evidence collected in a beautifully clear and compact state. Mr. Davager had walked to a public house just outside the town, in a lane leading to the high road.

On a bench outside the public house there sat a man smoking. He said "All right?" and gave a letter to Mr. Davager, who answered "All right," and walked back to the inn. In the hall he ordered hot rum and water, cigars, slippers and a fire to be lit in his room. After that he went upstairs, and Tom came away.

I now saw my road clear before me – not very far on but still clear. I had housed the letter, in all probability for that night, at the Gatliffe Arms. After tipping Tom, I gave him directions to play about the door of the inn and refresh himself when he was tired at the tart-shop opposite, eating as much as he pleased, on the understanding that he crammed all the time with his eye on the window. If Mr. Davager went out, or Mr. Davager's friend called on him, Tom was to let me know. He was also to take a little note from me to the head chambermaid – an old friend of mine – asking her to step over to my office on a private matter of business as soon as her work was done for that night. After settling these little matters, having half an hour to spare, I turned to and did myself a bloater at the office-fire, and had a drop of gin and hot water, and felt comparatively happy.

When the head chambermaid came, it turned out, as good luck would have it, that Mr. Davager had drawn her attention rather too closely to his ugliness, by offering her a testimony of his regard in the shape of a kiss. I no sooner mentioned him than she flew into a passion; and when I added, by way of clinching the matter, that I was retained to defend the interests of a very beautiful and deserving young lady (name not referred to, of course) against the most cruel underhand treachery on the part of Mr. Davager, the head chambermaid was ready to go any lengths that she could safely to serve my cause. In a few words I discovered that Boots was to call Mr. Davager at eight the next morning, and was to take his clothes downstairs to brush as usual. If Mr. D— had not emptied his own pockets overnight, we arranged that Boots was to forget to empty them for him, and was to bring the clothes downstairs just as he found them. If Mr. D—'s pockets were emptied, then, of course, it would be necessary to transfer the searching process to Mr. D—'s room.

Under any circumstances, I was certain of the head chambermaid;

and under any circumstances also, the head chambermaid was certain of Boots.

I waited till Tom came home, looking very puffy and bilious about the face, but as to his intellects, if anything, rather sharper than ever. His report was uncommonly short and pleasant. The inn was shutting up; Mr. Davager was going to bed in rather a drunken condition; Mr. Davager's friend had never appeared. I sent Tom (properly instructed about keeping our man in view all the next morning) to his shake-down behind the office-desk, where I heard him hiccupping half the night, as even the best boys will, when over-excited and too full of tarts.

At half-past seven next morning, I slipped quietly into Boots's pantry.

Down came the clothes. No pockets in trousers. Waistcoat pockets empty. Coat pockets with something in them. First, handkerchief; secondly, bunch of keys; thirdly, cigar-case; fourthly, pocket-book. Of course I wasn't such a fool as to expect to find the letter there, but I opened the pocket-book with a certain curiosity, notwithstanding.

Nothing in the two pockets of the book but some old advertisements cut out of newspapers, a lock of hair tied round with a dirty bit of ribbon, a circular letter about a loan society and some copies of verses not likely to suit any company that was not of an extremely free-and-easy description. On the leaves of the pocket-book, people's addresses scrawled in pencil and bets jotted down in red ink. On one leaf, by itself, this queer inscription:

"MEM. 5 ALONG. 4 ACROSS."

I understood everything but those words and figures, so of course I copied them out into my own book. Then I waited in the pantry till Boots had brushed the clothes and had taken them upstairs. His report when he came down was, that Mr. D— had asked if it was a fine morning. Being told that it was, he had ordered breakfast at nine and a saddle-horse to be at the door at ten to take him to Grimwith Abbey – one of the sights in our neighbourhood which I had told him of the evening before.

"I'll be here, coming in by the back way, at half-past ten," says I to the head chambermaid.

"What for?" says she.

"To take the responsibility of making Mr. Davager's bed off your hands for this morning only," says I.

"Any more orders?" says she.

"One more," says I. "I want to hire Sam for the morning. Put it down in the order-book that he's to be brought round to my office at ten."

In case you should think Sam was a man, I'd better perhaps tell you he was a pony. I'd made up my mind that it would be beneficial to Tom's health, after the tarts, if he took a constitutional airing on a nice hard saddle in the direction of Grimwith Abbey.

"Anything else?" says the head chambermaid.

"Only one more favour," says I. "Would my boy Tom be very much in the way if he came, from now till ten, to help with the boots and shoes, and stood at his work close by this window which looks out on the staircase?"

"Not a bit," says the head chambermaid.

"Thank you," says I, and stepped back to my office directly.

When I had sent Tom off to help with the boots and shoes, I reviewed the whole case exactly as it stood at that time.

There were three things Mr. Davager might do with the letter. He might give it to his friend again before ten – in which case, Tom would most likely see the said friend on the stairs. He might take it to his friend, or to some other friend, after tea – in which case Tom was ready to follow him on Sam the pony. And, lastly, he might leave it hidden somewhere in his room at the inn – in which case, I was all ready for him with a search-warrant of my own granting, under favour always of my friend the head chambermaid. So far I had my business arrangements all gathered up nice and compact in my own hands. Only two things bothered me: the terrible shortness of the time at my disposal, in case I failed in my first experiments for getting hold of the letter, and that queer inscription which I had copied out of the pocket-book –

"MEM. 5 ALONG. 4 ACROSS."

It was the measurement most likely of something, and he was afraid of forgetting it. Therefore, it was something important. Query – something about himself? Say "5" (inches) "along" – he doesn't wear a wig.

Say "5" (feet) "along" – it can't be coat, waistcoat, trousers, or under-clothing. Say "5" (yards) "along" – it can't be anything about himself, unless he wears round his body the rope that he's sure to be hanged with one of these days. Then it is *not* something about himself. What do I know of that is important to him besides? I know of nothing but the letter. Can the memorandum be connected with that? Say, yes. What do "5 along" and "4 across" mean, then? The measurement of some-thing he carries about with him? – or the measurement of something in his room? I could get pretty satisfactorily to myself as far as that, but I could get no further.

Tom came back to the office, and reported him mounted for his ride. His friend had never appeared. I sent the boy off, with his proper instructions, on Sam's back – wrote an encouraging letter to Mr. Frank to keep him quiet – then slipped into the inn by the back way a little before half-past ten. The head chambermaid gave me a signal when the landing was clear. I got into his room without a soul but her seeing me, and locked the door immediately.

The case was, to a certain extent, simplified now. Either Mr. Davager had ridden out with the letter about him, or he had left it in some safe hiding-place in his room. I suspected it to be in his room, for a reason that will a little astonish you – his trunk, his dressing-case, and all the drawers and cupboards, were left open. I knew my customer, and I thought this extraordinary carelessness on his part rather suspicious.

Mr. Davager had taken one of the best bedrooms at the Gatliffe Arms. Floor carpeted all over, walls beautifully papered, four-poster and general furniture first-rate. I searched, to begin with, on the usual plan, examining everything in every possible way, and taking more than an hour about it. No discovery. Then I pulled out a carpenter's rule which I had brought with me. Was there anything the room which – either in inches, feet, or yards – answered to "5 along" and "4 across?" Nothing. I put the rule back in my pocket – measurement was no good, evidently. Was there anything in the room that would count up to 5 one way and 4 another, seeing that nothing would measure up to it? I had got obstinately persuaded by this time that the letter must be in the room – principally because of the trouble I had had in looking after it.

And persuading myself of that, I took it into my head next, just as obstinately, that "5 along" and "4 across" must be the right clue to find the
letter by – principally because I hadn't left myself, after all my searching
and thinking, even so much as the ghost of another guide to go by. "5
along" – where could I count five along the room, in any part of it?

Not on the paper. The pattern there was pillars of trellis-work and
flowers, enclosing a plain green ground – only four pillars along the wall
and only two across. The furniture? There were not five chairs or five
separate pieces of any furniture in the room altogether. The fringes that
hung from the cornice of the bed? Plenty of them, at any rate. Up I
jumped on the counterpane, with my penknife in my hand. Every way
that "5 along" and "4 across" could be reckoned on those unlucky
fringes I reckoned on them – probed with my penknife – scratched with
my nails – crunched with my fingers. No use; not a sign of a letter; and
the time was getting on – oh, Lord! how the time did get on in Mr.
Davager's room that morning.

I jumped down from the bed, so desperate at my ill-luck that I
hardly cared whether anybody heard me or not. Quite a little cloud of
dust rose at my feet as they thumped on the carpet.

"Hullo!" thought I, "my friend the head chambermaid takes it easy
here. Nice state for a carpet to be in in one of the best bedrooms at the
Gatliffe Arms." Carpet! I had been jumping up on the bed and staring
up at the walls, but I had never so much as given a glance down at the
carpet. Think of me pretending to be a lawyer, and not knowing how to
look low enough!

The carpet! It had been a stout article in its time; had evidently
begun in a drawing-room; then descended to a coffee-room; then
gone upstairs altogether to a bedroom. The ground was brown, and
the pattern was bunches of leaves and roses speckled over the ground
at regular distances. I reckoned up the bunches. Ten along the room –
eight across it. When I had stepped out five one way and four the
other, and was down on my knees on the centre bunch, as true as I sit
on this chair I could hear my own heart beating so loud that it quite
frightened me.

I looked narrowly all over the bunch, and I felt all over it with the ends of my fingers, and nothing came of that. Then I scraped it over slowly and gently with my nails. My second finger-nail stuck a little at one place. I parted the pile of the carpet over that place, and saw a thin slit which had been hidden by the pile being smoothed over it – a slit about half an inch long, with a little end of brown thread, exactly the colour of the carpet ground, sticking out about a quarter of an inch from the middle of it. Just as I laid hold of the thread gently, I heard a footstep outside the door.

It was only the head chambermaid. "Haven't you done yet?" she whispers.

"Give me two minutes," says I, "and don't let anybody come near the door – whatever you do, don't let anybody startle me again by coming near the door.

I took a little pull at the thread, and heard something rustle. I took a longer pull, and out came a piece of paper, rolled up tight like those candle-lighters that the ladies make. I unrolled it – and, by George! There was the letter!

The original letter! – I knew it by the colour of the ink. The letter that was worth five hundred pounds to me! It was all that I could do to keep myself at first from throwing my hat into the air and hooraying like mad. I had to take a chair and sit quiet in it for a minute or two before I could cool myself down to my proper business level. I knew that I was safely down again when I found myself pondering how to let Mr. Davager know that he had been done by the innocent country attorney after all.

It was not long before a nice little irritating plan occurred to me. I tore a blank leaf out of my pocket-book, wrote on it with my pencil "Change for a five hundred pound note", folded up the paper, tied the thread to it, poked it back into the hiding-place, smoothed over the pile of the carpet, and then bolted off to Mr. Frank. He in his turn bolted off to show the letter to the young lady, who first certified to its genuineness, then dropped it into the fire, and then took the initiative for the first time since her marriage engagement, by flinging her arms round his neck, kissing him with all her might and going into hysterics in his arms. So at least Mr. Frank told me, but that's not evidence. It is evidence, however, that I saw them married with my own eyes on the Wednesday, and that while they went off in a carriage and four to spend the honeymoon, I went off on my own legs to open a credit at the Town and County Bank with a five hundred pound note in my pocket.

As to Mr. Davager, I can tell you nothing more about him, except what is derived from hearsay evidence, which is always unsatisfactory evidence, even in a lawyer's mouth.

My inestimable boy, Tom, although twice kicked off by Sam the pony, never lost hold of the bridle, and kept his man in sight from first to last. He had nothing particular to report, except that on the way out to the Abbey Mr. Davager had stopped at the public house, had spoken a word or two to his friend of the night before and had handed him what looked like a bit of paper. This was no doubt a clue to the thread that held the letter, to be used in case of accidents. In every other respect Mr. D. had ridden out and ridden in like an ordinary sightseer. Tom reported him to me as having dismounted at the hotel about two. At half-past, I locked my office door, nailed a card under the knocker with "not at home till to-morrow" written on it and retired to a friend's house a mile or so out of the town for the rest of the day.

Mr. Davager, I have been since given to understand, left the Gatliffe Arms that same night with his best clothes on his back and with all the valuable contents of his dressing-case in his pockets. I am not in a condition to state whether he ever went through the form of asking for his bill or not, but I can positively testify that he never paid it, and that the effects left in his bedroom did not pay it either. When I add to these fragments of evidence that he and I have never met (luckily for me, you will say) since I jockeyed him out of his bank-note, I have about fulfilled my implied contract as maker of a statement with you, sir, as hearer of a statement.

Observe the expression, will you? I said it was a Statement before I began; and I say it's a Statement now I've done. I defy you to prove it's a Story! How are you getting on with my portrait? I like you very well, Mr. Artist, but if you have been taking advantage of my talking to shirk your work, as sure as you're alive I'll split upon you to the Town Council!

John Gilbert   Henry Allard

The Dream Woman

I

I had not been settled much more than six weeks in my country practice, when I was sent for to a neighbouring town to consult with the
resident medical man there on a case of very dangerous illness.

My horse had come down with me, at the end of a long ride the
night before, and had hurt himself, luckily, much more than he had
hurt his master. Being deprived of the animal's services, I started for
my destination by the coach (there were no railways at that time), and
I hoped to get back again, towards the afternoon, in the same way.

After the consultation was over I went to the principal inn of the
town to wait for the coach. When it came up, it was full inside and
out. There was no resource left me but to get home as cheaply as I
could by hiring a gig. The price asked for this accommodation struck
me as being so extortionate that I determined to look out for an inn
of inferior pretensions and to try if I could not make a better bargain
with a less prosperous establishment.

I soon found a likely looking house, dingy and quiet, with an old-
fashioned sign, that had evidently not been repainted for many years
past. The landlord, in this case, was not above making a small profit,
and, as soon as we came to terms, he rang the yard-bell to order the
gig.

"Has Robert not come back from that errand?" asked the landlord,
appealing to the waiter who answered the bell.

"No, sir, he hasn't."

"Well, then, you must wake up Isaac."

"Wake up Isaac?" I repeated. "That sounds rather odd. Do your
ostlers go to bed in the day-time?"

"This one does," said the landlord, smiling to himself in rather a
strange way.

"And dreams, too," added the waiter.

"Never you mind about that," retorted his master. "You go and
rouse Isaac up. The gentleman's waiting for his gig."

The landlord's manner and the waiter's manner expressed a great deal more than they either of them said. I began to suspect that I might be on the trace of something professionally interesting to me as a medical man, and I thought I should like to look at the ostler, before the waiter awakened him.

"Stop a minute," I interposed. "I have rather a fancy for seeing this man before you wake him up. I am a doctor; and if this queer sleeping and dreaming of his comes from anything wrong in his brain, I may be able to tell you what to do with him."

"I rather think you will find his complaint past all doctoring, sir," said the landlord. "But if you would like to see him, you're welcome, I'm sure."

He led the way across a yard and down a passage to the stables, opened one of the doors and, waiting outside himself, told me to look in.

I found myself in a two-stall stable. In one of the stalls, a horse was munching his corn. In the other, an old man was lying asleep on the litter.

I stooped, and looked at him attentively. It was a withered, woe-begone face. The eyebrows were painfully contracted; the mouth was fast set and drawn down at the corners. The hollow wrinkled cheeks and the scanty grizzled hair told their own tale of past sorrow or suffering. He was drawing his breath convulsively when I first looked at him; and in a moment more he began to talk in his sleep.

"Wake up!" I heard him say, in a quick whisper, through his clenched teeth. "Wake up, there! Murder."

He moved one lean arm slowly till it rested over his throat, shuddered a little and turned on the straw. Then the arm left his throat, the hand stretched itself out and clutched at the side towards which he had turned, as if he fancied himself to be grasping at the edge of something. I saw his lips move, and bent lower over him. He was still talking in his sleep.

"Light-grey eyes," he murmured, "and a droop in the left eyelid – flaxen hair, with a gold-yellow streak in it – all right, mother – fair white arms, with a down on them – little lady's hand, with a reddish look under the finger-nails. The knife – always the cursed knife – first on one side, then on the other. Aha! you she-devil, where's the knife?"

At the last word his voice rose, and he grew restless on a sudden.

I saw him shudder on the straw; his withered face became distorted, and he threw up both his hands with a quick hysterical gasp. They struck against the bottom of the manger under which he lay, and the blow awakened him. I had just time to slip through the door and close it before his eyes were fairly open and his senses his own again.

"Do you know anything about that man's past life?" I said to the landlord.

"Yes, sir, I know pretty well all about it," was the answer, "and an uncommon queer story it is. Most people don't believe it. It's true, though, for all that. Why, just look at him," continued the landlord, opening the stable door again. "Poor devil! He's so worn out with his restless nights that he's dropped back into his sleep already."

"Don't wake him," I said, "I'm in no hurry for the gig. Wait till the other man comes back from his errand. And, in the meantime, suppose I have some lunch and a bottle of sherry; and suppose you come and help me to get through it."

The heart of mine host, as I had anticipated, warmed to me over his own wine. He soon became communicative on the subject of the man asleep in the stable, and, by little and little, I drew the whole story out of him. Extravagant and incredible as the events must appear to everybody, they are related here just as I heard them, and just as they happened.

II

Some years ago there lived in the suburbs of a large sea-port town, on the west coast of England, a man in humble circumstances, by name Isaac Scatchard. His means of subsistence were derived from any employment he could get as an ostler and, occasionally, when times went well with him, from temporary engagements in service as stable-helper in private houses. Although a faithful, steady and honest man, he got on badly in his calling. His ill-luck was proverbial among his neighbours. He was always missing good opportunities by no fault of his own; and always living longest in service with amiable people who were not punctual payers of wages. "Unlucky Isaac" was his nickname in his own neighbourhood – and no one could say that he did not richly deserve it.

With far more than one man's fair share of adversity to endure, Isaac had but one consolation to support him – and that was of the dreariest and most negative kind. He had no wife and children to increase his anxieties and add to the bitterness of his various failures in life. It might have been from mere insensibility, or it might have been from generous unwillingness to involve another in his own unlucky destiny, but the fact undoubtedly was, that he had arrived at the middle term of life without marrying; and, what is much more remarkable, without once exposing himself, from eighteen to eight-and-thirty, to the genial imputation of ever having had a sweetheart.

When he was out of service, he lived alone with his widowed mother. Mrs. Scatchard was a woman above the average in her lowly station, as to capacity and manners. She had seen better days, as the phrase is; but she never referred to them in the presence of curious visitors and, although perfectly polite to everyone who approached her, never cultivated any intimacies among her neighbours. She contrived to provide, hardly enough, for her simple wants, by doing rough work for the tailors, and always managed to keep a decent home for her son to return to, whenever his ill-luck drove him out helpless into the world.

One bleak autumn, when Isaac was getting fast towards forty, and when he was, as usual, out of place through no fault of his own, he set forth from his mother's cottage on a long walk inland to a gentleman's seat, where he had heard that a stable-helper was required.

It wanted then but two days of his birthday, and Mrs. Scatchard, with her usual fondness, made him promise, before he started, that he would be back in time to keep that anniversary with her, in as festive a way as their poor means would allow. It was easy for him to comply with this request, even supposing he slept a night each way on the road.

He was to start from home on Monday morning, and, whether he got the new place or not, he was to be back for his birthday dinner on Wednesday at two o'clock.

Arriving at his destination too late on the Monday night to make application for the stable-helper's place, he slept at the village inn, and, in good time on the Tuesday morning, presented himself at the gentleman's house to fill the vacant situation. Here again, his ill-luck pursued him as inexorably as ever. The excellent written testimonials to his character which he was able to produce availed him nothing; his long walk had been taken in vain – only the day before the stable-helper's place had been given to another man.

Isaac accepted this new disappointment resignedly and as a matter of course. Naturally slow in capacity, he had the bluntness of sensibility and phlegmatic patience of disposition which frequently distinguish men with sluggishly working mental powers. He thanked the gentleman's steward with his usual quiet civility for granting him an interview, and took his departure with no appearance of unusual depression in his face or manner.

Before starting on his homeward walk, he made some inquiries at the inn, and ascertained that he might save a few miles, on his return, by following a new road. Furnished with full instructions, several times repeated, as to the various turnings he was to take, he set forth on his homeward journey and walked on all day with only one stoppage for bread and cheese. Just as it was getting towards dark, the rain came on and the wind began to rise, and he found himself, to make matters worse, in a part of the country with which he was entirely unacquainted, although he knew himself to be some fifteen miles from home. The first house he found to inquire at was a lonely road-side inn, standing on the outskirts of a thick wood. Solitary as the place looked, it was welcome to a lost man who was also hungry, thirsty, footsore and wet. The landlord was civil and respectable-looking, and the price he asked for a bed was reasonable enough. Isaac, therefore, decided on stopping comfortably at the inn for that night.

He was constitutionally a temperate man. His supper simply consisted of two rashers of bacon, a slice of home-made bread and a pint of ale. He did not go to bed immediately after this moderate meal, but sat up with the landlord, talking about his bad prospects and his long run of ill-luck, and diverging from these topics to the subjects of horse flesh and racing. Nothing was said either by himself, his host or the few labourers who strayed into the tap-room, which could, in the slightest degree, excite the very small and very dull imaginative faculty which Isaac Scatchard possessed.

At a little after eleven the house was closed. Isaac went round with the landlord, and held the candle while the doors and lower-windows were being secured. He noticed with surprise the strength of the bolts, bars, and iron-sheathed shutters.

"You see, we are rather lonely here," said the landlord. "We never have had any attempts made to break in yet, but it's always as well to be on the safe side. When nobody is sleeping here I am the only man in the house. My wife and daughter are timid, and the servant-girl takes after her missuses. Another glass of ale before you turn in? No! Well, how such a sober man as you comes to be out of place, is more than I can make out, for one. Here's where you're to sleep. You're the only lodger to-night, and I think you'll say my missus has done her best to make you comfortable. You're quite sure you won't have another glass of ale? Very well. Good-night."

It was half-past eleven by the clock in the passage as they went upstairs to the bedroom, the window of which looked on to the wood at the back of the house.

Isaac locked the door, set his candle on the chest of drawers, and wearily got ready for bed. The bleak autumn wind was still blowing, and the solemn surging moan of it in the wood was dreary and awful to hear through the night-silence. Isaac felt strangely wakeful. He resolved, as he lay down in bed, to keep the candle alight until he began to grow sleepy, for there was something unendurably depressing in the bare idea of lying awake in the darkness, listening to the dismal, ceaseless moan of the wind in the wood.

Sleep stole on him before he was aware of it. His eyes closed, and he fell off insensibly to rest, without having so much as thought of extinguishing the candle.

The first sensation of which he was conscious, after sinking into slumber, was a strange shivering that ran through him suddenly from head to foot and a dreadful sinking pain at the heart, such as he had never felt before. The shivering only disturbed his slumbers; the pain woke him instantly. In one moment he passed from a state of sleep to a state of wakefulness – his eyes wide open – his mental perceptions cleared on a sudden as if by a miracle.

The candle had burnt down nearly to the last morsel of tallow, but the top of the unsnuffed wick had just fallen off, and the light in the little room was, for the moment, fair and full.

Between the foot of his bed and the closed door, there stood a woman with a knife in her hand, looking at him.

He was stricken speechless with terror, but he did not lose the pre-ternatural clearness of his faculties, and he never took his eyes off the woman. She said not a word as they stared each other in the face, but she began to move slowly towards the left-hand side of the bed.

His eyes followed her. She was a fair fine woman, with yellowish flaxen hair and light-grey eyes, with a droop in the left eyelid. He noticed these things and fixed them on his mind, before she was round at the side of the bed. Speechless, with no expression in her face, with no noise following her footfall, she came closer and closer – stopped – and slowly raised the knife. He laid his right arm over his throat to save it, but, as he saw the knife coming down, threw his hand across the bed to the right side and jerked his body over that way, just as the knife descended on the mattress within an inch of his shoulder.

His eyes fixed on her arm and hand, as she slowly drew her knife out of the bed. A white, well-shaped arm, with a pretty down lying lightly over the fair skin. A delicate, lady's hand, with the crowning beauty of a pink flush under and round the finger-nails.

She drew the knife out and passed back again slowly to the foot of the bed; stopped there for a moment looking at him; then came on – still speechless, still with no expression on the beautiful face, still with no sound following the stealthy footfalls – came on to the right side of the bed where he now lay.

As she approached, she raised the knife again, and he drew himself away to the left side. She struck, as before, right into the mattress, with a deliberate, perpendicularly downward action of the arm. This time his eyes wandered from her to the knife. It was like the large clasp-knives which he had often seen labouring men use to cut their bread and bacon with. Her delicate little fingers did not conceal more than two-thirds of the handle; he noticed that it was made of buckhorn, clean and shining as the blade was, and looking like new.

For the second time she drew the knife out, concealed it in the wide sleeve of her gown, then stopped by the bedside, watching him. For an instant he saw her standing in that position – then the wick of the spent candle fell over into the socket. The flame diminished to a little blue point, and the room grew dark.

A moment, or less if possible, passed so – and then the wick flamed up, smokily, for the last time. His eyes were still looking eagerly over the right-hand side of the bed when the final flash of light came, but they discerned nothing. The fair woman with the knife was gone.

The conviction that he was alone again, weakened the hold of the terror that had struck him dumb up to this time. The preternatural sharpness, which the very intensity of his panic had mysteriously imparted to his faculties, left them suddenly. His brain grew confused – his heart beat wildly – his ears opened for the first time since the appearance of the woman to a sense of the woeful, ceaseless moaning of the wind among the trees. With the dreadful conviction of the reality of what he had seen still strong within him, he leapt out of bed, and screaming – "Murder! – Wake up there, wake up!" – dashed headlong through the darkness to the door.

It was fast locked, exactly as he had left it on going to bed.

His cries, on starting up, had alarmed the house. He heard the terrified, confused exclamations of women; he saw the master of the house approaching along the passage, with his burning rush-candle in one hand and his gun in the other.

"What is it?" asked the landlord, breathlessly.

Isaac could only answer in a whisper. "A woman, with a knife in her hand," he gasped out. "In my room – a fair, yellow-haired woman; she jabbed at me with the knife, twice over."

The landlord's pale cheek grew paler. He looked at Isaac eagerly by the flickering light of his candle, and his face began to get red again – his voice altered, too, as well as his complexion.

"She seems to have missed you twice," he said.

"I dodged the knife as it came down," Isaac went on, in the same scared whisper. "It struck the bed each time."

The landlord took his candle into the bedroom immediately. In less than a minute he came out again into the passage in a violent passion.

"The devil fly away with you and your woman with the knife! There isn't a mark in the bed-clothes anywhere. What do you mean by coming into a man's place and frightening his family out of their wits by a dream?"

"I'll leave your house," said Isaac, faintly. "Better out on the road, in rain and dark, on my way home, than back again in that room, after what I've seen in it. Lend me a light to get my clothes by, and tell me what I'm to pay."

"Pay!" cried the landlord, leading the way with his light sulkily into the bedroom. "You'll find your score on the slate when you go downstairs. I wouldn't have taken you in for all the money you've got about you if I'd known your dreaming, screeching ways beforehand. Look at the bed. Where's the cut of a knife in it? Look at the window – is the lock bursted? Look at the door (which I heard you fasten yourself) – is it broke in? A murdering woman with a knife in my house! You ought to be ashamed of yourself!"

Isaac answered not a word. He huddled on his clothes, and then they went downstairs together.

"Nigh on twenty minutes past two!" said the landlord, as they passed the clock. "A nice time in the morning to frighten honest people out of their wits!"

Isaac paid his bill, and the landlord let him out at the front door, asking, with a grin of contempt, as he undid the strong fastenings, whether "the murdering woman got in that way?"

They parted without a word on either side. The rain had ceased, but the night was dark and the wind bleaker than ever. Little did the darkness, or the cold, or the uncertainty about the way home matter to Isaac. If he had been turned out into a wilderness in a thunderstorm, it would have been a relief, after what he had suffered in the bedroom of the inn.

What was the fair woman with the knife? The creature of a dream or that other creature from the unknown world, called among men by the name of ghost? He could make nothing of the mystery – had made nothing of it, even when it was mid-day on Wednesday, and when he stood, at last, after many times missing his road, once more on the door-step of home.

III

His mother came out eagerly to receive him. His face told her in a moment that something was wrong.

"I've lost the place; but that's my luck. I dreamt an ill dream last night, mother – or, maybe, I saw a ghost. Take it either way, it scared me out of my senses, and I'm not my own man again yet."

"Isaac! your face frightens me. Come in to the fire. Come in, and tell mother all about it."

He was as anxious to tell as she was to hear; for it had been his hope, all the way home, that his mother, with her quicker capacity and superior knowledge, might be able to throw some light on the mystery which he could not clear up for himself. His memory of the dream was still mechanically vivid, although his thoughts were entirely confused by it.

His mother's face grew paler and paler as he went on. She never interrupted him by so much as a single word; but when he had done, she moved her chair close to his, put her arm round his neck and said to him:

"Isaac, you dreamed your ill dream on this Wednesday morning.

What time was it when you saw the fair woman with the knife in her hand?"

Isaac reflected on what the landlord had said when they had passed by the clock on his leaving the inn – allowed as nearly as he could for the time that must have elapsed between the unlocking of his bedroom door and the paying of his bill just before going away, and answered:

"Somewhere about two o'clock in the morning."

His mother suddenly quitted her hold of his neck and struck her hands together with a gesture of despair.

"This Wednesday is your birthday, Isaac, and two o'clock in the morning is the time when you were born!"

Isaac's capacities were not quick enough to catch the infection of his mother's superstitious dread. He was amazed, and a little startled also, when she suddenly rose from her chair, opened her old writing-desk, took pen, ink and paper, and then said to him:

"Your memory is but a poor one, Isaac, and, now I'm an old woman, mine's not much better. I want all about this dream of yours to be as well known to both of us, years hence, as it is now. Tell me over again all you told me a minute ago, when you spoke of what the woman with the knife looked like."

Isaac obeyed, and marvelled much as he saw his mother carefully set down on paper the very words that he was saying.

"Light-grey eyes," she wrote as they came to the descriptive part, "with a droop in the left eyelid. Flaxen hair with a gold-yellow streak in it. White arms with a down upon them. Little lady's hand with a reddish look about the finger-nails. Clasp-knife with a buckhorn handle that seemed as good as new." To these particulars, Mrs. Scatchard added the year, month, day of the week and time in the morning when the woman of the dream appeared to her son. She then locked up the paper carefully in her writing-desk.

Neither on that day, nor on any day after, could her son induce her to return to the matter of the dream. She obstinately kept her thoughts about it to herself, and even refused to refer again to the paper in her writing-desk. Ere long, Isaac grew weary of attempting to make her break her resolute silence; and time, which sooner or later wears out all things, gradually wore out the impression produced on him by the dream. He began by thinking of it carelessly, and he ended by not thinking of it at all.

This result was the more easily brought about by the advent of some important changes for the better in his prospects, which commenced not long after his terrible night's experience at the inn. He reaped at last the reward of his long and patient suffering under adversity, by getting an excellent place, keeping it for seven years and leaving it, on the death of his master, not only with an excellent character but also with a comfortable annuity bequeathed to him as a reward for saving his mistress's life in a carriage accident. Thus it happened that Isaac Scatchard returned to his old mother, seven years after the time of the dream at the inn, with an annual sum of money at his disposal, sufficient to keep them both in ease and independence for the rest of their lives.

The mother, whose health had been bad of late years, profited so much by the care bestowed on her and by freedom from money anxieties that when Isaac's birthday came round, she was able to sit up comfortably at table and dine with him.

On that day, as the evening drew on, Mrs. Scatchard discovered that a bottle of tonic medicine – which she was accustomed to take, and in which she had fancied that a dose or more was still left – happened to be empty. Isaac immediately volunteered to go to the chemist's, and get it filled again. It was as rainy and bleak an autumn night as on the memorable past occasion when he lost his way and slept at the roadside inn.

On going into the chemist's shop, he was passed hurriedly by a poorly dressed woman coming out of it. The glimpse he had of her face struck him, and he looked back after her as she descended the doorsteps.

"You're noticing that woman?" said the chemist's apprentice behind the counter. "It's my opinion there's something wrong with her. She's been asking for laudanum to put to a bad tooth. Master's out for half an hour, and I told her I wasn't allowed to sell poison to strangers in his absence. She laughed in a queer way, and said she would come back in half an hour. If she expects master to serve her, I think she'll be disappointed. It's a case of suicide, sir, if ever there was one yet."

These words added immeasurably to the sudden interest in the woman which Isaac had felt at the first sight of her face. After he had got the medicine bottle filled, he looked about anxiously for her as soon as he was out in the street. She was walking slowly up and down on the opposite side of the road. With his heart, very much to his own surprise, beating fast, Isaac crossed over and spoke to her.

He asked if she was in any distress. She pointed to her torn shawl, her scanty dress, her crushed, dirty bonnet – then moved under a lamp so as to let the light fall on her stern, pale but still most beautiful face.

"I look like a comfortable, happy woman – don't I?" she said, with a bitter laugh.

She spoke with a purity of intonation which Isaac had never heard before from other than ladies' lips. Her slightest actions seemed to have the easy, negligent grace of a thoroughbred woman. Her skin, for all its poverty-stricken paleness, was as delicate as if her life had been passed in the enjoyment of every social comfort that wealth can purchase. Even her small, finely shaped hands, gloveless as they were, had not lost their whiteness.

Little by little, in answer to his questions, the sad story of the woman came out. There is no need to relate it here; it is told over and over again in Police reports and paragraphs descriptive of Attempted Suicides.

"My name is Rebecca Murdoch," said the woman, as she ended. "I have ninepence left, and I thought of spending it at the chemist's over the way in securing a passage to the other world. Whatever it is, it can't be worse to me than this – so why should I stop here?"

Besides the natural compassion and sadness moved in his heart by what he heard, Isaac felt within him some mysterious influence at work all the time the woman was speaking, which utterly confused his ideas and almost deprived him of his powers of speech. All that he could say in answer to her last reckless words was that he would prevent her from attempting her own life if he followed her about all night to do it. His rough, trembling earnestness seemed to impress her.

"I won't occasion you that trouble," she answered when he repeated his threat. "You have given me a fancy for living by speaking kindly to me. No need for the mockery of protestations and promises. You may believe me without them. Come to Fuller's Meadow to-morrow at twelve, and you will find me alive to answer for myself. No! – no money. My ninepence will do to get me as good a night's lodging as I want."

She nodded and left him. He made no attempt to follow – he felt no suspicion that she was deceiving him.

"It's strange, but I can't help believing her," he said to himself, and walked away bewildered towards home.

On entering the house, his mind was still so completely absorbed by its new subject of interest that he took no notice of what his mother was doing when he came in with the bottle of medicine. She had opened her old writing-desk in his absence and was now reading a paper attentively that lay inside it. On every birthday of Isaac's since she had written down the particulars of his dream from his own lips, she had been accustomed to read that same paper, and ponder over it in private.

The next day he went to Fuller's Meadow.

He had done only right in believing her so implicitly – she was there, punctual to a minute, to answer for herself. The last-left faint defences in Isaac's heart against the fascination which a word or look from her began inscrutably to exercise over him sank down and vanished before her for ever on that memorable morning.

When a man, previously insensible to the influence of women, forms an attachment in middle life, the instances are rare indeed, let the warning circumstances be what they may, in which he is found capable of freeing himself from the tyranny of the new ruling passion. The charm of being spoken to familiarly, fondly and gratefully by a woman whose language and manners still retained enough of their early refinement to hint at the high social station that she had lost would have been a dangerous luxury to a man of Isaac's rank at the age of twenty. But it was far more than that – it was certain ruin to him, now that his heart was opening unworthily to a new influence at that middle time of life when strong feelings of all kinds, once implanted, strike root most stubbornly in a man's moral nature. A few more stolen interviews after that first morning in Fuller's Meadow completed his infatuation. In less than a month from the time when he first met her, Isaac Scatchard had consented to give Rebecca Murdoch a new interest in existence, and a chance of recovering the character she had lost, by promising to make her his wife.

She had taken possession not of his passions only but of his faculties as well. All the mind he had he put into her keeping. She directed him on every point, even instructing him how to break the news of his approaching marriage in the safest manner to his mother.

"If you tell her how you met me and who I am at first," said the cunning woman, "she will move heaven and earth to prevent our marriage. Say I am the sister of one of your fellow-servants – ask her to see me before you go into any more particulars – and leave it to me to do the rest. I mean to make her love me next best to you, Isaac, before she knows anything of who I really am."

The motive of the deceit was sufficient to sanctify it to Isaac. The stratagem proposed relieved him of his one great anxiety and quieted his uneasy conscience on the subject of his mother. Still, there was something wanting to perfect his happiness, something that he could not realize, something mysteriously untraceable and yet something that perpetually made itself felt – not when he was absent from Rebecca Murdoch but, strange to say, when he was actually in her presence! She was kindness itself with him: she never made him feel his inferior capacities and inferior manners – she showed the sweetest anxiety to please him in the smallest trifles. But, in spite of all these attractions, he never could feel quite at his ease with her. At their first meeting, there had mingled with his admiration, when he looked in her face, a faint involuntary feeling of doubt whether that face was entirely strange to him. No after-familiarity had the slightest effect on this inexplicable, wearisome uncertainty.

Concealing the truth, as he had been directed, he announced his marriage engagement precipitately and confusedly to his mother, on the day when he contracted it. Poor Mrs. Scatchard showed her perfect confidence in her son by flinging her arms round his neck and giving him joy of having found at last, in the sister of one of his fellow-servants, a woman to comfort and care for him after his mother was gone. She was all eagerness to see the woman of her son's choice, and the next day was fixed for the introduction.

It was a bright sunny morning, and the little cottage parlour was full of light as Mrs. Scatchard, happy and expectant, dressed for the occasion in her Sunday gown, sat waiting for her son and her future daughter-in-law.

Punctual to the appointed time, Isaac hurriedly and nervously led his promised wife into the room. His mother rose to receive her, advanced a few steps, smiling, looked Rebecca full in the eyes and suddenly stopped. Her face, which had been flushed the moment before, turned white in an instant, her eyes lost their expression of softness and kindness and assumed a blank look of terror, her outstretched hands fell to her sides and she staggered back a few steps with a low cry to her son.

"Isaac!" she whispered, clutching him fast by the arm, when he asked alarmedly if she was taken ill. "Isaac! does that woman's face remind you of nothing?"

Before he could answer, before he could look round to where Rebecca stood, astonished and angered by her reception, at the lower end of the room, his mother pointed impatiently to her writing-desk and gave him the key.

"Open it," she said, in a quick, breathless whisper.

"What does this mean? Why am I treated as if I had no business here? Does your mother want to insult me?" asked Rebecca, angrily.

"Open it, and give me the paper in the left-hand drawer. Quick! quick! for heaven's sake!" said Mrs. Scatchard, shrinking further back in terror.

Isaac gave her the paper. She looked it over eagerly for a moment, then followed Rebecca, who was now turning away haughtily to leave the room, and caught her by the shoulder, abruptly raised the long, loose sleeve of her gown and glanced at her hand and arm. Something like fear began to steal over the angry expression of Rebecca's face as she shook herself free from the old woman's grasp.

"Mad!" she said to herself, "and Isaac never told me." With those few words she left the room.

Isaac was hastening after her, when his mother turned and stopped his further progress. It wrung his heart to see the misery and terror in her face as she looked at him.

"Light-grey eyes," she said, in low, mournful, awestruck tones, pointing towards the open door. "A droop in the left eyelid; flaxen hair with a gold-yellow streak in it; white arms with a down on them; little, lady's hand with a reddish look under the finger-nails. *The Dream Woman!* – Isaac, the Dream Woman!"

That faint cleaving doubt which he had never been able to shake off in Rebecca Murdoch's presence, was fatally set at rest for ever. He *had* seen her face, then, before – seven years before, on his birthday, in the bedroom of the lonely inn.

"Be warned! Oh, my son, be warned! Isaac! Isaac! Let her go, and do you stop with me!"

Something darkened the parlour window as those words were said. A sudden chill ran through him, and he glanced sidelong at the shadow. Rebecca Murdoch had come back. She was peering in curiously at them over the low window-blind.

"I have promised to marry, mother," he said, "and marry I must."

The tears came into his eyes as he spoke, and dimmed his sight; but he could just discern the fatal face outside, moving away again from the window.

His mother's head sank lower.

"Are you faint?" he whispered.

"Broken-hearted, Isaac."

He stooped down and kissed her. The shadow, as he did so, returned to the window, and the fatal face peered in curiously once more.

IV

Three weeks after that day Isaac and Rebecca were man and wife. All that was hopelessly dogged and stubborn in the man's moral nature seemed to have closed round his fatal passion and to have fixed it unassailably in his heart.

After that first interview in the cottage parlour, no consideration could induce Mrs. Scatchard to see her son's wife again or even to talk of her when Isaac tried hard to plead her cause after their marriage.

This course of conduct was not in any degree occasioned by a discovery of the degradation in which Rebecca had lived. There was no question of that between mother and son. There was no question of anything but the fearfully exact resemblance between the living, breathing woman and the spectre woman of Isaac's dream.

Rebecca, on her side, neither felt nor expressed the slightest sorrow at the estrangement between herself and her mother-in-law. Isaac, for the sake of peace, had never contradicted her first idea that age and long illness had affected Mrs. Scatchard's mind. He even allowed his wife to upbraid him for not having confessed this to her at the time of their marriage engagement, rather than risk anything by hinting at the truth. The sacrifice of his integrity before his one all-mastering delusion seemed but a small thing and cost his conscience but little after the sacrifices he had already made.

The time of waking from his delusion – the cruel and the rueful time – was not far off. After some quiet months of married life, as the summer was ending and the year was getting on towards the month of his birthday, Isaac found his wife altering towards him. She grew sullen and contemptuous; she formed acquaintances of the most dangerous kind, in defiance of his objections, his entreaties and his commands; and, worst of all, she learnt, ere long, after every fresh difference with her husband, to seek the deadly self-oblivion of drink. Little by little, after the first miserable discovery that his wife was keeping company with drunkards, the shocking certainty forced itself on Isaac that she had grown to be a drunkard herself.

He had been in a sadly desponding state for some time before the occurrence of these domestic calamities. His mother's health, as he could but too plainly discern every time he went to see her at the cottage, was failing fast, and he upbraided himself in secret as the cause of the bodily and mental suffering she endured. When, to his remorse on his mother's account, was added the shame and misery occasioned by the discovery of his wife's degradation, he sank under the double trial, his face began to alter fast, and he looked what he was, a spirit-broken man.

His mother, still struggling bravely against the illness that was hurrying her to the grave, was the first to notice the sad alteration in him, and the first to hear of his last, worst trouble with his wife. She could only weep bitterly on the day when he made his humiliating confession; but, on the next occasion when he went to see her, she had taken a resolution, in reference to his domestic afflictions, which astonished and even alarmed him. He found her dressed to go out, and, on asking the reason, received this answer:

"I am not long for this world, Isaac," she said, "and I shall not feel easy on my death-bed, unless I have done my best to the last to make my son happy. I mean to put my own fears and my own feelings out of the question and to go with you to your wife, and try what I can do to reclaim her. Give me your arm, Isaac, and let me do the last thing I can in this world to help my son before it is too late."

He could not disobey her, and they walked together slowly towards his miserable home.

It was only one o'clock in the afternoon when they reached the cottage where he lived. It was their dinner hour, and Rebecca was in the kitchen. He was thus able to take his mother quietly into the parlour and then prepare his wife for the interview. She had fortunately drank but little at that early hour, and she was less sullen and capricious than usual.

He returned to his mother with his mind tolerably at ease. His wife soon followed him into the parlour, and the meeting between her and Mrs. Scathard passed off better than he had ventured to anticipate, although he observed with secret apprehension that his mother, resolutely as she controlled herself in other respects, could not look his wife in the face when she spoke to her. It was a relief to him, therefore, when Rebecca began to lay the cloth.

She laid the cloth, brought in the bread-tray, and cut a slice from the loaf for her husband, then returned to the kitchen. At that moment, Isaac, still anxiously watching his mother, was startled by seeing the same ghastly change pass over her face which had altered it so awfully on the morning when Rebecca and she first met. Before he could say a word, she whispered with a look of horror:

"Take me back! – home, home again, Isaac! Come with me and never go back again!"

He was afraid to ask for an explanation; he could only sign to her to be silent, and help her quickly to the door. As they passed the bread-tray on the table, she stopped and pointed to it.

"Did you see what your wife cut your bread with?" she asked in a low whisper.

"No, Mother; I was not noticing. What was it?"

"Look?"

He did look. A new clasp-knife, with a buckhorn handle, lay with the loaf in the bread-tray. He stretched out his hand, shudderingly, to possess himself of it, but at the same time there was a noise in the kitchen, and his mother caught at his arm.

"The knife of the dream! Isaac, I'm faint with fear – take me away, before she comes back!"

He was hardly able to support her. The visible, tangible reality of the knife struck him with a panic and utterly destroyed any faint doubts he might have entertained up to this time, in relation to the mysterious dream-warning of nearly eight years before. By a last desperate effort, he summoned self-possession enough to help his mother but of the house – so quietly, that the "Dream Woman" (he thought of her by that name now) did not hear their departure.

"Don't go back, Isaac, don't go back!" implored Mrs. Scatchard, as he turned to go away after seeing her safely seated again in her own room.

"I must get the knife," he answered under his breath. His mother tried to stop him again, but he hurried out without another word.

On his return, he found that his wife had discovered their secret departure from the house. She had been drinking and was in a fury of passion. The dinner in the kitchen was flung under the grate; the cloth was off the parlour table. Where was the knife?

Unwisely, he asked for it. She was only too glad of the opportunity of irritating him, which the request afforded her. "He wanted the knife, did he? Could he give her a reason why? – No? Then he should not have it – not if he went down on his knees to ask for it." Further recriminations elicited the fact that she had bought it a bargain, and that she considered it her own especial property. Isaac saw the uselessness of attempting to get the knife by fair means, and determined to search for it, later in the day, in secret. The search was unsuccessful. Night came on, and he left the house to walk about the streets. He was afraid now to sleep in the same room with her.

Three weeks passed. Still sullenly enraged with him, she would not give up the knife; and still that fear of sleeping in the same room with her possessed him. He walked about at night, or dozed in the parlour, or sat watching by his mother's bed-side. Before the expiration of the first week in the new month his mother died. It wanted then but ten days of her son's birthday. She had longed to live till that anniversary. Isaac was present at her death, and her last words in this world were addressed to him:

"Don't go back, my son – don't go back!"

He was obliged to go back, if it were only to watch his wife. Exasperated to the last degree by his distrust of her, she had revenge-fully sought to add a sting to his grief during the last days of his mother's illness by declaring that she would assert her right to attend the funeral. In spite of all that he could do or say, she held with wicked pertinacity to her word, and on the day appointed for the burial, forced herself – inflamed and shameless with drink – into her husband's presence, and declared that she would walk in the funeral procession to his mother's grave.

This last worst outrage, accompanied by all that was most insulting in word and look, maddened him for the moment. He struck her.

The instant the blow was dealt he repented it. She crouched down, silent, in a corner of the room, and eyed him steadily. It was a look that cooled his hot blood and made him tremble. But there was no time now to think of a means of making atonement. Nothing remained but to risk the worst till the funeral was over. There was but one way of making sure of her. He locked her into her bedroom.

When he came back, some hours after, he found her sitting, very much altered in look and bearing, by the bed-side with a bundle on her lap. She rose and faced him quietly, and spoke with a strange still-ness in her voice, a strange repose in her eyes, a strange composure in her manner.

"No man has ever struck me twice," she said, "and my husband shall have no second opportunity. Set the door open and let me go. From this day forth we see each other no more."

Before he could answer she passed him and left the room. He saw her walk away up the street.

Would she return?

All that night he watched and waited; but no footstep came near the house. The next night, overcome by fatigue, he lay down in bed in his clothes, with the door locked, the key on the table and the candle burning. His slumber was not disturbed. The third night, the fourth, the fifth, the sixth passed and nothing happened. He lay down on the seventh, still in his clothes, still with the door locked, the key on the table and the candle burning, but easier in his mind.

Easier in his mind and in perfect health of body when he fell off to sleep. But his rest was disturbed. He woke twice without any sensation of uneasiness. But the third time it was that never-to-be-forgotten shivering of the night at the lonely inn, that dreadful sinking pain at the heart, which once more aroused him in an instant.

His eyes opened towards the left-hand side of the bed, and there stood –

The Dream Woman again? No! His wife; the living reality, with the dream-spectre's face – in the dream-spectre's attitude: the fair arm up; the knife clasped in the delicate white hand.

He sprang upon her, almost at the instant of seeing her, and yet not quickly enough to prevent her from hiding the knife. Without a word from him, without a cry from her, he pinioned her in a chair. With one hand he felt up her sleeve, and there, where the Dream Woman had hidden the knife, his wife had hidden it – the knife with the buckhorn handle, that looked like new.

In the despair of that fearful moment his brain was steady, his heart was calm. He looked at her fixedly, with the knife in his hand, and said these last words:

"You told me we should see each other no more, and you have come back. It is my turn now to go, and to go for ever. I say that we shall see each other no more, and *my* word shall not be broken."

He left her and set forth into the night. There was a bleak wind abroad, and the smell of recent rain was in the air. The distant church clocks chimed the quarter as he walked rapidly beyond the last houses in the suburb. He asked the first policeman he met what hour that was, of which the quarter past had just struck.

The man referred sleepily to his watch, and answered: "Two o'clock." Two in the morning. What day of the month was this day that had just begun? He reckoned it up from the date of his mother's funeral. The fatal parallel was complete – it was his birthday!

Had he escaped the mortal peril which his dream foretold? or had he only received a second warning?

As this ominous doubt forced itself on his mind, he stopped, reflected and turned back again towards the city. He was still resolute to hold to his word, and never to let her see him more, but there was a thought now in his mind of having her watched and followed. The knife was in his possession; the world was before him; but a new distrust of her – a vague, unspeakable, superstitious dread – had overcome him.

"I must know where she goes, now she thinks I have left her," he said to himself, as he stole back wearily to the precincts of his house.

It was still dark. He had left the candle burning in the bedchamber, but when he looked up to the window of the room now, there was no light in it. He crept cautiously to the house door. On going away, he remembered to have closed it; on trying it now, he found it open.

He waited outside, never losing sight of the house till daylight. Then he ventured indoors – listened and heard nothing; looked into kitchen, scullery, parlour and found nothing; went up at last into the bedroom – it was empty. A picklock lay on the floor, betraying how she had gained entrance in the night, and that was the only trace of her.

Whither had she gone? No mortal tongue could tell him. The darkness had covered her flight, and, when the day broke, no man could say where the light found her.

Before leaving the house and the town for ever, he gave instructions to a friend and neighbour to sell his furniture for anything that it would fetch and to apply the proceeds towards employing the police to trace her. The directions were honestly followed, and the money was all spent; but the inquiries led to nothing. The picklock on the bedroom floor remained the last useless trace of the Dream Woman.

At this part of the narrative the landlord paused and, turning towards the window of the room in which we were sitting, looked in the direction of the stable-yard.

"So far," he said, "I tell you what was told to me. The little that remains to be added lies within my own experience. Between two and three months after the events I have just been relating, Isaac Scatchard came to me, withered and old-looking before his time, just as you saw him to-day. He had his testimonials to character with him and he asked me for employment here. Knowing that my wife and he were distantly related, I gave him a trial, in consideration of that relationship, and liked him in spite of his queer habits. He is as sober, honest and willing a man as there is in England. As for his restlessness at night and his sleeping away his leisure time in the day, who can wonder at it after hearing his story? Besides, he never objects to being roused up when he's wanted, so there's not much inconvenience to complain of, after all."

"I suppose he is afraid of a return of that dreadful dream, and of waking out of it in the dark?"

"No," returned the landlord. "The dream comes back to him so often, that he has got to bear with it by this time resignedly enough. It's his wife keeps him waking at night, as he has often told me."

"What! Has she never been heard of yet?"

"Never. Isaac himself has the one perpetual thought, that she is alive and looking for him. I believe he wouldn't let himself drop off to sleep towards two in the morning for a king's ransom. Two in the morning, he says, is the time she will find him, one of these days. Two in the morning is the time, all the year round, when he likes to be most certain that he has got the clasp-knife safe about him. He does not mind being alone as long as he is awake, except on the night before his birthday, when he firmly believes himself to be in peril of his life. The birthday has only come round once since he has been here, and then he sat up along with the night-porter. 'She's looking for me,' is all he says, when anybody speaks to him about the one anxiety of his life. 'She's looking for me.' He may be right. She *may* be looking for him. Who can tell?"

"Who can tell?" said I.

The Diary of Anne Rodway
[Taken from her Diary]

MARCH 3RD, 1840. A long letter to-day from Robert, which surprised and vexed me so that I have been sadly behindhand with my work ever since. He writes in worse spirits than last time, and absolutely declares that he is poorer even than when he went to America, and that he has made up his mind to come home to London.

How happy I should be at this news, if he only returned to me a prosperous man! As it is, although I love him dearly, I cannot look forward to the meeting him again, disappointed and broken down, and poorer than ever, without a feeling almost of dread for both of us. I was twenty-six last birthday, and he was thirty-three, and there seems less chance now than ever of our being married. It is all I can do to keep myself by my needle, and his prospects, since he failed in the small stationery business three years ago, are worse, if possible, than mine.

Not that I mind so much for myself: women, in all ways of life, and especially in my dressmaking way, learn, I think, to be more patient than men. What I dread is Robert's despondency and the hard struggle he will have in this cruel city to get his bread – let alone making money enough to marry me. So little as poor people want to set up in house-keeping and be happy together, it seems hard that they can't get it when they are honest and hearty and willing to work. The clergyman said in his sermon last Sunday evening, that all things are ordered for the best and we are all put into the stations in life that are properest for us. I suppose he was right, being a very clever gentleman who fills the church to crowding, but I think I should have understood him better if I had not been very hungry at the time, in consequence of my own station in life being nothing but Plain Needlewoman.

MARCH 4TH. Mary Mallinson came down to my room to take a cup of tea with me. I read her bits of Robert's letter to show her that, if she has her troubles, I have mine, too. But I could not succeed in cheering her. She says she is born to misfortune and that, as long back as she can remember, she has never had the least morsel of luck to be thankful for. I told her to go and look in my glass, and to say if she had nothing to be thankful for then, for Mary is a very pretty girl, and would look still prettier if she could be more cheerful and dress neater. However, my compliment did no good. She rattled her spoon impatiently in her teacup, and said:

"If I was only as good a hand at needlework as you are, Anne, I would change faces with the ugliest girl in London."

"Not you!" says I, laughing. She looked at me for a moment and shook her head, and was out of the room before I could get up and stop her. She always runs off in that way when she is going to cry, having a kind of pride about letting other people see her in tears.

MARCH 5TH. A fright about Mary. I had not seen her all day, as she does not work at the same place where I do, and in the evening she never came down to have tea with me, or sent me word to go to her. So just before I went to bed, I ran upstairs to say good-night.

She did not answer when I knocked, and, when I stepped softly into the room, I saw her in bed, asleep, with her work not half done, lying about the room in the untidiest way. There was nothing remarkable in that, and I was just going away on tip-toe, when a tiny bottle and wine-glass on the chair by her bed-side caught my eye. I thought she was ill, and had been taking physic, and looked at the bottle. It was marked in large letters: "Laudanum – Poison".

My heart gave a jump, as if it was going to fly out of me. I laid hold of her with both hands, and shook her with all my might. She was sleeping heavily, and woke slowly, as it seemed to me – but still she did wake. I tried to pull her out of bed, having heard that people ought to be always walked up and down when they have taken laudanum, but she resisted and pushed me away violently.

"Anne!" says she, in a fright. "For gracious sake, what's come to you? Are you out of your senses?"

"Oh, Mary! Mary!" says I, holding up the bottle before her, "if I hadn't come in when I did –" And I laid hold of her to shake her again.

She looked puzzled at me for a moment, then smiled (the first time

I had seen her do so for many a long day), then put her arms round my neck.

"Don't be frightened about me, Anne," she says. "I am not worth it, and there is no need."

"No need!" says I, out of breath. "No need, when the bottle has got Poison marked on it!"

"Poison, dear, if you take it all," says Mary, looking at me very tenderly, "and a night's rest, if you only take a little."

I watched her for a moment, doubtful whether I ought to believe what she said, or to alarm the house. But there was no sleepiness now in her eyes and nothing drowsy in her voice, and she sat up in bed quite easily, without anything to support her.

"You have given me a dreadful fright, Mary," says I, sitting down by her in the chair, and beginning, by this time, to feel rather faint after being startled so.

She jumped out of bed to get me a drop of water, and kissed me, and said how sorry she was, and how undeserving of so much interest being taken in her. At the same time, she tried to possess herself of the laudanum bottle, which I still kept cuddled up tight in my own hands.

"No," says I. "You have got into a low-spirited, despairing way. I won't trust you with it."

"I am afraid I can't do without it," says Mary, in her usual quiet, hopeless voice. "What with work that I can't get through as I ought, and troubles that I can't help thinking of, sleep won't come to me unless I take a few drops out of that bottle. Don't keep it away from me, Anne. It's the only thing in the world that makes me forget myself."

"Forget yourself!" says I. "You have no right to talk in that way, at your age. There's something horrible in the notion of a girl of eighteen sleeping with a bottle of laudanum by her bedside every night. We all of us have our troubles. Haven't I got mine?"

"You can do twice the work I can, twice as well as me," says Mary. "You are never scolded and rated at for awkwardness with your needle, and I always am. You can pay for your room every week, and I am three weeks in debt for mine."

"A little more practice", says I, "and a little more courage, and you will soon do better. You have got all your life before you –"

"I wish I was at the end of it," says she, breaking in. "I'm alone in the world, and my life's no good to me."

"You ought to be ashamed of yourself for saying so," says I. "Haven't you got me for a friend? Didn't I take a fancy to you when first you left your stepmother and came to lodge in this house, and haven't I been sisters with you ever since? Suppose you are alone in the world, am I much better off? I'm an orphan, like you. I've almost as many things in pawn as you; and if your pockets are empty, mine have only got nine-pence in them, to last me for all the rest of the week."

"Your father and mother were honest people," says Mary obstinately. "My mother ran away from home and died in a hospital. My father was always drunk and always beating me. My stepmother is as good as dead, for all she cares about me. My only brother is thousands of miles away, in foreign parts, and never writes to me, and never helps me with a farthing. My sweetheart . . ."

She stopped, and the red flew into her face. I knew, if she went on that way, she would only get to the saddest part of her sad story, and give both herself and me unnecessary pain.

"My sweetheart is too poor to marry me, Mary," I said, "so I'm not so much to be envied even there. But let's give over disputing which is worst off. Lie down in bed and let me tuck you up. I'll put a stitch or two into that work of yours while you go to sleep."

Instead of doing what I told her, she burst out crying (being very like a child in some of her ways) and hugged me so tight round the neck that she quite hurt me. I let her go on till she had worn herself out, and was obliged to lie down. Even then, her last few words, before she dropped off to sleep, were such as I was half sorry, half frightened, to hear.

"I won't plague you long, Anne," she said. "I haven't courage to go out of the world you seem to fear I shall. But I began my life wretchedly, and wretchedly I am sentenced to end it."

It was of no use lecturing her again, for she closed her eyes.

I tucked her up as neatly as I could, and put her petticoat over her, for the bed-clothes were scanty and her hands felt cold. She looked so pretty and delicate as she fell asleep, that it quite made my heart ache to see her, after such talk as we had held together. I just waited long enough to be quite sure that she was in the land of dreams, then emptied the horrible laudanum bottle into the grate, took up her half-done work and, going out softly, left her for that night.

MARCH 6TH. Sent off a long letter to Robert, begging and entreating him not to he so downhearted, and not to leave America without making another effort. I told him I could bear any trial except the wretchedness of seeing him come back a helpless, broken-down man, trying uselessly to begin life again, when too old for a change.

It was not till after I had posted my own letter and read over parts of Robert's again that the suspicion suddenly floated across me, for the first time, that he might have sailed for England immediately after writing to me. There were expressions in the letter which seemed to indicate that he had some such headlong project in his mind. And yet, surely, if it were so, I ought to have noticed them at the first reading. I can only hope I am wrong in my present interpretation of much of what he has written to me – hope it earnestly, for both our sakes.

This has been a doleful day for me. I have been uneasy about Robert and uneasy about Mary. My mind is haunted by those last words of hers: "I began my life wretchedly, and wretchedly I am sentenced to end it." Her usual melancholy way of talking never produced the same impression on me that I feel now. Perhaps the discovery of the laudanum bottle is the cause of this. I would give many a hard day's work to know what to do for Mary's good. My heart warmed to her when we first met in the same lodging-house two years ago, and, although I am not one of the over-affectionate sort myself, I feel as if I could go to the world's end to serve that girl. Yet, strange to say, if I was asked why I was so fond of her, I don't think I should know how to answer the question.

MARCH 7TH. I am almost ashamed to write it down, even in this journal, which no eyes but mine ever look on; yet I must honestly confess to myself, that here I am, at nearly one in the morning, sitting up in a state of serious uneasiness, because Mary has not yet come home.

I walked with her this morning to the place where she works, and tried to lead her into talking of the relations she has got who are still alive. My motive in doing this was to see if she dropped anything in the course of conversation which might suggest a way of helping her interests with those who are bound to give her all reasonable assistance. But the little I could get her to say to me led to nothing. Instead of answering my questions about her stepmother and her brother, she persisted at first, in the strangest way, in talking of her father, who was dead and gone, and of one Noah Truscott, who had been the worst of all the bad friends he had, and had taught him to drink and game. When I did get her to speak of her brother, she only knew that he had gone out to a place called Assam, where they grew tea. How he was doing, or whether he was there still, she did not seem to know, never having heard a word from him for years and years past.

As for her stepmother, Mary, not unnaturally, flew into a passion the moment I spoke of her. She keeps an eating-house at Hammersmith, and could have given Mary good employment in it, but she seems always to have hated her and to have made her life so wretched with abuse and ill-usage that she had no refuge left but to go away from home and do her best to make a living for herself. Her husband (Mary's father) appears to have behaved badly to her, and, after his death, she took the wicked course of revenging herself on her stepdaughter. I felt, after this, that it was impossible Mary could go back, and that it was the hard necessity of her position, as it is of mine, that she should struggle on to make a decent livelihood without assistance from any of her relations. I confessed as much as this to her; but I added that I would try to get her employment with the persons for whom I work, who pay higher wages and show a little more indulgence to those under them than the people to whom she is now obliged to look for support.

I spoke much more confidently than I felt about being able to do this, and left her, as I thought, in better spirits than usual. She promised to be back to-night to tea, at nine o'clock, and now it is nearly one in the morning, and she is not home yet. If it was any other girl, I should not feel uneasy, for I should make up my mind that there was extra work to be done in a hurry, and that they were keeping her late and I should go to bed. But Mary is so unfortunate in everything that happens to her, and her own melancholy talk about herself keeps hanging on my mind so, that I have fears on her account which would not distress me about any one else. It seems inexcusably silly to think such a thing, much more to write it down; but I have a kind of nervous dread upon me that some accident –.

What does that loud knocking at the street door mean? And those voices and heavy footsteps outside? Some lodger who has lost his key, I suppose. And yet, my heart – What a coward I have become all of a sudden!

More knocking and louder voices. I must run to the door and see what it is. O Mary! Mary! I hope I am not going to have another fright about you; but I feel sadly like it.

MARCH 8TH.
MARCH 9TH.
MARCH 10TH.

MARCH 11TH. O me! all the troubles I have ever had in my life are as nothing to the trouble I am in now. For three days I have not been able to write a single line in this journal, which I have kept so regularly ever since I was a girl. For three days I have not once thought of Robert – I, who am always thinking of him at other times.

My poor, dear, unhappy Mary! the worst I feared for you on that night when I sat up alone was far below the dreadful calamity that has really happened. How can I write about it, with my eyes full of tears and my hand all of a tremble? I don't even know why I am sitting down at my desk now, unless it is habit that keeps me to my old everyday task, in spite of the grief and fear which seem to unfit me entirely for performing it.

The people of the house were asleep and lazy on that dreadful night, and I was the first to open the door. Never, never could I describe in writing, or even say in plain talk, although it is so much easier, what I felt when I saw two policemen come in, carrying between them what seemed to me to be a dead girl, and that girl Mary! I caught hold of her, and gave a scream that must have alarmed the whole house; for frightened people came crowding downstairs in their night-dresses. There was a dreadful confusion and noise of loud talking, but I heard nothing, and saw nothing, till I had got her into my room, and laid on my bed. I stooped down, frantic-like, to kiss her, and saw an awful mark of a blow on the left temple, and felt, at the same time, a feeble flutter of her breath on my cheek. The discovery that she was not dead seemed to give me back my senses again. I told one of the policemen where the nearest doctor was to be found, and sat down by the bedside, while he was gone, and bathed her poor head with cold water. She never opened her eyes, or moved or spoke, but she breathed, and that was enough for me, because it was enough for life.

The policeman left in the room was a big, thick-voiced, pompous man, with a horrible unfeeling pleasure in hearing himself talk before an assembly of frightened, silent people. He told us how he had found her, as if he had been telling a story in a tap-room, and began with saying:

"I don't think the young woman was drunk."

Drunk! My Mary, who might have been a born lady for all the spirits she ever touched – drunk! I could have struck the man for uttering the word, with her lying, poor suffering angel, so white and still and helpless before him. As it was, I gave him a look; but he was too stupid to understand it, and went droning on, saying the same thing over and over again in the same words. And yet the story of how they found her was, like all the sad stories I have ever heard told in real life, so very, very short. They had just seen her lying along on the kerb-stone, a few streets off, and had taken her to the station-house. There she had been searched, and one of my cards, that I give to ladies who promise me employment, had been found in her pocket, and so they had brought her to our house. This was all the man really had to tell. There was nobody near her when she was found, and no evidence to show how the blow on her temple had been inflicted.

What a time it was before the doctor came, and how dreadful to hear him say, after he had looked at her, that he was afraid all the medical men in the world could be of no use here; he could not get her to swallow anything, and the more he tried to bring her back to her senses, the less chance there seemed of his succeeding. He examined the blow on her temple, and said he thought she must have fallen down in a fit of some sort and struck her head against the pavement, and so have given her brain what he was afraid was a fatal shake. I asked what was to be done if she showed any return to sense in the night. He said:

"Send for me directly," and stopped for a little while afterwards, stroking her head gently with his hand, and whispering to himself: "Poor girl, so young and so pretty!" I had felt, some minutes before, as if I could have struck the policeman, and I felt now as if I could have thrown my arms round the doctor's neck and kissed him. I did put out my hand, when he took up his hat, and he shook it in the friendliest way.

"Don't hope, my dear," he said, and went out.

The rest of the lodgers followed him, all silent and shocked, except the inhuman wretch who owns the house and lives in idleness on the high rents he wrings from poor people like us.

"She's three weeks in my debt," says he, with a frown and an oath. "Where the devil is my money to come from now?" – Brute! brute!

I had a long cry alone with her, that seemed to ease my heart a little. She was not the least changed for the better when I had wiped away the tears and could see her clearly again. I took up her right hand, which lay nearest to me. It was tight clenched. I tried to unclasp the fingers, and succeeded after a little time. Something dark fell out of the palm of her hand as I straightened it.

I picked the thing up, and smoothed it out, and saw that it was an end of a man's cravat.

A very old, rotten, dingy strip of black silk, with thin lilac lines, all blurred and deadened with dirt, running across and across the stuff in a sort of trellis-work pattern. The small end of the cravat was hemmed in the usual way, but the other end was all jagged, as if the morsel then in my hands had been torn off violently from the rest of the stuff. A chill ran all over me as I looked at it, for that poor, stained, crumpled end of a cravat seemed to be saying to me, as though it had been in plain words – "If she dies, she has come to her death by foul means, and I am the witness of it."

I had been frightened enough before, lest she should die suddenly and quietly without my knowing it, while we were alone together; but I got into a perfect agony now, for fear this last worst affliction should take me by surprise. I don't suppose five minutes passed all that woeful night through, without my getting up and putting my cheek close to her mouth, to feel if the faint breaths still fluttered out of it. They came and went just the same as at first, although the fright I was in often made me fancy they were stilled for ever.

Just as the church clocks were striking four, I was startled by seeing the room door open. It was only Dusty Sal (as they call her in the house), the maid-of-all-work. She was wrapped up in the blanket off her bed, her hair was all tumbled over her face and her eyes were heavy with sleep, as she came up to the bedside where I was sitting.

"I've two hours good before I begin to work," says she, in her hoarse, drowsy voice, "and I've come to sit up and take my turn at watching her. You lay down and get some sleep on the rug. Here's my blanket for you – I don't mind the cold – it will keep me awake."

"You are very kind – very, very kind and thoughtful, Sally," says I, "but I am too wretched in my mind to want sleep or rest, or to do anything but wait where I am and try and hope for the best."

"Then I'll wait, too," says Sally. "I must do something; if there's nothing to do but waiting, I'll wait."

And she sat down opposite me at the foot of the bed, and drew the blanket close round her with a shiver.

"After working so hard as you do, I'm sure you must want all the little rest you can get," says I.

"Excepting only you," says Sally, putting her heavy arm very clumsily, but very gently at the same time, round Mary's feet, and looking hard at the pale still face on the pillow. "Excepting you, she's the only soul in this house as never swore at me or give me a hard word that I can remember. When you made puddings on Sundays and give her half, she always give me a bit. The rest of 'em calls me Dusty Sal. Excepting only you, again, she always called me Sally, as if she knowed me in a friendly way. I ain't no good here, but I ain't no harm neither, and I shall take my turn at the sitting up – that's what I shall do!"

She nestled her head down close at Mary's feet as she spoke those words, and said no more. I once or twice thought she had fallen asleep, but whenever I looked at her, her heavy eyes were always wide open. She never changed her position an inch till the church clocks struck six; then she gave one little squeeze to Mary's feet with her arm, and shuffled out of the room without a word. A minute or two after, I heard her down below lighting the kitchen fire just as usual.

A little later, the doctor stepped over before his breakfast-time to see if there had been any change in the night. He only shook his head when he looked at her, as if there was no hope. Having nobody else to consult that I could put trust in, I showed him the end of the cravat, and told him of the dreadful suspicion that had arisen in my mind when I found it in her hand.

"You must keep it carefully, and produce it at the inquest," he said. "I don't know, though, that it is likely to lead to anything. The bit of stuff may have been lying on the pavement near her, and her hand may have unconsciously clutched it when she fell. Was she subject to fainting fits?"

"Not more so, sir, than other young girls who are hard-worked and anxious, and weakly from poor living," I answered.

"I can't say that she may not have got that blow from a fall," the doctor went on, looking at her temple again. "I can't say that it presents any positive appearance of having been inflicted by another person. It will be important, however, to ascertain what state of health she was in last night. Have you any idea where she was yesterday evening?"

I told him where she was employed at work, and said I imagined she must have been kept there later than usual.

"I shall pass the place this morning," said the doctor, "in going my rounds among my patients, and I'll just step in and make some inquiries."

I thanked him, and we parted. Just as he was closing the door, he looked in again.

"Was she your sister?" he asked.

"No, sir, only my dear friend."

He said nothing more, but I heard him sigh, as he shut the door softly. Perhaps he once had a sister of his own and lost her. Perhaps she was like Mary in the face.

The doctor was hours gone away. I began to feel unspeakably forlorn and helpless. So much so, as even to wish selfishly that Robert might really have sailed from America, and might get to London in time to assist and console me.

No living creature came into the room but Sally. The first time she brought me some tea; the second and third times she only looked in to see if there was any change, and glanced her eye towards the bed. I had never known her so silent before; it seemed almost as if this dreadful accident had struck her dumb. I ought to have spoken to her, perhaps, but there was something in her face that daunted me; and, besides, the fever of anxiety I was in began to dry up my lips, as if they would never be able to shape any words again. I was still tormented by that frightful apprehension of the past night, that Mary would die without my knowing it – die without saying one word to clear up the awful mystery of this blow and set the suspicions at rest for ever which I still felt whenever my eyes fell on the end of the old cravat.

At last the doctor came back.

"I think you may safely clear your mind of any doubts to which that bit of stuff may have given rise," he said. "She was, as you supposed, detained late by her employers, and she fainted in the work-room. They most unwisely and unkindly let her go home alone, without giving her any stimulant, as soon as she came to her senses again. Nothing is more probable, under these circumstances, than that she should faint a second time on her way here. A fall on the pavement, without any friendly arm to break it, might have produced even a worse injury than the injury we see. I believe that the only ill-usage to which the poor girl was exposed was the neglect she met with in the work-room."

"You speak very reasonably, I own, sir," said I, not yet quite convinced. "Still, perhaps she may –"

"My poor girl, I told you not to hope," said the doctor, interrupting me. He went to Mary and lifted up her eyelids and looked at her eyes while he spoke, then added: "If you still doubt how she came by that blow, do not encourage the idea that any words of hers will ever enlighten you. She will never speak again."

"Not dead! Oh! sir, don't say she's dead!"

"She is dead to pain and sorrow – dead to speech and recognition. There is more animation in the life of the feeblest insect that flies than in the life that is left in her. When you look at her now, try to think that she is in heaven. That is the best comfort I can give you, after telling the hard truth."

I did not believe him. I could not believe him. So long as she breathed at all, so long I was resolved to hope. Soon after the doctor was gone, Sally came in again and found me listening (if I may call it so) at Mary's lips. She went to where my little hand-glass hangs against the wall, took it down and gave it to me.

"See if the breath marks it," she said.

Yes; her breath did mark it, but very faintly. Sally cleaned the glass with her apron, and gave it back to me. As she did so, she half stretched out her hand to Mary's face, but drew it in again suddenly, as if she was afraid of soiling the delicate skin with her hard, horny fingers. Going out, she stopped at the foot of the bed, and scraped away a little patch of mud that was on one of Mary's shoes.

"I always used to clean 'em for her," said Sally, "to save her hands from getting blacked. May I take 'em off now, and clean 'em again?"

I nodded my head, for my heart was too heavy to speak. Sally took the shoes off with a slow, awkward tenderness, and went out.

An hour or more must have passed, when, putting the glass over her lips again, I saw no mark on it. I held it closer and closer. I dulled it accidentally with my own breath, and cleaned it. I held it over her again. Oh! Mary, Mary, the doctor was right! I ought to have only thought of you in heaven!

Dead, without a word, without a sign – without even a look to tell the true story of the blow that killed her! I could not call to anybody, I could not cry, I could not so much as put the glass down and give her a kiss for the last time. I don't know how long I had sat there with my eyes burning and my hands deadly cold, when Sally came in with the shoes cleaned, and carried carefully in her apron for fear of a soil touching them. At the sight of that –

I can write no more. My tears drop so fast on the paper that I can see nothing.

MARCH 12TH. She died on the afternoon of the eighth. On the morning of the ninth, I wrote, as in duty bound, to her stepmother at Hammersmith. There was no answer. I wrote again; my letter was returned to me this morning, unopened. For all that woman cares, Mary might be buried with a pauper's funeral. But this shall never be, if I pawn everything about me, down to the very gown that is on my back.

The bare thought of Mary being buried by the workhouse gave me the spirit to dry my eyes and go to the undertaker's, and tell him how I was placed. I said, if he would get me an estimate of all that would have to be paid, from first to last, for the cheapest decent funeral that could be had, I would undertake to raise the money. He gave me the estimate, written in this way, like a common bill:

	£	s	d
A walking funeral complete	£1	13	8
Vestry	0	4	4
Rector	0	4	4
Clerk	0	1	0
Sexton	0	1	0
Beadle	0	1	0
Bell	0	1	0
Six feet of ground	0	2	0
Total	£2	8	4

If I had the heart to give any thought to it, I should be inclined to wish that the Church could afford to do without so many small charges for burying poor people, to whose friends even shillings are of consequence. But it is useless to complain: the money must be raised at once. The charitable doctor – a poor man himself, or he would not be living in our neighbourhood – has subscribed ten shillings towards the expenses; and the coroner, when the inquest was over, added five more.

Perhaps others may assist me. If not, I have fortunately clothes and furniture of my own to pawn. And I must set about parting with them without delay; for the funeral is to be to-morrow, the thirteenth.

The funeral – Mary's funeral! It is well that the straits and difficulties I am in, keep my mind on the stretch. If I had leisure to grieve, where should I find the courage to face to-morrow?

Thank God they did not want me at the inquest. The verdict given – with the doctor, the policeman and two persons from the place where she worked, for witnesses – was "Accidental Death". The end of the cravat was produced, and the coroner said that it was certainly enough to suggest suspicion, but the jury, in the absence of any positive evidence, held to the doctor's notion that she had fainted and fallen down, and so got the blow on her temple. They reproved the people where Mary worked for letting her go home alone, without so much as a drop of brandy to support her, after she had fallen into a swoon, from exhaustion, before their eyes. The coroner added, on his own account, that he thought the reproof was thoroughly deserved. After that, the cravat-end was given back to me, by my own desire, the police saying that they could make no investigations with such a slight clue to guide them. They may think so, and the coroner, and doctor, and jury may think so, but, in spite of all that has passed, I am now more firmly persuaded than ever that there is some dreadful mystery in connection with that blow on my poor lost Mary's temple which has yet to be revealed, and which may come to be discovered through this very fragment of a cravat that I found in her hand. I cannot give any good reason why I think so, but I know that if I had been one of the jury at the inquest, nothing should have induced me to consent to such a verdict as Accidental Death.

After I had pawned my things, and had begged a small advance of wages at the place where I work to make up what was still wanting to pay for Mary's funeral, I thought I might have had a little quiet time to prepare myself as I best could for to-morrow. But this was not to be. When I got home, the landlord met me in the passage. He was in liquor, and more brutal and pitiless in his way of looking and speaking than ever I saw him before.

"So you're going to be fool enough to pay for her funeral, are you?" were his first words to me.

I was too weary and heart-sick to answer – I only tried to get by him to my own door.

"If you can pay for burying her," he went on, putting himself in front of me, "you can pay her lawful debts. She owes me three weeks' rent. Suppose you raise the money for that next, and hand it over to me? I am not joking, I can promise you. I mean to have my rent; and if somebody don't pay it, I'll have her body seized and sent to the workhouse!"

Between terror and disgust, I thought I should have dropped to the floor at his feet. But I determined not to let him see how he had horrified me, if I could possibly control myself. So I mastered resolution enough to answer that I did not believe the Law gave him any such wicked power over the dead.

"I'll teach you what the Law is!" he broke in. "You'll raise money to bury her like a born lady when she's died in my debt, will you? And you think I'll let my rights be trampled upon like that, do you? See if I do! I'll give you till to-night to think about it. If I don't have the three weeks she owes, before to-morrow – dead or alive, she shall go to the workhouse!"

This time I managed to push by him and get to my own room, and lock the door in his face. As soon as I was alone, I fell into a breathless, suffocating fit of crying, that seemed to be shaking me to pieces. But there was no good and no help in tears. I did my best to calm myself after a little while, and tried to think whom I should run to for help and protection.

The doctor was the first friend I thought of, but I knew he was always out seeing his patients of an afternoon. The beadle was the next person who came into my head. He had the look of being a very dignified, unapproachable kind of man when he came about the inquest; but he talked to me a little then, and said I was a good girl, and seemed, I really thought, to pity me. So to him I determined to apply in my great danger and distress.

Most fortunately, I found him at home. When I told him of the landlord's infamous threats, and of the misery I was suffering in con-sequence of them, he rose up with a stamp of his foot, and sent for his gold-laced cocked hat that he wears on Sundays and his long cane with the ivory top to it.

"I'll give it to him," said the beadle. "Come along with me, my dear. I think I told you you were a good girl at the inquest – if I didn't, I tell you so now. I'll give it to him! Come along with me."

And he went out, striding along, with his cocked hat and his great cane, and I followed him.

"Landlord!" he cries, the moment he gets into the passage, with a thump of his cane on the floor. "Landlord!" with a look all round him as if he was king of England calling to a beast. "Come out!"

The moment the landlord came out and saw who it was his eyes fixed on the cocked hat, and he turned as pale as ashes.

"How dare you frighten this poor girl?" says the beadle. "How dare you bully her at this sorrowful time with threatening to do what you know you can't do? How dare you be a cowardly bullying braggadocio of an unmanly landlord? Don't talk to me – I won't hear you! I'll pull you up, sir! If you say another word to the young woman, I'll pull you up before the authorities of this metropolitan parish! I've had my eye on you, and the authorities have had their eye on you, and the rector has had his eye on you. We don't like the look of your small shop round the corner; we don't like the look of some of the customers who deal at it; we don't like disorderly characters; and we don't, by any manner of means, like *you*. Leave the young woman alone, or I'll pull you up! If he says another word, or interferes with you again, my dear, come and tell me; and, as sure as he's a bullying, unmanly braggadocio of a landlord, I'll pull him up!"

With those words, the beadle gave a loud cough to clear his throat and another thump of his cane on the floor, and so went striding out again, before I could open my lips to thank him. The landlord slunk back into his room without a word. I was left alone and unmolested at last, to strengthen myself for the hard trial of my poor love's funeral to-morrow.

MARCH 13TH. It is all over. A week ago, her head rested on my bosom. It is laid in the churchyard now – the fresh earth lies heavy over her grave. I, and my dearest friend, the sister of my love, are parted in this world for ever.

I followed her funeral alone through the cruel, bustling streets. Sally, I thought, might have offered to go with me, but she never so much as came into my room. I did not like to think badly of her for this, and I am glad I restrained myself – for, when we got into the church-yard, among the two or three people who were standing by the open grave, I saw Sally, in her ragged grey shawl and her patched black bonnet. She did not seem to notice me till the last words of the service had been read and the clergyman had gone away. Then she came up and spoke to me.

"I couldn't follow along with you," she said, looking at her ragged shawl, "for I haven't a decent suit of clothes to walk in. I wish I could get vent in crying for her like you, but I can't; all the crying's been drudged and starved out of me, long ago. Don't you think about lighting your fire when you get home. I'll do that, and get you a drop of tea to comfort you."

She seemed on the point of saying a kind word or two more; when, seeing the beadle coming towards me, she drew back as if she was afraid of him, and left the churchyard.

"Here's my subscription towards the funeral," said the beadle, giving me back his shilling fee. "Don't say anything about it, for it mightn't be approved of in a business point of view, if it came to some people's ears. Has the landlord said anything more to you? No, I thought not. He's too polite a man to give me the trouble of pulling him up. Don't stop crying here, my dear. Take the advice of a man familiar with funerals, and go home."

I tried to take his advice, but it seemed like deserting Mary to go away when all the rest forsook her.

I waited about till the earth was thrown in and the men had left the place – then I returned to the grave. Oh, how bare and cruel it was, without so much as a bit of green turf to soften it! Oh, how much harder it seemed to live than to die, when I stood alone looking at the heavy piled-up lumps of clay, and thinking of what was hidden beneath them.

I was driven home by my own despairing thoughts. The sight of Sally lighting the fire in my room eased my heart a little. When she was gone, I took up Robert's letter again to keep my mind employed on the only subject in the world that has any interest for me now.

This fresh reading increased the doubts I had already felt relative to his having remained in America after writing to me. My grief and forlornness have made a strange alteration in my former feelings about his coming back. I seem to have lost all my prudence and self-denial, and to care so little about his poverty and so much about himself, that the prospect of his return is really the only comforting thought I have now to support me. I know this is weak in me, and that his coming back poor can lead to no good result for either of us. But he is the only living being left me to love, and – I can't explain it – but I want to put my arms round his neck and tell him about Mary.

MARCH 14TH. I locked up the end of the cravat in my writing-desk. No change in the dreadful suspicions that the bare sight of it rouses in me. I tremble if I so much as touch it.

MARCH 15TH, 16TH, 17TH. Work, work, work. If I don't knock up, I shall be able to pay back the advance in another week, and then, with a little more pinching in my daily expenses, I may succeed in saving a shilling or two to get some turf to put over Mary's grave – and perhaps even a few flowers besides to grow round it.

MARCH 18TH. Thinking of Robert all day long. Does this mean that he is really coming back? If it does, reckoning the distance he is at from New York, and the time ships take to get to England, I might see him by the end of April or the beginning of May.

MARCH 19TH. I don't remember my mind running once on the end of the cravat yesterday, and I am certain I never looked at it, yet I had the strangest dream concerning it at night. I thought it was lengthened into a long clue, like the silken thread that led to Rosamond's Bower. I thought I took hold of it, and followed it a little way, and then got frightened and tried to go back but found that I was obliged, in spite of myself, to go on. It led me through a place like the Valley of the Shadow of Death, in an old print I remember in my mother's copy of the *Pilgrim's Progress*. I seemed to be months and months following it without any respite, till at last it brought me, on a sudden, face to face with an angel whose eyes were like Mary's. He said to me:

"Go on, still; the truth is at the end, waiting for you to find it." I burst out crying, for the angel had Mary's voice as well as Mary's eyes, and woke with my heart throbbing, and my cheeks all wet. What is the meaning of this? Is it always superstitious, I wonder, to believe that dreams may come true?

***

APRIL 30TH. I have found it! God knows to what results it may lead, but it is as certain as that I am sitting here before my journal, that I have found the cravat from which the end in Mary's hand was torn! I discovered it last night; but the flutter I was in, and the nervousness and uncertainty I felt, prevented me from noting down this most extraordinary and unexpected event at the time when it happened. Let me try if I can preserve the memory of it in writing now.

I was going home rather late from where I work, when I suddenly remembered that I had forgotten to buy myself any candles the evening before and that I should be left in the dark if I did not manage to rectify this mistake in some way. The shop close to me, at which I usually deal, would be shut up, I knew, before I could get to it; so I determined to go into the first place I passed where candles were sold. This turned out to be a small shop with two counters, which did business on one side in the general grocery way, and on the other in the rag and bottle and old iron line.

There were several customers on the grocery side when I went in, so I waited on the empty rag side till I could be served. Glancing about me here at the worthless-looking things by which I was surrounded, my eye was caught by a bundle of rags lying on the counter, as if they had just been brought in and left there. From mere idle curiosity, I looked close at the rags, and saw among them something like an old cravat. I took it up directly and held it under a gas-light. The pattern was blurred lilac lines, running across and across the dingy black ground in a trellis-work form. I looked at the ends; one of them was torn off.

How I managed to hide the breathless surprise into which this discovery threw me, I cannot say, but I certainly contrived to steady my voice somehow and to ask for my candles calmly, when the man and woman serving in the shop, having disposed of their other customers, inquired of me what I wanted.

As the man took down the candles, my brain was all in a whirl with trying to think how I could get possession of the old cravat without exciting any suspicion. Chance, and a little quickness on my part in taking advantage of it, put the object within my reach in a moment. The man, having counted out the candles, asked the woman for some paper to wrap them in. She produced a piece much too small and flimsy for the purpose, and declared, when he called for something better, that the day's supply of stout paper was all exhausted. He flew into a rage with her for managing so badly. Just as they were beginning to quarrel violently, I stepped back to the rag-counter, took the old cravat carelessly out of the bundle, and said, in as light a tone as I could possibly assume:

"Come, come! don't let my candles be the cause of hard words between you. Tie this ragged old thing round them with a bit of string, and I shall carry them home quite comfortably."

The man seemed disposed to insist on the stout paper being produced; but the woman, as if she was glad of an opportunity of spiting him, snatched the candles away and tied them up in a moment in the torn old cravat. I was afraid he would have struck her before my face, he seemed in such a fury, but, fortunately, another customer came in, and obliged him to put his hands to peaceable and proper uses.

"Quite a bundle of all sorts on the opposite counter there," I said to the woman, as I paid her for the candles.

"Yes, and all hoarded up for sale by a poor creature with a lazy brute of a husband, who lets his wife do all the work, while he spends all the money," answered the woman, with a malicious look at the man by her side.

"He can't surely have much money to spend, if his wife has no better work to do than picking up rags," said I.

"It isn't her fault if she hasn't got no better," says the woman, rather angrily. "She's ready to turn her hand to anything. Charring, washing, laying-out, keeping empty houses – nothing comes amiss to her. She's my half-sister, and I think I ought to know."

"Did you say she went out charing?" I asked, making believe as if I knew of somebody who might employ her.

"Yes, of course I did," answered the woman; "and if you can put a job into her hands, you'll be doing a good turn to a poor hard-working creature as wants it. She lives down the mews here to the right – name of Horlick, and as honest a woman as ever stood in shoe-leather. Now then, ma'am, what for you?"

Another customer came in just then and occupied her attention. I left the shop, passed the turning that led down to the Mews, looked up at the name of the street, so as to know how to find it again, and then ran home as fast as I could. Perhaps it was the remembrance of my strange dream striking me on a sudden, or perhaps it was the shock of the discovery I had just made, but I began to feel frightened, without knowing why, and anxious to be under shelter in my own room.

If Robert should come back! Oh, what a relief and help it would be now if Robert should come back!

MAY 1ST. On getting indoors last night, the first thing I did, after striking a light, was to take the ragged cravat off the candles, and smooth it out on the table. I then took the end that had been in poor Mary's hand out of my writing-desk, and smoothed that out, too. It matched the torn side of the cravat exactly. I put them together, and satisfied myself that there was not a doubt of it.

Not once did I close my eyes that night. A kind of fever got possession of me – a vehement yearning to go on from this first discovery and find out more, no matter what the risk might be. The cravat now really became, to my mind, the clue that I thought I saw in my dream

– the clue that I was resolved to follow. I determined to go to Mrs. Horlick this evening, on my return from work.

I found the Mews easily. A crook-backed dwarf of a man was lounging at the corner of it, smoking his pipe. Not liking his looks, I did not inquire of him where Mrs. Horlick lived, but went down the Mews till I met with a woman, and asked her. She directed me to the right number. I knocked at the door, and Mrs. Horlick herself – a lean, ill-tempered, miserable-looking woman – answered it. I told her at once that I had come to ask what her terms were for charring. She stared at me for a moment, then answered my question civilly enough.

"You look surprised at a stranger like me finding you out," I said. "I first came to hear of you last night, from a relation of yours, in rather an odd way."

And I told her all that had happened in the chandler's shop, bringing in the bundle of rags, and the circumstance of my carrying home the candles in the old torn cravat, as often as possible.

"It's the first time I've heard of anything belonging to *him* turning out any use," said Mrs. Horlick, bitterly.

"What, the spoilt old neck-handkerchief belonged to your husband, did it?" said I at a venture.

"Yes; I pitched his rotten rag of a neck-'andkercher into the bundle along with the rest; and I wish I could have pitched him in after it," said Mrs. Horlick. "I'd sell him cheap at any rag-shop. There he stands, smoking his pipe at the end of the Mews, out of work for weeks past, the idlest humpbacked pig in all London!"

She pointed to the man whom I had passed on entering the Mews. My cheeks began to burn and my knees to tremble, for I knew that in tracing the cravat to its owner I was advancing a step towards a fresh discovery. I wished Mrs. Horlick good evening, and said I would write and mention the day on which I wanted her.

"What I had just been told, put a thought into my mind that I was afraid to follow out. I have heard people talk of being light-headed, and I felt as I have heard them say they felt, when I retraced my steps up the Mews. My head got giddy and my eyes seemed able to see nothing but the figure of the little crook-backed man, still smoking his pipe in his former place, I could see nothing but that; I could think of nothing but the mark of the blow on my poor lost Mary's temple. I know that I must have been light-headed, for as I came close to the crook-backed man, I stopped without meaning it. The minute before, there had been no idea in me of speaking to him. I did not know how to speak, or in what way it would be safest to begin. And yet, the moment I came face to face with him, something out of myself seemed to stop me, and to make me speak without considering beforehand, without thinking of consequences; without knowing, I may almost say, what words I was uttering till the instant when they rose to my lips.

"When your old neck-tie was torn, did you know that one end of it went to the rag-shop, and the other fell into my hands?"

I said these bold words to him suddenly, and, as it seemed, without my own will taking any part in them.

He started, stared, changed colour. He was too much amazed by my sudden speaking to find an answer for me. When he did open his lips, it was to say, rather to himself than me:

"You're not the girl."

"No," I said, with a strange choking at my heart. "I'm her friend."

By this time he had recovered his surprise, and he seemed to be aware that he had let out more than he ought.

"You may be anybody's friend you like," he said brutally, "so long as you don't come jabbering nonsense here. I don't know you, and I don't understand your jokes."

He turned quickly away from me when he had said the last words. He had never once looked fairly at me since I first spoke to him.

Was it his hand that had struck the blow?

I had only sixpence in my pocket, but I took it out and followed him. If it had been a five-pound note, I should have done the same in the state I was in then.

"Would a pot of beer help you to understand me?" I said, and offered him the sixpence.

"A pot ain't no great things," he answered, taking the sixpence doubtfully.

"It may lead to something better," I said.

His eyes began to twinkle, and he came close to me. Oh, how my legs trembled! – How my head swam!

"This is all in a friendly way, is it?" he asked in a whisper.

I nodded my head. At that moment, I could not have spoken for worlds.

"Friendly, of course," he went on to himself, "or there would have been a policeman in it. She told you, I suppose, that I wasn't the man?"

I nodded my head again. It was all I could do to keep myself standing upright.

"I suppose it's a case of threatening to have him up, and make him settle it quietly for a pound or two? How much for me if you lay hold of him?"

"Half."

I began to be afraid that he would suspect something if I was still silent. The wretch's eyes twinkled again, and he came closer.

"I drove him to the Red Lion, corner of Dodd Street and Rudgely Street. The house was shut up, but he was let in at the jug and bottle-door, like a man who was known to the landlord. That's as much as I can tell you, and I'm certain I'm right. He was the last fare I took up at night. The next morning master give me the sack. Said I cribbed his corn and his fares. I wish I had!"

I gathered from this that the crook-backed man had been a cab-driver.

"Why don't you speak?" he asked suspiciously. "Has she been telling you a pack of lies about me? What did she say when she came home?"

"What ought she to have said?"

"She ought to have said my fare was drunk, and she came in the way as he was going to get into the cab. That's what she ought to have said, to begin with."

"But after."

"Well, after, my fare, by way of larking with her, puts out his leg for to trip her up, and she stumbles and catches at me for to save herself, and tears off one of the limp ends of my rotten old tie. 'What do you mean by that, you brute?' says she, turning round, as soon as she was steady on her legs, to my fare. Says my fare to her: 'I means to teach you to keep a civil tongue in your head.' And he ups with his fist, and – what's come to you, now? What are you looking at me like that for? How do you think a man of my size was to take her part, against a man big enough to have eaten me up? Look as much as you like, in my place you would have done what I done – drove off when he shook his fist at you, and swore he'd be the death of you if you didn't start your horse in no time."

I saw he was working himself up into a rage; but I could not, if my life had depended on it, have stood near him or looked at him any longer. I just managed to stammer out that I had been walking a long way, and that, not being used to much exercise, I felt faint and giddy with fatigue. He only changed from angry to sulky when I made that excuse. I got a little further away from him, and then added that if he would be at the Mews entrance the next evening, I should have something more to say, and something more to give him. He grumbled a few suspicious words in answer, about doubting whether he should trust me to come back. Fortunately, at that moment, a policeman passed on the opposite side of the way. He slunk down the Mews immediately, and I was free to make my escape.

How I got home, I can't say, except that I think I ran the greater part of the way. Sally opened the door, and asked if anything was the matter the moment she saw my face. I answered:

"Nothing! nothing." She stopped me as I was going into my room, and said:

"Smooth your hair a bit, and put your collar straight. There's a gentleman in there waiting for you."

My heart gave one great bound – I knew who it was in an instant, and rushed into the room like a mad woman.

"Oh, Robert! Robert!"

All my heart went out to him in those two little words.

"Good God, Anne! has anything happened? Are you ill?"

"Mary! my poor, lost, murdered, dear, dear Mary!"

That was all I could say before I fell on his breast.

MAY 2ND. Misfortunes and disappointments have saddened him a little, but towards me he is unaltered. He is as good, as kind, as gently and truly affectionate as ever. I believe no other man in the world could have listened to the story of Mary's death with such tenderness and pity as he. Instead of cutting me short anywhere, he drew me on to tell more than I had intended; and his first generous words, when I had done, were to assure me that he would see himself to the grass being laid and the flowers planted on Mary's grave. I could almost have gone on my knees and worshipped him when he made me that promise.

Surely, this best, and kindest, and noblest of men cannot always be unfortunate. My cheeks burn when I think that he has come back with only a few pounds in his pocket, after all his hard and honest struggles to do well in America. They must be bad people there, when such a man as Robert cannot get on among them. He now talks calmly and resignedly of trying for any one of the lowest employments by which a man can earn his bread honestly in this great city – he who knows French, who can write so beautifully! Oh, if the people who have places to give away only knew Robert as well as I do, what a salary he would have, what a post he would be chosen to occupy!

I am writing these lines alone, while he has gone to the Mews to treat with the dastardly, heartless wretch with whom I spoke yesterday.

Robert says the creature – I won't call him a man – must be humoured and kept deceived about poor Mary's end, in order that we may discover and bring to justice the monster whose drunken blow was the death of her. I shall know no ease of mind till her murderer is secured and till I am certain that he will be made to suffer for his crimes. I wanted to go with Robert to the Mews, but he said it was best that he should carry out the rest of the investigation alone, for my strength and resolution had been too hardly taxed already. He said more words in praise of me for what I have been able to do up to this time, which I am almost ashamed to write down with my own pen. Besides, there is no need – praise from his lips is one of the things that I can trust my memory to preserve to the latest day of my life.

MAY 3RD. Robert was very long last night before he came back to tell me what he had done. He easily recognized the hunchback at the corner of the Mews by my description of him; but he found it a hard matter, even with the help of money, to overcome the cowardly wretch's distrust of him as a stranger and a man. However, when this had been accomplished, the main difficulty was conquered. The hunchback, excited by the promise of more money, went at once to the Red Lion to inquire about the person whom he had driven there in his cab. Robert followed him and waited at the corner of the street. The tidings brought by the cabman were of the most unexpected kind. The murderer – I can write of him by no other name – had fallen ill on the very night when he was driven to the Red Lion, had taken to his bed there and then, and was still confined to it at that very moment. His disease was of a kind that is brought on by excessive drinking, and that affects the mind as well as the body. The people at the public house called it the Horrors.

Hearing these things, Robert determined to see if he could not find out something more for himself, by going and inquiring at the public house in the character of one of the friends of the sick man in bed upstairs. He made two important discoveries. First, he found out the name and address of the doctor in attendance. Secondly, he entrapped the barman into mentioning the murderous wretch by his name. This last discovery adds an unspeakably fearful interest to the dreadful misfortune of Mary's death. Noah Truscott, as she told me herself in the last conversation I ever had with her, was the name of the man whose drunken example ruined her father; and Noah Truscott is also the name of the man whose drunken fury killed her. There is something that makes one shudder, something supernatural in this awful fact. Robert agrees with me that the hand of Providence must have guided my steps to that shop from which all the discoveries since made took their rise. He says he believes we are the instruments of effecting a righteous retribution; and, if he spends his last farthing, he will have the investigation brought to its full end in a court of justice.

MAY 4TH. Robert went to-day to consult a lawyer whom he knew in former times. The lawyer was much interested, though not so seriously impressed as he ought to have been by the story of Mary's death and of the events that have followed it. He gave Robert a confidential letter to take to the doctor in attendance on the double-dyed villain at the Red

Lion. Robert left the letter, and called again and saw the doctor, who said his patient was getting better and would most likely be up again in ten days or a fortnight. This statement Robert communicated to the lawyer, and the lawyer has undertaken to have the public house properly watched, and the hunchback (who is the most important witness) sharply looked after for the next fortnight, or longer, if necessary. Here, then, the progress of this dreadful business stops for awhile.

MAY 5TH. Robert has got a little temporary employment in copying for his friend the lawyer. I am working harder than ever at my needle to make up for the time that has been lost lately.

MAY 6TH. To-day was Sunday, and Robert proposed that we should go and look at Mary's grave. He, who forgets nothing where a kindness is to be done, has found time to perform the promise he made to me on the night when we first met. The grave is already, by his orders, covered with turf and planted round with shrubs. Some flowers and a low headstone are to be added to make the place look worthier of my poor lost darling who is beneath it. Oh! I hope I shall live long after I am married to Robert! I want so much time to show him all my gratitude!

MAY 20TH. A hard trial to my courage to-day. I have given evidence at the police office, and have seen the monster who murdered her.

I could only look at him once. I could just see that he was a giant in size, and that he kept his dull, lowering, bestial face turned towards the witness box, and his bloodshot, vacant eyes staring on me. For an instant I tried to confront that look; for an instant I kept my attention fixed on him, on his blotched face, on the short grizzled hair above it – on his knotty, murderous right hand, hanging loose over the bar in front of him, like the paw of a wild beast over the edge of its den. Then the horror of him – the double horror of confronting him in the first place, and afterwards of seeing that he was an old man – overcame me, and I turned away, fain, sick, and shuddering. I never faced him again, and at the end of my evidence Robert considerately took me out.

When we met once more at the end of the examination, Robert told me that the prisoner never spoke and never changed his position. He was either fortified by the cruel composure of a savage or his faculties had not yet thoroughly recovered from the disease that had so lately shaken them. The magistrate seemed to doubt if he was in his right mind; but the evidence of the medical man relieved him from this uncertainty, and the prisoner was committed for trial on a charge of manslaughter.

Why not on a charge of murder? Robert explained the law to me when I asked that question. I accepted the explanation, but it did not satisfy me. Mary Mallinson was killed by a blow from the hand of Noah Truscott. That is murder in the sight of God. Why not murder in the sight of the Law also?

***

JUNE 18TH. To-morrow is the day appointed for the trial at the Old Bailey.

Before sunset this evening, I went to look at Mary's grave. The turf has grown so green since I saw it last and the flowers are springing up so prettily. A bird was perched, dressing his feathers, on the low white head-stone that bears the inscription of her name and age. I did not go near enough to disturb the little creature. He looked innocent and pretty on the grave, as Mary herself was in her life-time. When he flew away, I went and sat for a little by the headstone, and read the mournful lines on it. Oh! my love! my love! what harm or wrong had you ever done in this world, that you should die at eighteen by a blow from a drunkard's hand?

JUNE 19TH. The trial. My experience of what happened at it is limited, like my experience of the examination at the police office, to the time occupied in giving my own evidence. They made me say much more than I said before the magistrate. Between examination and cross-examination, I had to go into almost all the particulars about poor Mary and her funeral that I have written in this journal; the jury listening to every word I spoke with the most anxious attention. At the end, the judge said a few words to me approving of my conduct, and then there was a clapping of hands among the people in court. I was so agitated and excited that I trembled all over when they let me go out into the air again.

I looked at the prisoner both when I entered the witness-box and when I left it. The lowering brutality of his face was unchanged, but his faculties seemed to be more alive and observant than they were at the police office. A frightful blue change passed over his face; and he drew his breath so heavily that the gasps were distinctly audible, while I mentioned Mary by name and described the mark of the blow on her temple. When they asked me if I knew anything of the prisoner, and I answered that I only knew what Mary herself had told me about his having been her father's ruin, he gave a kind of groan and struck both his hands heavily on the dock. And when I passed beneath him on my way out of court, he leaned over suddenly, whether to speak to me or to strike me I can't say, for he was immediately made to stand upright again by the turnkeys on either side of him. While the evidence proceeded (as Robert described it to me), the signs that he was suffering under superstitious terror became more and more apparent, until, at last, just as the lawyer appointed to defend him was rising to speak, he suddenly cried out, in a voice that startled everyone, up to the very judge on the bench:

"Stop!"

There was a pause, and all eyes looked at him. The perspiration was pouring over his face like water, and he made strange, uncouth signs with his hands to the judge opposite. "Stop all this!" he cried out. "I've been the ruin of the father and the death of the child. Hang me before I do more harm! Hang me, for God's sake, out of the way!" As soon as the shock produced by this extraordinary interruption had subsided, he was removed, and there followed a long discussion about whether he was of sound mind, or not. The matter was left to the jury to decide by their verdict. They found him guilty of the charge of manslaughter, without the excuse of insanity. He was brought up again, and condemned to transportation for life. All he did, on hearing the dreadful sentence, was to reiterate his desperate words:

"Hang me before I do more harm! Hang me, for God's sake, out of the way!"

JUNE 20TH. I made yesterday's entry in sadness of heart, and I have not been better in my spirits to-day. It is something to have brought the murderer to the punishment that he deserves. But the knowledge that this most righteous act of retribution is accomplished brings no consolation with it. The Law does indeed punish Noah Truscott for his crime, but can it raise up Mary Mallinson from her last resting-place in the churchyard?

While writing of the Law, I ought to record that the heartless wretch who allowed Mary to be struck down in his presence without making an attempt to defend her, is not likely to escape with perfect impunity. The policeman who looked after him, to insure his attendance at the trial, discovered that he had committed past offences for which the Law can make him answer. A summons was executed upon him, and he was taken before the magistrate the moment he left the court after giving his evidence.

I had just written these few lines, and was closing my journal, when there came a knock at the door. I answered it, thinking Robert had called on his way home to say good-night, and found myself face to face with a strange gentleman who immediately asked for Anne Rodway. On hearing that I was the person inquired for, he requested five minutes' conversation with me. I showed him into the little empty room at the back of the house and waited, rather surprised and fluttered, to hear what he had to say.

He was a dark man, with a serious manner and a short, stern way of speaking. I was certain that he was a stranger, and yet there seemed something in his face not unfamiliar to me. He began by taking a newspaper from his pocket and asking me if I was the person who had given evidence at the trial of Noah Truscott on a charge of manslaughter? I answered immediately that I was.

"I have been for nearly two years in London, seeking Mary Mallinson, and always seeking her in vain," he said. "The first and only news I have had of her is found in the report of the trial yesterday."

He still spoke calmly, but there was something in the look of his eyes which showed me that he was suffering in spirit. A sudden nervousness overcame me, and I was obliged to sit down.

"You knew Mary Mallinson, sir?" I asked, as quietly as I could.

"I am her brother."

I clasped my hands, and hid my face in despair. Oh, the bitterness of heart with which I heard him say those simple words.

"You were very kind to her," said the calm, tearless man. "In her name, and for her sake, I thank you."

"Oh, sir," I said, "why did you never write to her when you were in foreign parts?"

"I wrote often," he answered, "but each of my letters contained a remittance of money. Did Mary tell you she had a stepmother? If she did, you may guess why none of my letters were allowed to reach her. I now know that this woman robbed my sister. Has she lied in telling me that she was never informed of Mary's place of abode?"

I remembered that Mary had never communicated with her stepmother after the separation, and could therefore assure him that the woman had spoken the truth.

He paused for a moment after that, and sighed. Then he took out a pocket-book, and said:

"I have already arranged for the payment of any legal expenses that may have been incurred by the trial, but I have still to reimburse you for the funeral charges which you so generously defrayed. Excuse my speaking bluntly on this subject; I am accustomed to look on all matters where money is concerned purely as matters of business."

I saw that he was taking several bank-notes out of the pocket-book, and stopped him.

"I will gratefully receive back the little money I actually paid, sir, because I am not well off, and it would be an ungracious act of pride in me to refuse it from you," I said. "But I see you handling bank-notes, any one of which is far beyond the amount you have to repay me. Pray put them back, sir. What I did for your poor lost sister, I did from my love and fondness for her. You have thanked me for that; and your thanks are all I can receive."

He had hitherto concealed his feelings, but I saw them now begin to get the better of him. His eyes softened, and he took my hand and squeezed it hard.

"I beg your pardon," he said. "I beg your pardon, with all my heart."

There was silence between us, for I was crying; and I believe, at heart, he was crying, too. At last, he dropped my hand, and seemed to change back, by an effort, to his former calmness.

"Is there no one belonging to you to whom I can be of service?" he asked. "I see among the witnesses on the trial the name of a young man who appears to have assisted you in the inquiries which led to the prisoner's conviction. Is he a relation?"

"No, sir; at least, not now – but I hope –"

"What?"

"I hope that he may, one day, be the nearest and dearest relation to me that a woman can have." I said those words boldly, because I was afraid of his otherwise taking some wrong view of the connection between Robert and me.

"One day?" he repeated. "One day may be a long time hence."

"We are neither of us well off, sir," I said. "One day means the day when we are a little richer than we are now."

"Is the young man educated? Can he produce testimonials to his character? Oblige me by writing his name and address down on the back of that card."

When I had obeyed, in a handwriting which I am afraid did me no credit, he took out another card and gave it to me.

"I shall leave England to-morrow," he said. "There is nothing now to keep me in my own country. If you are ever in any difficulty or distress (which, I pray God, you may never be), apply to my London agent, whose address you have there."

He stopped, and looked at me attentively – then took my hand again.

"Where is she buried?" he said suddenly, in a quick whisper, turning his head away.

I told him, and added that we had made the grave as beautiful as we could with grass and flowers.

I saw his lips whiten and tremble.

"God bless and reward you!" he said, and drew me towards him quickly, and kissed my forehead. I was quite overcome, and sank down and hid my face on the table. When I looked up again, he was gone.

***

JUNE 25TH, 1841. I write these lines on my wedding morning, when little more than a year has passed since Robert returned to England.

His salary was increased yesterday to one hundred and fifty pounds a year. If I only knew where Mr. Mallinson was, I would write and tell him of our present happiness. But for the situation which his kindness procured for Robert, we might still have been waiting vainly for the day that has now come.

I am to work at home for the future, and Sally is to help us in our new abode. If Mary could have lived to see this day! I am not ungrateful for my blessings; but, oh, how I miss that sweet face, on this morning of all others!

I got up to-day early enough to go alone to the grave, and to gather the nosegay that now lies before me from the flowers that grow round it. I shall put it in my bosom when Robert comes to fetch me to the church. Mary would have been my bridesmaid if she had lived; and I can't forget Mary, even on my wedding day!

A Marriage Tragedy

I

The first place I got, when I began going out to service, was not a very profitable one. I certainly gained the advantage of learning my business thoroughly, but I never had my due in the matter of wages. My master was made a bankrupt, and his servants suffered with the rest of his creditors.

My second situation, however, amply compensated me for my want of luck in the first. I had the good fortune to enter the service of Mr. and Mrs. Norcross. My master was a very rich gentleman. He had the Darrock house and lands in Cumberland, an estate also in Yorkshire and a very large property in Jamaica, which produced at that time, and for some years afterwards, a great income. Out in the West Indies he met with a pretty young lady, a governess in an English family, and, taking a violent fancy to her, married her, although she was a good five-and-twenty years younger than himself. After the wedding they came to England, and it was at this time that I was lucky enough to be engaged by them as a servant.

I lived with my new master and mistress three years. They had no children. At the end of that period Mr. Norcross died. He was sharp enough to foresee that his young widow would marry again, and he bequeathed his property so that it all went to Mrs. Norcross first and then to any children she might have by a second marriage, and, failing that, to relations and friends of his own. I did not suffer by my master's death, for his widow kept me in her service. I had attended on Mr. Norcross all through his last illness, and had made myself useful enough to win my mistress's favour and gratitude. Besides me, she also retained her maid in her service – a quadroon woman named Josephine, whom she brought with her from the West Indies. Even at that time I disliked the half-breed's wheedling manners and her cruel, tawny face, and wondered how my mistress could be so fond of her as she was. Time showed that I was right in distrusting this woman. I shall have much more to say about her when I get further advanced with my story.

Meanwhile, I have next to relate that my mistress broke up the rest of her establishment, and, taking me and the lady's maid with her, went to travel on the Continent.

Among other wonderful places, we visited Paris, Genoa, Venice, Florence, Rome and Naples, staying in some of those cities for months together. The fame of my mistress's riches followed her wherever she went, and there were plenty of gentlemen, foreigners as well as Englishmen, who were anxious enough to get into her good graces and to prevail on her to marry them. Nobody succeeded, however, in producing any very strong or lasting impression on her, and when we came back to England, after more than two years of absence, Mrs. Norcross was still a widow, and showed no signs of wanting to change her condition.

We went to the house on the Yorkshire estate first, but my mistress did not fancy some of the company round about, so we moved again to Darrock Hall, and made excursions from time to time in the Lake District, some miles off. On one of these trips, Mrs. Norcross met with some old friends, who introduced her to a gentleman of their party, bearing the very common and very uninteresting name of Mr. James Smith.

He was a tall, fine young man enough, with black hair which grew very long, and the biggest, bushiest pair of black whiskers I ever saw. Altogether he had a rakish, unsettled look and a bounceable way of talking, which made him the prominent person in company. He was poor enough himself, as I heard from his servant, but well connected – a gentleman by birth and education, although his manners were so free. What my mistress saw to like in him I don't know, but when she asked her friends to stay with her at Darrock, she included Mr. James Smith in the invitation. We had a fine, gay, noisy time of it at the Hall – the strange gentleman, in particular, making himself as much at home as if the place belonged to him. I was surprised at Mrs. Norcross putting up with him as she did; but I was fairly thunderstruck, some months afterwards, when I heard that she and her free-and-easy visitor were actually going to be married! She had refused offers by dozens abroad, from higher and richer and better-behaved men. It seemed next to impossible that she could seriously think of throwing herself away upon such a hare-brained, headlong, penniless young gentleman as Mr. James Smith.

Married, nevertheless, they were, in due course of time; and, after spending the honeymoon abroad, they came back to Darrock Hall.

I soon found that my new master had a very variable temper. There were some days when he was as easy and familiar and pleasant with his servants as any gentleman need be. At other times some devil within him seemed to get possession of his whole nature. He flew into violent passions and took wrong ideas into his head, which no reasoning or remonstrance could remove. It rather amazed me, considering how gay he was in his tastes and how restless his habits were, that he should consent to live at such a quiet, dull place as Darrock. The reason for this, however, soon came out. Mr. James Smith was not much of a sportsman – he cared nothing for indoor amusements, such as reading, music and so forth – and he had no ambition for representing the county in Parliament. The one pursuit that he was really fond of was yachting. Darrock was within sixteen miles of a sea-port town, with an excellent harbour; and to this accident of position the Hall was entirely indebted for recommending itself as a place of residence to Mr. James Smith.

He had such an untiring enjoyment and delight in cruising about at sea, and all his ideas of pleasure seemed to be so closely connected with his remembrance of the sailing trips he had taken on board the different yachts belonging to his friends, that I verily believe his chief object in marrying my mistress was to get the command of money enough to keep a vessel for himself. Be that as it may, it is certain that he prevailed on her, some time after their marriage, to make him a present of a fine schooner yacht, which was brought round from Cowes to our coast-town, and kept always waiting ready for him in the harbour.

His wife required some little persuasion before she could make up her mind to let him have the vessel. She suffered so much from sea-sickness, that pleasure-sailing was out of the question for her; and, being very fond of her husband, she was naturally unwilling that he should engage in an amusement which took him away from her. However, Mr. James Smith used his influence over her cleverly, promising that he would never go away without first asking her leave, and engaging that his terms of absence at sea should never last more than a week or ten days at a time. Accordingly, my mistress, who was the kindest and most unselfish woman in the world, put her own feelings aside, and made her husband happy in the possession of a vessel of his own.

While my master was away cruising, my mistress had a dull time of it at the Hall. The few gentlefolks there were in our part of the county lived at a distance, and could only come to Darrock when they were asked to stay there for some days together. As for the village near us, there was but one person living in it whom my mistress could think of asking to the Hall, and that person was the clergyman who did duty at the church.

This gentleman's name was Mr. Meeke. He was a single man, very young, and very lonely in his position. He had a mild, melancholy, pasty-looking face, and was as shy and soft spoken as a little girl – altogether, what one may call, without being unjust or severe, a poor weak creature, and, out of all sight, the very worst preacher I ever sat under in my life. The one thing he did, which, as I heard, he could really do well, was playing on the fiddle. He was uncommonly fond of music – so much so that he often took his instrument out with him when he went for a walk. This taste of his was his great recommendation to my mistress, who was a wonderfully fine player on the piano, and who was delighted to get such a performer as Mr. Meeke to play duets with her. Besides liking his society for this reason, she felt for him in his lonely position; naturally enough, I think, considering how often she was left in solitude herself. Mr. Meeke, on his side, when he got over his first shyness, was only too glad to leave his lonesome little parsonage for the fine music room at the Hall and for the company of a handsome, kind-hearted lady, who made much of him and admired his fiddle-playing with all her heart. Thus it happened that, whenever my master was away at sea, my mistress and Mr. Meeke were always together, playing duets as if they had their living to get by it. A more harmless connection than the connection between those two never existed in this world; and yet, innocent as it was, it turned out to be the first cause of all the misfortunes that afterward happened.

My master's treatment of Mr. Meeke was, from the first, the very opposite of my mistress's. The restless, rackety, bounceable Mr. James Smith felt a contempt for the weak, womanish, fiddling little parson; and, what was more, did not care to conceal it. For this reason, Mr. Meeke (who was dreadfully frightened by my master's violent language and rough ways) very seldom visited at the Hall, except when my mistress was alone there. Meaning no wrong, and therefore stooping to no concealment, she never thought of taking any measures to keep Mr. Meeke out of the way, when he happened to he with her at the time of her husband's coming home – whether it was only from a riding excursion in the neighbourhood, or from a cruise in the schooner. In this way, it so turned out that whenever my master came home, after a long or short absence, in nine cases out of ten he found the parson at the Hall.

At first he used to laugh at this circumstance, and to amuse himself with some coarse jokes at the expense of his wife and her companion. But, after a while, his variable temper changed, as usual. He grew sulky, rude, angry and, at last, downright jealous of Mr. Meeke. Although too proud to confess it in so many words, he still showed the state of his mind clearly enough to my mistress to excite her indignation. She was a woman who could be led anywhere by anyone for whom she had a regard; but there was a firm spirit within her that rose at the slightest show of injustice or oppression, and that resented tyrannical usage of any sort, perhaps a little too warmly. The bare suspicion that her husband could feel any distrust of her, set her all in aflame, and she took the most unfortunate, and yet, at the same time, the most natural way for a woman, of resenting it. The ruder her husband was to Mr. Meeke, the more kindly she behaved to him. This led to serious disputes and dissensions, and thence, in time, to a violent quarrel. I could not avoid hearing the last part of the altercation between them, for it took place in the garden-walk, outside the dining-room window, while I was occupied in laying the table for lunch.

Without repeating their words – which I have no right to do, having heard by accident what I had no business to hear – I may say generally, to show how serious the quarrel was, that my mistress charged my master with having married from mercenary motives, with keeping out of her company as much as he could and with insulting her by a suspicion which it would be hard ever to forgive and impossible ever to forget. He replied by violent language directed against herself and by commanding her never to open the doors again to Mr. Meeke; she, on her side, declaring that she would never consent to insult a clergyman and a gentleman in order to satisfy the whim of a tyrannical husband. Upon that he called out, with a great oath, to have his horse saddled directly, declaring that he would not stop another instant under the same roof with a woman who had set him at defiance – and warning his wife that he would come back, if Mr. Meeke entered the house again, and horsewhip him, in spite of his black coat, all through the village.

With those words he left her and rode away to the sea-port where his yacht was lying. My mistress kept up her spirit till he was out of sight, and then burst into a dreadful screaming passion of tears, which ended by leaving her so weak that she had to be carried to her bed like a woman who was at the point of death.

The same evening my master's horse was ridden back by a messenger, who brought a scrap of note-paper with him, addressed to me. It only contained these lines: "Pack up my clothes, and deliver them immediately to the bearer. You may tell your mistress that I sail to-night, at eleven o'clock, for a cruise to Sweden. Forward my letters to the Post Office, Stockholm."

I obeyed the orders given to me, except that relating to my mistress. The doctor had been sent for, and was still in the house. I consulted him on the propriety of my delivering the message. He positively forbade me to do so that night, and told me to give him the slip of paper, and leave it to his discretion to show it to her, or not, the next morning.

The messenger had hardly been gone an hour, when Mr. Meeke's housekeeper came to the Hall with a roll of music for my mistress. I told the woman of my master's sudden departure and of the doctor being in the house. This news brought Mr. Meeke himself to the Hall in a great flutter.

I felt so angry with him for being the cause – innocent as he might be – of the shocking scene which had taken place, that I exceeded the bounds of my duty and told him the whole truth. The poor, weak, wavering, childish creature flushed up red in the face, then turned as pale as ashes and dropped into one of the hall chairs, crying – literally crying fit to break his heart!

"Oh, William!" says he, wringing his little, frail, trembling, white hands, as helpless as a baby. "Oh, William! What am I to do?"

"As you ask me that question, sir," says I, "you will excuse me, I hope, if, being a servant, I plainly speak my mind, notwithstanding. I know my station well enough to be aware that, strictly speaking, I have done wrong, and far exceeded my duty, in telling you as much as I have told you already. But I would go through fire and water, sir," says I, feeling my own eyes getting moist, "for my mistress's sake. She has no relation here who can speak to you; and it is even better that a servant like me should risk being guilty of an impertinence than that dreadful and lasting mischief should arise from the right remedy not being applied at the right time. This is what I should do, sir, in your place. Saving your presence, I should leave off crying, and go back home and write to Mr. James Smith, saying that I would not, as a clergyman, give him railing for railing, but would prove how unworthily he had suspected me, by ceasing to visit at the Hall from this time forth rather than be a cause of dissension between man and wife. If you will put that into proper language, sir, and will have the letter ready for me in half an hour's time, I will call for it on the fastest horse in our stables, and, at my own risk, will give it to my master before he sails to-night. I have nothing more to say, sir, except to ask your pardon for forgetting my proper place and for making bold to speak on a very serious matter as equal to equal, and as man to man."

To do Mr. Meeke justice, he had a heart, although it was a very small one. He shook hands with me, and said he accepted my advice as the advice of a friend, and so went back to his parsonage to write the letter.

In half an hour I called for it on horseback, but it was not ready for me. Mr. Meeke was ridiculously nice about how he should express himself when he got a pen into his hand. I found him with his desk littered with rough copies, in a perfect agony about how to turn his phrases delicately enough in referring to my mistress. Every minute being precious, I hurried him as much as I could, without standing on any ceremony. It took half an hour more, with all my efforts, before he could make up his mind that the letter would do. I started off with it at a gallop, and never drew rein till I got to the sea-port town.

The harbour-clock chimed the quarter past eleven as I rode by it, and, when I got down to the jetty, there was no yacht to be seen. She had been cast off from her moorings ten minutes before eleven, and as the clock struck she had sailed out of the harbour. I would have followed in a boat, but it was a fine starlight night, with a fresh wind blowing, and the sailors on the pier laughed at me when I spoke of rowing after a schooner-yacht, which had got a quarter of an hour's start of us, with the wind abeam and the tide in her favour.

I rode back with a heavy heart. All I could do now was to send the letter to the Post Office, Stockholm.

The next day the doctor showed my mistress the scrap of paper with the message on it from my master; and an hour or two after that, a letter was sent to her in Mr. Meeke's handwriting, explaining the reason why she must not expect to see him at the Hall, and referring to me in terms of high praise, as a sensible and faithful man, who had spoken the right word at the right time. I am able to repeat the substance of the letter, because I heard all about it from my mistress, under very unpleasant circumstances so far as I was concerned.

The news of my master's departure did not affect her as the doctor had supposed it would. Instead of distressing her, it roused her spirit and made her angry; her pride, as I imagine, being wounded by the contemptuous manner in which her husband had notified his intention of sailing to Sweden, at the end of a message to a servant about packing his clothes. Finding her in that temper of mind, the letter from Mr. Meeke only irritated her the more. She insisted on getting up, and as soon as she was dressed and downstairs, she vented her violent humour on me, reproaching me for impertinent interference in the affairs of my betters and declaring that she had almost made up her mind to turn me out of my place for it. I did not defend myself, because I respected her sorrows and the irritation that came from them; also, because I knew the kindness of her nature well enough, to be assured that she would make amends to me for her harshness, the moment her mind was composed again. The result showed that I was right. That same evening she sent for me, and begged me to forgive and forget the hasty words she had spoken in the morning, with a grace and sweetness that would have won the heart of any man who listened to her.

Weeks passed after this, till it was more than a month since the day of my master's departure, and no letter in his handwriting came to Darrock Hall.

My mistress, taking this treatment of her more angrily than sorrowfully, went to London to consult her nearest relations, who lived there. On leaving home, she stopped the carriage at the parsonage, and went in (as I thought, rather defiantly) to say good-bye to Mr. Meeke. She had answered his letter, and received others from him, and had answered them likewise. She had also, of course, seen him every Sunday at church, and had always stopped to speak to him after the service. But this was the first occasion on which she had visited him at his house.

As the carriage stopped, the little parson came out, in great hurry and agitation, to meet her at the garden gate.

"Don't look alarmed, Mr. Meeke," says my mistress, getting out. "Though you have engaged not to come near the Hall, I have made no promise to keep away from the parsonage." With those words she went into the house.

The quadroon maid, Josephine, was sitting with me in the rumble of the carriage, and I saw a smile on her tawny face as the parson and his visitor went into the house together. Harmless as Mr. Meeke was, and innocent of all wrong as I knew my mistress to be, I regretted that she should be so rash as to despise appearances, considering the situation she was placed in. She had already exposed herself to be thought of disrespectfully by her own maid, and it was hard to say what worse consequences might not happen after that.

Half an hour later, we were away on our journey. My mistress stayed in London two months. Throughout all that long time no letter from my master was forwarded to her from the country house.

II

When the two months had passed, we returned to Darrock Hall. Nobody there had received any news in our absence of the whereabouts of my master and his yacht.

Six more weary weeks elapsed, and in that time but one event happened at the Hall, to vary the dismal monotony of the lives we now led in the solitary place. One morning Josephine came down, after dressing my mistress, with her face downright livid to look at, except on one cheek, where there was a mark as red as burning fire. I was in the kitchen at the time, and I asked what was the matter.

"The matter!" says she, in her shrill voice and her half-foreign English. "Use your own eyes, if you please, and look at this cheek of mine. What! have you lived so long a time with your mistress, and don't you know the mark of her hand yet?"

I was at a loss to understand what she meant, but she soon explained herself. My mistress, whose temper had been sadly altered for the worse by the trials and humiliations she had gone through, had got up that morning more out of humour than usual; and, in answer to her maid's inquiry as to how she had passed the night, had begun talking about her weary miserable life in an unusually fretful and desperate way. Josephine, in trying to cheer her spirits, had ventured, most improperly, on making a light, jesting reference to Mr. Meeke, which had so enraged my mistress that she turned round sharp on the halfbreed, and gave her – to use the common phrase – a smart box on the ear. Josephine confessed that the moment after she had done this, her better sense appeared to tell her that she had taken a most improper way of resenting undue familiarity. She had immediately expressed her regret for having forgotten herself, and had proved the sincerity of it by a gift of half a dozen cambric handkerchiefs, presented as a peace-offering on the spot. After that, I thought it impossible that Josephine could bear any malice against a mistress whom she had served ever since she had been a girl, and I said as much to her when she had done telling me what had happened upstairs.

"Malice!" cries Miss Josephine, in her hard, sharp, snappish way. "Fie upon you for mentioning the word! If my mistress smacks my cheek with one hand, she gives me handkerchiefs to wipe it with the other. Ah, you bad man, to suspect me of malice! Fie, fie, fie! I am quite ashamed of you."

She burst out laughing – the harshest laugh I ever heard from a woman's lips. Turning away from me directly after, she said no more, and never referred to the subject again on any subsequent occasion.

From that time, however, I noticed an alteration in Miss Josephine; not in her way of doing her work, for she was just as sharp and careful about it as ever, but in her manners and habits. She grew amazingly quiet, and passed almost all her leisure time alone. I could bring no charge against her which authorized me to speak a word of warning, but, for all that, I could not help feeling that if I had been in my mistress's place, I would have followed up the present of the cambric handkerchiefs by paying her a month's wages in advance and sending her away from the house the same evening.

With the exception of this little domestic matter, which appeared trifling enough at the time but which led to very serious consequences afterwards, nothing happened at all out of the ordinary way during the six weary weeks to which I have referred. At the beginning of the seventh week, however, an event occurred at last.

One morning the postman brought a letter to the Hall, addressed to my mistress. I took it upstairs, and looked at the direction as I put it on the salver. The handwriting was not my master's; was not, as it appeared to me, the handwriting of any well-educated person. The outside of the letter was also very dirty, and the seal a common office-seal of the usual lattice-work pattern. This must be a begging-letter, I thought to myself as I entered the breakfast-room and took it to my mistress.

She held up her hand before she opened it, as a sign to me that she had some order to give and that I was not to leave the room till I had received it. Then she broke the seal, and began to read the letter.

Her eyes had hardly been on it a moment before her face turned as pale as death and the paper began to tremble in her fingers. She read on to the end, and suddenly turned from pale to scarlet, started out of her chair, crumpled the letter up violently in her hand and took several turns backwards and forwards in the room, without seeming to notice me as I stood by the door.

"You villain! you villain! you villain!" I heard her whisper to herself many times over. She stopped, and said on a sudden: "Can it be true?" Then she looked up, and seeing me standing at the door, started as if I had been a stranger, changed colour again, and told me, in a stifled voice, to leave her and come back again in half an hour. I obeyed, feeling certain that she must have received some very bad news of her husband, and wondering, anxiously enough, what it might be.

When I returned to the breakfast-room, her face was as much discomposed as ever. Without speaking a word, she handed me two sealed letters. One, a note to be left for Mr. Meeke, at the parsonage; the other, a letter marked "Immediate", and addressed to her solicitor in London, who was also, I should add, her nearest living relative.

I left one of these letters and posted the other. When I came back, I heard that my mistress had taken to her room. She remained there for four days, keeping her new sorrow, whatever it was, strictly to herself. On the fifth day, the lawyer from London arrived at the Hall. My mistress went down to him in the library, and was shut up there with him for nearly two hours. At the end of that time the bell rang for me.

"Sit down, William," said my mistress when I came into the room. "I feel such entire confidence in your fidelity and attachment that I am about, with the full concurrence of this gentleman, who is my nearest relative and my legal adviser, to place a very serious secret in your keeping, and to employ your services on a matter which is as important to me as a matter of life and death."

Her poor eyes were very red, and her lips quivered as she spoke to me. I was so startled by what she had said that I hardly knew which chair to sit in. She pointed to one placed near herself at the table, and seemed about to speak to me again when the lawyer interfered.

"Let me entreat you", he said, "not to agitate yourself unnecessarily. I will put this person in possession of the facts; and if I omit anything, you shall stop me and set me right."

My mistress leaned back in her chair and covered her face with her handkerchief. The lawyer waited a moment and then addressed himself to me.

"You are already aware", he said, "of the circumstances under which your master left this house; and you also know, I have no doubt, that no direct news of him has reached your mistress up to this time?"

I bowed to him, and said I knew of the circumstances so far.

"Do you remember", he went on, "taking a letter to your mistress five days ago?"

"Yes, sir," I replied. "A letter which seemed to distress and alarm her very seriously."

"I will read you that letter before we say any more," continued the lawyer. "I warn you beforehand that it contains a terrible charge against your master, which, however, is not attested by the writer's signature. I have already told your mistress that she must not attach too much importance to an anonymous letter, and I now tell you the same thing."

Saying that, he took up a letter from the table and read it aloud. I had a copy of it given to me afterwards, which I looked at often enough to fix the contents of the letter in my memory. I can now repeat them, I think, word for word.

Madam – I cannot reconcile it to my conscience to leave you in total ignorance of your husband's atrocious conduct towards you. If you have ever been disposed to regret his absence, do so no longer. Hope and pray, rather, that you and he may never meet face to face again in this world. I write in great haste and in great fear of being observed. Time fails me to prepare you as you ought to be prepared for what I have now to disclose. I must tell you plainly, with much respect for you and sorrow for your misfortune, that your husband *has married another wife*. I saw the ceremony performed, unknown to him. If I could not have spoken of this infamous act as an eye-witness, I would not have spoken of it at all.

I dare not acknowledge who I am, for I believe Mr. James Smith would stick at no crime to revenge himself on me, if he ever came to a knowledge of the step I am now taking, and of the means by which I got my information. Neither have I time to enter into particulars. I simply warn you of what has happened, and leave you to act on that warning as you please. You may disbelieve this letter, because it is not signed by any name. In that case, if Mr. James Smith should ever venture into your presence, I recommend you to ask him suddenly what he has done with his *new wife* and to see if his countenance does not immediately testify that the truth has been spoken by

YOUR UNKNOWN FRIEND

Poor as my opinion was of my master, I had never believed him to be capable of such villainy as this; and I could not believe it when the lawyer had done reading the letter.

"Oh, sir!" I said. "Surely this is some base imposition? Surely it cannot be true?"

"That is what I have told your mistress," he answered. "But she says in return –"

"I feel it to be true," my mistress broke in, speaking behind the handkerchief, in a faint smothered voice.

"We need not debate the question," the lawyer went on. "Our business now is to prove the truth or falsehood of this letter. That must be done at once. I have written to one of my clerks, who is accustomed to conducting delicate investigations, to come to this house without loss of time. He is to be trusted with anything, and he will pursue the needful inquiries immediately. It is absolutely necessary, to make sure of committing no mistakes, that he should be accompanied by someone who is well acquainted with Mr. James Smith's habits and personal appearance; and your mistress has fixed upon you to be that person. However well the inquiry is managed, it may be attended by much trouble and delay, may necessitate a long journey and may involve some personal danger. Are you," said the lawyer, looking hard at me, "ready to suffer any inconvenience and to run any risk for your mistress's sake?"

"There is nothing I *can* do, sir," said I, "that I will not do. I am afraid I am not clever enough to be of much use. But so far as troubles and risks are concerned, I am ready for anything from this moment."

My mistress took the handkerchief from her face, looked at me with her eyes full of tears and held out her hand. How I came to do it I don't know, but I stooped down and kissed the hand she offered me, feeling half startled, half ashamed at my own boldness the moment after.

"You will do, my man," said the lawyer, nodding his head. "Don't trouble yourself about the cleverness or the cunning that may be wanted. My clerk has got head enough for two. I have only one word to say before you go downstairs again. Remember that this investigation, and the cause that leads to it, must be kept a profound secret. Except us three and the clergyman here (to whom your mistress has written word of what has happened), nobody knows anything about it. I will let my clerk into the secret when he joins us. As soon as you and he are away from the house, you may talk about it. Until then, you will close your lips on the subject."

The clerk did not keep us long waiting. He came as fast as the mail from London could bring him.

I had expected, from his master's description, to see a serious, sedate man, rather sly in his looks and rather reserved in his manner. To my amazement, this practised hand at delicate investigations was a brisk, plump, jolly little man, with a comfortable double chin, a pair of very bright black eyes and a big bottle-nose of the true groggy red colour. He wore a suit of black and a limp, dingy white cravat, took snuff perpetually out of a very large box, walked with his hands crossed behind his back and looked, upon the whole, much more like a parson of free-and-easy habits than a lawyer's clerk.

"How d'ye do?" says he, when I opened the door to him.

"I'm the man you expect from the office in London. Just say Mr. Dark, will you? I'll sit down here till you come back; and, young man, if there is such a thing as a glass of ale in the house, I don't mind committing myself so far as to say that I'll drink it."

I got him the ale before I announced him. He winked at me as he put it to his lips.

"Your good health," says he. "I like you. Don't forget that the name's Dark; and just leave the jug and glass, will you, in case my master keeps me waiting."

I announced him at once, and was told to show him into the library.

When I got back to the hall the jug was empty, and Mr. Dark was comforting himself with a pinch of snuff, snorting over it like a perfect grampus. He had swallowed more than a pint of the strongest old ale in the house; and, for all the effect it seemed to have had on him, he might just as well have been drinking so much water.

As I led him along the passage to the library, Josephine passed us. Mr. Dark winked at me again, and made her a low bow.

"Lady's maid," I heard him whisper to himself. "A fine woman to look at, but a damned bad one to deal with." I turned round on him, rather angry at his cool ways, and looked hard at him just before I opened the library door. Mr. Dark looked hard at *me*. "All right," says he. "I can show myself in." And he knocks at the door, and opens it, and goes in with another wicked wink, all in a moment.

Half an hour later, the bell rang for me. Mr. Dark was sitting between my mistress (who was looking at him in amazement) and the lawyer (who was looking at him with approval). He had a map open on his knee, and a pen in his hand. Judging by his face, the communication of the secret about my master did not seem to have made the smallest impression on him.

"I've got leave to ask you a question," says he the moment I appeared. "When you found your master's yacht gone, did you hear which way she sailed? Was it northward towards Scotland? Speak up, young man, speak up!"

"Yes," I answered. "The boatmen told me that when I made inquiries at the harbour."

"Well, sir," says Mr. Dark, turning to the lawyer, "if he said he was going to Sweden, he seems to have started on the road to it, at all events. I think I have got my instructions now?"

The lawyer nodded, and looked at my mistress, who bowed her head to him. He then said, turning to me:

"Pack up your bag for travelling at once, and have a conveyance got ready to go to the nearest post town. Look sharp, young man – look sharp!"

"And whatever happens in the future," added my mistress, her kind voice trembling a little, "believe, William, that I shall never forget the proof you now give of your devotion to me. It is still some comfort to know that I have your fidelity to depend on in this dreadful trial – your fidelity and the extraordinary intelligence and experience of Mr. Dark."

Mr. Dark did not seem to hear the compliment. He was busy writing, with his paper upon the map on his knee.

A quarter of an hour later, when I had ordered the dog-cart and had got down into the hall with my bag packed, I found him there waiting for me. He was sitting in the same chair which he had occupied when he first arrived, and he had another jug of the old ale on the table by his side.

"Got any fishing-rods in the house?" says he, when I put my bag down in the hall.

"Yes," I replied, astonished at the question. "What do you want with them?"

"Pack a couple in cases for travelling," says Mr. Dark, "with lines and hooks and fly-books all complete. Have a drop of the ale before you go – and don't stare, William, don't stare. I'll let the light in on you, as soon as we are out of the house. Off with you for the rods! I want to be on the road in five minutes."

When I came back with the rods and tackle, I found Mr. Dark in the dog-cart.

"Money, luggage, fishing-rods, papers of directions, copy of anonymous letter, guide-book, map," says he, running over in his mind the things wanted for the journey. "All right so far. Drive off."

I took the reins and started the horse. As we left the house, I saw my mistress and Josephine looking after us from two of the windows on the second floor. The memory of those two attentive faces – one so fair and so good – the other so yellow and so wicked – haunted my mind perpetually for many days afterwards.

"Now, William," says Mr. Dark, when we were clear of the lodge gates, "I'm going to begin by telling you that you must step out of your own character till further notice. You are a clerk in a bank, and I'm another. We have got our regular holiday, that comes, like Christmas, once a year, and we are taking a little tour in Scotland to see the curiosities and to breathe the sea air and to get some fishing whenever we can. I'm the fat cashier who digs holes in a drawerful of gold with a copper shovel. And you're the arithmetical young man who sits on a perch behind me and keeps the books. Scotland's a beautiful country, William. Can you make whisky toddy? I can. And what's more, unlikely as the thing may seem to you, I can actually drink it into the bargain."

"Scotland!" says I. "What are we going to Scotland for?"

"Question for question," says Mr. Dark. "What are we starting on a journey for?"

"To find my master," I answered, "and to make sure if the letter about him is true."

"Very good," says he. "How would *you* set about doing that, eh?"

"I should go and ask about him at Stockholm, in Sweden, where he said his letters were to be sent."

"Should you indeed?" says Mr. Dark. "If you were a shepherd, William, and had lost a sheep in Cumberland, would you begin looking for it at the Land's End, or would you try a little nearer home?"

"You're attempting to make a fool of me now," says I.

"No," says Mr. Dark, "I'm only letting the light in on you, as I said I would. Now listen to reason, William, and profit by it as much as you can. Mr. James Smith says he is going on a cruise to Sweden, and makes his word good, at the beginning, by starting northward toward the coast of Scotland. What does he go in? A yacht. Do yachts carry live beasts and a butcher on board? No. Will joints of meat keep fresh all the way from Cumberland to Sweden? No. Do gentlemen like living on salt provisions? No. What follows from these three Noes? That Mr. James Smith must have stopped somewhere, on the way to Sweden, to supply his sea-larder with fresh provisions. Where, in that case, must he stop?

Somewhere in Scotland, supposing he didn't alter his course when he was out of sight of your sea-port. Where in Scotland? Northward on the mainland or westward at one of the islands? Most likely on the mainland, where the sea-side places are largest and where he is sure of getting all the stores he wants. Next, what is our business? Not to risk losing a link in the chain of evidence by missing any place where he has put his foot on shore. Not to overshoot the mark when we want to hit it in the bull's-eye. Not to waste money and time by taking a long trip to Sweden, till we know that we must absolutely go there. Where is our journey of discovery to take us to first, then? Clearly to the north of Scotland. What do you say to that, Mr. William? Is my catechism all correct, or has your strong ale muddled my head?"

It was evident by this time that no ale could do that, and I told him so. He chuckled, winked at me and, taking another pinch of snuff, said he would now turn the whole case over in his mind again, and make sure that he had got all the bearings of it quite clear.

By the time we reached the post-town, he had accomplished this mental effort to his own perfect satisfaction, and was quite ready to compare the ale at the inn with the ale at Darrock Hall. The dog-cart was left to be taken back the next morning by the ostler. A post-chaise and horses were ordered out. A loaf of bread, a Bologna sausage and two bottles of sherry were put into the pockets of the carriage. We took our seats, and started briskly on our doubtful journey.

"One word more of friendly advice," says Mr. Dark, settling himself comfortably in his corner of the carriage. "Take your sleep, William, whenever you feel that you can get it. You won't find yourself in bed again till we get to Glasgow."

III

Although the events that I am now relating happened many years ago, I shall still, for caution's sake, avoid mentioning by name the various places visited by Mr. Dark and myself for the purpose of making inquiries. It will be enough if I describe generally what we did, and if I mention in substance only the result at which we ultimately arrived.

On reaching Glasgow, Mr. Dark turned the whole case over in his mind once more. The result was that he altered his intention of going straight to the north of Scotland, considering it safer to make sure, if possible, of the course the yacht had taken in her cruise along the western coast.

The carrying out of this new resolution involved the necessity of delaying our onward journey by perpetually diverging from the direct road. Three times we were sent uselessly to wild places in the Hebrides by false reports. Twice we wandered away inland, following gentlemen who answered generally to the description of Mr. James Smith but who turned out to be the wrong men as soon as we set eyes on them. These vain excursions – especially the three to the western islands – consumed time terribly. It was more than two months from the day when we had left Darrock Hall before we found ourselves up at the very top of Scotland at last, driving into a considerable sea-side town with a harbour attached to it. Thus far, our journey had led to no results, and I began to despair of success. As for Mr. Dark, he never got to the end of his sweet temper and his wonderful patience.

"You don't know how to wait, William," was his constant remark whenever he heard me complaining. "I do."

We drove into the town towards evening, in a modest little gig, and put up, according to our usual custom, at one of the inferior inns.

"We must begin at the bottom," Mr. Dark used to say. "High company in a coffee-room won't be familiar with us. Low-company in a tap-room will." And he certainly proved the truth of his own words. The like of him for making intimate friends of total strangers at the shortest notice, I have never met with before or since. Cautious as the Scotch are, Mr. Dark seemed to have the knack of twisting them round his finger as he pleased. He varied his way artfully with different men, but there were three standing opinions of his, which he made a point of expressing in all varieties of company while we were in Scotland. In the first place, he thought the view of Edinburgh from Arthur's seat the finest in the world. In the second place, he considered whisky to be the most wholesome spirit in the world. In the third place, he believed his late beloved mother to have been the best woman in the world. It may be worthy of note that, whenever he expressed this last opinion in Scotland, he invariably added that her maiden name was Macleod.

Well, we put up at a modest little inn near the harbour. I was dead tired with the journey, and lay down on my bed to get some rest. Mr. Dark, whom nothing ever fatigued, left me to take his toddy and pipe among the company in the tap-room.

I don't know how long I had been asleep when I was roused by a shake on my shoulder. The room was pitch dark, and I felt a hand suddenly clapped over my mouth. Then a strong smell of whisky and tobacco saluted my nostrils, and a whisper stole into my ear:

"William! We have got to the end of our journey."

"Mr. Dark," I stammered out, "is that you? What in heaven's name do you mean?"

"The yacht put in here," was the answer, still in a whisper, "and your blackguard of a master came ashore –"

"Oh, Mr. Dark," I broke in, "don't tell me that the letter is true!"

"Every word of it," says he. "He was married here, and he was off again to the Mediterranean with Number Two a good three weeks before we left your mistress's house. Hush! don't say a word. Go to sleep again, or strike a light and read if you like it better. Do anything but come downstairs with me. I'm going to find out all the particulars, without seeming to want to know one of them. Yours is a very good-looking face, William, but it's so infernally honest that I can't trust it in the tap-room. I'm making friends with the Scotchmen already. They know my opinion of Arthur's Seat; they *see* what I think of whisky; and I rather fancy it won't be long before they hear that my mother's maiden name was Macleod." With those words he slipped out of the room and left me as he had found me, in the dark.

I was far too much agitated by what I had heard to think of going to sleep again, so I struck a light and tried to amuse myself as well as I could with an old newspaper that had been stuffed into my carpet bag. It was then nearly ten o'clock. Two hours later, when the house shut up, Mr. Dark came back to me again in high spirits.

"I have got the whole case here," says he, tapping his forehead, "the whole case, as neat and clean as if it was drawn in a brief. That master of yours doesn't stick at a trifle, William. It's my opinion that your mistress and you have not seen the last of him yet."

We were sleeping that night in a double-bedded room. As soon as Mr. Dark had secured the door and disposed himself comfortably in his bed, he entered on a detailed narrative of the particulars communicated to him in the tap-room. The substance of what he told me may be related as follows:

The yacht had had a wonderful run all the way to Cape Wrath. On rounding that headland, she had met the wind nearly dead against her, and had beaten every inch of the way to the sea-port town, where she had put in to get a supply of provisions and to wait for a change in the wind.

Mr. James Smith had gone ashore to look about him and to see whether the principal hotel was the sort of house at which he would like to stop for a few days. In the course of his wandering about the town, his attention had been attracted to a decent house where lodgings were to be let by the sight of a very pretty girl sitting at work at the parlour window. He was so struck by her face that he came back twice to look at it, determining, the second time, to try if he could not make acquaintance with her by asking to see the lodgings. He was shown the rooms by the girl's mother, a very respectable woman, whom he discovered to be the wife of the master and part owner of a small coasting vessel, then away at sea. With a little manœuvring, he managed to get into the parlour where the daughter was at work and to exchange a few words with her. Her voice and manner completed the attraction of her face. Mr. James Smith decided, in his headlong way, that he was violently in love with her, and, without hesitating another instant, he took the lodgings on the spot for a month certain.

It is unnecessary to say that his designs on the girl were of the most disgraceful kind, and that he represented himself to the mother and daughter as a single man. Helped by his advantages of money, position and personal appearance, he had made sure that the ruin of the girl might be effected with very little difficulty – but he soon found that he had undertaken no easy conquest.

The mother's watchfulness never slept, and the daughter's presence of mind never failed her. She admired Mr. James Smith's tall figure and splendid whiskers; she showed the most encouraging partiality for his society; she smiled at his compliments and blushed whenever he looked at her; but, whether it was cunning or whether it was innocence, she seemed incapable of understanding that his advances toward her were of any other than an honourable kind. At the slightest approach to undue familiarity, she drew back with a kind of contemptuous surprise in her face, which utterly perplexed Mr. James Smith. He had not calculated on that sort of resistance, and he could not see his way to overcoming it. The weeks passed; the month for which he had taken the lodgings expired. Time had strengthened the girl's hold on him, till his admiration for her amounted to downright infatuation – and he had not advanced one step yet towards the fulfilment of the vicious purpose with which he had entered the house.

At this time he must have made some fresh attempt on the girl's virtue, which produced a coolness between them, for, instead of taking the lodgings for another term, he removed to his yacht in the harbour and slept on board for two nights.

The wind was now fair and the stores were on board, but he gave no orders to the sailing-master to weigh anchor. On the third day, the cause of the coolness, whatever it was, appears to have been removed, and he returned to his lodgings on shore. Some of the more inquisitive among the townspeople observed soon afterwards, when they met him in the street, that he looked rather anxious and uneasy. The conclusion had probably forced itself upon his mind, by this time, that he must decide on pursuing one of two courses. Either he must resolve to make the sacrifice of leaving the girl altogether or he must commit the villainy of marrying her.

Scoundrel as he was, he hesitated at encountering the risk – perhaps, also, at being guilty of the crime – involved in this last alternative. While he was still in doubt, the father's coasting vessel sailed into the harbour, and the father's presence on the scene decided him at last. How this new influence acted, it was impossible to find out from the imperfect evidence of persons who were not admitted to the family councils. The fact, however, was certain, that the date of the father's return, and the date of Mr. James Smith's first wicked resolution to marry the girl, might both be fixed, as nearly as possible, at one and the same time.

Having once made up his mind to the commission of the crime, he proceeded, with all possible coolness and cunning, to provide against the chances of detection.

Returning on board his yacht, he announced that he had given up his intention of cruising to Sweden and that he intended to amuse himself by a long fishing tour in Scotland. After this explanation, he ordered the vessel to be laid up in the harbour, gave the sailing-master leave of absence to return to his family at Cowes and paid off the whole of the crew, from the mate to the cabin-boy. By these means he cleared the scene, at one blow, of the only people in the town who knew of the existence of his unhappy wife. After that, the news of his approaching marriage might be made public without risk of discovery; his own common name being of itself a sufficient protection, in case the event was mentioned in the Scotch newspapers. All his friends, even his wife herself, might read a report of the marriage of Mr. James Smith, without having the slightest suspicion of who the bridegroom really was.

A fortnight after the paying off of the crew, he was married to the merchant-captain's daughter. The father of the girl was well known among his fellow-townsmen as a selfish, grasping man, who was too anxious to secure a rich son-in-law to object to any proposals for hastening the marriage. He and his wife, and a few intimate relations, had been present at the ceremony, and, after it had been performed, the newly married couple left the town at once for a honeymoon trip to the Highland Lakes.

Two days later, however, they unexpectedly returned, announcing a complete change in their plans. The bridegroom (thinking, probably, that he would be safer out of England than in it) had been pleasing the bride's fancy by his descriptions of the climate and the scenery of southern parts. The new Mrs. James Smith was all curiosity to see Spain and Italy, and, having often proved herself an excellent sailor on board her father's vessel, was anxious to go to the Mediterranean in the easiest way by sea. Her affectionate husband, having now no other object in life than to gratify her wishes, had given up the Highland excursion and had returned to have his yacht got ready for sea immediately. In this explanation there was nothing to awaken the suspicions of the lady's parents. The mother thought Mr. James Smith a model among bridegrooms. The father lent his assistance to man the yacht at the shortest notice, with as smart a crew as could be picked up about the town. Principally through his exertions, the vessel was got ready for sea with extraordinary dispatch. The sails were bent, the provisions were put on board and Mr. James Smith sailed for the Mediterranean with the unfortunate woman who believed herself to be his wife, before Mr. Dark and myself set forth to look after him from Darrock Hall.

Such was the true account of my master's infamous conduct in Scotland as it was related to me. On concluding, Mr. Dark hinted that he had something still left to tell me, but declared that he was too sleepy to talk any more that night. As soon as we were awake the next morning, he returned to the subject.

"I didn't finish all I had to say last night, did I?" he began.

"You unfortunately told me enough, and more than enough, to prove the truth of the statement in the anonymous letter," I answered.

"Yes," says Mr. Dark. "But did I tell you who wrote the anonymous letter?"

"You don't mean to say you have found that out!" says I.

"I think I have," was the cool answer. "When I heard about your precious master paying off the regular crew of the yacht, I put the circumstance by in my mind, to be brought out again and sifted a little as soon as the opportunity offered. It offered in about half an hour. Says I to the gauger, who was the principal talker in the room: 'How about those men that Mr. Smith paid off? Did they all go as soon as they got their money, or did they stop here till they had spent every farthing of it in the public houses?' The gauger laughed. 'No such luck,' says he, in the broadest possible Scotch (which I'll translate into English, William, for your benefit). 'No such luck; they all went south to spend their money among finer people than us. All that is to say, with one exception. It was thought the steward of the yacht had gone along with the rest when, the very day Mr. Smith sailed for the Mediterranean, who should turn up unexpectedly but the steward himself! Where he had been hiding, and why he had been hiding, nobody could tell.' 'Perhaps he had been imitating his master, and looking out for a wife,' says I. 'Likely enough,' says the gauger. 'He gave a very confused account of himself, and he cut all questions short by going away south in a violent hurry.' That was enough for me. I let the subject drop. Clear as daylight, isn't it, William? The steward suspected something wrong – the steward waited and watched – the steward wrote that anonymous letter to your mistress. We can find him, if we want him, by inquiring at Cowes, and we can send to the church for legal evidence of the marriage as soon as we are instructed to do so. All that we have got to do now is to go back to your mistress, and see what course she means to take under the circumstances. It's a pretty case, William, so far – an uncommonly pretty case, as it stands at present."

We returned to Darrock Hall as fast as coaches and post-horses could carry us.

Having from the first believed that the statement in the anonymous letter was true, my mistress received the bad news we brought calmly and resignedly – so far, at least, as outward appearances went. She astonished and disappointed Mr. Dark, by declining to act, in any way, on the information that he had collected for her, and by insisting that the whole affair should still be buried in the profoundest secrecy. For the first time since I had known my travelling companion, he became depressed in spirits on hearing that nothing more was to be done, and, although he left the Hall with a handsome present, he left it discontentedly.

"Such a pretty case, William," says he, quite sorrowfully, as we shook hands. "Such an uncommonly pretty case! It's a thousand pities to stop it in this way before it's half over."

"You don't know what a proud lady and what a delicate lady my mistress is," I answered. "She would die rather than expose her forlorn situation in a public court for the sake of punishing her husband."

"Bless your simple heart," says Mr. Dark. "Do you really think, now, that such a case as this can be hushed up?"

"Why not," I asked, "if we all keep the secret?"

"That for the secret!" cries Mr. Dark, snapping his fingers. "Your master will let the cat out of the bag if nobody else does."

"My master!" I repeated, in amazement.

"Yes, your master," says Mr. Dark. "I have had some experience in my time, and I say you have not seen the last of him yet. Mark my words, William. Mr. James Smith will come back."

With that prophecy Mr. Dark fretfully treated himself to a last pinch of snuff, and departed in dudgeon on his return to his master in London. His last words hung heavily on my mind for days after he had gone. It was some weeks before I got over a habit of starting whenever the bell was rung at the front door.

IV

Our life at the Hall soon returned to its old dreary course. The lawyer in London wrote to my mistress to ask her to come and stay for a little while with his wife. But she declined the invitation, being averse to facing company after what had happened to her. Although she tried hard to keep the real state of her mind concealed from all about her, I, for one, could see plainly enough that she was pining under the bitter injury that had been inflicted on her. What effect continued solitude might have had on her spirits, I tremble to think.

Fortunately for herself, it occurred to her, before long, to send and invite Mr. Meeke to resume his musical practising with her at the Hall. She told him – and, as it seemed to me, with perfect truth – that any implied engagement which he had made with Mr. James Smith was now cancelled, since the person so named had morally forfeited all his claims as a husband – first, by his desertion of her; and, secondly, by his criminal marriage with another woman. After stating this view of the matter, she left it with Mr. Meeke to decide whether the perfectly innocent connection between them should be resumed or not.

The little parson, after hesitating and pondering in his helpless way, ended by agreeing with my mistress and by coming back once more to the Hall with his fiddle under his arm. This renewal of their old habits might have been imprudent enough, as tending to weaken my mistress's case in the eyes of the world; but, for all that, it was the most sensible course she could take for her own sake. The harmless company of Mr. Meeke, and the relief of playing the old tunes again in the old way, saved her, I verily believe, from sinking altogether under the oppression of the shocking situation in which she was now placed.

So, with the assistance of Mr. Meeke and his fiddle, my mistress got through the weary time. The winter passed, the spring came, and no fresh tidings reached us of Mr. James Smith. It had been a long, hard winter that year, and the spring was backward and rainy. The first really fine day we had was the day that fell on March 14th.

I am particular in mentioning this date merely because it is fixed for ever in my memory. As long as there is life in me, I shall remember that March 14th and the smallest circumstances connected with it.

The day began ill, with what superstitious people would think a bad omen. My mistress remained late in her room in the morning, amusing herself by looking over her clothes and by setting to rights some drawers in her cabinet which she had not opened for some time past. Just before luncheon, we were startled by hearing the drawing-room bell rung violently. I ran up to see what was the matter, and the quadroon, Josephine, who had heard the bell in another part of the house, hastened to answer it also. She got into the drawing-room first, and I followed close on her heels. My mistress was standing alone on the hearth-rug, with an appearance of great discomposure in her face and manner.

"I have been robbed!" she said, vehemently. "I don't know when or how. But I miss a pair of bracelets, three rings and a quantity of old-fashioned lace pocket handkerchiefs."

"If you have any suspicions, ma'am," said Josephine, in, a sharp, sudden way, "say who they point at. My boxes, for one, are quite at your disposal."

"Who asked you about your boxes?" said my mistress, angrily. "Be a little less ready with your answer, if you please, the next time I speak."

She then turned to me, and began explaining the circumstances under which she had discovered her loss. I suggested that the missing things should be well searched for first, and then, if nothing came of that, that I should go for the constable and place the matter under his direction.

My mistress agreed to this plan, and the search was undertaken immediately. It lasted till dinner time, and led to no results. I then proposed going for the constable. But my mistress said it was too late to do anything that day, and told me to wait at table as usual, and to go on my errand the first thing the next morning. Mr. Meeke was coming with some new music in the evening, and I suspect she was not willing to be disturbed at her favourite occupation by the arrival of the constable.

When dinner was over, the parson came, and the concert went on as usual through the evening. At ten o'clock I took up the tray, with the wine and soda-water and biscuits. Just as I was opening one of the bottles of soda-water, there was a sound of wheels on the drive outside, and a ring at the bell.

I had unfastened the wires of the cork, and could not put the bottle down to run at once to the door. One of the female servants answered it. I heard a sort of half-scream – then the sound of a footstep that was familiar to me.

My mistress turned round from the piano and looked me hard in the face.

"William," she said, "do you know that step?"

Before I could answer, the door was pushed open and Mr. James Smith walked into the room.

He had his hat on. His long hair flowed down under it over the collar of his coat; his bright black eyes, after resting an instant on my mistress, turned to Mr. Meeke. His heavy eyebrows met together and one of his hands went up to one of his bushy black whiskers, and pulled at it angrily.

"You here again!" he said, advancing a few steps toward the little parson, who sat trembling all over, with his fiddle hugged up in his arms as if it had been a child.

Seeing her villainous husband advance, my mistress moved, too, so as to face him. He turned round on her at the first step she took, as quick as lightning.

"You shameless woman," he said. "Can you look me in the face, in the presence of that man?" He pointed, as he spoke, to Mr. Meeke.

My mistress never shrank when he turned upon her. Not a sign of fear was in her face when they confronted each other. Not the faintest flush of anger came into her cheeks when he spoke. The sense of the insult and injury that he had inflicted on her, and the consciousness of knowing his guilty secret, gave her all her self-possession at that trying moment.

"I ask you again," he repeated, finding that she did not answer him, "how dare you look me in the face in the presence of that man?"

She raised her steady eyes to his hat, which he still kept on his head.

"Who has taught you to come into a room and speak to a lady with your hat on?" she asked, in quiet, contemptuous tones. "Is that a habit which is sanctioned *by your new wife?*"

My eyes were on him as she said those last words. His complexion, naturally dark and swarthy, changed instantly to a livid yellow white, his hand caught at the chair nearest to him and he dropped into it heavily.

"I don't understand you," he said, after a moment of silence, looking about the room unsteadily while he spoke.

"You do," said my mistress. "Your tongue lies, but your face speaks the truth."

He called back his courage and audacity by a desperate effort, and started up from the chair again with an oath.

The instant before this happened, I thought I heard the sound of a rustling dress in the passage outside, as if one of the women servants was stealing up to listen outside the door. I should have gone at once to see whether this was the case or not, but my master stopped me just after he had risen from the chair.

"Get the bed made in the Red Room, and light a fire there directly," he said, with his fiercest look and in his roughest tones. "When I ring the bell, bring me a kettle of boiling water and a bottle of brandy. As for you," he continued, turning towards Mr. Meeke, who still sat pale and speechless, with his fiddle hugged up in his arms, "leave the house, or you won't find your cloth any protection to you."

At this insult the blood flew into my mistress's face. Before she could say anything, Mr. James Smith raised his voice loud enough to drown hers.

"I won't hear another word from you," he cried out, brutally. "You have been talking like a mad woman, and you look like a mad woman. You are out of your senses. As sure as you live, I'll have you examined by the doctors to-morrow. Why the devil do you stand there, you scoundrel?" he roared, wheeling round on his heel to me. "Why don't you obey my orders?"

I looked at my mistress. If she had directed me to knock Mr. James Smith down – big as he was, I think at that moment I could have done it.

"Do as he tells you, William," she said, squeezing one of her hands firmly over her bosom, as if she was trying to keep down the rising indignation in that way. "This is the last order of his giving that I shall ask you to obey."

"Do you threaten me, you mad —?"

He finished the question by a word I shall not repeat.

"I tell you," she answered, in clear, ringing, resolute tones, "that you have outraged me past all forgiveness and all endurance, and that you shall never insult me again as you have insulted me to-night."

After saying those words, she fixed one steady look on him, then turned away, and walked slowly to the door.

A minute previously, Mr. Meeke had summoned courage enough to get up and leave the room quietly. I noticed him walking demurely away, close to the wall, with his fiddle held under one tail of his long frock coat, as if he was afraid that the savage passions of Mr. James Smith might be wreaked on that unoffending instrument. He got to the door before my mistress. As he softly pulled it open, I saw him start, and the rustling of the gown caught my ear again from outside.

My mistress followed him into the passage, turning, however, in the opposite direction to that taken by the little parson, in order to reach the staircase that led to her own room. I went out next, leaving Mr. James Smith alone.

I overtook Mr. Meeke in the hall, and opened the door for him.

"I beg your pardon, sir," I said, "but did you come upon anybody listening outside the music-room when you left it just now?"

"Yes, William," said Mr. Meeke, in a faint voice. "I think it was Josephine. But I was so dreadfully agitated that I can't be quite certain about it."

Had she surprised our secret? That was the question I asked myself as I went away to light the fire in the Red Room. Calling to mind the exact time at which I had first detected the rustling outside the door, I came to the conclusion that she had only heard the last part of the quarrel between my mistress and her rascal of a husband. These bold words about the "new wife" had been assuredly spoken before I heard Josephine stealing up to the door.

As soon as the fire was alight and the bed made, I went back to the music-room to announce that my orders had been obeyed. Mr. James Smith was walking up and down in a perturbed way, still keeping his hat on. He followed me to the Red Room without saying a word.

Ten minutes later, he rang for the kettle and the bottle of brandy. When I took them in, I found him unpacking a small carpet-bag, which was the only luggage he had brought with him. He still kept silence, and did not appear to take any notice of me. I left him immediately, without our having so much as exchanged a single word.

So far as I could tell, the night passed quietly. The next morning, I heard that my mistress was suffering so severely from a nervous attack that she was unable to rise from her bed. It was no surprise to me to be told that, knowing, as I did, what she had gone through the night before.

About nine o'clock I went with the hot water to the Red Room. After knocking twice, I tried the door, and, finding it not locked, went in with the jug in my hand.

I looked at the bed; I looked all round the room. Not a sign of Mr. James Smith was to be seen anywhere.

Judging by appearances, the bed had certainly been occupied. Thrown across the counterpane lay the night-gown he had worn. I took it up, and saw some spots on it. I looked at them a little closer. They were spots of blood.

V

The first amazement and alarm produced by this discovery deprived me of my presence of mind. Without stopping to think what I ought to do first, I ran back to the servants' hall, calling out that something had happened to my master.

All the household hurried directly into the Red Room, Josephine among the rest. I was first brought to my senses, as it were, by observing the strange expression of her countenance when she saw the bed-gown and the empty room. All the other servants were bewildered and frightened. She alone, after giving a little start, recovered herself directly. A look of devilish satisfaction broke out on her face, and she left the room quickly and quietly, without exchanging a word with any of us. I saw this, and it aroused my suspicions. There is no need to mention what they were, for, as events soon showed, they were entirely wide of the mark.

Having come to myself a little, I sent them all out of the room, except the coachman. We two then examined the place.

The Red Room was usually occupied by visitors. It was on the ground floor, and looked out into the garden. We found the window-shutters, which I had barred over-night, open, but the window itself was down. The fire had been out long enough for the grate to be quite cold. Half the bottle of brandy had been drunk. The carpet-bag was gone. There were no marks of violence or struggling anywhere about the bed or the room. We examined every corner carefully, but made no other discoveries than these.

When I returned to the servants' hall, bad news of my mistress was awaiting me there. The unusual noise and confusion in the house had reached her ears, and she had been told what had happened, without sufficient caution being exercised in preparing her to hear it. In her weak, nervous state, the shock of the intelligence had quite prostrated her. She had fallen into a swoon, and had been brought back to her senses with the greatest difficulty. As to giving me or anybody else directions what to do, under the embarrassing circumstances which had now occurred, she was totally incapable of the effort.

I waited till the middle of the day, in the hope that she might get strong enough to give her orders, but no message came from her. At last I resolved to send and ask her what she thought it best to do. Josephine was the proper person to go on this errand; but when I asked for Josephine, she was nowhere to be found. The housemaid, who had searched for her ineffectually, brought word that her bonnet and shawl were not hanging in their usual places. The parlour-maid, who had been in attendance in my mistress's room, came down while we were all aghast at this new disappearance. She could only tell us that Josephine had begged her to do lady's-maid's duty that morning as she was not well. Not well! And the first result of her illness appeared to be that she had left the house.

I cautioned the servants on no account to mention this circumstance to my mistress, and then went upstairs myself to knock at her door. My object was to ask if I might count on her approval if I wrote in her name to the lawyer in London, and if I afterwards went and gave information of what had occurred to the nearest justice of the peace. I might have sent to make this inquiry through one of the female servants, but by this time, although not naturally suspicious, I had got to distrust everybody in the house, whether they deserved it or not.

So I asked the question myself, standing outside the door. My mistress thanked me in a faint voice, and begged me to do what I had proposed immediately.

I went into my own bedroom and wrote to the lawyer, merely telling him that Mr. James Smith had appeared unexpectedly at the Hall, and that events had occurred in consequence which required his immediate presence. I made the letter up like a parcel and sent the coachman with it to catch the mail on its way through to London.

The next thing was to go to the justice of the peace. The nearest lived about five miles off and was well acquainted with my mistress. He was an old bachelor, and he kept house with his brother, who was a widower. The two were much respected and beloved in the county, being kind, unaffected gentlemen, who did a great deal of good among the poor. The Justice was Mr. Robert Nicholson, and his brother, the widower, was Mr. Philip.

I had got my hat on, and was asking the groom which horse I had better take, when an open carriage drove up to the house. It contained Mr. Philip Nicholson and two persons in plain clothes, not exactly servants, and not exactly gentlemen, as far as I could judge. Mr. Philip looked at me, when I touched my hat to him, in a very grave, downcast way, and asked for my mistress. I told him she was ill in bed. He shook his head at hearing that, and said he wished to speak to me in private. I showed him into the library. One of the men in plain clothes followed us and sat in the hall. The other waited with the carriage.

"I was just going out, sir," I said, as I set a chair for him, "to speak to Mr. Robert Nicholson about a very extraordinary circumstance –"

"I know what you refer to," said Mr. Philip, cutting me short rather abruptly, "and I must beg, for reasons which will presently appear, that you will make no statement of any sort to me until you have first heard what I have to say. I am here on a very serious and a very shocking errand, which deeply concerns your mistress and you."

His face suggested something worse than his words expressed. My heart began to beat fast, and I felt that I was turning pale.

"Your master, Mr. James Smith," he went on, "came here unexpectedly, yesterday evening, and slept in this house last night. Before he retired to rest, he and your mistress had high words together, which ended, I am sorry to hear, in a threat of a serious nature addressed by Mrs. James Smith to her husband. They slept in separate rooms. This morning you went into your master's room and saw no sign of him there. You only found his night-gown on the bed, spotted with blood."

"Yes, sir," I said, in as steady a voice as I could command. "Quite true."

"I am not examining you," said Mr. Philip. "I am only making a certain statement, the truth of which you can admit or deny before my brother."

"Before your brother, sir!" I repeated. "Am I suspected of anything wrong?"

"There is a suspicion that Mr. James Smith has been murdered," was the answer I received to that question.

My flesh began to creep all over from head to foot.

"I am shocked, I am horrified to say," Mr. Philip went on, "that the suspicion affects your mistress in the first place, and you in the second."

I shall not attempt to describe what I felt when he said that. No words of mine, no words of anybody's could give an idea of it. What other men would have done in my situation, I don't know. I stood before Mr. Philip, staring straight at him, without speaking, without moving, almost without breathing. If he, or any other man, had struck me at that moment, I do not believe I should have felt the blow.

"Both my brother and myself", said Mr. Philip, "have such unfeigned respect for your mistress, such sympathy for her under these frightful circumstances and such an implicit belief in her capability of proving her innocence, that we are desirous of sparing her in this dreadful emergency as much as possible. For those reasons, I have undertaken to come here with the persons appointed to execute my brother's warrant –"

"Warrant, sir?" I said, getting command of my voice as he pronounced that word. "A warrant against my mistress?"

"Against her and against you," said Mr. Philip. "The suspicious circumstances have been sworn to by a competent witness, who has declared on oath that your mistress is guilty and that you are an accomplice."

"What witness, sir?"

"Your mistress's quadroon maid, who came to my brother this morning, and who has made her deposition in due form."

"And who is as false as hell," I cried out passionately, "in every word she says against my mistress and against me."

"I hope – no, I will go further and say I believe she is false," said

Mr. Philip. "But her perjury must be proved, and the necessary examination must take place. My carriage is going back to my brother's, and you will go in it, in charge of one of my men, who has the warrant to take you into custody. I shall remain here with the man who is waiting in the hall, and, before any steps are taken to execute the other warrant, I shall send for the doctor to ascertain when your mistress can be removed."

"Oh, my poor mistress!" I said. "This will be the death of her, sir."

"I will take care that the shock shall strike her as tenderly as possible," said Mr. Philip. "I am here for that express purpose. She has my deepest sympathy and respect, and shall have every help and alleviation that I can afford her."

The hearing him say that, and the seeing how sincerely he meant what he said, was the first gleam of comfort in the dreadful affliction that had befallen us. I felt this: I felt a burning anger against the wretch who had done her best to ruin my mistress's fair name and mine, but in every other respect, I was like a man who had been stunned and whose faculties had not perfectly recovered from the shock. Mr. Philip was obliged to remind me that time was of importance, and that I had better give myself up immediately, on the merciful terms which his kindness offered to me. I acknowledged that, and wished him good morning. But a mist seemed to come over my eyes as I turned round to go away, a mist that prevented me from finding my way to the door. Mr. Philip opened it for me, and said a friendly word or two, which I could hardly hear. The man waiting outside took me to his companion in the carriage at the door, and I was driven away – a prisoner for the first time in my life.

On our way to the Justice's, what little thinking faculty I had left in me was all occupied in the attempt to trace a motive for the inconceivable treachery and falsehood of which Josephine had been guilty.

Her words, her looks and her manner, on that unfortunate day when my mistress so far forgot herself as to strike her, came back dimly to my memory and led to the inference that part of the motive, at least, of which I was in search, might be referred to what had happened on that occasion. But was this the only reason for her devilish vengeance against my mistress? And, even if it were so, what fancied injuries had I done her? Why should I be included in the false accusation? In the dazed state of my faculties, at that time, I was quite incapable of seeking the answer to these questions. My mind was clouded all over, and I gave up the attempt to clear it in despair.

I was brought before Mr. Robert Nicholson that day, and the fiend of a quadroon was examined in my presence. The first sight of her face – with its wicked self-possession, with its smooth, leering triumph – so sickened me that I turned my head away, and never looked at her a second time throughout the proceedings. The answers she gave amounted to a mere repetition of the deposition to which she had already sworn. I listened to her with the most breathless attention, and was thunder-struck at the inconceivable artfulness with which she had mixed up truth and falsehood in her charge against my mistress and me.

This was, in substance, what she now stated in my presence:

After describing the manner of Mr. James Smith's arrival at the Hall, the witness, Josephine Durand, confessed that she had been led to listen at the music-room door, by hearing angry voices inside, and she then described, truly enough, the latter part of the altercation between husband and wife. Fearing, after this, that something serious might happen, she had kept watch in her room, which was on the same floor as her mistress's. She had heard her mistress's door open softly, between one and two in the morning; had followed her mistress, who carried a small lamp, along the passage and down the stairs into the hall; had hidden herself in the porter's chair; had seen her mistress take a dagger in a green sheath from a collection of Eastern curiosities kept in the hall; had followed her again and seen her softly enter the Red Room; had heard the heavy breathing of Mr. James Smith, which gave token that he was asleep; had slipped into an empty room next door to the Red Room, and had waited there about a quarter of an hour, when her mistress came out again with the dagger in her hand; had followed her mistress again into the hall, where she had put the dagger back into its place; had seen her mistress turn into a side passage that led to my room; had heard her knock at my door, and heard me answer and open it; had hidden again in the porter's chair; had, after a while, seen me and my mistress pass together into the passage that led to the Red Room; had watched us both into the Red Room; and had then, through fear of being discovered and murdered herself if she risked detention any longer, stolen back to her own room for the rest of the night.

After deposing, on oath, to the truth of these atrocious falsehoods, and declaring, in conclusion, that Mr. James Smith had been murdered by my mistress, and that I was an accomplice, the quadroon had further asserted, in order to show a motive for the crime, that Mr. Meeke was my mistress's lover; that he had been forbidden the house by her husband; and that he was found in the house, and alone with her, on the evening of Mr. James Smith's return. Here again, there were some grains of truth cunningly mixed up with a revolting lie, and they had their effect in giving to the falsehood a look of probability.

I was cautioned in the usual manner, and asked if I had anything to say.

I replied that I was innocent, but that I would wait for legal assistance before I defended myself. The Justice remanded me, and the examination was over. Three days later, my unhappy mistress was subjected to the same trial. I was not allowed to communicate with her. All I knew was that the lawyer had arrived from London to help her. Towards the evening, he was admitted to see me. He shook his head sorrowfully when I asked after my mistress.

"I am afraid," he said, "that she has sunk under the horror of the situation in which that vile woman has placed her. Weakened by her previous agitation, she seems to have given way under this last shock, tenderly and carefully as Mr. Philip Nicholson broke the bad news to her. All her feelings appeared to be strangely blunted at the examination to-day. She answered the questions put to her quite correctly, but, at the same time, quite mechanically, with no change in her complexion, or in her tone of voice, or in her manner, from beginning to end. It is a sad thing, William, when women cannot get their natural vent of weeping, and your mistress has not shed a tear since she left Darrock Hall."

"But surely, sir," I said, "if my examination has not proved

Josephine's perjury, my mistress's examination must have exposed it?"

"Nothing will expose it", answered the lawyer, "but producing Mr. James Smith, or, at least, legally proving that he is alive. Morally speaking, I have no doubt that the Justice before whom you have been examined is as firmly convinced as we can be that the quadroon has perjured herself. Morally speaking, he believes that those threats which your mistress unfortunately used, referred (as she said they did, to-day) to her intention of leaving the Hall early in the morning, with you for her attendant, and coming to me, if she had been well enough to travel, to seek effectual legal protection from her husband for the future. Mr. Nicholson believes that, and I, who know more of the circumstances than he does, believe also that Mr. James Smith stole away from Darrock Hall in the night, under fear of being indicted for bigamy. But if I can't find him, if I can't prove him to be alive, if I can't account for those spots of blood on the night-gown, the accidental circumstances of the case remain unexplained – your mistress's rash language, the bad terms on which she has lived with her husband and her unlucky disregard of appearances in keeping up her intercourse with Mr. Meeke, all tell dead against us – and the Justice has no alternative, in a legal point of view, but to remand you both, as he has now done, for the production of further evidence."

"But how, then, in heaven's name, is our innocence to be proved, sir?" I asked.

"In the first place," said the lawyer, "by finding Mr. James Smith; and, in the second place, by persuading him, when he is found, to come forward and declare himself."

"Do you really believe, sir," said I, "that he would hesitate to do that, when he knows the horrible charge to which his disappearance has exposed his wife? He is a heartless villain, I know, but surely –"

"I don't suppose", said the lawyer, cutting me short, "that he is quite scoundrel enough to decline coming forward, supposing he ran no risk by doing so. But remember that he has placed himself in a position to be tried for bigamy, and that he believes your mistress will put the Law in force against him."

I had forgotten that circumstance. My heart sank within me when it was recalled to my memory, and I could say nothing more.

"It is a very serious thing," the lawyer went on. "It is a downright offence against the law of the land to make any private offer of a compromise to this man. Knowing what we know, our duty as good citizens is to give such information as may bring him to trial. I tell you plainly, that if I did not stand towards your mistress in the position of a relation as well as a legal adviser, I should think twice about running the risk – the very serious risk – on which I am now about to venture for her sake. As it is, I have taken the right measures to assure Mr. James Smith that he will not be treated according to his deserts. When he knows what the circumstances are, he will trust us – supposing always that we can find him. The search about this neighbourhood has been quite useless. I have sent private instructions by to-day's post to Mr. Dark in London, and with them a carefully worded form of advertisement for the public newspapers. You may rest assured that every human means of tracing him will be tried forthwith. In the meantime, I have an important question to put to you about Josephine. She may know more than we think she does. She may have surprised the secret of the second marriage, and may be keeping it in reserve to use against us. If this should turn out to be the case, I shall want some other chance against her besides the chance of indicting her for perjury. As to her motive now for making this horrible accusation, what can you tell me about that, William?"

"Her motive against me, sir?"

"No, no, not against you. I can see plainly enough that she accuses you because it is necessary to do so to add to the probability of her story – which, of course, assumes that you helped your mistress to dispose of the dead body. You are coolly sacrificed to some devilish vengeance against her mistress. Let us get at that first. Has there ever been a quarrel between them?"

I told him of the quarrel, and of how Josephine had looked and talked when she showed me her cheek.

"Yes," he said, "that is a strong motive for revenge with a naturally pitiless, vindictive woman. But is that all? Had your mistress any hold over her? Is there any self-interest mixed up along with this motive of vengeance? Think a little, William. Has anything ever happened in the house to compromise this woman, or to make her fancy herself compromised?"

The remembrance of my mistress's lost trinkets and handkerchiefs, which later and greater troubles had put out of my mind, flashed back into my memory while he spoke. I told him immediately of the alarm in the house when the loss was discovered.

"Did your mistress suspect Josephine and question her?" he asked, eagerly.

"No, sir," I replied. "Before she could say a word, Josephine impudently asked who she suspected, and boldly offered her own boxes to be searched."

The lawyer's face turned red as scarlet. He jumped out of his chair and hit me such a smack on the shoulder that I thought he had gone mad.

"By Jupiter!" he cried out. "We have got the whip hand of that she-devil at last."

I looked at him in astonishment.

"Why, man alive," he said, "don't you see how it is? Josephine's the thief! I am as sure of it as that you and I are talking together. This vile accusation against your mistress answers another purpose besides the vindictive one – it is the very best screen that the wretch could possibly set up to hide herself from detection. It has stopped your mistress and you from moving in the matter; it exhibits her in the false character of an honest witness against a couple of criminals; it gives her time to dispose of the goods, or to hide them, or to do anything she likes with them. Stop! let me be quite sure that I know what the lost things are. A pair of bracelets, three rings and a lot of lace pocket-handkerchiefs – is that what you said?"

"Yes, sir."

"Your mistress will describe them particularly, and I will take the right steps the first thing to-morrow morning. Good evening, William, and keep up your spirits. It shan't be my fault if you don't see the quadroon in the right place for her – at the prisoner's bar."

With that farewell he went out.

The days passed, and I did not see him again until the period of my remand had expired. On this occasion, when I once more appeared before the Justice, my mistress appeared with me. The first sight of her absolutely startled me – she was so sadly altered. Her face looked so pinched and thin that it was like the face of an old woman. The dull, vacant resignation of her expression was something shocking to see. It changed a little when her eyes first turned heavily towards me; and she whispered, with a faint smile, "I am sorry for *you*, William; I am very, very sorry for *you*." But as soon as she had said those words, the blank look returned and she sat with her head drooping forward, quiet, and inattentive, and hopeless – so changed a being that her oldest friends would hardly have known her.

Our examination was a mere formality. There was no additional evidence, either for or against us, and we were remanded again for another week.

I asked the lawyer, privately, if any chance had offered itself of tracing Mr. James Smith. He looked mysterious, and only said in answer: "Hope for the best." I inquired, next, if any progress had been made toward fixing the guilt of the robbery on Josephine.

"I never boast," he replied, "but, cunning as she is, I should not be surprised if Mr. Dark and I together turned out to be more than a match for her."

Mr. Dark! There was something in the mere mention of his name that gave me confidence in the future. If I could only have got my poor mistress's dazed face out of my mind, I should not have had much depression of spirits to complain of during the interval of time that elapsed between the second examination and the third.

VI

On the third appearance of my mistress and myself before the Justice, I noticed some faces in the room which I had not seen there before. Greatly to my astonishment – for the previous examinations had been conducted as privately as possible – I remarked the presence of two of the servants from the Hall, and of three or four of the tenants on the Darrock estate who lived nearest to the house. They all sat together on one side of the justice-room. Opposite to them, and close at the side of a door, stood my old acquaintance, Mr. Dark, with his big snuff-box, his jolly face and his winking eye. He nodded to me, when I looked at him, as jauntily as if we were meeting at a party of pleasure. The quadroon woman, who had been summoned to the examination, had a chair placed opposite to the witness-box, and in a line with the seat occupied by my poor mistress, whose looks, as I was grieved to see, were not altered for the better. The lawyer from London was with her, and I stood behind her chair.

We were all quietly disposed in the room in this way, when the Justice, Mr. Robert Nicholson, came in with his brother. It might have been only fancy, but I thought I could see in both their faces that something remarkable had happened since we had met at the last examination.

The deposition of Josephine Durand was then read over by the clerk, and she was asked if she had anything to add to it. She replied in the negative. The Justice then appealed to my mistress's relation, the lawyer, to know if he could produce any evidence relating to the charge against his clients.

"I have evidence," answered the lawyer, getting briskly on his legs, "which, I believe, sir, will justify me in asking for their discharge."

"Where are your witnesses?" inquired the Justice, looking hard at Josephine while he spoke.

"One of them is in waiting, your worship," said Mr. Dark, opening the door near which he was standing.

He went out of the room, remained away about a minute and returned with his witness at his heels.

My heart gave a bound as if it would jump out of my body. There, with his long hair cut short, and his bushy whiskers shaved off – there, in his own proper person, safe and sound as ever, was Mr. James Smith!

The quadroon's iron nature resisted the shock of his unexpected presence on the scene, with a steadiness that was nothing short of marvellous. Her thin lips closed together convulsively, and there was a slight movement in the muscles of her throat. But not a word, not a sign betrayed her. Even the yellow tinge of her complexion remained unchanged.

"It is not necessary, sir, that I should waste time and words in referring to the wicked and preposterous charge against my clients," said the lawyer, addressing Mr. Robert Nicholson. "The one sufficient justification for discharging them immediately is before you, at this moment, in the person of that gentleman. There, sir, stands the murdered Mr. James Smith, of Darrock Hall, alive and well, to answer for himself."

"That is not the man!" cried Josephine, her shrill voice just as high, clear and steady as ever. "I denounce that man as an impostor! Of my own knowledge I deny that he is Mr. James Smith!"

"No doubt you do," said the lawyer. "But we will prove his identity for all that."

The first witness called was Mr. Philip Nicholson. He could swear that he had seen Mr. James Smith, and spoken to him, at least a dozen times. The person now before him was Mr. James Smith – altered as to personal appearance by having his hair cut short and his whiskers shaved off, but still unmistakably the man he assumed to be.

"It will sooner meet the ends of justice," said Mr. Robert Nicholson, addressing the lawyer, "if you prove the question of identity by witnesses who have been in habits of daily communication with Mr. James Smith."

Upon this, one of the servants from the Hall was placed in the box.

The alteration in his master's appearance evidently puzzled the man. Besides the perplexing change already adverted to, there was also a change in Mr. James Smith's expression and manner. Rascal as he was, I must do him the justice to say that he looked startled and ashamed, when he first caught sight of his unfortunate wife. The servant, who was used to be eyed tyrannically by him and ordered about roughly, seeing him now for the first time abashed and silent, stammered and hesitated on being asked to swear to his identity.

"I can hardly say for certain, sir," said the man, addressing the Justice in a bewildered manner. "He is like my master, and yet he isn't.

If he wore whiskers and had his hair long, and if he was, saving your presence, sir, a little more rough and ready in his way, I could swear to him anywhere with a safe conscience."

Fortunately for us, at this moment Mr. James Smith's feeling of uneasiness at the situation in which he was placed, changed to a feeling of irritation at being coolly surveyed and then stupidly doubted in the matter of his identity by one of his own servants.

"Can't you say in plain words, you idiot, whether you know me, or whether you don't?" he called out, angrily.

"That's his voice!" cried the servant, starting in the box. "Whiskers or no whiskers, that's him!"

"If there is any difficulty, your worship, about the gentleman's hair," said Mr. Dark, coming forward with a grin, "here's a small parcel which, I may make so bold as to say, will remove it." Saying that, he opened the parcel, took some locks of hair out of it, and held them close up to Mr. James Smith's head. "A pretty good match, your worship," continued Mr. Dark. "I have no doubt the gentleman's head feels cooler now it's off. We can't put the whiskers on, I'm afraid, but they match the hair; and there they are in the paper (if one may say such a thing of whiskers) to speak for themselves."

At this stage of the proceedings, Josephine lost her wicked self-control, and burst out with vixenish abuse of the witnesses. The Justice made a sign to two of the constables present, and the men removed her to an adjoining room.

A second servant from the Hall was then put in the box, and was followed by one of the tenants. After what they had heard and seen, neither of these men had any hesitation in swearing positively to their master's identity.

"It is quite unnecessary", said the Justice, as soon as the box was empty again, "to examine any more witnesses as to the question of identity. All the legal formalities are accomplished, and the charge against the prisoners falls to the ground. I have great pleasure in ordering the immediate discharge of both the accused persons, and in declaring from this place that they leave the court without the slightest stain on their characters."

He bowed low to my mistress as he said that, paused a moment, and then looked inquiringly at Mr. James Smith.

"I have hitherto refrained from making any remark unconnected with the immediate matter in hand," he went on. "But now that my duty is done, I cannot leave this chair without expressing my strong sense of disapprobation of the conduct of Mr. James Smith – conduct which, whatever may be the motives that occasioned it, has given a false colour of probability to a most horrible charge against a lady of unspotted reputation, and against a person in a lower rank of life, whose good character ought not to have been imperilled, even for a moment. Mr. Smith may or may not choose to explain his mysterious disappearance from Darrock Hall, and the equally unaccountable change which he has chosen to make in his personal appearance. There is no legal charge against him, but, speaking morally, I should be unworthy of the place I hold if I hesitated to declare my present conviction that his conduct has been deceitful, inconsiderate and unfeeling in the highest degree."

To this sharp reprimand, Mr. James Smith (evidently tutored beforehand as to what he was to say) replied that in attending before the Justice, he wished to perform a plain duty and to keep himself strictly within the letter of the Law. He apprehended that the only legal obligation laid on him was to attend in that court to declare himself and to enable competent witnesses to prove his identity. This duty accomplished, he had merely to add that he preferred submitting to a reprimand from the Bench to entering into explanations which would involve the disclosure of domestic circumstances of a very unhappy nature. After that brief reply, he had nothing further to say, and he would respectfully request the Justice's permission to withdraw.

The permission was accorded. As he crossed the room, he stopped near his wife and said confusedly, in a very low tone:

"I have done you many injuries, but I never intended this. I am sorry for it. Have you anything to say to me before I go?"

My mistress shuddered and hid her face. He waited a moment, and, finding that she did not answer him, bowed his head politely and went out. I did not know it then, but I had seen him for the last time.

After he had gone, the lawyer, addressing Mr. Robert Nicholson, said that he had an application to make, in reference to the woman, Josephine Durand.

At the mention of that name, my mistress hurriedly whispered a few words into her relation's ear. He looked towards Mr. Philip Nicholson, who immediately advanced, offered his arm to my mistress and led her out. I was about to follow, when Mr. Dark stopped me and begged that I would wait a few minutes longer, in order to give myself the pleasure of seeing "the end of the case".

In the meantime, the Justice had pronounced the necessary order to have the quadroon brought back. She came in, as bold and confident as ever. Mr. Robert Nicholson looked away from her in disgust, and said to the lawyer:

"Your application is to have her committed for perjury, of course?"

"For perjury?" said Josephine, with her wicked smile. "Very good! I shall explain some little matters that I have not explained before. I shall make myself a thorn in your sides, yet!"

"She has got scent of the second marriage," whispered Mr. Dark to me.

There could be no doubt of it. She had evidently been listening at the door, on the night when my master came back, longer than I had supposed. She must have heard those words about "the new wife" – she might even have seen the effect of them on Mr. James Smith.

"We do not, at present, propose to charge Josephine Durand with perjury", said the lawyer, "but with another offence, for which it is important to try her immediately. I charge her with stealing from her mistress, while in her service at Darrock Hall, a pair of bracelets, three rings and a dozen and a half of lace pocket-handkerchiefs. The articles in question were taken this morning from between the mattresses of her bed, and a letter was found in the same place, which clearly proves that she had represented the property as belonging to herself, and that she had tried to dispose of it to a purchaser in London." While he was speaking, Mr. Dark produced the jewellery, the handkerchiefs and the letter, and laid them before the Justice.

Even Josephine's extraordinary powers of self-control now gave way at last. At the first words of the unexpected charge against her, she struck her hands together violently, gnashed her sharp white teeth and burst out with a torrent of fierce sounding words in some foreign language, the meaning of which I did not understand then, and cannot explain now.

"I think that's check-mate for Marmzelle," whispered Mr. Dark, with his invariable wink. "Suppose you go back to the Hall now, William, and draw a jug of that very remarkable old ale of yours? I'll be after you in five minutes, as soon as the charge is made out."

I could hardly realize it, when I found myself walking back to Darrock a free man again.

In a quarter of an hour's time Mr. Dark joined me, and drank to my health, happiness and prosperity, in three separate tumblers. After performing this ceremony, he wagged his head and chuckled with an appearance of such excessive enjoyment that I could not avoid remarking on his high spirits. "It's the Case, William; it's the beautiful neatness of the Case that quite intoxicates me!" cries Mr. Dark, slapping his stumpy hands on his fat knees in a sort of ecstasy.

I had a very different opinion of the case, for my own part, but I did not venture on expressing it. I was too anxious to know how Mr. James Smith had been discovered and produced at the examination, to enter into any arguments. Mr. Dark guessed what was passing in my mind, and telling me to sit down and make myself comfortable, volunteered of his own accord to inform me of all that I wanted to know.

"When I got my instructions and my statement of particulars," he began, "I was not at all surprised to hear that Mr. James Smith had come back (I prophesied that, if you remember, William, the last time we met). But I was a good deal astonished, nevertheless, at the turn things had taken – and I can't say I felt very hopeful about finding our man. However, I followed my master's directions, and put the advertisement in the papers. It addressed Mr. James Smith by name, but it was very carefully worded as to what was wanted of him. Two days after it appeared, a letter came to our office in a woman's handwriting. It was my business to open the letters, and I opened that. The writer was short and mysterious. She requested that somebody would call from our office, at a certain address, between the hours of two and four that afternoon, in reference to the advertisement which we had inserted in the newspapers. Of course I was the somebody who went. I kept myself from building up hopes, by the way, knowing what a lot of Mr. James Smiths there were in London. On getting to the house, I was shown into the drawing-room, and there, dressed in a wrapper and lying on a sofa, was an uncommonly pretty woman, who looked as if she was just recovering from an illness. She had a newspaper by her side, and came to the point at once: 'My husband's name is James Smith,' she says, 'and I have my reasons for wanting to know if he is the person you are in search of.' I described our man as Mr. James Smith of Darrock Hall, Cumberland. 'I know no such person,' says she –"

"What! was it not the second wife, after all?" I broke out.

"Wait a bit," says Mr. Dark. "I mentioned the name of the yacht next, and she started up on the sofa as if she had been shot. 'I think you were married in Scotland, ma'am?' says I. She turns as pale as ashes, and drops back on the sofa, and says, faintly: 'It *is* my husband. Oh, sir, what has happened? What do you want with him? Is he in debt?' I took a minute to think, and then made up my mind to tell her everything – feeling that she would keep her husband (as she called him) out of the way, if I frightened her by any mysteries. A nice job I had, William, as you may suppose, when she knew about the bigamy business. What with screaming, fainting, crying and blowing me up (as if I was to blame), she kept me by that sofa of hers the best part of an hour – kept me there, in short, till Mr. James Smith himself came back. I leave you to judge if that mended matters. He found me mopping the poor woman's temples with scent and water, and he would have pitched me out of the window, as sure as I sit here, if I had not met him and staggered him at once with the charge of murder against his wife. That stopped him when he was in full cry, I can promise you. 'Go and wait in the next room,' says he, 'and I'll come in and speak to you directly.'"

"And did you go?" I asked.

"Of course I did," says Mr. Dark. "I knew he couldn't get out by the drawing-room windows, and I knew I could watch the door, so away I went, leaving him alone with the lady, who didn't spare him, by any manner of means, as I could easily hear in the next room. However, all rows in this world come to an end sooner or later; and a man with any brains in his head may do what he pleases with a woman who is fond of him. Before long I heard her crying and kissing him. 'I can't go home,' she says, after this. 'You have behaved like a villain and a monster to me – but oh, Jemmy, I can't give you up to anybody. Don't go back to your wife! Oh, don't, don't go back to your wife!' 'No fear of that,' says he. 'My wife wouldn't have me if I did go back to her.' After that, I heard the door open, and went out to meet him on the landing. He began swearing the moment he saw me, as if that was any good. 'Business first, if you please, sir,' says I, 'and any pleasure you like, in the way of swearing, afterwards.' With that beginning I mentioned our terms to him, and asked the pleasure of his company to Cumberland in return. He was uncommonly suspicious at first, but I promised to draw out a legal document (mere waste paper, of no earthly use, except to pacify him) engaging to hold him harmless throughout the proceedings; and what with that, and telling him of the frightful danger his wife was in, I managed, at last, to carry my point."

"But did the second wife make no objection to his going away with you?" I inquired.

"Not she," said Mr. Dark. "I stated the case to her, just as it stood; and soon satisfied her that there was no danger of Mr. James Smith's first wife laying any claim to him. After hearing that, she joined me in persuading him to do his duty, and said she pitied your mistress from the bottom of her heart. With her influence to back me, I had no great fear of our man changing his mind. I had the door watched that night, however, so as to make quite sure of him. The next morning he was ready to time when I called; and a quarter of an hour after that, we were off together for the north road. We made the journey with post-horses, being afraid of chance passengers, you know, in public conveyances. On the way down, Mr. James Smith and I got on as comfortably together as if we had been a pair of old friends. I told the story of our tracing him to the north of Scotland, and he gave me the particulars, in return, of his bolting from Darrock Hall. They are rather amusing, William – would you like to hear them?"

I told Mr. Dark that he had anticipated the very question I was about to ask him.

"Well," he said, "this is how it was. To begin at the beginning, our man really took Mrs. Smith Number Two to the Mediterranean, as we heard. He sailed up the Spanish Coast and, after short trips ashore, stopped at a sea-side place in France called Cannes. There he saw a house and grounds to be sold, which took his fancy as a nice retired place to keep Number Two in. Nothing particular was wanted but the money to buy it; and, not having the little amount in his own possession, Mr. James Smith makes a virtue of necessity, and goes back overland to his wife, with private designs on her purse-strings. Number Two, who objects to be left behind, goes with him as far as London. There he trumps up the first story that comes into his head, about rents in the country and a house in Lincolnshire that is too damp for her to trust herself in, and so, leaving her for a few days in London, starts boldly for Darrock Hall. His notion was to wheedle your mistress out of the money by good behaviour, but it seems he started badly by quarrelling with her about a fiddle-playing parson –"

"Yes, yes, I know all about that part of the story," I broke in, seeing, by Mr. Dark's manner, that he was likely to speak both ignorantly and impertinently of my mistress's unlucky friendship for Mr. Meeke. "Go on to the time when I left my master alone in the Red Room, and tell me what he did between midnight and nine the next morning."

"Did?" said Mr. Dark. "Why, he went to bed with the unpleasant conviction on his mind that your mistress had found him out, and with no comfort to speak of except what he could get out of the brandy bottle. He couldn't sleep, and the more he tossed and tumbled, the more certain he felt that his wife intended to have him tried for bigamy. At last, towards the grey of the morning, he could stand it no longer, and he made up his mind to give the Law the slip while he had the chance. As soon as he was dressed, it struck him that there might be a reward offered for catching him, and he determined to make that slight change in his personal appearance which puzzled the witnesses so much before the magistrate to-day. So he opens his dressing-case and crops his hair in no time, and takes off his whiskers next. The fire was out, and he had to shave in cold water. What with that, and what with the flurry of his mind, naturally enough he cut himself –"

"And dried the blood with his night-gown!" says I.

"With his night-gown," repeated Mr. Dark. "It was the first thing that lay handy, and he snatched it up. Wait a bit, though, the cream of the thing is to come. When he had done being his own barber, he couldn't for the life of him hit on a way of getting rid of the loose hair. The fire was out, and he had no matches, so he couldn't burn it. As for throwing it away, he didn't dare do that in the house, or about the house, for fear of its being found and betraying what he had done. So he wraps it all up in paper, crams it into his pocket to be disposed of when he is at a safe distance from the Hall, takes his bag, gets out at the window, shuts it softly after him and makes for the road as fast as his long legs will carry him. There he walks on till a coach overtakes him, and so travels back to London, to find himself in a fresh scrape as soon as he gets there. An interesting situation, William – and hard travelling from one end of France to the other had not agreed together in the case of Number Two. Mr. James Smith found her in bed, with doctor's orders that she was not to be moved. There was nothing for it, after that, but to lie by in London till the lady got better. Luckily for us, she didn't hurry herself, so that, after all, your mistress has to thank the very woman who supplanted her, for clearing her character by helping us to find Mr. James Smith!"

"And pray how did you come by that loose hair of his which you showed before the Justice to-day?" I asked.

"Thank Number Two again," says Mr. Dark. "I was put up for asking after it by what she told me. While we were talking about the advertisement, I made so bold as to inquire what first set her thinking that her husband and the Mr. James Smith whom we wanted, might be one and the same man. 'Nothing,' says she, 'but seeing him come home with his hair cut short and his whiskers shaved off, and, finding that he could not give me any good reason for disfiguring himself in that way, I had my suspicions that something was wrong, and the sight of your advertisement strengthened them directly.' The hearing her say that, suggested to my mind that there might be a difficulty in identifying him after the change in his looks, and I asked him what he had done with the loose hair, before we left London. It was found in the pocket of his travelling coat, just as he had huddled it up there on leaving the Hall, worry and fright and vexation having caused him to forget all about it. Of course I took charge of the parcel – and you know what good it did as well as I do. So to speak, William, it just completed this beautifully neat case. Looking at the matter in a professional point of view, I don't hesitate to say that we have managed our business with Mr. James Smith to perfection. We have produced him at the right time, and we are going to get rid of him at the right time. By to-night he will be on his way to foreign parts with Number Two, and he won't show his nose in England again if he lives to the age of Methuselah."

It was a relief to hear that, and it was almost as great a comfort to find, from what Mr. Dark said next, that my mistress need fear nothing that Josephine could do for the future.

The charge of theft, on which she was about to be tried, did not afford the shadow of an excuse in Law, any more than in logic, for alluding to the crime which her master had committed. If she meant to talk about it, she might do so in her place of transportation, but she would not have the slightest chance of being listened to previously in a court of law.

"In short," said Mr. Dark, rising to take his leave, "as I have told you already, William, it's check-mate for Marmzelle. She didn't manage the business of the robbery half as sharply as I should have expected. She certainly began well enough, by staying modestly at a lodging in the village, to give her attendance at the examinations as it might be required. Nothing could look more innocent and respectable so far. But her hiding the property between the mattresses of her bed – the very first place that any experienced man would think of looking in – was such an amazingly stupid thing to do, that I really can't account for it, unless her mind had more weighing on it than it was able to bear – which, considering the heavy stakes she played for, is likely enough.

Anyhow, her hands are tied now, and her tongue, too, for the matter of that. Give my respects to your mistress, and tell her that her run-away husband and her lying maid will never either of them harm her again as long as they live. She has nothing to do now but to pluck up her spirits and live happy. Here's long life to her and to you, William, in the last glass of ale, and here's the same toast to myself in the bottom of the jug."

With those words, Mr. Dark pocketed his large snuff-box, gave a last wink with his bright eye and walked away, whistling, to catch the London coach. From that time to this, he and I have never met again.

A few last words relating to my mistress, and to the other persons chiefly concerned in this narrative, will conclude all that it is now necessary for me to say.

For some months, the relatives and friends, and I myself, felt sad misgivings on my poor mistress's account. We doubted if it was possible, with such a quick sensitive nature as hers, that she could support the shock which had been inflicted on her, But our powers of endurance are, as I have learnt to believe, more often equal to the burdens laid upon us than we are apt to imagine. I have seen many surprising recoveries from illness, after all hope had been lost, and I have lived to see my mistress recover from the grief and terror which we once thought would prove fatal to her. It was long before she began to hold up her head again, but care and kindness, and time and change, wrought their effect on her at last. She is not now, and never will be again, the woman she was once: her manner is altered, and she looks older by many a year than she really is. But her health causes us no anxiety now, her spirits are calm and equal and I have good hope that many quiet years of service in her house are left for me still. I myself have married during the long interval of time which I am now passing over in a few words. This change in my life is, perhaps, not worth mentioning – but I am reminded of my two little children, when I speak of my mistress in her present position. I really think they make the great happiness and interest and amusement of her life, and prevent her from feeling lonely and dried up at heart. It is a pleasant reflection to me to remember this, and perhaps it may be the same to you – for which reason only I speak of it.

As for the other persons connected with the troubles at Darrock Hall, I may mention the vile woman Josephine first, so as to have the sooner done with her. Mr. Dark's guess, when he tried to account for her want of cunning in hiding the stolen property, by saying that her mind might have had more weighing on it than she was able to bear, turned out to be nothing less than the plain and awful truth. After she had been found guilty of the robbery, and had been condemned to seven years' transportation, a worse sentence fell upon her, from a higher tribunal than any in this world. While she was still in the county gaol, previous to her removal, her mind gave way; the madness breaking out in an attempt to set fire to the prison. Her case was pronounced to be hopeless from the first. The lawful asylum received her, and the lawful asylum will keep her to the end of her days.

Mr. James Smith, who, in my humble opinion, deserved hanging by law, or drowning by accident at least, lived quietly abroad with his Scotch wife (or no wife) for two years, and then died in the most quiet and customary manner, in his bed, after a short illness. His end was described to me as a "highly edifying one". But as he was also reported to have sent his forgiveness to his wife – which was as much as to say that *he* was the injured person of the two – I take leave to consider that he was the same impudent vagabond in his last moments that he had been all his life. His Scotch widow has married again and is now settled in London. I hope her husband is all her own property this time.

Mr. Meeke must not be forgotten, although he has dropped out of the latter part of my story, because he had nothing to do with the serious events which followed Josephine's perjury. In the confusion and wretchedness of that time, he was treated with very little ceremony, and was quite passed over when we left the neighbourhood. After pining and fretting for some time, as we afterwards heard, in his lonely parsonage, he resigned his living at the first chance he got and took a sort of under-chaplain's place in an English chapel abroad. He writes to my mistress once or twice a year to ask after her health and well-being, and she writes back to him. That is all the communication they are ever likely to have with each other. The music they once played together will never sound again. Its last notes have long since died out – and the last words of this story, trembling on the lips of the teller, may now pass away with them.

Who Is the Thief?
[Extracted from the Correspondence of the London Police]

FROM CHIEF INSPECTOR THEAKSTONE, OF THE DETECTIVE POLICE,
TO SERGEANT BULMER OF THE SAME FORCE

London, July 4th, 18—

Sergeant Bulmer – This is to inform you that you are wanted to assist
in looking up a case of importance, which will require all the attention
of an experienced member of the force. The matter of the robbery on
which you are now engaged, you will please to shift over to the young
man who brings you this letter. You will tell him all the circumstances
of the case, just as they stand; you will put him up to the progress you
have made (if any) towards detecting the person or persons by whom
the money has been stolen; and you will leave him to make the best
he can of the matter now in your hands. He is to have the whole
responsibility of the case and the whole credit of his success, if he
brings it to a proper issue.

So much for the orders that I am desired to communicate to you.

A word in your ear, next, about this new man who is to take your
place. His name is Matthew Sharpin, and he is to have the chance
given him of dashing into our office at a jump – supposing he turns out
strong enough to take it. You will naturally ask me how he comes by
this privilege. I can only tell you that he has some uncommonly strong
interest to back him in certain high quarters which you and I had better not mention except under our breaths. He has been a lawyer's
clerk, and he is wonderfully conceited in his opinion of himself as well
as mean and underhand to look at. According to his own account, he
leaves his old trade and joins ours of his own free will and preference.
You will no more believe that than I do. My notion is that he has managed to ferret out some private information in connection with the
affairs of one of his master's clients, which makes him rather an awkward customer to keep in the office for the future, and which, at the
same time, gives him hold enough over his employer to make it dangerous to drive him into a corner by turning him away. I think the giving

him this unheard-of chance among us is, in plain words, pretty much like giving him hush-money to keep him quiet. However that may be, Mr. Matthew Sharpin is to have the case now in your hands, and if he succeeds with it, he pokes his ugly nose into our office, as sure as fate. I put you up to this, Sergeant, so that you may not stand in your own light by giving the new man any cause to complain of you at headquarters, and remain yours,

FRANCIS THEAKSTONE

FROM MR. MATTHEW SHARPIN TO CHIEF INSPECTOR THEAKSTONE

London, July 5th, 18—

Dear Sir – Having now been favoured with the necessary instructions from Sergeant Bulmer, I beg to remind you of certain directions which I have received relating to the report of my future proceedings which I am to prepare for examination at headquarters.

The object of my writing, and of your examining what I have written before you send it in to the higher authorities, is, I am informed, to give me, as an untried hand, the benefit of your advice in case I want it (which I venture to think I shall not) at any stage of my proceedings. As the extraordinary circumstances of the case on which I am now engaged make it impossible for me to absent myself from the place where the robbery was committed, until I have made some progress towards discovering the thief, I am necessarily precluded from consulting you personally. Hence the necessity of writing down the various details which might, perhaps, be better communicated by word of mouth. This, if I am not mistaken, is the position in which we are now placed. I state my own impressions on the subject, in writing, in order that we may clearly understand each other at the outset, and have the honour to remain, your obedient servant,

MATTHEW SHARPIN

FROM CHIEF INSPECTOR THEAKSTONE TO MR. MATTHEW SHARPIN

London, July 6th, 18—

Sir – You have begun by wasting time, ink and paper. We both of us perfectly well knew the position we stood in towards each other when I sent you with my letter to Sergeant Bulmer. There was not the least need to repeat it in writing. Be so good as to employ your pen, in future, on the business actually in hand.

You have now three separate matters on which to write to me. First, you have to draw up a statement of your instructions received from Sergeant Bulmer, in order to show us that nothing has escaped your memory and that you are thoroughly acquainted with all the circumstances of the case which has been entrusted to you. Secondly, you are to inform me what it is you propose to do. Thirdly, you are to report every inch of your progress (if you make any) from day to day, and, if need be, from hour to hour as well. This is *your* duty. As to what *my* duty may be, when I want you to remind me of it, I will write and tell you so. In the meantime, I remain, yours,

FRANCIS THEAKSTONE

FROM MR. MATTHEW SHARPIN TO CHIEF INSPECTOR THEAKSTONE

London, July 6th, 18—

Sir – You are rather an elderly person, and, as such, naturally inclined to be a little jealous of men like me, who are in the prime of their lives and their faculties. Under these circumstances, it is my duty to be considerate towards you and not to bear too hardly on your small failings. I decline, therefore, altogether, to take offence at the tone of your letter; I give you the full benefit of the natural generosity of my nature; I sponge the very existence of your surly communication out of my memory – in short, Chief Inspector Theakstone, I forgive you, and proceed to business.

My first duty is to draw up a full statement of the instructions I have received from Sergeant Bulmer. Here they are at your service, according to my version of them.

At number 13 Rutherford Street, Soho, there is a stationer's shop. It is kept by one Mr. Yatman. He is a married man, but has no family. Besides Mr. and Mrs. Yatman, the other inmates in the house are: a young single man named Jay, who lodges in the front room on the second floor; a shopman, who sleeps in one of the attics; and a servant-of-all-work, whose bed is in the back-kitchen. Once a week a charwoman comes for a few hours in the morning only, to help this servant. These are all the persons who, on ordinary occasions, have means of access to the interior of the house, placed, as a matter of course, at their disposal.

Mr. Yatman has been in business for many years, carrying on his affairs prosperously enough to realize a handsome independence for a person in his position. Unfortunately for himself, he endeavoured to increase the amount of his property by speculating. He ventured boldly in his investments, luck went against him, and rather less than two years ago he found himself a poor man again. All that was saved out of the wreck of his property was the sum of two hundred pounds.

Although Mr. Yatman did his best to meet his altered circumstances by giving up many of the luxuries and comforts to which he and his wife had been accustomed, he found it impossible to retrench so far as to allow of putting by any money from the income produced by his shop. The business has been declining of late years – the cheap advertising stationers having done it injury with the public. Consequently, up to the last week, the only surplus property possessed by Mr. Yatman consisted of the two hundred pounds which had been recovered from the wreck of his fortune. This sum was placed as a deposit in a joint-stock bank of the highest possible character.

Eight days ago, Mr. Yatman and his lodger Mr. Jay held a conversation on the subject of the commercial difficulties which are hampering trade in all directions at the present time. Mr. Jay (who lives by supplying the newspapers with short paragraphs relating to accidents, offences and brief records of remarkable occurrences in general – who is, in short, what they call a penny-a-liner) told his landlord that he had been in the City that day, and had heard unfavourable rumours on the subject of the joint-stock banks. The rumours to which he alluded had already reached the ears of Mr. Yatman from other quarters, and the confirmation of them by his lodger had such an effect on his mind – predisposed as it was to alarm by the experience of his former losses – that he resolved to go at once to the bank and withdraw his deposit.

It was then getting on towards the end of the afternoon, and he arrived just in time to receive his money before the bank closed.

He received the deposit in bank-notes of the following amounts: one fifty-pound note, three twenty-pound notes, six ten-pound notes and six five-pound notes. His object in drawing the money in this form was to have it ready to lay out immediately in trifling loans, on good security, among the small tradespeople of his district, some of whom are sorely pressed for the very means of existence at the present time. Investments of this kind seemed to Mr. Yatman to be the most safe and the most profitable on which he could now venture.

He brought the money back in an envelope placed in his breast-pocket, and asked his shopman, on getting home, to look for a small, flat tin cash-box, which had not been used for years, and which, as Mr. Yatman remembered it, was exactly of the right size to hold the bank-notes. For some time the cash-box was searched for in vain. Mr. Yatman called to his wife to know if she had any idea where it was. The question was overheard by the servant-of-all-work, who was taking up the tea-tray at the time, and by Mr. Jay, who was coming downstairs on his way out to the theatre. Ultimately the cash-box was found by the shopman. Mr. Yatman placed the bank-notes in it, secured them by a padlock, and put the box in his coat-pocket. It stuck out of the coat pocket a very little, but enough to be seen. Mr. Yatman remained at home, upstairs, all the evening. No visitors called. At eleven o'clock he went to bed, and put the cash-box along with his clothes on a chair by the bedside.

When he and his wife woke the next morning the box was gone. Payment of the notes was immediately stopped at the Bank of England, but no news of the money has been heard of since that time.

So far, the circumstances of the case are perfectly clear. They point unmistakably to the conclusion that the robbery must have been committed by some person living in the house. Suspicion falls, therefore, upon the servant-of-all-work, upon the shopman and upon Mr. Jay. The two first knew that the cash-box was being inquired for by their master, but did not know what it was he wanted to put into it. They would assume, of course, that it was money. They both had opportunities (the servant when she took away the tea, and the shopman when he came, after shutting up, to give the keys of the till to his master) of seeing the cash-box in Mr. Yatman's pocket and of inferring, naturally, from its position there, that he intended to take it into his bedroom with him at night.

Mr. Jay, on the other hand, had been told, during the afternoon's conversation on the subject of joint-stock banks, that his landlord had a deposit of two hundred pounds in one of them. He also knew that Mr. Yatman left him with the intention of drawing that money out, and he heard the inquiry for the cash-box, afterwards, when he was coming downstairs. He must, therefore, have inferred that the money was in the house, and that the cash-box was the receptacle intended to contain it. That he could have had any idea, however, of the place in which Mr. Yatman intended to keep it for the night, is impossible, seeing that he went out before the box was found and did not return till his landlord was in bed. Consequently, if he committed the robbery, he must have gone into the bedroom purely on speculation.

Speaking of the bedroom reminds me of the necessity of noticing the situation of it in the house, and the means that exist of gaining easy access to it at any hour of the night.

The room in question is the back room on the first floor. In consequence of Mrs. Yatman's constitutional nervousness on the subject of fire (which makes her apprehend being burnt alive in her room, in case of accident, by the hampering of the lock if the key is turned in it) her husband has never been accustomed to lock the bedroom door. Both he and his wife are, by their own admission, heavy sleepers. Consequently the risk to be run by any evil-disposed persons wishing to plunder the bedroom, was of the most trifling kind. They could enter the room by merely turning the handle of the door; and if they moved with ordinary caution, there was no fear of their waking the sleepers inside. This fact is of importance. It strengthens our conviction that the money must have been taken by one of the inmates of the house because it tends to show that the robbery, in this case, might have been committed by persons not possessed of the superior vigilance and cunning of the experienced thief.

Such are the circumstances, as they were related to Sergeant Bulmer, when he was first called in to discover the guilty parties, and, if possible, to recover the lost bank-notes. The strictest inquiry which he could institute failed of producing the smallest fragment of evidence against any of the persons on whom suspicion naturally fell. Their language and behaviour, on being informed of the robbery, was perfectly consistent with the language and behaviour of innocent people. Sergeant Bulmer felt from the first that this was a case for private inquiry and secret observation. He began by recommending Mr. and Mrs. Yatman to affect a feeling of perfect confidence in the innocence of the persons living under their roof, and he then opened the campaign by employing himself in following the goings and comings and in discovering the friends, the habits and the secrets of the maid-of-all-work.

Three days and nights of exertion on his own part, and on that of others who were competent to assist his investigations, were enough to satisfy him that there was no sound cause for suspicion against the girl.

He next practised the same precaution in relation to the shopman. There was more difficulty and uncertainty in privately clearing up this person's character without his knowledge, but the obstacles were at last smoothed away with tolerable success; and although there is not the same amount of certainty, in this case, which there was in that of the girl, there is still fair reason for supposing that the shopman has had nothing to do with the robbery of the cash-box.

As a necessary consequence of these proceedings, the range of suspicion now becomes limited to the lodger, Mr. Jay.

When I presented your letter of introduction to Sergeant Bulmer, he had already made some inquiries on the subject of this young man. The result, so far, has not been at all favourable. Mr. Jay's habits are irregular: he frequents public houses, and seems to be familiarly acquainted with a great many dissolute characters; he is in debt to most of the tradespeople whom he employs; he has not paid his rent to Mr. Yatman for the last month; yesterday evening he came home excited by liquor, and last week he was seen talking to a prize-fighter. In short, although Mr. Jay does call himself a journalist in virtue of his penny-a-line contributions to the newspapers, he is a young man of low tastes, vulgar manners and bad habits. Nothing has yet been discovered in relation to him which redounds to his credit in the smallest degree.

I have now reported, down to the very last details, all the particulars communicated to me by Sergeant Bulmer. I believe you will not find an omission anywhere, and I think you will admit, although you are prejudiced against me, that a clearer statement of facts was never laid before you than the statement I have now made. My next duty is to tell you what I propose to do, now that the case is confided to my hands.

In the first place, it is clearly my business to take up the case at the point where Sergeant Bulmer has left it. On his authority, I am justified in assuming that I have no need to trouble myself about the maid-of-all-work and the shopman. Their characters are now to be considered as cleared up. What remains to be privately investigated is the question of the guilt or innocence of Mr. Jay. Before we give up the notes for lost, we must make sure, if we can, that he knows nothing about them.

This is the plan that I have adopted, with the full approval of Mr. and Mrs. Yatman, for discovering whether Mr. Jay is or is not the person who has stolen the cash-box:

I propose, to-day, to present myself at the house in the character of a young man who is looking for lodgings. The back room on the second floor will be shown to me as the room to let, and I shall establish myself there to-night, as a person from the country who has come to London to look for a situation in a respectable shop or office.

By this means, I shall be living next to the room occupied by Mr. Jay. The partition between us is mere lath and plaster. I shall make a small hole in it, near the cornice, through which I can see what Mr. Jay does in his room and hear every word that is said when any friend happens to call on him. Whenever he is at home, I shall be at my post of observation. Whenever he goes out, I shall be after him. By employing these means of watching him, I believe I may look forward to the discovery of his secret – if he knows anything about the lost bank-notes – as to a dead certainty.

What you may think of my plan of observation I cannot undertake to say. It appears to me to unite the invaluable merits of boldness and simplicity. Fortified by this conviction, I close the present communication with feelings of the most sanguine description in regard to the future, and remain your obedient servant,

MATTHEW SHARPIN

FROM THE SAME TO THE SAME

July 7th

Sir – As you have not honoured me with any answer to my last communication, I assume that, in spite of your prejudices against me, it has produced the favourable impression on your mind which I ventured to anticipate. Gratified beyond measure by the token of approval which your eloquent silence conveys to me, I proceed to report the progress that has been made in the course of the last twenty-four hours.

I am now comfortably established next door to Mr. Jay, and I am delighted to say that I have two holes in the partition instead of one. My natural sense of humour has led me into the pardonable extravagance of giving them appropriate names. One I call my peep-hole, and the other my pipe-hole. The name of the first explains itself; the name of the second refers to a small tin pipe, or tube, inserted in the hole, and twisted so that the mouth of it comes close to my ear, while I am standing at my post of observation. Thus, while I am looking at Mr. Jay through my peep-hole, I can hear every word that may be spoken in his room through my pipe-hole.

Perfect candour – a virtue which I have possessed from my childhood – compels me to acknowledge, before I go any further, that the ingenious notion of adding a pipe-hole to my proposed peep-hole originated with Mrs. Yatman. This lady – a most intelligent and accomplished person, simple, and yet distinguished in her manners – has entered into all my little plans with an enthusiasm and intelligence which I cannot too highly praise. Mr. Yatman is so cast down by his loss that he is quite incapable of affording me any assistance. Mrs. Yatman, who is evidently most tenderly attached to him, feels her husband's sad condition of mind even more acutely than she feels the loss of the money, and is mainly stimulated to exertion by her desire to assist in raising him from the miserable state of prostration into which he has now fallen.

"The money, Mr. Sharpin," she said to me yesterday evening, with tears in her eyes, "the money may be regained by rigid economy and strict attention to business. It is my husband's wretched state of mind that makes me so anxious for the discovery of the thief. I may be wrong, but I felt hopeful of success as soon as you entered the house, and, I believe, if the wretch who has robbed us is to be found, you are the man to discover him." I accept this gratifying compliment in the spirit in which it was offered – firmly believing that I shall be found, sooner or later, to have thoroughly deserved it.

Let me now return to business; that is to say, to my peephole and my pipe-hole.

I have enjoyed some hours of calm observation of Mr. Jay. Although rarely at home, as I understand from Mrs. Yatman, on ordinary occasions, he has been indoors the whole of this day. That is suspicious to begin with. I have to report, further, that he rose at a late hour this morning (always a bad sign in a young man) and that he lost a great deal of time, after he was up, in yawning and complaining to himself of headache. Like other debauched characters, he ate little or nothing for breakfast. His next proceeding was to smoke a pipe – a dirty clay pipe, which a gentleman would have been ashamed to put between his lips. When he had done smoking, he took out pen, ink and paper, and sat down to write with a groan – whether of remorse for having taken the bank-notes or of disgust at the task before him, I am unable to say. After writing a few lines (too far away from my peephole to give me a chance of reading over his shoulder), he leaned back in his chair and amused himself by humming the tunes of certain popular songs. Whether these do or do not represent secret signals by which he communicates with his accomplices remains to be seen. After he had amused himself for some time by humming, he got up and began to walk about the room, occasionally stopping to add a sentence to the paper on his desk. Before long, he went to a locked cupboard and opened it. I strained my eyes eagerly, in expectation of making a discovery. I saw him take something carefully out of the cupboard – he turned round – and it was only a pint bottle of brandy!

Having drunk some of the liquor, this extremely indolent reprobate lay down on his bed again, and in five minutes was fast asleep.

After hearing him snoring for at least two hours, I was recalled to my peep-hole by a knock at his door. He jumped up and opened it with suspicious activity.

A very small boy, with a very dirty face, walked in, said "Please, sir, they're waiting for you," sat down on a chair, with his legs a long way from the ground, and instantly fell asleep! Mr. Jay swore an oath, tied a wet towel round his head, and, going back to his paper, began to cover it with writing as fast as his fingers could move the pen. Occasionally getting up to dip the towel in water and tie it on again, he continued at this employment for nearly three hours, then folded up the leaves of writing, woke the boy and gave them to him, with this remarkable expression:

"Now, then, young sleepy-head, quick – march! If you see the governor, tell him to have the money ready when I call for it." The boy grinned and disappeared. I was sorely tempted to follow "sleepy-head", but, on reflection, considered it safest still to keep my eye on the proceedings of Mr. Jay.

In half an hour's time, he put on his hat and walked out. Of course, I put on my hat and walked out also. As I went downstairs, I passed Mrs. Yatman going up. The lady has been kind enough to undertake, by previous arrangement between us, to search Mr. Jay's room while he is out of the way and while I am necessarily engaged in the pleasing duty of following him wherever he goes. On the occasion to which I now refer, he walked straight to the nearest tavern and ordered a couple of mutton chops for his dinner. I placed myself in the next box to him and ordered a couple of mutton chops for my dinner. Before I had been in the room a minute, a young man of highly suspicious manners and appearance, sitting at a table opposite, took his glass of porter in his hand and joined Mr. Jay. I pretended to be reading the newspaper, and listened, as in duty bound, with all my might.

"Jack has been here inquiring after you," says the young man.

"Did he leave any message?" asks Mr. Jay.

"Yes," says the other. "He told me, if I met with you, to say that he wished very particularly to see you to-night, and that he would give you a look in, at Rutherford Street, at seven o'clock."

"All right," says Mr. Jay. "I'll get back in time to see him."

Upon this, the suspicious-looking young man finished his porter, and saying that he was rather in a hurry, took leave of his friend (perhaps I should not be wrong if I said his accomplice) and left the room.

At twenty-five minutes and a half past six – in these serious cases it is important to be particular about time – Mr. Jay finished his chops and paid his bill. At twenty-six minutes and three-quarters I finished my chops and paid mine. In ten minutes more I was inside the house in Rutherford Street, and was received by Mrs. Yatman in the passage. That charming woman's face exhibited an expression of melancholy and disappointment which it quite grieved me to see.

"I am afraid, Ma'am," says I, "that you have not hit on any little criminating discovery in the lodger's room?"

She shook her head and sighed. It was a soft, languid, fluttering sigh – and, upon my life, it quite upset me. For the moment, I forgot business and burned with envy of Mr. Yatman.

"Don't despair, Ma'am," I said, with an insinuating mildness which seemed to touch her. "I have heard a mysterious conversation – I know of a guilty appointment – and I expect great things from my peep-hole and my pipe-hole to-night. Pray, don't be alarmed, but I think we are on the brink of a discovery."

Here my enthusiastic devotion to business got the better of my tender feelings. I looked, winked, nodded, left her.

When I got back to my observatory, I found Mr. Jay digesting his mutton chops in an arm-chair, with his pipe in his mouth. On his table were two tumblers, a jug of water, and the pint bottle of brandy. It was then close upon seven o'clock. As the hour struck, the person described as "Jack" walked in.

He looked agitated – I am happy to say he looked violently agitated. The cheerful glow of anticipated success diffused itself (to use a strong expression) all over me, from head to foot. With breathless interest I looked through my peep-hole, and saw the visitor – the "Jack" of this delightful case – sit down, facing me, at the opposite side of the table to Mr. Jay. Making allowance for the difference in expression which their countenances just now happened to exhibit, these two abandoned villains were so much alike in other respects as to lead at once to the conclusion that they were brothers. Jack was the cleaner man and the better dressed of the two. I admit that, at the outset. It is, perhaps, one of my failings to push justice and impartiality to their utmost limits. I am no Pharisee, and where Vice has its redeeming point, I say, let Vice have its due – yes, yes, by all manner of means, let Vice have its due.

"What's the matter now, Jack?" says Mr. Jay.

"Can't you see it in my face?" says Jack. "My dear fellow, delays are dangerous. Let us have done with suspense and risk it the day after to-morrow."

"So soon as that?" cried Mr. Jay, looking very much astonished. "Well, I'm ready, if you are. But, I say, Jack, is Somebody Else ready, too? Are you quite sure of that?"

He smiled as he spoke – a frightful smile – and laid a very strong emphasis on those two words, "Somebody Else". There is evidently a third ruffian, a nameless desperado, concerned in the business.

"Meet us to-morrow," says Jack, "and judge for yourself. Be in the Regent's Park at eleven in the morning, and look out for us at the turning that leads to the Avenue Road."

"I'll be there," says Mr. Jay. "Have a drop of brandy and water? What are you getting up for? You're not going already?"

"Yes, I am," says Jack. "The fact is, I'm so excited and agitated that I can't sit still anywhere for five minutes together. Ridiculous as it may appear to you, I'm in a perpetual state of nervous flutter. I can't, for the life of me, help fearing that we shall be found out. I fancy that every man who looks twice at me in the street is a spy –"

At those words, I thought my legs would have given way under me. Nothing but strength of mind kept me at my peep-hole – nothing else, I give you my word of honour.

"Stuff and nonsense!" cried Mr. Jay, with all the effrontery of a veteran in crime. "We have kept the secret up to this time, and we will manage cleverly to the end. Have a drop of brandy and water, and you will feel as certain about it as I do."

Jack steadily refused the brandy and water, and steadily persisted in taking his leave.

"I must try if I can't walk it off," he said. "Remember to-morrow morning – eleven o'clock, Avenue Road side of the Regent's Park."

With those words he went out. His hardened relative laughed desperately, and resumed the dirty clay pipe.

I sat down on the side of my bed, actually quivering with excitement.

It is clear to me that no attempt has yet been made to change the stolen bank-notes; and I may add that Sergeant Bulmer was of that opinion also, when he left the case in my hands. What is the natural conclusion to draw from the conversation which I have just set down? Evidently, that the confederates meet to-morrow to take their respective shares in the stolen money, and to decide on the safest means of getting the notes changed the day after. Mr. Jay is, beyond a doubt, the leading criminal in this business, and he will probably run the chief risk – that of changing the fifty-pound note. I shall, therefore, still make it my business to follow him – attending at the Regent's Park to-morrow and doing my best to hear what is said there. If another appointment is made for the day after, I shall, of course, go to it. In the meantime, I shall want the immediate assistance of two competent persons (supposing the rascals separate after their meeting) to follow the two minor criminals. It is only fair to add that, if the rogues all retire together, I shall probably keep my subordinates in reserve. Being naturally ambitious, I desire, if possible, to have the whole credit of discovering this robbery to myself.

July 8th

I have to acknowledge, with thanks, the speedy arrival of my two subordinates – men of very average abilities, I am afraid, but, fortunately, I shall always be on the spot to direct them.

My first business this morning was, necessarily, to prevent mistakes by accounting to Mr. and Mrs. Yatman for the presence of two strangers on the scene. Mr. Yatman (between ourselves, a poor feeble man) only shook his head and groaned. Mrs. Yatman (that superior woman) favoured me with a charming look of intelligence.

"Oh, Mr. Sharpin!" she said. "I am so sorry to see those two men! Your sending for their assistance looks as if you were beginning to be doubtful of success."

I privately winked at her (she is very good in allowing me to do so without taking offence), and told her, in my facetious way, that she laboured under a slight mistake.

"It is because I am sure of success, Ma'am, that I send for them. I am determined to recover the money, not for my own sake only, but for Mr. Yatman's sake – and for yours."

I laid a considerable amount of stress on those last three words. She said "Oh, Mr. Sharpin!" again – and blushed of a heavenly red – and looked down at her work. I could go to the world's end with that woman, if Mr. Yatman would only die.

I sent off the two subordinates to wait, until I wanted them, at the Avenue Road gate of the Regent's Park. Half an hour afterwards I was following in the same direction myself, at the heels of Mr. Jay.

The two confederates were punctual to the appointed time, I blush to record it, but it is nevertheless necessary to state, that the third rogue – the nameless desperado of my report, or if you prefer it, the mysterious "Somebody Else" of the conversation between the two brothers – is a woman! and, what is worse, a young woman! and what is more lamentable still, a nice-looking woman! I have long resisted a growing conviction that, wherever there is mischief in this world, an individual of the fair sex is inevitably certain to be mixed up in it. After the experience of this morning, I can struggle against that sad conclusion no longer. I give up the sex – excepting Mrs. Yatman, I give up the sex.

The man named "Jack" offered the woman his arm. Mr. Jay placed himself on the other side of her. The three then walked away slowly among the trees. I followed them at a respectful distance. My two subordinates, at a respectful distance also, followed me.

It was, I deeply regret to say, impossible to get near enough to them to overhear their conversation, without running too great a risk of being discovered. I could only infer from their gestures and actions that they were all three talking with extraordinary earnestness on some subject which deeply interested them. After having been engaged in this way a full quarter of an hour, they suddenly turned round to retrace their steps. My presence of mind did not forsake me in this emergency. I signed to the two subordinates to walk on carelessly and pass them, while I myself slipped dextrously behind a tree. As they came by me, I heard "Jack" address these words to Mr. Jay:

"Let us say half-past ten to-morrow morning. And mind you come in a cab. We had better not risk taking one in this neighbourhood."

Mr. Jay made some brief reply, which I could not overhear. They walked back to the place at which they had met, shaking hands there with an audacious cordiality which it quite sickened me to see. They then separated. I followed Mr. Jay; my subordinates paid the same delicate attention to the other two.

Instead of taking me back to Rutherford Street, Mr. Jay led me to the Strand. He stopped at a dingy, disreputable-looking house, which, according to the inscription over the door, was a newspaper office, but which, in my judgement, had all the external appearance of a place devoted to the reception of stolen goods.

After remaining inside for a few minutes, he came out, whistling with his finger and thumb in his waistcoat pocket. A less discreet man than myself would have arrested him on the spot. I remembered the necessity of catching the two confederates and the importance of not interfering with the appointment that had been made for the next morning. Such coolness as this, under trying circumstances, is rarely to be found, I should imagine, in a young beginner, whose reputation as a detective policeman is still to make.

From the house of suspicious appearance, Mr. Jay betook himself to a cigar-divan, and read the magazines over a cheroot. I sat at a table near him, and read the magazines likewise over a cheroot. From the divan he strolled to the tavern and had his chops. I strolled to the tavern and had my chops. When he had done, he went back to his lodging. When I had done, I went back to mine. He was overcome with drowsiness early in the evening and went to bed. As soon as I heard him snoring, I was overcome with drowsiness and went to bed also.

Early in the morning my two subordinates came to make their report.

They had seen the man named "Jack" leave the woman near the gate of an apparently respectable villa-residence, not far from the Regent's Park. Left to himself, he took a turning to the right, which led to a sort of suburban street, principally inhabited by shopkeepers. He stopped at the private door of one of the houses and let himself in with his own key – looking about him as he opened the door and staring suspiciously at my men as they lounged along on the opposite side of the way. These were all the particulars which the subordinates had to communicate. I kept them in my room to attend on me, if needful, and mounted to my peep-hole to have a look at Mr. Jay.

He was occupied in dressing himself, and was taking extraordinary pains to destroy all traces of the natural slovenliness of his appearance. This was precisely what I expected. A vagabond like Mr. Jay knows the importance of giving himself a respectable look when he is going to run the risk of changing a stolen bank-note. At five minutes past ten o'clock, he had given the last brush to his shabby hat and the last scouring with bread-crumb to his dirty gloves. At ten minutes past ten, he was in the street, on his way to the nearest cab-stand, and I and my subordinates were close on his heels.

He took a cab, and we took a cab. I had not overheard them appoint a place of meeting when following them in the Park on the previous day, but I soon found that we were proceeding in the old direction of the Avenue Road gate.

The cab in which Mr. Jay was riding turned into the Park slowly. We stopped outside, to avoid exciting suspicion. I got out to follow the cab on foot. Just as I did so, I saw it stop, and detected the two confederates approaching it from among the trees. They got in, and the cab was turned about directly. I ran back to my own cab, and told the driver to let them pass him and then to follow as before.

The man obeyed my directions, but so clumsily as to excite their suspicions. We had been driving after them about three minutes (returning along the road by which we had advanced) when I looked out of the window to see how far they might be ahead of us. As I did this, I saw two hats popped out of the windows of their cab and two faces looking back at me. I sank into my place in a cold sweat; the expression is coarse, but no other form of words can describe my condition at that trying moment.

"We are found out!" I said faintly to my two subordinates. They stared at me in astonishment. My feelings changed instantly from the depth of despair to the height of indignation.

"It is the cabman's fault. Get out, one of you," I said, with dignity. "Get out and punch his head."

Instead of following my directions (I should wish this act of disobedience to be reported at head-quarters) they both looked out of the window. Before I could pull them back, they both sat down again. Before I could express my just indignation, they both grinned, and said to me:

"Please to look out, sir!"

I did look out. The thieves' cab had stopped.

Where?

At a church door!!!

What effect this discovery might have had upon the ordinary run of men, I don't know. Being of a strong religious turn myself, it filled me with horror. I have often read of the unprincipled cunning of criminal persons, but I never before heard of three thieves attempting to double on their pursuers by entering a church! The sacrilegious audacity of that proceeding is, I should think, unparalleled in the annals of crime.

I checked my grinning subordinates by a frown. It was easy to see what was passing in their superficial minds. If I had not been able to look below the surface, I might, on observing two nicely dressed men and one nicely dressed woman enter a church before eleven in the morning on a week day, have come to the same hasty conclusion at which my inferiors had evidently arrived. As it was, appearances had no power to impose on *me*. I got out, and, followed by one of my men, entered the church. The other man I sent round to watch the vestry door. You may catch a weasel asleep – but not your humble servant, Matthew Sharpin!

We stole up the gallery stairs, diverged to the organ loft and peered through the curtains in front. There they were all three, sitting in a pew below – yes, incredible as it may appear, sitting in a pew below!

Before I could determine what to do, a clergyman made his appearance in full canonicals, from the vestry door, followed by a clerk. My brain whirled, and my eyesight grew dim. Dark remembrances of robberies committed in vestries floated through my mind. I trembled for the excellent man in full canonicals – I even trembled for the clerk.

The clergyman placed himself inside the altar rails. The three desperadoes approached him. He opened his book, and began to read. What? – you will ask.

I answer, without the slightest hesitation, the first lines of the Marriage Service.

My subordinate had the audacity to look at me, and then to stuff his pocket-handkerchief into his mouth. I scorned to pay any attention to him. After I had discovered that the man "Jack" was the bridegroom, and that the man Jay acted the part of father and gave away the bride, I left the church, followed by my man, and joined the other subordinate outside the vestry door. Some people in my position would now have felt rather crestfallen and would have begun to think that they had made a very foolish mistake. Not the faintest misgiving of any kind troubled me. I did not feel in the slightest degree depreciated in my own estimation. And even now, after a lapse of three hours, my mind remains, I am happy to say, in the same calm and hopeful condition.

As soon as I and my subordinates were assembled together outside the church, I intimated my intention of still following the other cab, in spite of what had occurred. My reason for deciding on this course will appear presently. The two subordinates were astonished at my resolution. One of them had the impertinence to say to me:

"If you please, sir, who is it that we are after? A man who has stolen money, or a man who has stolen a wife?"

The other low person encouraged him by laughing. Both have deserved an official reprimand; and both, I sincerely trust, will be sure to get it.

When the marriage ceremony was over, the three got into their cab; and once more our vehicle (neatly hidden round the corner of the church, so that they could not suspect it to be near them) started to follow theirs.

We traced them to the terminus of the South-Western Railway. The newly married couple took tickets for Richmond – paying their fare with a half-sovereign, and so depriving me of the pleasure of arresting them, which I should certainly have done, if they had offered a banknote. They parted from Mr. Jay, saying:

"Remember the address – 14 Babylon Terrace. You dine with us tomorrow week." Mr. Jay accepted the invitation, and added, jocosely, that he was going home at once to get off his clean clothes and to be comfortable and dirty again for the rest of the day. I have to report that I saw him home safely, and that he is comfortable and dirty again (to use his own disgraceful language) at the present moment.

Here the affair rests, having by this time reached what I may call its first stage.

I know very well what persons of hasty judgement will be inclined to say of my proceedings thus far. They will assert that I have been deceiving myself all through, in the most absurd way; they will declare that the suspicious conversations which I have reported referred solely to the difficulties and dangers of successfully carrying out a runaway match; and they will appeal to the scene in the church as offering undeniable proof of the correctness of their assertions. So let it be. I dispute nothing up to this point. But I ask a question, out of the depths of my own sagacity as a man of the world, which the bitterest of my enemies will not, I think, find it particularly easy to answer.

Granted the fact of the marriage, what proof does it afford me of the innocence of the three persons concerned in that clandestine transaction? It gives me none. On the contrary, it strengthens my suspicions against Mr. Jay and his confederates, because it suggests a distinct motive for their stealing the money. A gentleman who is going to spend his honeymoon at Richmond wants money; and a gentleman who is in debt to all his tradespeople wants money. Is this an unjustifiable imputation of bad motives? In the name of outraged morality, I deny it.

These men have combined together and have stolen a woman. Why should they not combine together and steal a cash-box? I take my stand on the logic of rigid virtue; and I defy all the sophistry of vice to move me an inch out of my position.

Speaking of virtue, I may add that I have put this view of the case to Mr. and Mrs. Yatman. That accomplished and charming woman found it difficult, at first; to follow the close chain of my reasoning, I am free to confess that she shook her head, and shed tears, and joined her husband in premature lamentation over the loss of the two hundred pounds. But a little careful explanation on my part, and a little attentive listening on hers, ultimately changed her opinion. She now agrees with me that there is nothing in this unexpected circumstance of the clandestine marriage which absolutely tends to divert suspicion from Mr. Jay, or Mr. "Jack", or the runaway lady. "Audacious hussy" was the term my fair friend used in speaking of her, but let that pass. It is more to the purpose to record that Mrs. Yatman has not lost confidence in me and that Mr. Yatman promises to follow her example and do his best to look hopefully for future results.

I have now, in the new turn that circumstances have taken, to wait advice from your office. I pause for fresh orders with all the composure of a man who has got two strings to his bow. When I traced the three confederates from the church door to the railway terminus, I had two motives for doing so. First, I followed them as a matter of official business, believing them still to have been guilty of the robbery. Secondly, I followed them as a matter of private speculation, with a view of discovering the place of refuge to which the runaway couple intended to retreat and of making my information a marketable commodity to offer to the young lady's family and friends. Thus, whatever happens, I may congratulate myself beforehand on not having wasted my time. If the office approves of my conduct, I have my plan ready for further proceedings. If the office blames me, I shall take myself off, with my marketable information, to the genteel villa-residence in the neighbourhood of the Regent's Park. Anyway, the affair puts money into my pocket, and does credit to my penetration as an uncommonly sharp man.

I have only one word more to add, and it is this: If any individual ventures to assert that Mr. Jay and his confederates are innocent of all share in the stealing of the cash-box, I, in return, defy that individual – although he may even be Chief Inspector Theakstone himself – to tell me who has committed the robbery at Rutherford Street, Soho.

I have the honour to be,

Your very obedient servant,

MATTHEW SHARPIN

FROM CHIEF INSPECTOR THEAKSTONE TO SERGEANT BULMER

Birmingham, July 9th

Sergeant Bulmer – That empty-headed puppy, Mr. Matthew Sharpin, has made a mess of the case at Rutherford Street, exactly as I expected he would. Business keeps me in this town; so I write to you to set the matter straight. I enclose, with this, the pages of feeble scribble-scrabble which the creature, Sharpin, calls a report. Look them over, and, when you have made your way through all the gabble, I think you will agree with me that the conceited booby has looked for the thief in every direction but the right one. You can lay your hand on the guilty person in five minutes, now. Settle the case at once, forward your report to me at this place and tell Mr. Sharpin that he is suspended till further notice.

Yours,

FRANCIS THEAKSTONE

FROM SERGEANT BULMER TO CHIEF INSPECTOR THEAKSTONE

London, July 10th

Inspector Theakstone – Your letter and enclosure came safe to hand. Wise men, they say, may always learn something, even from a fool. By the time I had got through Sharpin's maundering report of his own folly, I saw my way clear enough to the end of the Rutherford Street case, just as you thought I should. In half an hour's time I was at the house. The first person I saw there was Mr. Sharpin himself.

"Have you come to help me?" says he.

"Not exactly," says I. "I've come to tell you that you are suspended till further notice."

"Very good," says he, not taken down by so much as a single peg in his own estimation. "I thought you would be jealous of me. It's very natural, and I don't blame you. Walk in, pray, and make yourself at home. I'm off to do a little detective business on my own account, in the neighbourhood of the Regent's Park. Ta-ta, Sergeant, ta-ta!"

With those words he took himself out of the way – which was exactly what I wanted him to do.

As soon as the maid-servant had shut the door, I told her to inform her master that I wanted to say a word to him in private. She showed me into the parlour behind the shop, and there was Mr. Yatman, all alone, reading the newspaper.

"About this matter of the robbery, sir," says I.

He cut me short, peevishly enough – being naturally a poor, weak, womanish sort of man.

"Yes, yes, I know," says he. "You have come to tell me that your wonderfully clever man, who has bored holes in my second-floor partition, has made a mistake and is off the scent of the scoundrel who has stolen my money."

"Yes, sir," says I. "That *is* one of the things I came to tell you. But I have got something else to say, besides that."

"Can you tell me who the thief is?" says he, more pettish than ever.

"Yes, sir," says I, "I think I can."

He put down the newspaper, and began to look rather anxious and frightened.

"Not my shopman?" says he. "I hope, for the man's own sake, it's not my shopman."

"Guess again, sir," says I.

"That idle slut, the maid?" says he.

"She is idle, sir," says I, "and she is also a slut – my first inquiries about her proved as much as that. But she's not the thief."

"Then in the name of heaven, who is?" says he.

"Will you please to prepare yourself for a very disagreeable surprise, sir?" says I. "And in case you lose your temper, will you excuse my remarking that I am the stronger man of the two and that, if you allow yourself to lay hands on me, I may unintentionally hurt you, in pure self-defence?"

He turned as pale as ashes, and pushed his chair two or three feet away from me.

"You have asked me to tell you, sir, who has taken your money," I went on. "If you insist on my giving you an answer –"

"I do insist," he said faintly. "Who has taken it?"

"Your wife has taken it," I said very quietly and very positively at the same time.

He jumped out of the chair as if I had put a knife into him, and struck his fist on the table, so heavily that the wood cracked again.

"Steady, sir," says I. "Flying into a passion won't help you to the truth."

"It's a lie!" says he, with another smack of his fist on the table, "a base, vile, infamous lie! How dare you –"

He stopped, and fell back into the chair again, looked about him in a bewildered way and ended by bursting out crying.

"When your better sense comes back to you, sir," says I, "I am sure you will be gentleman enough to make an apology for the language you have just used. In the meantime, please to listen, if you can, to a word of explanation. Mr. Sharpin has sent in a report to our inspector of the most irregular and ridiculous kind, setting down not only all his own foolish doings and sayings but the doings and sayings of Mrs. Yatman as well. In most cases, such a document would have been fit for the waste-paper basket, but, in this particular case, it so happens that Mr. Sharpin's budget of nonsense leads to a certain conclusion, which the simpleton of a writer has been quite innocent of suspecting from the beginning to the end. Of that conclusion I am so sure, that I will forfeit my place if it does not turn out that Mrs. Yatman has been practising upon the folly and conceit of this young man, and that she has tried to shield herself from discovery by purposely encouraging him to suspect the wrong persons. I tell you that confidently; and I will even go further. I will undertake to give a decided opinion as to why Mrs. Yatman took the money, and what she has done with it, or with a part of it. Nobody can look at that lady, sir, without being struck by the great taste and beauty of her dress —"

As I said those last words, the poor man seemed to find his powers of speech again. He cut me short directly, as haughtily as if he had been a duke instead of a stationer.

"Try some other means of justifying your vile calumny against my wife," says he. "Her milliner's bill for the past year is on my file of receipted accounts at this moment."

"Excuse me, sir," says I, "but that proves nothing. Milliners, I must tell you, have a certain rascally custom which comes within the daily experience of our office. A married lady who wishes it can keep two accounts at her dressmaker's: one is the account which her husband sees and pays; the other is the private account, which contains all the extravagant items, and which the wife pays secretly, by instalments, whenever she can. According to our usual experience, these instalments are mostly squeezed out of the housekeeping money. In your case, I suspect no instalments have been paid, proceedings have been threatened, Mrs. Yatman, knowing your altered circumstances, has felt herself driven into a corner and she has paid her private account out of your cash-box."

"I won't believe it," says he. "Every word you speak is an abominable insult to me and to my wife."

"Are you man enough, sir," says I, taking him up short, in order to save time and words, "to get that receipted bill you spoke of just now off the file, and come with me at once to the milliner's shop where Mrs. Yatman deals?"

He turned red in the face at that, got the bill directly and put on his hat. I took out of my pocket-book the list containing the numbers of the lost notes, and we left the house together immediately.

Arrived at the milliner's (one of the expensive West End houses, as I expected), I asked for a private interview, on important business, with the mistress of the concern. It was not the first time that she and I had met over the same delicate investigation. The moment she set eyes on me, she sent for her husband. I mentioned who Mr. Yatman was and what we wanted.

"This is strictly private?" inquires her husband. I nodded my head.

"And confidential?" says the wife. I nodded again.

"Do you see any objection, dear, to obliging the sergeant with a sight of the books?" says the husband.

"None in the world, love, if you approve of it," says the wife.

All this while poor Mr. Yatman sat looking the picture of astonishment and distress, quite out of place at our polite conference. The books were brought – and one minute's look at the pages in which Mrs. Yatman's name figured was enough, and more than enough, to prove the truth of every word I had spoken.

There, in one book, was the husband's account, which Mr. Yatman had settled. And there, in the other, was the private account, crossed off also, the date of settlement being the very day after the loss of the cash-box. This said private account amounted to the sum of a hundred and seventy-five pounds, odd shillings, and it extended over a period of three years. Not a single instalment had been paid on it. Under the last line was an entry to this effect: "Written to for the third time, June 23rd." I pointed to it, and asked the milliner if that meant "last June". Yes, it did mean last June; and she now deeply regretted to say that it had been accompanied by a threat of legal proceedings.

"I thought you gave good customers more than three years' credit?" says I.

The milliner looks at Mr. Yatman, and whispers to me: "Not when a lady's husband gets into difficulties."

She pointed to the account as she spoke. The entries after the time when Mr. Yatman's circumstances became involved were just as extravagant, for a person in his wife's situation, as the entries for the year before that period. If the lady had economized in other things, she had certainly not economized in the matter of dress.

There was nothing left now but to examine the cash-book for form's sake. The money had been paid in notes, the amounts and numbers of which exactly tallied with the figures set down in my list.

After that, I thought it best to get Mr. Yatman out of the house immediately. He was in such a pitiable condition that I called a cab and accompanied him home in it. At first he cried and raved like a child, but I soon quieted him – and I must add, to his credit, that he made me a most handsome apology for his language as the cab drew up at his house door. In return, I tried to give him some advice about how to set matters right, for the future, with his wife. He paid very little attention to me, and went upstairs muttering to himself about a separation. Whether Mrs. Yatman will come cleverly out of the scrape or not, seems doubtful. I should say, myself, that she will go into screeching hysterics, and so frighten the poor man into forgiving her. But this is no business of ours. So far as we are concerned, the case is now at an end, and the present report may come to a conclusion along with it.

I remain, accordingly, yours to command,

THOMAS BULMER

P.S. – I have to add, that, on leaving Rutherford Street, I met Mr. Matthew Sharpin coming to pack up his things.

"Only think!" says he, rubbing his hands in great spirits, "I've been to the genteel villa-residence, and the moment I mentioned my business, they kicked me out directly. There were two witnesses of the assault, and it's worth a hundred pounds to me if it's worth a farthing."

"I wish you joy of your luck," says I.

"Thank you," says he. "When may I pay you the same compliment on finding the thief?"

"Whenever you like," says I, "for the thief is found."

"Just what I expected," says he. "I've done all the work, and now you cut in and claim all the credit – Mr. Jay of course?"

"No," says I.

"Who is it then?" says he.

"Ask Mrs. Yatman," says I. "She's waiting to tell you."

"All right! I'd much rather hear it from that charming woman than from you," says he, and goes into the house in a mighty hurry.

What do you think of that, Inspector Theakstone? Would you like to stand in Mr. Sharpin's shoes? I shouldn't, I can promise you!

FROM CHIEF INSPECTOR THEAKSTONE TO MR. MATTHEW SHARPIN

July 12th

Sir – Sergeant Bulmer has already told you to consider yourself suspended until further notice, I have now authority to add that your services as a member of the Detective Police are positively declined. You will please to take this letter as notifying officially your dismissal from the force.

I may inform you, privately, that your rejection is not intended to cast any reflections on your character. It merely implies that you are not quite sharp enough for our purpose. If we *are* to have a new recruit among us, we should infinitely prefer Mrs. Yatman.

Your obedient servant,

FRANCIS THEAKSTONE

NOTE ON THE PRECEDING CORRESPONDENCE,
ADDED BY MR. THEAKSTONE

The Inspector is not in a position to append any explanations of importance to the last of the letters. It has been discovered that Mr. Matthew Sharpin left the house in Rutherford Street five minutes after his interview outside of it with Sergeant Bulmer – his manner expressing the liveliest emotions of terror and astonishment, and his left cheek displaying a bright patch of red, which might have been the result of a slap on the face from a female hand. He was also heard, by the shopman at Rutherford Street, to use a very shocking expression in reference to Mrs. Yatman, and was seen to clench his fist vindictively as he ran round the corner of the street. Nothing more has been heard of him, and it is conjectured that he has left London with the intention of offering his valuable services to the provincial police.

On the interesting domestic subject of Mr. and Mrs. Yatman still less is known. It has, however, been positively ascertained that the medical attendant of the family was sent for in a great hurry on the day when Mr. Yatman returned from the milliner's shop. The neighbouring chemist received, soon afterwards, a prescription of a soothing nature to make up for Mrs. Yatman. The day after, Mr. Yatman purchased some smelling-salts at the shop, and afterwards appeared at the circulating library to ask for a novel, descriptive of high life, that would amuse an invalid lady. It has been inferred from these circumstances that he has not thought it desirable to carry out his threat of separating himself from his wife – at least in the present (presumed) condition of that lady's sensitive nervous system.

The Clergyman's Confession

I

My brother, the clergyman, looked over my shoulder before I was aware of him, and discovered that the volume which completely absorbed my attention was a collection of famous Trials, published in a new edition and in a popular form.

He laid his finger on the Trial which I happened to be reading at the moment. I looked up at him. His face startled me: he had turned pale; his eyes were fixed on the open page of the book with an expression which puzzled and alarmed me.

"My dear fellow," I said, "what in the world is the matter with you?"

He answered in an odd absent manner, still keeping his finger on the open page.

"I had almost forgotten," he said. "And this reminds me."

"Reminds you of what?" I asked. "You don't mean to say you know anything about the Trial?"

"I know this," he said. "The prisoner was guilty."

"Guilty?" I repeated. "Why, the man was acquitted by the jury, with the full approval of the judge! What can you possibly mean?"

"There are circumstances connected with that Trial," my brother answered, "which were never communicated to the judge or the jury – which were never so much as hinted or whispered in court. I know them – of my own knowledge, by my own personal experience. They are very sad, very strange, very terrible. I have mentioned them to no mortal creature. I have done my best to forget them. You – quite innocently – have brought them back to my mind. They oppress, they distress me. I wish I had found you reading any book in your library, except *that* book!"

My curiosity was now strongly excited. I spoke out plainly.

"Surely", I suggested, "you might tell your brother what you are unwilling to mention to persons less nearly related to you. We have followed different professions, and have lived in different countries, since we were boys at school. But you know you can trust me."

He considered a little with himself.

"Yes," he said. "I know I can trust you." He waited a moment, and then he surprised me by a strange question.

"Do you believe", he asked, "that the spirits of the dead can return to earth and show themselves to the living?"

I answered cautiously – adopting as my own the words of a great English writer, touching the subjects of ghosts.

"You ask me a question," I said, "which, after five thousand years, is yet undecided. On that account alone, it is a question not to be trifled with."

My reply seemed to satisfy him.

"Promise me," he resumed, "that you will keep what I tell you a secret as long as I live. After my death I care little what happens. Let the story of my strange experience he added to the published experience of those other men who have seen what I have seen, and who believe what I believe. The world will not be the worse, and may be the better, for knowing one day what I am now about to trust to your ear alone."

My brother never again alluded to the narrative which he had confided to me, until the later time when I was sitting by his deathbed. He asked if I still remembered the story of Jéromette. "Tell it to others," he said, "as I have told it to you."

I repeat it after his death – as nearly as I can in his own words.

II

On a fine summer evening, many years since, I left my chambers in the Temple, to meet a fellow-student who had proposed to me a night's amusement in the public gardens at Cremorne.

You were then on your way to India, and I had taken my degree at Oxford. I had sadly disappointed my father by choosing the Law as my profession in preference to the Church. At that time, to own the truth, I had no serious intention of following any special vocation. I simply wanted an excuse for enjoying the pleasures of a London life. The study of the Law supplied me with that excuse. And I chose the Law as my profession accordingly.

On reaching the place at which we had arranged to meet, I found that my friend had not kept his appointment. After waiting vainly for ten minutes, my patience gave way, and I went into the Gardens by myself.

I took two or three turns round the platform devoted to the dancers without discovering my fellow-student, and without seeing any other person with whom I happened to be acquainted at that time.

For some reason which I cannot now remember, I was not in my usual good spirits that evening. The noisy music jarred on my nerves, the sight of the gaping crowd round the platform irritated me, the blandishments of the painted ladies of the profession of pleasure saddened and disgusted me. I opened my cigar-case, and turned aside into one of the quiet by-walks of the Gardens.

A man who is habitually careful in choosing his cigar has this advantage over a man who is habitually careless. He can always count on smoking the best cigar in his case, down to the last. I was still absorbed in choosing *my* cigar, when I heard these words behind me – spoken in a foreign accent and in a woman's voice:

"Leave me directly, sir! I wish to have nothing to say to you."

I turned round and discovered a little lady very simply and tastefully dressed, who looked both angry and alarmed as she rapidly passed me on her way to the more frequented part of the Gardens. A man (evidently the worse for the wine he had drunk in the course of the evening) was following her, and was pressing his tipsy attentions on her with the coarsest insolence of speech and manner. She was young and pretty, and she cast one entreating look at me as she went by, which it was not in manhood – perhaps I ought to say, in young-manhood – to resist.

I instantly stepped forward to protect her, careless whether I involved myself in a discreditable quarrel with a blackguard or not. As a matter of course, the fellow resented my interference, and my temper gave way. Fortunately for me, just as I lifted my hand to knock him down, a policeman appeared who had noticed that he was drunk, and who settled the dispute officially by turning him out of the Gardens.

I led her away from the crowd that had collected. She was evidently frightened – I felt her hand trembling on my arm – but she had one great merit: she made no fuss about it.

"If I can sit down for a few minutes," she said in her pretty foreign accent, "I shall soon be myself again, and I shall not trespass any farther on your kindness. I thank you very much, sir, for taking care of me."

We sat down on a bench in a retired part of the Gardens, near a little fountain. A row of lighted lamps ran round the outer rim of the basin. I could see her plainly.

I have said that she was "a little lady". I could not have described her more correctly in three words.

Her figure was slight and small; she was a well-made miniature of a woman from head to foot. Her hair and her eyes were both dark; the hair curled naturally; the expression of the eyes was quiet, and rather sad; the complexion, as I then saw it, very pale; the little mouth perfectly charming. I was especially attracted, I remembered, by the carriage of her head: it was strikingly graceful and spirited; it distinguished her, little as she was and quiet as she was, among the thousands of other women in the Gardens, as a creature apart. Even the one marked defect in her – a slight cast in the left eye – seemed to add, in some strange way, to the quaint attractiveness of her face. I have already spoken of the tasteful simplicity of her dress. I ought now to add that it was not made of any costly material, and that she wore no jewels or ornaments of any sort. My little lady was not rich. Even a man's eye could see that.

She was perfectly unembarrassed and unaffected. We fell as easily into talk as if we had been friends instead of strangers.

I asked how it was that she had no companion to take care of her. "You are too young and too pretty," I said in my blunt English way, "to trust yourself alone in such a place as this."

She took no notice of the compliment. She calmly put it away from her as if it had not reached her ears.

"I have no friend to take care of me," she said simply. "I was sad and sorry this evening, all by myself, and I thought I would go to the Gardens and hear the music, just to amuse me. It is not much to pay at the gate. Only a shilling."

"No friend to take care of you?" I repeated. "Surely there must be one happy man who might have been here with you to-night?"

"What man do you mean?" she asked.

"The man," I answered thoughtlessly, "whom we call, in England, a sweetheart."

I would have given worlds to have recalled those foolish words the moment they passed my lips. I felt that I had taken a vulgar liberty with her. Her face saddened; her eyes dropped to the ground. I begged her pardon.

"There is no need to beg my pardon," she said. "If you wish to know, sir – yes, I had once a sweetheart, as you call it in England. He has gone away and left me. No more of him, if you please. I am rested now. I will thank you again, and go home."

She rose to leave me.

I was determined not to part with her in that way. I begged to be allowed to see her safely back to her own door. She hesitated. I took a man's unfair advantage of her, by appealing to her fears. I said: "Suppose the blackguard who annoyed you should be waiting outside the gates?" That decided her. She took my arm. We went away together by the bank of the Thames, in the balmy summer night.

A walk of half an hour brought us to the house in which she lodged – a shabby little house in a by-street, inhabited evidently by very poor people.

She held out her hand at the door, and wished me good-night. I was too much interested in her to consent to leave my little foreign lady without the hope of seeing her again. I asked permission to call on her the next day. We were standing under the light of the street-lamp. She studied my face with a grave and steady attention before she made any reply.

"Yes," she said at last. "I think I do know a gentleman when I see him. You may come, sir, if you please, and call upon me to-morrow."

So we parted. So I entered – doubting nothing, foreboding nothing – on a scene in my life, which I now look back on with unfeigned repentance and regret.

III

I am speaking at this later time in the position of a clergyman, and in the character of a man of mature age. Remember that; and you will understand why I pass as rapidly as possible over the events of the next year of my life – why I say as little as I can of the errors and the delusion of my youth.

I called on her the next day. I repeated my visits during the days and weeks that followed, until the shabby little house in the by-street had become a second and (I say it with shame and self-reproach) a dearer home to me.

All of herself and her story which she thought fit to confide to me under these circumstances may be repeated to you in few words.

The name by which letters were addressed to her was "Mademoiselle Jéromette". Among the ignorant people of the house and the small tradesmen of the neighbourhood – who found her name not easy of pronunciation by the average English tongue – she was known by the friendly nickname of "The French Miss". When I knew her, she was resigned to her lonely life among strangers. Some years had elapsed since she had lost her parents and had left France. Possessing a small, very small, income of her own, she added to it by colouring miniatures for the photographers. She had relatives still living in France, but she had long since ceased to correspond with them. "Ask me nothing more about my family," she used to say. "I am as good as dead in my own country and among my own people."

This was all – literally all – that she told me of herself. I have never discovered more of her sad story from that day to this.

She never mentioned her family name – never even told me what part of France she came from or how long she had lived in England. That she was, by birth and breeding, a lady, I could entertain no doubt: her manners, her accomplishments, her ways of thinking and speaking, all proved it. Looking below the surface, her character showed itself in aspects not common among young women in these days. In her quiet way, she was an incurable fatalist and a firm believer in the ghostly reality of apparitions from the dead. Then again, in the matter of money she had strange views of her own. Whenever my purse was in my hand, she held me resolutely at a distance from first to last. She refused to move into better apartments: the shabby little house was clean inside, and the poor people who lived in it were kind to her – and that was enough. The most expensive present that she ever permitted me to offer her was a little enamelled ring, the plainest and cheapest thing of the kind in the jeweller's shop. In all relations with me she was sincerity itself. On all occasions, and under all circumstances, she spoke her mind (as the phrase is) with the same uncompromising plainness.

"I like you," she said to me. "I respect you. I shall always be faithful to you while you are faithful to me. But my love has gone from me. There is another man who has taken it away with him, I know not where."

Who was the other man?

She refused to tell me. She kept his rank and his name strict secrets from me. I never discovered how he had met with her, or why he had left her, or whether the guilt was his of making of her an exile from her country and her friends. She despised herself for still loving him, but the passion was too strong for her – she owned it and lamented it with the frankness which was so pre-eminently a part of her character. More than this, she plainly told me, in the early days of our acquaintance, that she believed he would return to her. It might be to-morrow, or it might be years hence. Even if he failed to repent of his own cruel conduct, the man would still miss her, as something lost out of his life, and, sooner or later, he would come back.

"And will you receive him if does come back?" I asked.

"I shall receive him," she replied, "against my own better judgement – in spite of my own firm persuasion that the day of his return to me will bring with it the darkest days of my life."

I tried to remonstrate with her.

"You have a will of your own," I said. "Exert it if he attempts to return to you."

"I have no will of my own", she answered quietly, "where *he* is concerned. It is my misfortune to love him." Her eyes rested for a moment on mine, with the utter self-abandonment of despair. "We have said enough about this," she added abruptly. "Let us say no more."

From that time we never spoke again of the unknown man. During the year that followed our first meeting, she heard nothing of him directly or indirectly. He might be living, or he might be dead. There came no word of him or from him. I was fond enough of her to be satisfied with this – he never disturbed us.

IV

The year passed – and the end came. Not the end as you may have anticipated it or as I might have foreboded it.

You remember the time when your letters from home informed you of the fatal termination of our mother's illness? It is the time of which I am now speaking. A few hours only before she breathed her last, she called me to her bedside, and desired that we might be left together alone. Reminding me that her death was near, she spoke of my prospects in life. She noticed my want of interest in the studies which were then supposed to be engaging my attention, and she ended by entreating me to reconsider my refusal to enter the Church.

"Your father's heart is set upon it," she said. "Do what I ask of you, my dear, and you will help to comfort him when I am gone."

Her strength failed her: she could say no more. Could I refuse the last request she would ever make to me? I knelt at the bedside, and took her wasted hand in mine, and solemnly promised her the respect which a son owes to his mother's last wishes.

Having bound myself by this sacred engagement, I had no choice but to accept the sacrifice which it imperatively exacted from me. The time had come when I must tear myself free from all unworthy associations. No matter what the effort cost me, I must separate myself at once and for ever from the unhappy woman who was not, who never could be, my wife.

At the close of a dull, foggy day, I set forth with a heavy heart to say the words which were to part us for ever.

Her lodging was not far from the banks of the Thames. As I drew near the place the darkness was gathering, and the broad surface of the river was hidden from me in a chill white mist. I stood for awhile, with my eyes fixed on the vaporous shroud that brooded over the flowing water – I stood, and asked myself in despair the one dreary question: "What am I to say to her?"

The mist chilled me to the bones. I turned from the riverbank, and made my way to her lodgings hard by. "It must be done!" I said to myself, as I took out my key and opened the house door.

She was not at her work as usual, when I entered her little sitting-room. She was standing by the fire, with her head down, and with an open letter in her hand.

The instant she turned to meet me, I saw in her face that something was wrong. Her ordinary manner was the manner of an unusually placid and self-restrained person. Her temperament had little of the liveliness which we associate in England with the French nature. She was not ready with her laugh; and in all my previous experience, I had never yet known her to cry. Now, for the first time, I saw the quiet face disturbed; I saw tears in the pretty brown eyes. She ran to meet me, and laid her head on my breast, and burst into a passionate fit of weeping that shook her from head to foot.

Could she by any human possibility have heard of the coming change in my life? Was she aware, before I had opened my lips, of the hard necessity which had brought me to the house?

It was simply impossible; the thing could not be.

I waited until her first burst of emotion had worn itself out. Then I asked – with an uneasy conscience, with a sinking heart – what had happened to distress her.

She drew herself away from me, sighing heavily, and gave me the open letter which I had seen in her hand.

"Read that," she said. "And remember I told you what might happen when we first met."

I read the letter.

It was signed in initials only, but the writer plainly revealed himself as the man who had deserted her. He had repented; he had returned to her. In proof of his penitence he was willing to do her the justice which he had hitherto refused – he was willing to marry her, on the condition that she would engage to keep the marriage a secret so long as his parents lived. Submitting this proposal, he waited to know whether she would consent, on her side, to forgive and forget.

I gave her back the letter in silence. This unknown rival had done me the service of paving the way for our separation. In offering her the atonement of marriage, he had made it, on my part, a matter of duty to *her*, as well as to myself, to say the parting words. I felt this instantly. And yet, I hated him for helping me!

She took my hand and led me to the sofa. We sat down, side by side. Her face was composed to a sad tranquillity. She was quiet; she was herself again:

"I have refused to see him", she said, "until I had first spoken to you. You have read his letter. What do you say?"

I could make but one answer. It was my duty to tell her what my own position was in the plainest terms. I did my duty – leaving her free to decide on the future for herself. Those sad words said, it was useless to prolong the wretchedness of our separation. I rose, and took her hand for the last time.

I see her again now, at that final moment, as plainly as if it had happened yesterday. She had been suffering from an affection of the throat, and she had a white silk handkerchief tied loosely round her neck. She wore a simple dress of purple merino, with a black-silk apron over it. Her face was deadly pale; her fingers felt icily cold as they closed round my hand.

"Promise me one thing", I said, "before I go. While I live, I am your friend – if I am nothing more. If you are ever in trouble, promise that you will let me know it."

She started, and drew back from me as if I had struck her with a sudden terror.

"Strange!" she said, speaking to herself. "He feels as I feel. *He* is afraid of what may happen to me, in my life to come."

I attempted to reassure her. I tried to tell her what was indeed the truth – that I had only been thinking of the ordinary chances and changes of life when I spoke.

She paid no heed to me; she came back and put her hands on my shoulders, and thoughtfully and sadly looked up in my face.

"My mind is not your mind in this matter," she said. "I once owned to you that I had my forebodings when we first spoke of this man's return. I may tell you now more than I told you then. I believe I shall die young, and die miserably. If I am right, have you interest enough still left in me to wish to hear of it?"

She paused, shuddering – and added these startling words:

"You *shall* hear of it."

The tone of steady conviction in which she spoke alarmed and distressed me. My face showed her how deeply and how painfully I was affected.

"There, there!" she said, returning to her natural manner. "Don't take what I say too seriously. A poor girl who has led a lonely life like mine thinks strangely and talks strangely – sometimes. Yes, I give you my promise. If I am ever in trouble, I will let you know it. God bless you – you have been very kind to me – good-bye!"

A tear dropped on my face as she kissed me. The door closed between us. The dark street received me.

It was raining heavily. I looked up at her window, through the drifting shower. The curtains were parted. She was standing in the gap, dimly lit by the lamp on the table behind her, waiting for our last look at each other. Slowly lifting her hand, she waved her farewell at the window, with the unsought native grace which had charmed me on the night when we first met. The curtain fell again. She disappeared. Nothing was before me, nothing was round me, but the darkness and the night.

V

In two years from that time, I had redeemed the promise given to my mother on her deathbed. I had entered the Church.

My father's interest made my first step in my new profession an easy one. After serving my preliminary apprenticeship as a curate, I was appointed, before I was thirty years of age, to a living in the West of England.

My new benefice offered me every advantage that I could possibly desire – with the one exception of a sufficient income. Although my wants were few, and although I was still an unmarried man, I found it desirable, on many accounts, to add to my resources. Following the example of other young clergymen in my position, I determined to receive pupils who might stand in need of preparation for a career at the Universities. My relatives exerted themselves, and my good fortune still befriended me. I obtained two pupils to start with. A third would complete the number which I was at present prepared to receive. In course of time, this third pupil made his appearance, under circumstances sufficiently remarkable to merit being mentioned in detail.

It was the summer vacation, and my two pupils had gone home. Thanks to a neighbouring clergyman, who kindly undertook to perform my duties for me, I, too, obtained a fortnight's holiday, which I spent at my father's house in London.

During my sojourn in the metropolis, I was offered an opportunity of preaching in a church made famous by the eloquence of one of the popular pulpit-orators of our time. In accepting the proposal, I felt naturally anxious to do my best before the unusually large and unusually intelligent congregation which would be assembled to hear me.

At the period of which I am now speaking, all England had been startled by the discovery of a terrible crime, perpetrated under circumstances of extreme provocation. I chose this crime as the main subject of my sermon. Admitting that the best among us were frail mortal creatures, subject to evil promptings and provocations like the worst among us, my object was to show how a Christian man may find his certain refuge from temptation in the safeguards of his religion. I dwelt minutely on the hardship of the Christian's first struggle to resist the evil influence, on the help which his Christianity inexhaustibly held out to him in the worst relapses of the weaker and viler part of his nature, on the steady and certain gain which was the ultimate reward of his faith and his firmness and on the blessed sense of peace and happiness which accompanied the final triumph. Preaching to this effect, with the fervent conviction which I really felt, I may say for myself, at least, that I did no discredit to the choice which had placed me in the pulpit. I held the attention of my congregation from the first word to the last.

While I was resting in the vestry on the conclusion of the service, a note was brought to me written in pencil. A member of my congregation – a gentleman – wished to see me on a matter of considerable importance to himself. He would call on me at any place and at any hour which I might choose to appoint. If I wished to be satisfied of his respectability, he would beg leave to refer me to his father, with whose name I might possibly be acquainted.

The name given in the reference was undoubtedly familiar to me, as the name of a man of some celebrity and influence in the world of London. I sent back my card, appointing an hour for the visit of my correspondent on the afternoon of the next day.

VI

The stranger made his appearance punctually. I guessed him to be some two or three years younger than myself. He was undeniably handsome; his manners were the manners of a gentleman – and yet, without knowing why, I felt a strong dislike to him the moment he entered the room.

After the first preliminary words of politeness had been exchanged between us, my visitor informed me as follows of the object which he had in view.

"I believe you live in the country, sir?" he began.

"I live in the West of England," I answered.

"Do you make a long stay in London?"

"No. I go back to my rectory to-morrow."

"May I ask if you take pupils?"

"Yes."

"Have you any vacancy?"

"I have one vacancy."

"Would you object to let me go back with you to-morrow, as your pupil?"

The abruptness of the proposal took me by surprise. I hesitated.

In the first place (as I have already said), I disliked him. In the second place, he was too old to be a fit companion for my other two pupils – both lads in their teens. In the third place, he had asked me to receive him at least three weeks before the vacation came to an end. I had my own pursuits and amusements in prospect during that interval, and saw no reason why I should inconvenience myself by setting them aside.

He noticed my hesitation, and did not conceal from me that I had disappointed him.

"I have it very much at heart," he said, "to repair without delay the time that I have lost. My age is against me, I know. The truth is – I have wasted my opportunities since I left school, and I am anxious, honestly anxious, to mend my ways before it is too late. I wish to prepare myself for one of the Universities – I wish to show, if I can, that I am not quite unworthy to inherit my father's famous name. You are the man to help me, if I can only persuade you to do it. I was struck by your sermon yesterday, and, if I may venture to make the confession in your presence, I took a strong liking to you. Will you see my father, before you decide to say No? He will be able to explain whatever may seem strange in my present application, and he will be happy to see you this afternoon, if you can spare the time. As to the question of terms, I am quite sure it can be settled to your entire satisfaction."

He was evidently in earnest – gravely, vehemently in earnest. I unwillingly consented to see his father.

Our interview was a long one. All my questions were answered fully and frankly.

The young man had led an idle and desultory life. He was weary of it and ashamed of it. His disposition was a peculiar one. He stood sorely in need of a guide, a teacher and a friend, in whom he was disposed to confide. If I disappointed the hopes which he had centred in me, he would be discouraged, and he would relapse into the aimless and indolent existence of which he was now ashamed. Any terms for which I might stipulate were at my disposal if I would consent to receive him, for three months to begin with, on trial.

Still hesitating, I consulted my father and my friends.

They were all of opinion (and justly of opinion so far) that the new connection would be an excellent one for me. They all reproached me for taking a purely capricious dislike to a well-born and well-bred young man, and for permitting it to influence me, at the outset of my career, against my own interests. Pressed by these considerations, I allowed myself to be persuaded to give the new pupil a fair trial. He accompanied me the next day on my way back to the rectory.

VII

Let me be careful to do justice to a man whom I personally disliked. My senior pupil began well: he produced a decidedly favourable impression on the persons attached to my little household.

The women, especially, admired his beautiful light hair, his crisply curling beard, his delicate complexion, his clear blue eyes and his finely shaped hands and feet. Even the inveterate reserve in his manner and the downcast, almost sullen, look which had prejudiced *me* against him, aroused a common feeling of romantic enthusiasm in my servants' hall. It was decided, on the high authority of the housekeeper herself, that "the new gentleman" was in love – and, more interesting still, that he was the victim of an unhappy attachment which had driven him away from his friends and his home.

For myself, I tried hard, and tried vainly, to get over my first dislike to the senior pupil.

I could find no fault with him. All his habits were quiet and regular, and he devoted himself conscientiously to his reading. But, little by little, I became satisfied that his heart was not in his studies. More than this, I had my reasons for suspecting that he was concealing something from me, and that he felt painfully the reserve on his own part which he could not, or dared not, break through. There were moments when I almost doubted whether he had not chosen my remote country rectory as a safe place of refuge from some person or persons of whom he stood in dread.

For example, his ordinary course of proceeding, in the matter of his correspondence, was, to say the least of it, strange.

He received no letters at my house. They waited for him at the village post office. He invariably called for them himself and invariably forbore to trust any of my servants with his own letters for the post. Again, when we were out walking together, I more than once caught him looking furtively over his shoulder, as if he suspected some person of following him for some evil purpose. Being constitutionally a hater of mysteries, I determined, at an early stage of our intercourse, on making an effort to clear matters up. There might be just a chance of my winning the senior pupil's confidence if I spoke to him while the last days of the summer vacation still left us alone together in the house.

"Excuse me for noticing it," I said to him one morning, while we engaged over our books. "I cannot help observing that you appear to have some trouble on your mind. Is it indiscreet on my part to ask if I can be of any use to you?"

He changed colour, looked up at me quickly, looked down again at his book, struggled hard with some secret fear or secret reluctance that was in him and suddenly burst out with this extraordinary question:

"I suppose you were in earnest when you preached that sermon in London?"

"I am astonished that you should doubt it," I replied.

He paused again, struggled with himself again and startled me by a second outbreak, even stranger than the first.

"I am one of the people you preached at in your sermon." he said. 'That's the true reason why I asked you to take me for your pupil. Don't turn me out! When you talked to your congregation of tortured and tempted people, you talked of Me."

I was so astonished by the confession, that I lost my presence of mind. For the moment, I was unable to answer him.

"Don't turn me out!" he repeated. "Help me against myself. I am telling you the truth. As God is my witness, I am telling you the truth!"

"Tell me the *whole* truth," I said, "and rely on my consoling and helping you – rely on my being your friend."

In the fervour of the moment, I took his hand. It lay cold and still in mine: it mutely warned me that I had a sullen and a secret nature to deal with.

"There must be no concealment between us," I resumed. "You have entered my house, by your own confession, under false pretences. It is your duty to me and your duty to yourself to speak out."

The man's inveterate reserve – cast off for the moment only – renewed its hold on him. He considered, carefully considered, his next words before he permitted them to pass his lips.

"A person is in the way of my prospects in life," he began slowly, with his eyes cast down on his book. "A person provokes me horribly. I feel dreadful temptations (like the man you spoke of in your sermon) when I am in the person's company. Teach me to resist temptation! I am afraid of myself if I see the person again. You are the only man who can help me. Do it while you can."

He stopped, and passed his handkerchief over his forehead.

"Will that do?" he asked – still with his eyes on his book

"It will *not* do," I answered. "You are so far from really opening your heart to me that you won't even let me know whether it is a man or a woman who stands in the way of your prospects in life. You used the word 'person' over and over again – rather than say 'he' or 'she' when you speak of the provocation which is trying you. How can I help a man who has so little confidence in me as that?"

My reply evidently found him at the end of his resources. He tried, tried desperately, to say more than he had said yet. No! The words seemed to stick in his throat. Not one of them would pass his lips.

"Give me time," he pleaded piteously. "I can't bring myself to it, all at once. I mean well. Upon my soul, I mean well. But I am slow at this sort of thing. Wait till to-morrow."

To-morrow came – and again he put it off.

"One more day!" he said. "You don't know how hard it is to speak plainly. I am half afraid; I am half ashamed. Give me one more day."

I had hitherto only disliked him. Try as I might (and did) to make merciful allowance for his reserve, I began to despise him now.

VIII

The day of the deferred confession came, and brought an event with it for which both he and I were alike unprepared. Would he really have confided in me but for that event? He must either have done it or have abandoned the purpose which had led him into my house.

We met as usual at the breakfast-table. My housekeeper brought in my letters of the morning. To my surprise, instead of leaving the room again as usual, she walked round to the other side of the table and laid a letter before my senior pupil – the first letter, since his residence with me, which had been delivered to him under my roof.

He started, and took up the letter. He looked at the address. A spasm of suppressed fury passed across his face, his breath came quickly, his hand trembled as it held the letter. So far, I said nothing. I waited to see whether he would open the envelope in my presence or not.

He was afraid to open it in my presence. He got on his feet. He said, in tones so low that I could barely bear him:

"Please excuse me for a minute," and left the room.

I waited for half an hour – for a quarter of an hour, after that – and then I sent to ask if he had forgotten his breakfast.

In a minute more, I heard his footstep in the hall. He opened the breakfast-room door, and stood on the threshold, with a small travelling-bag in his hand.

"I beg your pardon," he said, still standing at the door. "I must ask for leave of absence for a day or two. Business in London."

"Can I be of any use?" I asked. "I am afraid your letter has brought you bad news?"

"Yes," he said shortly. "Bad news. I have no time for breakfast."

"Wait a few minutes," I urged. "Wait long enough to treat me like your friend – to tell me what your trouble is before you go."

He made no reply. He stepped into the hall, and closed the door –

then opened it again a little way, without showing himself.

"Business in London," he repeated, as if he thought it highly important to inform me of the nature of his errand. The door closed for the second time. He was gone.

I went into my study, and carefully considered what had happened.

The result of my reflections is easily described. I determined on discontinuing my relations with my senior pupil. In writing to his father (which I did, with all due courtesy and respect, by that day's post), I mentioned as my reason for arriving at this decision. First, that I had found it impossible to win the confidence of his son. Secondly, that his son had that morning suddenly and mysteriously left my house for London, and that I must decline accepting any further responsibility towards him as the necessary consequence.

I had put my letter in the post-bag, and was beginning to feel a little easier after having written it, when my housekeeper appeared in the study, with a very grave face and with something hidden apparently in her closed hand.

"Would you please look, sir, at what we have found in the gentleman's bedroom, since he went away this morning?"

I knew the housekeeper to possess a woman's full share of that amiable weakness of the sex which goes by the name of "Curiosity". I had also, in various indirect ways, become aware that my senior pupil's strange departure had largely increased the disposition among the women of my household to regard him as the victim of an unhappy attachment. The time was ripe, as it seemed to me, for checking any further gossip about him and any renewed attempts at prying into his affairs in his absence.

"Your only business in my pupil's bedroom", I said to the housekeeper, "is to see that it is kept clean and that it is properly aired. There must be no interference, if you please, with his letters, or his papers, or with anything else that he has left behind him. Put back directly whatever you may have found in his room."

The housekeeper had her full share of a woman's temper as well as of a woman's curiosity. She listened to me with a rising colour and a just perceptible toss of the head.

"Must I put it back, sir, on the floor between the bed and the wall?" she inquired, with an ironical assumption of the humblest deference to my wishes. "*That's* where the girl found it when she was sweeping the room. Anybody can see for themselves," pursued the housekeeper indignantly, "that the poor gentleman has gone away broken-hearted. And there, in my opinion, is the hussy who is the cause of it!"

With those words, she made me a low curtsey, and laid a small photographic portrait on the desk at which I was sitting.

I looked at the photograph.

In an instant, my heart was beating wildly, my head turned giddy, the housekeeper, the furniture, the walls of the room, all swayed and whirled round me.

The portrait that had been found in my senior pupil's bedroom was the portrait of Jéromette!

IX

I had sent the housekeeper out of my study. I was alone, with the photograph of the Frenchwoman on my desk.

There could surely be little doubt about the discovery that had burst upon me. The man who had stolen his way into my house, driven by the terror of a temptation that he dared not reveal, and the man who had been my unknown rival in the bygone time, were one and the same!

Recovering self-possession enough to realize this plain truth, the inferences that followed forced their way into my mind as a matter of course. The unnamed person who was the obstacle to my pupil's prospects in life, the unnamed person in whose company he was assailed by temptations which made him tremble for himself, stood revealed to me now as being, in all human probability, no other than Jéromette. Had she bound him in the fetters of the marriage which he had himself proposed? Had she discovered his place of refuge in my house? And was the letter that had been delivered to him of her writing? Assuming these questions to be answered in the affirmative, what, in that case, was his "business in London"? I remembered how he had spoken to me of his temptations, I recalled the expression that had crossed his face when he recognized the handwriting on the letter – and the conclusion that followed literally shook me to the soul. Ordering my horse to be saddled, I rode instantly to the railway station.

The train by which he had travelled to London had reached the terminus nearly an hour since. The one useful course that I could take, by way of quieting the dreadful misgivings crowding one after another on my mind, was to telegraph to Jéromette at the address at which I had last seen her. I sent the subjoined message – prepaying the reply:

"If you are in any trouble, telegraph to me. I will be with you by the first train. Answer, in any case."

There was nothing in the way of the immediate dispatch of my message. And yet the hours passed and no answer was received. By the advice of the clerk, I sent a second telegram to the London office requesting an explanation. The reply came back in these terms:

"Improvements in street. Houses pulled down. No trace of person named in telegram."

I mounted my horse, and rode back slowly to the rectory.

"The day of his return to me will bring with it the darkest days of my life . . . I shall die young, and die miserably . . . Have you interest enough still left in me to wish to hear of it? . . . You *shall* hear of it." Those words were in my memory while I rode home in the cloudless moonlight night. They were so vividly present to me that I could hear again her pretty foreign accent, her quiet clear tones, as she spoke them. For the rest, the emotions of that memorable day had worn me out. The answer from the telegraph-office had struck me with a strange and stony despair. My mind was a blank. I had no thoughts. I had no tears.

I was about half-way on my road home, and I had just heard the clock of a village church strike ten, when I became conscious, little by little, of a chilly sensation slowly creeping through and through me to the bones. The warm balmy air of a summer night was abroad. It was the month of July. In the month of July, was it possible that any living creature (in good health) could feel cold? It was *not* possible – and yet, the chilly sensation still crept through and through me to the bones.

I looked up. I looked all round me.

My horse was walking along an open highroad. Neither trees nor waters were near me. On either side, the flat fields stretched away bright and broad in the moonlight.

I stopped my horse, and looked round me again.

Yes. I saw it. With my own eyes I saw it. A pillar of white mist – between five and six feet high, as well as I could judge – was moving beside me at the edge of the road, on my left hand. When I stopped, the white mist stopped. When I went on, the white mist went on. I pushed my horse to a trot, the pillar of mist was with me. I urged him to a gallop, the pillar of mist was with me. I stopped him again, the pillar of mist stood still.

The white colour of it was the white colour of the fog which I had seen over the river – on the night when I had gone to bid her farewell. And the chill which had then crept through me to the bones was the chill that was creeping through me now.

I went on again slowly. The white mist went on again slowly, with the clear bright night all round it.

I was awed rather than frightened. There was one moment, and one only, when the fear came to me that my reason might be shaken. I caught myself keeping time to the slow tramp of the horse's feet with the slow utterances of these words, repeated over and over again: "Jéromette is dead. Jéromette is dead." But my will was still my own: I was able to control myself, to impose silence on my own muttering lips. And I rode on quietly. And the pillar of mist went quietly with me.

My groom was waiting for my return at the rectory gate. I pointed to the mist passing through the gate with me.

"Do you see anything there?" I said.

The man looked at me in astonishment.

I entered the rectory. The housekeeper met me in the hall. I pointed to the mist entering with me.

"Do you see anything at my side?" I asked.

The housekeeper looked at me as the groom had looked at me.

"I am afraid you are not well, sir," she said. "Your colour is all gone – you are shivering. Let me get you a glass of wine."

I went into my study, on the ground-floor, and took the chair at my desk. The photograph still lay where I had left it. The pillar of mist floated round the table and stopped opposite to me, behind the photograph.

The housekeeper brought in the wine. I put the glass to my lips and set it down again. The chill of the mist was in the wine. There was no taste, no reviving spirit in it. The presence of the housekeeper oppressed me. My dog had followed her into the room. The presence of the animal oppressed me. I said to the woman:

"Leave me by myself, and take the dog with you."

They went out and left me alone in the room.

I sat looking at the pillar of mist, hovering opposite to me.

It lengthened slowly, until it reached to the ceiling. As it lengthened, it grew bright and luminous. A time passed, and a shadowy appearance showed itself in the centre of the light. Little by little, the shadowy appearance took the outline of a human form. Soft brown eyes, tender and melancholy, looked at me through the unearthly light in the mist. The head and the rest of the face broke next slowly on my view. Then the figure gradually revealed itself, moment by moment, downward and downward to the feet. She stood before me as I had last seen her, in her purple merino dress, with the black silk apron, with the white handkerchief tied loosely round her neck. She stood before me, in the gentle beauty that I remembered so well, and looked at me as she had looked when she gave me her last kiss, when her tears had dropped on my cheek.

I fell on my knees at the table. I stretched out my hands to her imploringly. I said: "Speak to me – O, once again speak to me, Jéromette."

Her eyes rested on me with a divine compassion in them. She lifted her hand, and pointed to the photograph on my desk, with a gesture which bade me turn the card. I turned it. The name of the man who had left my house that morning was inscribed on it, in her own handwriting.

I looked up at her again when I had read it. She lifted her hand once more and pointed to the handkerchief round her neck. As I looked at it, the fair white silk changed horribly in colour – the fair white silk became darkened and drenched in blood.

A moment more, and the vision of her began to grow dim. By slow degrees, the figure, then the face, faded back into the shadowy appearance that I had first seen. The luminous inner light died out in the white mist. The mist itself dropped slowly downwards, floated a moment in airy circles on the floor, vanished. Nothing was before me but the familiar wall of the room and the photograph lying face downwards on my desk.

X

The next day, the newspapers reported the discovery of a murder in London. A Frenchwoman was the victim. She had been killed by a wound in the throat. The crime had been discovered between ten and eleven o'clock on the previous night.

I leave you to draw your conclusion from what I have related. My own faith in the reality of the apparition is immovable. I say, and believe, that Jéromette kept her word with me. She died young and died miserably. And I heard of it from herself.

Take up the Trial again, and look at the circumstances that were revealed during the investigation in court. His motive for murdering her is there.

You will see that she did indeed marry him privately; that they lived together contentedly until the fatal day when she discovered that his fancy had been caught by another woman; that violent quarrels took place between them, from that time to the time when my sermon showed him his own deadly hatred towards her, reflected in the case of another man; that she discovered his place of retreat in my house, and threatened him by letter with the public assertion of her conjugal rights; lastly, that a man, variously described by different witnesses, was seen leaving the door of her lodgings on the night of the murder. The Law – advancing no farther than this – may have discovered circumstances of suspicion, but no certainty. The Law, in default of direct evidence to convict the prisoner, may have rightly decided in letting him go free.

But *I* persist in believing that the man was guilty. *I* declare that he, and he alone, was the murderer of Jéromette. And now, you know why.

Love's Random Shot

I

The scene is a famous city in Scotland. The chief personage is the best police officer we had in the time when I served the office of sheriff. He was an old man, about to retire on a well-earned pension at the period of his life to which my narrative refers. A theft of a priceless picture, which had escaped discovery by the other members of our police force, roused old Benjamin Parley to exert himself for the last time. The money motive was not the motive that mainly influenced him, although the large reward originally offered for the recovery of the picture had been doubled.

"If the rest of you can't find the thief," he said, "I must take the case in hand, for the honour of Scotland."

Having arrived at this decision, Parley presented himself at my house. I gave him a letter of introduction to the proprietor of the picture – then on the point of applying for help to London.

You have heard of Lord Dalton's famous gallery. A Madonna, by Raphael, was the gem of the collection. Early one morning the servants discovered the empty frame, without finding a trace of the means by which the audacious robbery had been committed. Having allowed our veteran officer to make his own preliminary investigations, my lord (a man of rare ability and of marked originality of character) was at once impressed by the startling novelty of the conclusion at which Parley arrived, and by the daring nature of the plan that he devised for solving the mystery of the theft.

Lord Dalton pointed to a letter on his library table, addressed to the Chief of the London Detective Police Force.

"I will delay posting this for a week," he said. "If, at the end of the time, you send me a sufficiently encouraging first report, the case shall be left unreservedly in your hands."

At the end of the week the report was sent in. Lord Dalton first destroyed his letter to London and then spoke to Parley on the subject of the reward.

"As a well-informed police officer," he said, "you are no doubt aware that I am one of the three richest men in Scotland. Have you also heard that I am a stingy man?"

"I have heard exactly the contrary, my lord," Parley answered, with perfect truth.

"Very good. You will be inclined to believe me when I tell you that the money value of my picture (large as it may be) is the least part of its value in my estimation. The sheriff tells me that you have a wife and two daughters at home, and that you were about to retire on a pension when you offered your services. At your age, I must take that circumstance into consideration. Do you mind telling me what income you have to look forward to, adding your other pecuniary resources (if you have any) to your pension?"

Parley answered the question without hesitation and without reserve. He was not an easy man to astonish, but Lord Dalton's next words literally struck him speechless.

"Put my Raphael back in the frame within a month from this day," said his lordship, "and I will treble your income, and secure it to your widow and children after you."

In less than three weeks from that date, Benjamin Parley (just arrived from Brussels) walked into the picture gallery and put the Raphael back into the frame with his own hands. He refused to say how he had recovered the picture. But he announced, with an appearance of self-reproach which entirely failed to deceive Lord Dalton, the disastrous escape of his prisoner on the journey to Scotland. At a later period, scandal whispered that this same prisoner was a vagabond member of my lord's family, and that Parley's success had been due, in the first instance, to his wise courage in daring to suspect a nobleman's relative. I don't know what your experience may be. For my own part, I have now and then found scandal building on a well-secured foundation.

II

In relating the circumstances which made the generous nobleman and the skilled police officer acquainted with each other, I have borne in mind certain results, the importance of which you have yet to estimate. The day on which Benjamin Parley received his magnificent reward proved to be the fatal day in his life.

He had originally planned to retire to the village in Perthshire in which he had been born. Being now possessed of an income which enabled him to indulge the ambition of his wife and daughters, it was decided that he should fix his residence in one of the suburbs of the city. Mrs. Parley and her two girls, established in "a genteel villa", assumed the position of "ladies", and old Benjamin, when time hung heavy on his hands, was within half an hour's walk of his colleagues in the police force.

"But for my lord's generosity," his wife remarked, "he would not have had the resource. If we had gone to Perthshire, he would never, in all likelihood, have seen our city again."

To give you some idea of this poor fellow's excellent character, and of the high estimation in which he was deservedly held, I may mention that his retirement was celebrated by the presentation of a testimonial. It assumed the quaint form of a receipted bill, representing the expenses incurred in furnishing his new house. I took the chair at the meeting. The landed gentry, the lawyers and the merchants were present in large numbers, all equally desirous of showing their respect for a man who, in a position beset by temptations, had set an example of incorruptible integrity from first to last.

Some family troubles of mine at that time obliged me to apply for leave of absence. For two months my duties were performed by deputy.

Examining the letters and cards which covered the study-table on my return, I found a morsel of paper with some lines of writing on it in pencil, signed by Parley's wife: "When you can spare a little time, sir, pray be so good as to let me say a word to you at your house."

The handwriting showed plain signs of agitation, and the last three words were underlined. Was the good woman burdened with a domestic secret, and were her husband and children not admitted to her confidence?

I was so busily occupied after my absence that I could only make an appointment to see Mrs. Parley at my breakfast time. The hour was so early that she would be sure to find me alone.

The moment she entered the room I saw a change in her which prepared me for something serious. It may be, perhaps, desirable to add, by way explaining a certain tendency to excitement and exaggeration in Mrs. Parley's ways of thinking and speaking, that she was a Welsh woman.

"Is there anything wrong at home?" I asked.

She began to cry. "You know how proud I was, sir, of our grand house and our splendid income. I wish we had gone where we first thought of going – hundreds of miles away from this place! I wish Parley had never seen his lordship, and never earned the great reward!"

"You don't mean to tell me," I said, "that you and your husband have quarrelled?"

"Worse, sir, worse than that. Parley is so changed that my own husband is like a stranger to me. For God's sake, don't mention it! In your old age, after sleeping together for thirty years and more, I'm cast off. Parley has his bedroom, and I have mine!" She looked at me – and blushed. At nearly sixty years of age, the poor creature blushed like a young girl!

It is needless to say that the famous question of the French philosopher was on the tip of my tongue: "Who is she?" But I owed it to Parley's unblemished reputation to hesitate before I committed myself to a positive opinion. The question of the beds was clearly beyond the reach of my interference.

"In what other ways does Parley seem to be changed?" I inquired.

"Seem?" she repeated. "Why even the girls notice it! That their father doesn't care about them now. And it's true! In our present prosperity, we can afford to pay a governess, and when we first settled in the new house, Parley agreed with me that the poor things ought to be better educated. He has lost all interest in their welfare. If I only mention the matter now, he says: 'Oh! bother!' and discourages me in that way. You know, sir, he always dressed respectably, according to his station and time of life. That's all altered now. He has gone to a new tailor: he wears smart cutaway coats, like the young men; I found an elastic belt among his clothes – the sort of thing they advertise to keep down fat and preserve the figure. You were so kind as to give him a snuff-box on his last birthday. It's of no more use to him now. Benjamin has given up taking snuff."

Here I thought it desirable, in the interests of good Mrs. Parley herself, to bring the recital of her grievances to a close. The domestic situation (to speak the language of the stage) was more than sufficiently revealed to me. After an exemplary life, the model husband and father had fallen in the way of one of those temptations which are especially associated with the streets of a great city, and had yielded at the end of his career. A disastrous downfall – not altogether without precedent in the history of frail humanity, even at the wintry period of life! I was sorry, truly sorry, but in my position what could I do?

"I am at your service," I said, "if you will only tell me how I can advise you."

"Some hussy has got hold of Benjamin!" cried the poor woman. "And I don't know where to find her. What am I to do? Benjamin's too deep for me – I believe I shall go mad!"

She fell back on her chair, and began to beat her hands on her lap. If I permitted this hysterical agitation to proceed in its usual course of development, the household would be alarmed by an outburst of screaming. There was but one way of composing Mrs. Parley, and I took it.

"Suppose I speak to your husband?" I suggested.

"Oh, Mr. Sheriff . . . !"

In Mrs. Parley's excitable Welsh nature even gratitude threatened to express itself hysterically. I checked the new outbreak by putting some necessary questions. The few facts which I succeeded in eliciting did not present my coming interview with the husband in an encouraging light.

After moving into the new house, Parley had found some difficulty (naturally enough) in reconciling himself to the change in his life. From time to time (as his wife had suggested) he looked in at the police office, and had offered the benefit of his experience to his colleagues when they were in need of advice. For a while these visits to the city produced the good results which had been anticipated. Then followed the very complete and very suspicious change in him, already related to me. While the husband and wife still occupied the same room at night, Mrs. Parley discovered that Benjamin was disturbed by dreams. For the first time in all her experience, she heard him talking in his sleep. Here and there, words escaped him which seemed to allude to a woman – a woman whom he called "my dear" – a woman who had apparently placed some agitating confidence in him. Sensible enough under other circumstances, Mrs. Parley's jealousy had hurried her into an act of folly. She woke her husband and insisted on an explanation. The result had been the institution of separate bedrooms – on the pretence that Parley's sense of conjugal duty would not permit him to be the means of disturbing his wife's rest. Arriving, correctly enough, at the conclusion that he was afraid of betraying himself, Mrs. Parley had tried the desperate experiment of following him privately when he next left the house. A police officer of forty years' experience, with a secret to keep, sees before him and behind him, and on his right hand and his left, at one and the same time. Poor Mrs. Parley, discovered as a spy, felt the look that her husband gave her (to use her own expression) "in the marrow of her bones". His language had been equally alarming. "Try it again," he said, "and you will have seen the last of me." She had naturally been afraid to try it again; and there she was, at my breakfast table, with but one hope left – the hope that the sheriff would assist her!

III

Such was my interview with the wife. My interview with the husband produced one result, for which I was in some degree prepared. It satisfied me that any interference on my part would be worse than useless.

I had certain claims on Parley's gratitude and respect, which he had hitherto recognized with heartfelt sincerity. When we now stood face to face – before a word had passed between us – I saw one thing clearly: my hold over him was lost.

For Mrs. Parley's sake I could not allow myself to be discouraged at the outset.

"Your wife was with me yesterday," I said, "in great distress."

His voice told me that he had suffered – and was still suffering – keenly. I also noticed that the lines marked by age in his face had deepened. He evidently felt that he stood before me a man self-degraded in his old age. On the other hand, it was just as plain that he was determined to deceive me if I attempted to penetrate his secret.

My one chance of producing the right impression was to appeal to his sense of self-respect, if any such sense was still left in him.

"Don't suppose that I presume to interfere between you and your wife," I resumed. "In what little I have now to say to you, I shall bear in mind the high character that you have always maintained, not only among your own friends but among persons like myself, who are placed above you by the accidents of birth and position."

"You are very good, sir. I assure you I feel . . ."

He paused. I waited to let him go on. His eyes dropped before mine. He seemed to be afraid to follow the good impulse that I had roused in him. I tried again.

"Without repeating what Mrs. Parley has said to me," I proceeded, "I may tell you at what conclusion I have myself arrived. It is only doing you justice to suppose that your wife has been mislaid by false appearances. Will you go back to her, and satisfy that she has been mistaken?"

"She wouldn't believe me, sir."

"Will you at least try the experiment?"

He shook his head doggedly. "Quite useless," he answered. "My wife's temper –"

I stopped him there.

"Make some allowance for your wife's temper," I said, "and don't forget that you owe some consideration to your daughters. Spare them the shame and distress of seeing their father and mother at enmity."

His manner changed: I had said something which appeared to give him confidence.

"Did my wife say anything to you about our girls?" he asked.

"Yes."

"What did she say?"

"She thought you neglectful of your daughters."

"Anything else, sir?"

"She said you had, at one time, acknowledged that the girls ought to have a good governess, but she now finds you indifferent to the best interests of your children."

He lifted one of his hands, with a theatrical exaggeration of gesture quite new in my experience of him.

"She said that, did she? Now, Mr. Sheriff, judge for yourself what my wife's complaints of me are worth! I have this day engaged a governess for my children."

I looked at him.

Once more his eyes dropped before mine.

"Does Mrs. Parley know what you have done?" I inquired.

"She shall know", he answered loudly, almost insolently, "when I return home."

"I am obliged to you for coming here, Mr. Parley. Don't let me detain you any longer."

"Does that mean, sir, that you disapprove of what I have done?"

"I pronounce no opinion."

"Does it mean that you doubt the governess's character?"

"It means that I regret having troubled you to come here – and that I have no more to say."

He walked to the door, opened it, hesitated and came back to me.

"I ask your pardon, sir, if I have been in any way rough in speaking to you. You will understand, perhaps, that I am a little troubled in my mind." He considered with himself, and took from his pocket the snuff-box to which his wife had alluded. "I've given up the habit, sir, of taking snuff. It's slovenly, and – and not good for the health. But I don't feel the less honoured by your gift. I shall prize it gratefully, as long as I live."

He turned his head away – but not quickly enough to hide the tears that filled his eyes. For a moment all that was best and truest in the nature of Benjamin Parley had forced its way to expression. But the devil in possession of him was not to be cast out. He became basely ashamed of the good impulse that did him honour.

"The sun is very bright this morning," he muttered confusedly. "My eyes are rather weak, sir. I wish you good morning."

IV

Left by myself I rang the bell and gave the servant his instructions. If Mr. or Mrs. Parley called again at the house they were to be told that I was not able to see them.

Was this a harsh act on my part? Let us look the matter fairly in the face and see.

It is possible that some persons, not having had my experience of the worst aspects of human nature, might have been inclined to attribute Mrs. Parley's suspicions to her jealous temper, and might have been not unwilling to believe that her husband had engaged a governess for his children in perfect good faith. No such merciful view of the matter presented itself to my mind. Nothing could be plainer to me than that Parley was an instrument in the hands of a bold and wicked woman, who had induced him, for reasons of her own, to commit an act which was nothing less than an outrage on his wife. To what purpose could I interfere? The one person who could help poor Mrs. Parley must be armed with the authority of a relation. And, even in this case, what good result could be anticipated if the woman played her part as governess discreetly and if Parley held firm? A more hopeless domestic prospect, so far, had never presented itself to my view. It vexed and humiliated me to find myself waiting helplessly for events. What else could I do?

On the next day, Mrs. Parley called, and the servant followed his instructions.

On the day after (with the pardonable pertinacity of a woman in despair), she wrote to me.

The letter has been long since destroyed, but the substance of it remains in my memory. It informed me that the governess was actually established in the house, and described her, it is needless to say, as the most shameless wretch that had ever breathed the breath of life. Asked if he had obtained a reference to her character, Parley had replied that he was old enough to know how to engage a governess, that he refused to answer impertinent questions and that he had instructed "Miss Beaumont" (this was the lady's well-sounding name) to follow his example. She had already contrived to steal her way into the confidence of her two innocent pupils and to produce a favourable impression on a visitor who had called at the house that morning. In one word, Mrs. Parley's position was, on her own showing, beyond the reach of help. As I had anticipated, the false governess played her part with discretion, and the infatuated husband asserted his authority.

Ten days later, I happened to be driving through the suburb of our city, and I discovered Mrs. Parley in close conversation with one of the younger members of the detective police force, named Butler. They were walking slowly along a retired path which led out of the high road, so interested, apparently, in what they had to say to each other that they failed to notice me, although I passed close by them.

The next morning, Butler presented himself at my office, and asked leave to speak to me. Being busy that day, I sent a message back, inquiring if the matter was of any importance. The answer was: "Of most serious importance". He was immediately admitted to my private room.

V

The little I had heard of this young police officer represented him to be "a rising man", resolute and clever, and not very scrupulous in finding his way to his own ends. Thoroughly useful, but wants looking after. There was the superintendent's brief description of Mr. Butler.

I warned him at the outset that I had but little time to spare. "Say what is necessary, but put it in few words. What is your business with me?"

"My business relates, sir, to something that has happened in the house of Benjamin Parley. He has got himself into a serious scrape."

I should have made a bad detective policeman. When I hear anything that interests or excites me, my face has got a habit of owning it.

Butler had merely to look at me, and to see that he might pass over certain explanations which he had been prepared to offer.

"Mrs. Parley told me, sir, that you had permitted her husband to speak to you. May I take it for granted that you have heard of the governess? Parley met the woman in the street. He was struck by her personal appearance; he got into conversation with her; he took her into a restaurant and gave her a dinner; he heard her interesting story; he fell in love with her, like an infernal old fool – oh, I beg your pardon!"

"Quite needless to apologize, Mr. Butler. When he permitted the woman to be governess to his children, he behaved like a scoundrel as well as a fool. Go on. You have discovered, of course, what object she has in establishing herself in Parley's house?"

"I will ask leave to tell you first, sir, how I made the discovery."

"Why?"

"Because you won't believe who the woman really is, unless I convince you beforehand that I have committed no mistake."

"Is she a person of celebrity?"

"She is known wherever there is a newspaper published."

"And conceals herself, of course," I said, "under an assumed name?"

"And what is more, sir, she would never have been found out – but for the wife's jealousy. Everybody but that old woman was wheedled into liking Miss Beaumont. Mrs. Parley believed the charming governess to be an impostor, and, being determined to expose her, applied to me for advice. The one morsel of evidence that induced me to look into the matter, came from the servant girl. Miss Beaumont's bedroom was at the back of the house. One night the servant heard her softly open her window, and saw her empty her wash-hand basin into the garden. The customary means of emptying her basin, were, of course, ready and waiting in her room. Have you ever dropped into an actor's dressing-room, sir, when he has done his work on the stage?"

"Sometimes."

"Have you accidentally looked at the basin when he washes his face before he goes home?"

"Not that I remember."

"In such cases, sir, the actor often leaves, what you may call, a tinge of his complexion in the water; and the colour might strike an observant person. If I had not begun life on the stage, it would never have occurred to me that Miss Beaumont's reason for privately emptying her basin might be connected with a false complexion – occasionally removed, you know, at night, and put on again the next morning. A mere guess, you will say, and more likely to be wrong than right, I don't dispute it; I only say that my guess encouraged me to make one or two inquiries. It's needless to trouble you, sir, by speaking of the difficulties that I found in my way. Let me only say that I contrived to get the better of them. Last night, after old Parley was safe in bed, his wife and his servant and I invaded the sanctuary of Miss Beaumont's room. We were not at all afraid of waking the lady, having taken the precaution (at supper time) of giving her, let us say, the blessing of a good night's rest. She had seemingly been a little irritable and restless before she went to sleep. At any rate, her wig was thrown on the floor. We passed by that, and went to the bed. She lay on her back; her mouth was open and her arms were flung out on either side of her. Her own pretty fair hair was not very long, and her false colour (she was disguised, sir, as a dark lady in public) was left that night on her face and neck and hands. So far, we had only discovered that she was, what Mrs. Parley believed her to be: an impostor, unknown. It was left for *me* to find out who the woman really was. The fastening of her night-dress round the throat had given way. Her bosom was exposed. Upon my soul I was terrified when the truth burst on me! There it was, sir, and no mistake – there, on the right side, under the right breast –"

I started out of my chair. On my writing-table lay a handbill, which I had read and re-read till I knew it by heart. It had been distributed by the London authorities throughout the United Kingdom, and it contained the description of a woman suspected of a terrible crime, who had baffled the pursuit of the police. I looked at the handbill; I looked at the man who was speaking to me.

"Good God!" I cried. "Did you see the scar?"

"I saw it, Mr. Sheriff, as plainly as I see you."

"And the false eye-tooth on the left side of her mouth?"

"Yes, sir – with the gold fastening to speak for it."

Years have passed since the conversation took place which I have just related. But some persons must remember a famous criminal trial in London – and would recognize, if I felt myself at liberty to mention it, the name of the most atrocious murderess of modern times.

VI

The warrant was issued for the woman's arrest. Competent witnesses identified her, and the preliminaries of the Law took their course.

To me, the serious part of the discovery was the part which cast suspicion on the unfortunate Benjamin Parley. Appearances were indisputably against him. He was not only suspected, he was actually charged with assisting the murderess to escape from justice. For the trouble that had now fallen on him, I could be of some use in assisting Parley and in comforting his unhappy family.

You will hardly believe the assertion, but I declare it to be true, the man's infatuation kept its hold on him more firmly than ever. His own interests were of no sort of importance to him; he seemed to be but little affected even by the distress of his wife and family; his one overwhelming anxiety was for the prisoner.

"I believe in her innocence," he actually said to me, "as I believe in my religion. She is falsely accused, sir, of that horrible crime." He was incapable of resenting, he was even incapable of appreciating, the cruel deception that she had practised on him. In one word, he was more devotedly in love with her than ever.

And, mind, there was no madness in this! I can answer for it, from my own experience: he was in perfect possession of his faculties.

The order came to have the woman removed to London, to be tried at the Central Criminal Court. Parley had heard of it. In the most moving terms he entreated me to have him set at liberty, and to trust him with the duty of taking charge of the prisoner!

It was my business to see her placed in the railway carriage, under proper guard. The train started in the morning. She refused to leave her bed. As a matter of course, I was sent for in this emergency.

The murderess was not a beautiful woman; she was not even a pretty woman. But she had a voluptuous smile, a singularly musical voice, a fine figure and a supreme confidence in herself. The moment I entered the room, the horrible creature tried her powers of fascination on the sheriff: she assumed the character of an innocent victim, overwhelmed by suffering of body and mind. I looked at my watch, and told her she had no time to lose. Not in the least disconcerted, she shifted to a new character: she took me, gayly and cynically, into her confidence.

"My dear sir, you would never have caught me," she said, "if I had not made one mistake. As governess in the family of an ex-police officer I should have been safe from discovery if I had not taken for granted that I could twist Parley's old woman round my little finger, like the rest of them. Who would have thought she could have been jealous of an ugly old husband at her time of life? Wouldn't you have said yourself: 'All that sort of thing must have been over long ago, when a woman is sixty years old and more?' Can there be jealousy without love? And do we love when we are hideously flabby creatures covered with wrinkles? Oh, fie! fie!"

I took out my watch once more.

"If I don't hear that you are up and dressed in ten minutes," I said, "I will have you wrapped in a blanket and taken to the railway by main force."

With that warning I left the room. The women in charge of her told me afterward that her language was too terrible to be repeated. But she was quick enough to see that I was in earnest, and she was up and dressed in time for the train.

VII

When I tell you that Parley was one of the witnesses examined at the trial, you will understand that we had relieved him from the serious charge of being (in the legal phrase) "an accessory after the fact". He went to London as firmly convinced of her innocence as ever. She was found guilty on irresistible evidence, and sentenced to death.

On the conclusion of the trial, Parley had not returned to his family; he had not even written. His wife followed him to London. He seemed hardly to know her again.

The one idea in possession of him was the hopeless idea of obtaining a reprieve. He was absolutely indifferent to every other earthly consideration. Ignorant people thought him mad. He wrote to the newspapers; he haunted the Government offices; he forced his way into the house of the judge who had presided at the trial. An eminent medical man was consulted. After careful examination he pronounced the patient to be perfectly sane.

Through the influence of friends in London, who were known to the city authorities, the poor wretch gained admittance to the prison, while the criminal was waiting for execution. His wife heard what happened at the interview, but was never able to repeat it, to me or to any one. The same miserable cry always escaped her if she was pressed on the subject:

"Oh don't ask me! Don't ask me!"

On the evening before the execution, he burst into a fit of hysterical crying. That outbreak of violent emotion was followed by a cataleptic seizure. More than eight and forty hours passed before consciousness returned. They feared the loss of reason when he had gained the capacity to feel and suffer. No such result attended his recovery.

On the same day he spoke of her to others for the first and last time. He said, very quietly, with a remarkable stillness in his face:

"Is she dead?" They answered, Yes. He said no more.

The next morning his wife asked if he would go back to Scotland with her. He was quite ready to do anything that she wished. Two or three days after their return I saw him. His grey hair had become perfectly white; his manner was subdued; his face, full of vivid expression in past days, seemed to have fallen into a state of changeless repose. That was all.

After an interval, I asked his wife and children if they noticed any change for the worse in him. Except that he was very silent, they noticed no change for the worse. He was once more the good husband

and kind father of their past happy experience. Did he ever speak of the woman? Never.

I was not quite satisfied. A month later Mrs. Parley asked me if I thought a friend of mine, who was one of our greatest living physicians, could do Benjamin any good. I asked what was the matter with him.

"He seems to be getting weak," was the only reply.

The same day, I took my friend with me to Parley's house. After looking at the patient, and putting some questions, he asked to be allowed to make a complete examination. The two retired. When they returned, Mrs. Parley was naturally a little alarmed.

"Is there anything that's wrong, sir?" she asked. And to my astonishment, the doctor answered:

"Nothing that I can find out."

When we had left the house, I put the question to him:

"What does this mean?"

"It means," he answered, "that the old man is dying, and I can't find out why."

Once in every week, the great physician visited Parley, always refusing to take his fee, but now and then asking permission to bring a medical friend with him. One day he called on me, and said:

"If you want to say 'good-bye' to the old police officer, you have no time to lose." I went to the house the same day. Parley was asleep. I returned some hours later. Parley was dead. I asked what he had died of, and the doctor said:

"We have obtained the widow's permission to make a post-mortem examination. Wait a little."

I waited until the funeral was over, and then returned to the subject.

"What discoveries did you make at the post-mortem examination?"

"We made no discoveries."

"But there must have been some cause for his death?"

"I called it 'decay of nature' on the certificate," my friend answered. "A mere pretence! The man's constitution was sound, and he had not reached seventy years of age. A registrar of deaths has nothing to do with questions of sentiment. A doctor's certificate is bound to deal with facts, otherwise . . ."

He paused, and drew me out of hearing of the mourners lingering in the churchyard.

"Don't mention it among my colleagues," he said. "If there really *is* such a thing – Benjamin Parley has died of a broken heart."